Miss Read, or in real life Dora Saint, was a school teacher by profession who started writing after the Second World War, beginning with light essays written for *Punch* and other journals. She then wrote on educational and country matters and worked as a scriptwriter for the BBC. Miss Read was married to a schoolmaster for sixty-four years until his death in 2004, and they have one daughter.

In the 1998 New Year Honours list Miss Read was awarded an MBE for her services to literature. She is the author of many immensely popular books, including two autobiographical works, but it is her novels of English rural life for which she is best known. The first of these, *Village School*, was published in 1955, and Miss Read continued to write about the fictitious villages of Fairacre and Thrush Green until her retirement in 1996. She lives in Berkshire.

Books by Miss Read

NOVELS

Village School * Village Diary * Storm in the Village
Thrush Green * Fresh from the Country
Winter in Thrush Green * Miss Clare Remembers
Over the Gate * The Market Square * Village Christmas
The Howards of Caxley * Fairacre Festival
News from Thrush Green * Emily Davis * Tyler's Row
The Christmas Mouse * Farther Afield
Battles at Thrush Green * No Holly for Miss Quinn
Village Affairs * Return to Thrush Green * The White Robin
Village Centenary * Gossip from Thrush Green
Affairs at Thrush Green * Summer at Fairacre
At Home in Thrush Green * The School at Thrush Green
Mrs Pringle * Friends at Thrush Green * Changes at Fairacre
Celebrations at Thrush Green * Farewell to Fairacre
Tales from a Village School * The Year at Thrush Green
A Peaceful Retirement

ANTHOLOGIES

Country Bunch * Miss Read's Christmas Book

OMNIBUSES

Chronicles of Fairacre * Life at Thrush Green
More Stories from Thrush Green
Further Chronicles of Fairacre * Christmas at Fairacre
Fairacre Roundabout * Tales from Thrush Green
Fairacre Affairs * Encounters at Thrush Green
The Caxley Chronicles * Farewell, Thrush Green
The Last Chronicle of Fairacre

NON-FICTION

Miss Read's Country Cooking * Tiggy
The World of Thrush Green * Early Days (comprising
A Fortunate Grandchild & Time Remembered)

Miss Read

Over the Gate
Farther Afield

Over the Gate
First published in Great Britain by Michael Joseph Ltd in 1964

Farther Afield
First published in Great Britain by Michael Joseph Ltd in 1974

This omnibus edition published in 2009
by Orion Books Ltd
Orion House, 5 Upper St Martin's Lane
London WC2H 9EA

An Hachette UK company

A CIP catalogue record for this book is available
from the British Library.

ISBN 9781407221083

Printed in Great Britain by Clays Ltd, St Ives plc

www.orionbooks.co.uk

Over the Gate

Over the Gate

For
Kit and Ivor
with love

CONTENTS

* * *

1. THE PORTRAIT

If you walk down the village street of Fairacre you will come before long to The Beetle and Wedge on the left-hand side. It is a long, low public house, sturdily built of brick and flint, and so attractive to the eye that it is easy to miss the narrow lane which runs between its side and the three cottages, also of brick and flint, which stand next to it.

This lane leads to the downs which shelter our village from the north-east wind. It begins, fairly respectably, with a tarred and gravelled surface, but after a quarter of a mile such refinement ends; the road narrows suddenly, the tarmac finishes, and only a muddy track makes its way uphill to peter out eventually on the windy slopes high above the village.

Here, where the hard surface ends and the rutted lane begins, stands a pair of dour grey houses which bear no resemblance to the cheerful brick-and-thatch architecture of most of Fairacre. They are faced with grey cement which has fallen off, here and there, leaving several scabrous patches. Each has a steep gable terminating in a formidable spike, and the roofs are of cold grey slate. Even on a day of shimmering heat, when the small blue butterflies of the chalk downs hover in the still gardens before them, these two houses present a chilly visage to the passer-by.

They were built in the latter half of Queen Victoria's reign by a well-to-do retired ironmonger from Caxley. At the same time he had built a larger and more imposing residence in the village street for his own use. This was called Jasmine Villa and boasted a black and white tiled path, an ornate verandah of iron trelliswork, and was magnificently out of keeping with the modest dwellings nearby.

Laburnum Villas, as the two were called, had housed the ironmonger's aged mother and two spinster sisters in one, and a married couple with two sons, all of whom worked for the family, in the other.

When I first took up the headship of Fairacre village school, some years ago, the property belonged to a descendant of the ironmonger's, and was pathetically shabby. The owner lived in Caxley, but Jasmine Villa became familiar to me, inside and out, for the tenant, Mrs Pratt, played the church organ and sometimes invited me in to hear one of my pupils practising his solo part in an anthem. At one time too she let a room to one of the school staff so that I became well acquainted with the chill of the late ironmonger's drawing-room and the gloom of his stairway.

But Laburnum Villas remained a mystery. The windows of one were shrouded in dirty lace, and inside, I heard, dwelt an old lady of ninety, who supped innumerable cups of strong tea and dozed between whiles. The tea was made when she rose in the morning and the pot kept hot on the hob all day, the kettle steaming comfortably beside it, ready for refilling. Sometimes, when the children and I walked past on our way to the downs, I thought of that somnolent room murmurous with the humming of the kettle, the gentle snoring of the old lady and the purring of her great black cat which was sometimes to be seen sitting in the window sunning itself.

Next door seemed a little livelier. The windows were clean, the curtains fresh, and a trim lawn sloped down to the front gate. Occasionally we saw a middle-aged man and woman working in the garden, but we rarely met them in the village street, a bare two hundred yards away. They seemed to lead a retired life tucked away from the main street of Fairacre and, like all curious country people, I was interested to hear more about them from Mrs Pringle, the school caretaker.

'A very respectable pair,' was Mrs Pringle's dictum when I asked. This was high praise from my curmudgeonly school cleaner and she must have noticed my surprise.

'I always speaks fair of folks when I can,' continued Mrs Pringle self-righteously, putting down her dustpan and settling herself on the front desk for a good gossip. The desk groaned under her thirteen stone but knew better than to let the lady down. 'There's mighty few these days as can be spoke fair of in Fairacre – a proper lazy, shiftless, godless, money-grubbing lot as they be. As I said to Mr Pringle only last night: "If this is the age of flatulence," I says, "then there's something in being poor but honest!"'

'But tell me about Laburnum Villas,' I urged, steering Mrs Pringle back to the point. Once launched on a sea of invective she will sail on for hours, as well I know. The great clock on the wall, ticking ponderously, already said ten minutes to nine, and very soon the children would be called in from the playground.

'Well, these Hursts,' said Mrs Pringle dismissively, 'have only been here two or three years, but before that the Fletchers were there. As nice a family as ever come to Fairacre,' boomed Mrs Pringle, warming to her theme, 'despite their old grandad being a byword in Caxley for pinching things he never had no need of off the market stalls. A real affliction he was to them – everlasting having his name in the *Caxley Chronicle* for all to see.'

'But the Hursts –' I persisted, one eye on the clock.

'Highly respectable,' replied Mrs Pringle, inclining her head graciously. 'Chapel-goers, but none the worse for that, I dare-say.' The parish church of St Patrick's has Mrs Pringle's support and the choir stalls there reverberate to her powerful contralto lowing, so that this was magnanimous indeed.

'Both been in good service,' continued the lady, 'and was with Sir Edmund over Springbourne way for donkey's years. When the old gentleman passed on, they went to one of his relations, I seem to recall. Some long way away it was. Let me think.'

There was a pause while Mrs Pringle frowned with concentration. New Zealand, I thought, or the Argentine, perhaps. The sound of children's voices stirred my conscience and I rose from behind my desk.

'Leicester!' said she triumphantly. 'I knew I'd get it in the end! That's right, it was Leicester they went to.'

At this point a small girl appeared dramatically between us. 'Please, miss, Ernie made me give him half of my toffee bar and now his tooth's come out in it,' she gabbled agitatedly, 'and what's more he says it's all my fault.'

'Rubbish!' I said, advancing to the door. 'It's nothing more or less than rough justice.'

'I was about to tell you,' boomed Mrs Pringle's voice behind me, heavy with outraged dignity.

'Sorry!' I called back above the rising din. 'It'll have to wait!'

Slowly, Mrs Pringle collected her paraphernalia together and limped heavily from the room, her back expressing outrage in every sturdy line. Mrs Pringle's bad leg 'flares up', as she puts it, whenever anything goes wrong. It looked as though I should have to wait some time before she would be in a fit state to tell me more about the mysterious Hursts.

But, before long, I had occasion to call at Laburnum Villas. The leg of a small brass trivet came off in Mrs Pringle's massive hand whilst she was polishing it. As she explained: 'When things are let get that filthy, they needs a bit of purchase put on them.' It was apparent that the purchase this time had been too much for my elderly trivet. I looked at it sadly.

'I'd take it to Fred Hurst,' advised Mrs Pringle. 'I daresay Mr Willet would have a go if he had a soldering iron, but he hasn't, so there you are.'

'How do you know Mr Hurst has one?' I asked.

'Because he fixed the twiddly-bits up to the chapel pulpit real lovely,' replied Mrs Pringle proudly. 'Mr Lamb told me at the Post Office, and what's more he says he likes doing soldering jobs any time he's asked.'

I must have looked a little diffident for Mrs Pringle's normal bellow rose to a crescendo of hearty encouragement.

'You pop down after school and see him,' she advised. 'Better than taking it to Caxley. You won't see it again this side of Christmas if it gets in there.'

There was some truth in this remark. Urged by Mrs Pringle's exhortations and my own curiosity I decided to walk down the lane after tea carrying my trivet with me.

It was one of those bell-like May evenings described by Edmund Blunden. A sharp shower had left the village street glistening and the bushes and trees quivering with bright drops. Now, bathed in evening sunlight, the village sparkled. Scent rose from the wallflowers and polyanthuses in the cottage gardens, and blackbirds scolded from the plumed lilac bushes. Our village of Fairacre is no lovelier than many others. We have rats as well as roses in our back gardens, scoundrels as well as stalwarts ploughing our fields, and plenty of damp and dirt hidden behind the winsome exteriors of our older cottages. But at times it is not only home to us but heaven, too, and this was just such an occasion.

As I waited in the porch, cradling the trivet, I wondered if there would be the usual delay in answering a country front door. A back door is usually open, or quickly answered, but I knew from experience that rusty bolts and heavy chains are often involved in front-door transactions in Fairacre. Only on formal occasions do we call at front doors, but this, I felt, was one of them.

To my surprise, the door opened quickly and quietly, showing an elegant white-painted hall and staircase. Mrs Hurst greeted me politely.

'I wondered if your husband –' I began diffidently.

'Come in,' she smiled, and I followed her into the drawing-room on the right-hand side of the corridor. The sight that greeted me was so unexpected that I almost gasped. Instead of the gloomy interior which I had imagined would match Laburnum Villas' unlovely exterior I found a long light room with a large window at each end, one overlooking the front, and the other the back garden. The walls were papered with a white-striped paper and the woodwork was white to match. At the windows hung long velvet curtains in deep blue, faded but beautiful, and a square carpet echoed the colour. Each piece of furniture was fine and old, shining with daily polishing by a loving hand.

But by far the most dominating feature of the room was a large portrait in oils of a black-haired man dressed in clothes of the early nineteenth century. It was not a handsome face, but it showed strength of character and kindliness. Surrounded by an ornate wide gold frame it glowed warmly above the white marble fireplace.

'What a lovely room!' I exclaimed.

'I'm glad you like it,' replied Mrs Hurst. 'My husband and I got nearly everything here at sales. We go whenever we can. It makes a day out and we both like nice things. Our landlord let us have the wall down between these two rooms, so that it's made one good long one, which is a better shape than before, and much lighter too.'

I nodded appreciatively.

'Sit down, do,' she continued. 'I'll get Fred. We live at the back mostly, and I'll tell him you're here.'

I waited in an elegant round armchair with a walnut rim running round its back, and gazed at this amazing room. What a contrast it was, I thought, to Mrs Pratt's counterpart at Jasmine Villa! There the room was crowded with a conglomeration of furniture, from bamboo to bog oak, each hideous piece bearing an equally hideous collection of malformed pottery. That was, to my mind, the most distracting room in

Fairacre, whereas this was perhaps the most tranquil one I had yet encountered.

Fred Hurst returned with his wife. He was short while she was tall, rosy while she was pale, and certainly more inclined to gossip than his dignified wife. He examined my trivet carefully.

'Nice little piece,' he said admiringly. 'A good hundred years old. I can mend it so as you'll never know it was broken.'

He told me that he could get it done in a week, and we talked generally about our gardens and the weather for a little while before I rose to go.

'I envy you this room,' I said truthfully. 'The school house has tiny rooms and furniture always looks so much better with plenty of space for it.'

'Pictures, too,' added Fred Hurst. He pointed to the portrait. 'One of my ancestors,' he continued.

I heard Mrs Hurst draw in her breath sharply.

'Fred!' she said warningly.

Her husband looked momentarily uncomfortable, then moved towards me with hand outstretched. 'We mustn't keep you, Miss Read,' he said politely. 'I'll do my best with the trivet.'

I made my farewells, promised to return in a week, and walked to the gate. There I turned to wave to Mrs Hurst who stood regally still upon her doorstep. She wore upon her pale face such an expression of stony distaste that I forbore to raise my hand, but set off soberly for home.

What in the world, I asked myself in astonishment, had happened in those few minutes to make Mrs Hurst look like that?

A week later, in some trepidation, I called again. Somewhat to my relief, only Fred Hurst was at home. He took me into the charming drawing-room again and lifted my mended trivet from a low table. The repair had been neatly done. It was clear that he was a clever workman.

'My wife's gone down to the shop,' he said. 'She'll be sorry to miss you.'

I murmured something polite and began to look in my purse for the modest half-crown which was all that he charged for his job.

'She doesn't see many people, living down here,' he went on. 'Bit quiet for her, I think, though she don't complain. I'm the one that likes company more, you know. Take after my old great-great-grandad here.'

He waved proudly at the portrait. The dark painted eyes seemed to follow us about the room.

'A very handsome portrait,' I commented.

'A fine old party,' agreed Fred Hurst, smiling at him. 'Had a tidy bit of money too, which none of us saw, I may say. Ran through it at the card table, my dad told me, and spent what was left on liquor. They do say, some people, that he had some pretty wild parties, but you don't have to believe all you hear.'

It was quite apparent that Fred Hurst's ancestor had a very soft place in his descendant's heart. He spoke of his weaknesses with indulgence, and almost with envy, it seemed to me. Certainly he was fascinated by the portrait, returning its inscrutable gaze with an expression of lively regard.

I could hear the sound of someone moving about in the kitchen, but Mr Hurst, engrossed as he was, seemed unaware of it.

'I should like to think that I took after him in some ways,' he continued boisterously. 'He got a good deal out of life, one way and another, did my old great-great-grandad.'

The door opened and Mrs Hurst swept into the room like a chilly wind.

'That'll do, Fred,' she said quenchingly. 'Miss Read don't want to hear all those old tales.' She bent down to pick an imaginary piece of fluff from the carpet. I could have sworn that she wanted to avoid my eyes.

'Your husband has mended my trivet beautifully,' I said hastily. 'I was just going.'

'I'll come to the gate with you,' said Mrs Hurst more gently.

We made our way down the sloping path to the little lane.

'My husband enjoys a bit of company,' she said, over the gate. 'I'm afraid he gets carried away at times. He dearly likes an audience.' She sounded apologetic and her normally pale face was suffused with pink, but whether with shame for her own tartness to him or with some secret anger, I could not tell. Ah well, I thought, as I returned to the school house, people are kittle-cattle, as Mr Willet is fond of reminding me.

'A pack of lies,' announced Mrs Pringle forthrightly when I mentioned Mr Hurst's portrait. 'That's no more his great-great-grandad than the Duke of Wellington!'

'Fred Hurst should know!' I pointed out mildly. I knew that this was the best way of provoking Mrs Pringle to further tirades and waited for the explosion.

'And so he does!' boomed Mrs Pringle, her three chins wobbling self-righteously. 'He knows quite well it's a pack of lies he's telling – that's when he stops to consider, which he don't. That poor wife of his,' went on the lady, raising hands and eyes heavenward, 'what she has to put up with nobody knows! Such a god-fearing pillar of truth as she is too! Them as really knows 'em, Miss Read, will tell you what that poor soul suffers with his everlasting taradiddles.'

'Perhaps he embroiders things to annoy her,' I suggested. 'Six of one and a half-dozen of the other, so to speak.'

'Top and bottom of it is that he don't fairly know truth, from lies,' asserted Mrs Pringle, brows beetling. 'This picture, for instance, everyone knows was bought at Ted Purdy's sale three years back. It's all of a piece with Fred Hurst's goings-on to say it's a relation. He starts in fun, maybe, but after a time or two he gets to believe it.'

'If people know that, then there's not much harm done,' I replied.

Mrs Pringle drew an outraged breath so deeply and with such volume that her stout corsets creaked with the strain.

'Not much harm done?' she echoed. 'There's such a thing as mortal sin, which is what plain lying is, and his poor wife knows it. My brother-in-law worked at Sir Edmund's when the Hursts was there and you should hear what went on between the two. Had a breakdown that poor soul did once, all on account of Fred Hurst's lies. "What'll become of you when you stand before your Maker, Fred Hurst?" she cried at him in the middle of a rabbit pie! My brother-in-law saw what harm lying does all right. And to the innocent, what's more! To the innocent!'

Mrs Pringle thrust her belligerent countenance close to mine and I was obliged to retreat.

'Yes, of course,' I agreed hastily. 'You are quite right, Mrs Pringle.'

Mrs Pringle sailed triumphantly towards the school kitchen with no trace of a limp. Victory always works wonders with Mrs Pringle's bad leg.

In the weeks that followed I heard other people's accounts of the tension which existed between volatile Fred Hurst and his strictly truthful wife. It was this one regrettable trait evidently in the man's character which caused unhappiness to Mrs Hurst. In all other ways they were a devoted couple.

'I reckons they're both to be pitied,' said Mr Willet, our school caretaker one afternoon. He was busy at the never-ending job of sweeping the coke into its proper pile at one end of the playground. Thirty children can spread a ton of coke over an incredibly large area simply by running up and down it. Mr Willet and I do what we can by exhortation, threats and occasional cuffs, but it does not seem to lessen his time wielding a stout broom. Now he rested upon it, blowing out his ragged grey moustache as he contemplated the idiosyncrasies of his neighbours.

'They've both got a fault, see?' he went on. 'He tells fibs. She's too strict about it. But she ain't so much to blame really when you know how she was brought up. Her ol' dad was a Tartar. Speak-when-you're-spoken-to, Dad's-always-right sort of chap. Used to beat the livin' daylights out o' them kids of his. She's still afeared that Fred'll burn in hell-fire because of his whoppers. I calls it a tragedy, when you come to think of it.'

He returned to his sweeping, and I to my classroom. I was to remember his words later.

Time passed and the autumn term was more than half gone. The weather had been rough and wet, and the village badly smitten with influenza. Our classes were small and there were very few families which had escaped the plague. Fred Hurst was one of the worst hit, Mrs Pringle told me.

It was some months since the incident of the trivet and I had forgotten the Hursts in the press of daily affairs. Suddenly I remembered that lovely room, the portrait, and the passions it aroused.

'Very poorly indeed,' announced Mrs Pringle, with lugubrious satisfaction. 'Doctor's been twice this week and Ted Prince says Fred's fallen away to a thread of what he was.'

'Let's hope he'll soon get over it,' I answered briskly, making light of Mrs Pringle's dark news. One gets used to believing a tenth of all that one hears in a village. To believe everything would be to sink beneath the sheer weight of all that is thrust upon one. Seeing my mood Mrs Pringle swept out, her leg dragging slightly.

At the end of that week I set off for Caxley. It was a grey day, with the downs covered in thick mist. The trees dripped sadly along the road to the market town, and the wet pavements were even more depressing. My business done, I was about to drive home again when I saw Mrs Hurst waiting at the bus stop. She was clutching a medicine bottle, and her face was drawn and white.

She climbed in gratefully, and I asked after her husband. She answered in a voice choked with suppressed tears.

'He's so bad, miss, I don't think he'll see the month out. Doctor don't say much, but I know he thinks the same.'

I tried to express my shock and sympathy. So Mrs Pringle had been right, I thought, with secret remorse.

'There seems no help anywhere,' went on the poor woman.

She seemed glad to talk to someone and I drove slowly to give her time. 'I pray, of course,' she said, almost perfunctorily. 'We was all brought up very strict that way by my father. He was a lay preacher, and a great one for us speaking the truth. Not above using the strap on us children, girls as well as boys, and once, I remember, he made me wash my mouth out with carbolic soap because he said I hadn't told the truth. He was wrong that time, but it didn't make no difference to dad. He was a man that always knew best.'

She sighed very sadly and the bottle trembled in her fingers.

'He never took to Fred, nor Fred to him, but there's no doubt my dad was right. There's laws laid down to be kept and them that sin against them must answer for it. "As ye sow, so shall ye reap," it says in the Bible, and no one can get over that one.'

She seemed to be talking to herself and I could do nothing but make comforting noises.

'Fred's the best husband in the world,' she continued, staring through the rain-spattered windscreen with unseeing eyes, 'but he's got his failings, like the rest of us. He don't seem to know fact from fancy, and sometimes I tremble to think what he's storing up for himself. I've reasoned with him – I've told him straight – I've always tried to set him an example –'

Her voice quivered and she fell silent. We drove down the village street between the shining puddles and turned into the lane leading to the misty downs. I stopped the car outside Laburnum Villas. It was suddenly very quiet. Somewhere nearby a rivulet of rainwater trickled along unseen, hidden by the dead autumn grasses.

'You see,' said Mrs Hurst, 'I've never told a lie in my life. I can't do it – not brought up as I was. It's made a lot of trouble between Fred and me, but it's the way I am. You can't change a thing like that.'

She scrubbed at her eyes fiercely with the back of her hand, then opened the door.

'Can I come and see him?' I asked impulsively. She nodded, her face expressionless.

I followed her up the steep wet path to the forlorn house. Its ugly exterior, blotched with damp, was more hideous than ever. Inside, in the lovely room, Fred Hurst lay asleep on a bed which had been brought from upstairs. He faced the portrait above the mantelpiece.

The sleeping man woke as we entered and tried to struggle up, but weakness prevented him. I was aghast at the change in him. It was apparent that he had very little time to live. His eyes wandered vaguely about the room, and his breathing was painful to hear. His wife crossed quickly to his side and took his hand. Her face softened as she gazed on him.

'Fred dear, it's me. And I've brought Miss Read to see you,' she said gently.

A flicker passed across his face and the dull eyes rolled in my direction.

'Come to see me?' he asked slowly. 'Me, or my great –' he took a shuddering breath, 'or my great-great-grandad? He is my kin, ain't he, my love?'

There was a terrible urgency in the hoarse voice as he turned to his wife. Across his wasted body her eyes met mine. They had become dark and dilated as though they looked upon hell itself, but her voice rang out defiantly.

'Of course he's your kin,' she cried, tightening her grip on his hand. 'Miss Read can see the likeness, can't you?'

I responded to the challenge.

'A strong family likeness,' I lied unfalteringly, and felt no regret.

2. STRANGE, BUT TRUE?

Poor Fred Hurst died a fortnight before Christmas, and Mr Willet, who is sexton of St Patrick's as well as caretaker of Fairacre school, had the melancholy task of digging his grave. We could hear the ring of his spade as it met sundry flints embedded in the chalk only a foot or so below the surface of the soil.

It was a dark grey December afternoon outside, but within the classroom was warmth, colour and a cheerful hum as the children made Christmas cards. Above their bent heads swung the paper chains they had made. Here and there a pendent star circled slowly in the keen cross draughts which play constantly between the Gothic windows at each end of the school building. A fir branch, cut from the Vicarage garden, leant in a corner giving out its sweet resinous breath as it awaited its metamorphosis into a glittering Christmas tree.

Crayons stuttered like machine guns as snow scenes were created. Reindeer, with colossal antlers which took up far too much room, tottered on legs – inevitably short – across the paper. Robins, fat as footballs, stood on tiptoe; Father Christmas, all boots and whiskers, appeared on every side at once; holly, Christmas puddings, bells and stars flowed from busy fingers throughout the afternoon. And every now and then, during the rare quiet pauses in their activity, we could hear the distant sound of Mr Willet at work, in the desolate solitude of an empty grave.

The winter afternoon was merging into twilight when the

children shouted and skipped their way homeward from Fair-acre village school. Mr Willet, coming from the churchyard next door, propped his spade against the lych gate and paused to light his pipe. In the murk, his wrinkled countenance was illumined, standing out against the dark background like a Rembrandt portrait. Hands cupped over the bowl of his pipe, he squinted sideways at me.

'Finished your day, I s'pose,' he commented. 'Nice work being a school teacher,' he added mischievously.

'What about you?' I retorted.

Mr Willet flung back his head and blew a fragrant blue cloud into the mist around him. 'Got your plaguey coke to sweep up now I've dug poor old Fred's last bed,' he answered equably. He reached for the spade with a massive muddy hand.

'My kettle's on,' I said. 'Come and have a cup of tea before you start again.'

'Well now,' said my caretaker, eyes brightening, 'I don't mind if I do, Miss Read. I'm fair shrammed. Grave-digging be mortal clammy work this weather.'

We strolled back together, across the empty playground, to the school house.

'Here, I can't come in like this!' protested Mr Willet at the kitchen door. 'All cagged up with mud! What'll old Mrs Pringle say when she comes to wash your floor?'

'No more than she says every week. This house is the dirtiest in the village, so she tells me.'

'Miserable ol' faggot!' Mr Willet smiled indulgently. 'How she do love a good moan! Still, this mud's a bit much, I will say. Give us a bit of newspaper and I'll 'ave it under me boots.'

We settled in the warm kitchen, the tea tray between us on the table. We were both tired and cold, and sipped the tea gratefully. It was good to have company and Mr Willet always has something new to impart. He did not fail me on this occasion.

'Poor old Fred Hurst,' he mused, stirring his cup

thoughtfully. 'I've got him right at the end of a row next to the old bit of the churchyard. Funny thing, he's lying aside Sally Gray. Two fanciful ones together there, I reckons.'

'Sally Gray?'

At the querying tone of my voice, the spoon's rotation stopped suddenly. Mr Willet looked at me in astonishment.

'You don't tell me you ain't heard of Sally Gray! Been here all this time and missed Sally?'

I nodded apologetically, and pushed the fruit cake across to him to atone for my short-comings. Mr Willet waved it aside, his eyes wide with amazement.

'Can't hardly credit it. She's about the most famous person in Fairacre. Why, come to think of it, we had a young chap down from some magazine or other writing a bit about her. Before your time, no doubt. Nice enough chap he seemed, although he had a beard.'

Mr Willet checked himself, blew out his own thick walrus moustache, and resumed his tale.

'Well, *beard*, I calls it. 'Twasn't hardly that. More like one of those pan cleaners, the bristly ones, and much the same colour. For two pins I'd have advised him to have it off, but you knows how touchy young fellers get about their bits of whisker, and I was allus one for peace. "Civility costs nothing," my old ma used to say. She were full of useful sayings.'

I began to see where Mr Willet got his own fund of maxims. No matter what the occasion, tragic or farcical, our caretaker-cum-sexton at Fairacre always has some snippet of homely wisdom to fit the case.

'And what did he write?' I prompted, edging him back towards the subject.

'Nest to nothin', when it come to it!' Mr Willet was disgusted. 'I thought at the time, watching him put down these 'ere twiddles and dots and dashes and that –'

'Shorthand,' I interpolated.

'Maybe,' said Mr Willet dismissively, 'but I thought at the

23

time, as I were saying, that he'd never make head nor tail of that rigmarole, and I bet you a quid that's just what happened. You know why?' Mr Willet raised his teaspoon threateningly. 'After us talking to 'im best part of a January afternoon, up the churchyard there, with an east wind fit to cut the liver and lights out of you, all 'e 'ad to show for it was a measly little bit in the corner of a page. And most of that was a picture of the gravestone, what you could make out through the fog, that is. Proper disappointing it was.'

'Which paper?' I asked.

'Some fiddle-faddling thing they brings out the other side of the county. Not worth looking at. All about flowers, and old ruins and history and that. Waste of time really, and not a patch on the *Caxley Chronicle*.' Mr Willet drained his cup and set it carefully down on the saucer. 'Well, must be off to me coke-sweeping, I s'pose.' He began to push back his chair.

'Not yet,' I begged. 'You haven't told me a word about Sally Gray.'

'Well, now –' began Mr Willet, weakening. 'I daresay the coke'd keep till morning, and it don't seem hardly right that you don't know nothing about our Sally.'

He watched me refill his cup without demur, rearranged his muddy boots on the newspaper and settled, with evident relish, to his task of enlightenment.

Sally Gray, Mr Willet told me, died a good ten years or more before he was born, in 1890 to be exact, and as her gravestone bore testimony, 'in her 63rd year'. Consequently, as he pointed out, he was not speaking at first hand, although he could vouch for this strange story, for his mother and grandmother had both heard it from Sally's own lips during her last illness.

Evidently she had always been 'a funny little party', to quote Mr Willet. She was the only child of elderly parents and was brought up in the end cottage of Tyler's Row. Her father was a carter, her mother took in washing, and the child grew up used to hard work and little reward for great labour. Nevertheless, she was happy enough, although the other children in the village found her prim and shy and tended to tease her. She was small of stature, so that she was called 'Mouse' by the boys, and dressed in cut-me-downs of her mother's which gave her a ludicrous dowdiness which invited the ridicule of the girls. No doubt her primness and shyness were the outcome of this treatment.

Her greatest joy was in reading, which she mastered at an early age. Books were scarce, but tattered volumes cast out from the vicarage nursery came her way and gave her endless pleasure. Sometimes a newspaper became available and she read the account of Victoria's coronation to her parents, to their wonder and pride.

When she was twelve or so she entered into service at the Parrs, a well-to-do family who lived in a Queen Anne house at the end of the village. She was quick and neat, obedient and dutiful, and gave satisfaction to the mistress of the house and, more important still, to the housekeeper who ruled the staff with a rod of iron. She lived in as a matter of course, although only five minutes' trot from her own home, but was often allowed to slip along the village street to see her family. Sometimes the cook gave her a bowlful of dripping, or a stout marrow-bone for the stock pot, to eke out the meagre commons of the Grays' diet. Sally was always careful to hide these titbits under her cloak, safe from the eyes of the housekeeper or village gossips who might be encountered on the brief journey.

Time passed. Housemaids came and went at the Parrs' house, but Sally remained. Girls who had worked beside her, dusting, brushing stair carpets, carrying interminable cans of hot water to bedrooms, married and left. They showed their fat offspring to Sally in the fullness of time, and commiserated with her about her state of spinsterhood. Sally did not appear to mind. She was as spry and nimble as ever, although a few grey hairs now mingled with the dark ones, and she continued to trot briskly about Fairacre.

One bitterly cold winter, the two old Grays fell desperately ill, and Sally asked leave to sleep at home and to work part-time at the Parrs. Mrs Parr, who was an autocratic person, did not care for the idea. By now, Sally was senior housemaid. It was she who carried in the early morning tea, pulled back the heavy curtains on their massive brass rings, and announced the weather conditions prevailing to her comatose mistress. She disliked the thought of someone else taking on these duties and told Sally that she must 'give it much consideration'. However, Mrs Parr knew full well that if she wished to keep Sally in her service then there must be some slackening of the reins whilst the old people were in need, and graciously gave her consent. 'But understand,' added the lady severely, 'you are to bring in the morning tea whenever it is *humanly possible*.' Sally promised, obedient as ever, to do all in her power.

For the next few months she scurried between the great house and the little thatched cottage and more often than not was early enough to take up the tea to her mistress and prepare her for the return to consciousness.

One summer morning, just before seven o'clock, she hastened by the dew-spangled shrubbery and was amazed to see the doctor's carriage outside the front door. In the kitchen a woebegone staff, sketchily dressed and with hair in curlers, poured forth the dramatic news. The master was dead! A heart attack, said the doctor, and mistress must be kept lying down to get over it!

Within a month poor Mr Parr was buried, his widow was settled in France, and his son was directing the decoration and alteration of his heritage. To Sally's stupefaction she found that she had been left the fabulous sum of one hundred pounds by her late employer. Young Mr Parr took her into Caxley and deposited it for her in the safety of a bank.

The village was agog with the news. Sally's parents were

beyond understanding her good fortune. Their days and nights were spent in fitful dozing, hovering between life and death, stirring occasionally to sup a bowl of gruel before sliding down thankfully upon the pillows again. In the thick of harvest time, as Fairacre folk sweated beneath a blazing sun, they slipped away within three days of each other and were buried together not far from Mr Parr's newly-erected marble angel.

Although she mourned her parents sincerely, there was no doubt that Sally's life now became very much easier. She still worked for the new master, but lived at home enjoying being mistress of her own small domain. Always an avid reader, she now had more time to indulge in this pleasure, and often took a book in one hand and her candle in the other and made her way to bed before nine o'clock, there to read until St Patrick's great clock struck midnight and the candle must be blown out.

She had been given a pile of books from her dead master's library when things were being sorted out, and these were to keep her occupied in her leisure moments for many years to come. Contentment of mind, more rest, and plenty of good country air and food began to show their effect on Sally. Hitherto small and rather skinny, she now began to put on flesh and soon became a little dumpling of a woman, albeit as quick on her feet as ever despite a certain breathlessness. She was now well on in her forties and her neighbours gave her no comfort.

'You be bound to put it on at your age,' said one.

'Better be fat and happy,' said another, 'than a bag o' bones.'

'You won't lose it now, my dear,' said a third smugly. ''Tis on for good when 'tis put on at your time of life.'

Sally was secretly nettled at this embarrassment of flesh. She let out seams, moved buttons and unpicked waistbands hoping, in vain, that one day she might revert to her former size. But the months grew into years and Sally's bulk grew too.

One sunny evening she sat in her back porch with a very

strange book in her hand. It was one of those bequeathed to her by her late master, a leather-covered exercise book which she had not troubled to open before. In it she found a number of recipes written out in a crabbed angular hand, in ink which had faded to a dull brown. They were not particularly interesting to Sally. Cooking was not one of her major interests and such household hints as: 'A Useful Polish for Ebonised Mahogany,' or 'A Valuable Amelioration for Children's Croup', which were also included in the book, did not stir her imagination. She yawned widely, and was about to put the book away and prepare her simple supper, when a heading caught her eye. It said: 'An Infallible Receipt for Losing Weight'.

Tilting the book to get the maximum light from the setting sun, Sally read with growing excitement.

To be sure, some of the ingredients sounded perfectly horrid. A basinful of pig's blood beaten with a pound of honey, some goose grease and a plover's egg was bad enough, thought Sally, but when an impressive list of ground herbs, moistened with cuckoo-spit, was to be added to it, then the concoction would surely be nauseating.

'Seal Top of Paste with Pig's Lard to Exclude Air,' said the recipe, and added in capital letters: 'PARTAKE SPARINGLY.'

Sally considered the page. Revolting it might be, but it was supposed to be infallible. The title said so. Would it be worth trying? She read the list of ingredients over again with close attention. The herbs would be easy to obtain, either from her own garden or the Parrs'. Cuckoo-spit glistened in all the meadows of Fairacre, honey stood ready in its comb on her pantry shelf, pig's blood and goose-grease could be obtained fairly readily. The plover's egg would be the most difficult article to procure, but somewhere on the flanks of the downs which sheltered Fairacre a boy's sharp eyes would be able to find a plover's nest, she felt sure.

The biggest problem was the assembling of all these ingredients without arousing suspicion. There are no secrets capable of being hidden in a village, as Sally well knew. It was not that she feared ridicule alone. Within her time she had seen old women ducked in the horse pond because their neighbours had suspected them of dabbling in witchcraft, and although the exercise book purported to be a straightforward recipe book there was something suspiciously sinister about the weight-reducing recipe. Sally decided to go about her task with the greatest circumspection. Who knows, in a few months' time she might have the trim slim figure of her youth? It was worth the trouble.

All went well. Even the plover's egg was obtained with comparative ease from a shepherd boy who, carrying six eggs to her cottage in his cap, was glad to earn a silver sixpence. One evening, after work, Sally prudently drew the curtain in her kitchen against prying eyes, and set about making the paste.

It smelt terrible and looked worse. It was yellowish-grey in colour, and speckled abominably with the ground herbs. Sally felt that she could not bring herself to taste it that evening, but would hope for strength in the morning. She retired to bed, with the reek of the concoction still in her nostrils.

It looked singularly unattractive by morning light, but after breakfast Sally put the tip of a spoon into the jar and bravely swallowed a morsel.

'I must do as it says and partake sparingly,' she told herself as she washed the spoon.

All that week she continued with the treatment. There seemed to be no result, but Sally was patient, and in any case expected to wait some weeks before her bulk began to diminish. Sometimes she felt a slight giddiness a few minutes after swallowing the stuff, but when one considered the nature of the ingredients this was hardly surprising.

One morning she decided to take a slightly larger dose. The clock on the mantel shelf told her it was later than usual, so that she flung the spoon in the washing-up bowl and set off at a brisk trot to the big house at the end of the village. She was perturbed to find that her gait was impaired. It seemed almost impossible to keep her heels on the ground, and Sally found herself tripping along on her toes, scarcely touching the ground at all. At the same time the giddiness occurred with some strength.

'Very strong stuff,' thought Sally to herself. 'Small wonder one's bid to partake sparingly!'

She took care to reduce the dose during the next week or two. By now it was high summer. Plumes of scented meadow-sweet tossed by the roadside, and the bright small birds kept up a gay clamour as they flashed from hedge to meadow and meadow to garden. Sally tried on her summer print gowns with growing despair. They were as tight as ever. Buttons burst from the strained bodices and waistbands gaped as Sally strove in vain to ram her bulk into the protesting garments.

'Dratted stuff!' panted Sally. 'Never done me a' aporth of good!' She surveyed herself in the small mirror which she had tilted forward in order to get a better view of her figure. Exasperation flooded her bulky frame. It was no good. She would simply have to make new dresses. These had been let out to their furthest limit.

She struggled out of the useless frocks, dressed in her former gown, and went sadly downstairs. The offending pot stood on the kitchen shelf.

'For two pins,' exclaimed Sally aloud, 'I'd throw you where you belongs – out on the rubbish heap!'

She was about to bustle about her household chores, when a thought struck her.

'Maybe I ain't been taking quite enough,' thought Sally. 'It's worth trying.'

Today was the perfect day to make an experiment. It was Sunday, and she need not go out anywhere. If a giddy attack followed the taking of too much medicine, then she could simply lie down until she recovered.

'And if it do make me giddy, but it works, then 'twill be worth it,' said Sally aloud. 'I can always take it at nights afore going to bed and sleep the giddiness off afore morning.'

She took a large spoon, dipped it deeply into the reeking mixture, and bravely downed it.

For a moment, nothing happened, apart from a slight feeling of nausea which taking the stuff habitually gave her. And then, to Sally's horror and alarm, her feet left the ground and she began to rise steadily to the ceiling. She bumped her head against the central rafter with some violence, and was about to scream loudly with combined pain and terror when prudence checked her.

'A fine thing if the neighbours saw you now,' she told herself severely. 'Look a proper fool, you would.' She tried to quieten her panicky heart, and the fear of ridicule, as well as being suspected of witchcraft, helped to keep her tongue silent.

It was uncomfortable and strange bobbing loosely about the ceiling trying to dodge the iron-hard rafter and the hanging oil lamp suspended from it, but Sally had always been of a philosophical strain and decided to make the best of a bad job.

' "What can't be cured must be endured," ' quoted Sally, running a finger along the top of the white china lamp shade. It was thick with dust, and Sally clucked disapprovingly at such filth in her house.

'No doubt about it: "Out of sight is out of mind." I must take this lot down and give it a real good wash in some suds.' A pang seized her. 'If I ever do get down,' she added despairingly. She propelled herself by pushing her hands against the ceiling until she was level with the high shelf where she stored bottling jars and preserving pans. To her horror she saw a large black beetle, dead and on its back, in the pan she kept for making pickles and chutney.

''Tis really shameful,' Sally scolded herself. 'If it hadn't been for this misfortune I'd never have realized what a slut I am.'

Below her the potatoes waited in a bowl of water to be

peeled. The cat mewed by his empty saucer, and the big black kettle on the oil stove began to hum.

'Lawks!' thought Sally. 'How long do I have to stick up here, I wonder? Them dizzy turns went over in ten minutes or so. With any luck I'll be down in half an hour.' Would the kettle boil over before then, she thought agitatedly? Really, it was too bad! It would teach her a lesson to go dabbling in things she didn't understand!

She had realized, as soon as her head cracked against the beam, that she had misconstrued the heading of the recipe. She had indeed lost weight, but not size. It was only now, in the first half-hour or so of her bizarre imprisonment, that she began to foresee the possibilities of her discovery. As a short woman, she had always found difficulty in reaching shelves and cupboards put into the cottage by her tall father. A stout stool accompanied Sally on many a job in the house such as window-cleaning, or storing preserves, or the winter blankets, in high little-used cupboards.

'If I takes just the right amount,' pondered Sally, picking a particularly thick cobweb from the top of the curtains, 'I can float just where I need to.' She began to dally with the idea of picking apples and plums without needing to borrow a ladder, but reason told her at once of the dangers.

'Too many prying eyes,' decided Sally sagaciously, 'and dear knows how high I might go if the wind got me! It's got to be faced. I'm more like a balloon than anything else when I've that stuff inside me.'

At that moment she heard footsteps. Her front door stood open, as was its custom in fine weather, and this gave direct access to the living-room. Luckily, the door between that room and the kitchen was securely shut. Sally edged her way, silently and painfully, to a shadowy corner of the ceiling. Her heart pounded. Would she be discovered?

'You in, my dear?' called her neighbour. Sally preserved a frozen silence.

'Be you upstairs?' went on the voice. Sally heard the clang of the metal door scraper. Lawks a mercy, what if she came in? Sally's throat dried at the very thought. She clung to the pan shelf with trembling fingers, praying with all her might. The kettle began to bubble steadily, and the cat jumped noisily on to the table among the dishes.

'You home, Sal?' said the voice, a little louder. The door scraper clanged again, then silence fell. At last, there was the sound of muttering and the slow fading of footsteps along the brick path to Sally's gate. Sally covered her face with her grimy hands and wept with relief. Ten minutes later, her body began to feel more solid and manageable. She found she could control the direction of her legs and arms with growing accuracy, and slowly she sank groundwards.

The first thing she did was to make a good strong pot of tea and carry it into the living-room to recover. A fine cabbage, obviously brought by her neighbour, waited on the threshold. She must go and thank her, when her legs stopped trembling, and explain that she must have been 'down the garden' when she called.

Meanwhile, sipping and thinking, Sally regained her composure and turned over in her mind the best way of making use of the secret and surprising accomplishment with which she was now endowed.

There now began, for Sally, a period of engrossing interest and pleasure. After her duties at the big house, she hurried home to experiment with her essays in levitation. She found that by taking a small amount of the concoction she could hover about a foot above the ground for a period of roughly ten minutes. This gave her ample time to tidy shelves, wash out high cupboards, dust the picture rail and so on, tasks which had always been irksome to one of her low stature.

She found it wholly delightful to be without weight, and became skilled at balancing herself, with one hand touching a wall, whilst the other performed its task. Naturally, she did not indulge in this secret practice every day. For one thing, she still feared that it might be discovered by her neighbours in Fairacre, and she had no intention of giving them cause for gossip. She found it prudent to keep her 'floating periods' for Thursdays. Market day in Caxley was on a Thursday, and usually the other inhabitants of Tyler's Row spent their Thursdays hunting for bargains, meeting their friends and catching up with their news amidst the market-day bustle. Alone in her cottage, Sally felt safe from unexpected visitors, and experimented with the mixture.

One day she noticed that both the plum tree and the ancient Bramley Seedling apple tree were heavy with fruit. She had wondered for some time if she might dare to practise floating out of doors, and this seemed the time to experiment. There was much to consider before she began.

Of course she must remain unseen by the neighbours. That was the first consideration. It would be wise, therefore, to wait until nightfall to make her first attempt. Then she must be careful to leave a considerable amount of fruit to be picked in the normal way or her neighbours would wonder why she had not borrowed a ladder as was her usual practice.

Then, of course, there was the question of staying in her own garden. She shuddered at the thought of floating out into the blue, as well she might, if she did not take care. It was not so much the *danger* that worried Sally as the *impropriety* of such a mode of travelling. After considerable thought she decided to tie a stout length of clothes line round her waist and to tie a brick to the other end. She would carry the brick, already tied, up in the basket with her. On attaining the correct height she would throw the brick to the ground, remain safely tethered level with the fruit, pick it and place it in the basket, and so get the job done.

Of course, there was more to it than the general plan. For one thing Sally had to calculate the height of the fruit from the ground, how much the brick would weigh and how much of her mixture she needed to take to balance all these factors. But she was determined to try her luck, and one moonless night she crept from the cottage to embark on this adventure.

It was very still and quiet. The windows in the row of cottages were dark. Not a soul stirred. St Patrick's clock had struck one as Sally tip-toed down her stairs, and all Fairacre slept the dreamless sleep of those who live and work in the bracing air of the downs.

A spoonful and a half of the revolting brew was doing its best to settle in Sally's affronted stomach as she approached the plum tree. Already her feet were skimming the grass and she had hardly reached the gnarled old trunk before she began to rise swiftly. For a moment Sally was torn with panic. She felt horribly vulnerable out here in the open and would have welcomed the painful crack of the kitchen rafter on her head, at that moment. She clawed frantically at a substantial branch, as she floated by, and paused to get her breath. Taking a tight grip with one hand, she groped inside the basket on her arm, found the brick and cast it downward.

It seemed to make the most appalling shindy and also jerked Sally cruelly round the waist. Breathless, she listened. Supposing the neighbours were disturbed and looked out of their windows? Supposing the rope broke? Sally gripped the tree even more desperately in her agitation. But the silence engulfed her, and only the distant yelping of a stoat stirred the blackness, as a falling leaf might ruffle the satin smoothness of a still pool.

Emboldened, Sally turned to her task. It was not easy, but it was wonderfully exhilarating to be at large in the tree tops and her basket was soon full. Weight returned to her in roughly half an hour, and Sally crept back to the cottage, basket in one hand, brick in the other, and went, highly elated, to bed.

*

Time passed. A pot of the mixture stood permanently on Sally's larder shelf and she began to take her ability to levitate almost for granted. She was wonderfully lucky in preserving her secret, although over the years she had one or two dangerous moments. One day, for example, she was cleaning her bedroom window inside, floating about eight inches above the rush matting, when her neighbour appeared on the garden path below her and asked if she might borrow some sugar.

'I'll be down in a minute,' Sally replied, doing her best to keep her feet hidden from sight below the window sill.

'Shall I take a cupful myself?' suggested the woman. 'Save you leaving the windows, like?'

'No, no,' answered Sally, trying to sound airy, as indeed she felt. 'I'll bring it round the minute I've finished.'

If she gets in here, thought Sally frantically, she'll be upstairs in double-quick time and I'm aloft here for a good five minutes yet. The woman watched her closely, as she undulated from one pane to the next.

'What you standin' on, gal?' she asked suspiciously.

'My little old stool,' responded Sally, tightening her hold on the curtain and concentrating her attention on one pane. 'Don't you trouble to wait,' she added hastily. 'I'll be round in two shakes.'

To her infinite relief the woman departed, but the incident left Sally severely shaken. It was several weeks before she dared to take another dose.

Under cover of darkness she often repeated her first outdoor experiment and picked fruit for pies and puddings, jamming and bottling. On one occasion the landlord of The Beetle and Wedge had asked her curiously how she had picked her apple tree so clean, and she had said quickly that she had 'given it a good old shake' and the wind had done the rest. He seemed to believe her.

One late October day, when Sally was almost sixty years of age, she gazed with a speculative eye upon her walnut tree.

This was a lofty beauty, of great age, and heavy this year with magnificent nuts. Sally decided to lengthen her rope and to make an assault upon it.

''Tis Thursday,' said Sally aloud, 'and they all be safely at market. By teatime it'll be dark enough to try.'

She made her preparations and made her way to the tree as dusk began to fall. The neighbours' cottages were empty and would remain so for a full hour, as well she knew. What she had not reckoned with was a freshening wind and the enormous collie puppy which came from the farm.

The brick lay at the foot of the tree, half hidden in wet grass. Higher than she had ever been before Sally plucked swiftly at the green walnuts, staining her fingers brown as the basket filled. The wind made things difficult, tugging at her skirts and lifting the boughs from her reach. It grew more boisterous each minute and Sally began to feel alarmed.

'I'll be downright thankful when this lightness wears off,' she said to herself, clinging to a sturdy branch. At that moment she became conscious of a rhythmic tremor running up the rope. There, busily gnawing at it, just above the brick, was the collie puppy. Caution thrown to the winds, Sally screamed at him.

'Be off, sir! Get away, you rascal!'

The puppy wagged a delighted tail and continued his gnawing. His strong white teeth, busy at their task, seemed to grin at her. Sally began to pelt him with walnuts, but he was unperturbed. Slowly but surely the strands were severed, until a particularly fierce gust of wind caught Sally unawares, broke the rope completely, and jerked her violently from the walnut tree. Still screaming, Sally rose abruptly another twenty or thirty feet, and began to twirl this way and that as the wind blew her on an erratic course clean across the village.

Over and over Sally rolled, like an escaped balloon, and soon she felt sick as well as frightened. But her innate common sense began to assert itself, and just as she had accepted the first ridiculous position against her own kitchen ceiling so, in this present predicament, she did her best to come to terms with the situation.

First, she stopped screaming. On no account would she draw attention to herself. She'd got herself in this pickle, and she'd get herself out of it. Dusk was falling fast and with luck her progress through the sky would pass unnoticed. The roaring of the wind would distract people's attention from unusual sounds above them. Heads down against the onslaught, they would probably be intent on getting home, Sally comforted herself.

Her own travelling arrangements next occupied her thoughts. The rope trailed behind her like an unwieldy tail. She hauled it painfully in towards her, rolling the end loosely round one arm. This steadied her a little, and by gripping it between her feet, a few inches below her billowing skirts, she was more likely to stay upright, she discovered. True, she still twirled and bobbed in a highly distracting fashion, but at least she was travelling with a little more decorum and her skirts were hanging in approximately the right direction. Her bun had come down and her locks streamed in the wind, but Sally found this remarkably refreshing. It was years since she had felt the wind blowing through her loose hair.

She floated dangerously close to the spire of St Patrick's and noticed how remarkably dirty the weather cock was at its tip. Below her she could see the new village school and the little playground, now mercifully empty. The village street wound its way beneath her, and she was thankful that it too appeared to be empty. Her pace was brisk, for the wind was now a gale and the noise from the topmost branches of the elms beyond the school almost deafened her. She looked down upon the untidy rooks' nests swaying dizzily at the top of the trees, and then swirled onwards towards the open fields between Fairacre and Springbourne.

At last, she began to lose height. Her weight began to return and she braced herself for the descent to earth. Alas, by this

time she was in the great park of Springbourne Manor and heading at incredible speed towards the avenue of lime trees which bordered the drive to the house. Closing her eyes and gripping the rope tightly, Sally awaited the crash. It came with a vast rending of boughs and garments. Dazed and bruised, Sally came to rest a good thirty feet above ground, securely enmeshed in lime branches and the remains of a squirrel's drey.

She was discovered by a cowman, who was making his way home after milking. By that time she had thrown the rope off and descended carefully as low as she could. The last twelve feet, unfortunately, consisted of trunk alone and it was while she was trying to brace herself to jump that the man arrived.

To Sally's relief he was a man of few words.

"Old on,' he said. 'I'll get a ladder.'

He returned in a few minutes and helped her down. They walked part of the way to Fairacre together in silence. At length he turned in to his cottage gate.

'Good night,' he bade her and then added: 'How d'yer get up there?'

Sally began the tale she had already manufactured. It involved being chased by a bull, and was the best she could manage under the trying circumstances. She was aware, as she came to a faltering halt, that her rescuer was not impressed.

'Must be a damn good leaper,' he observed drily, and went indoors.

Sally, bruised and weary, dragged herself homeward, took the pot from the larder shelf and threw it resolutely on to the rubbish heap.

Later that evening she thrust the exercise book into her fire and, holding it firmly down with the poker, she watched it burn to ashes.

She had flown for the last time.

'Well, there it is, Miss Read,' said Mr Willet, rising from his chair. 'Take it or leave it. That's what Sally told my mother a year or two later, just afore she died.'

'I don't disbelieve you,' I said slowly. 'It's a wonderful story. It's just that – somehow –'

'Well, what?' asked Mr Willet, blowing out his moustache fiercely. 'Proper doubting Thomases, some people be!'

'It's just that it seems extraordinary that no one ever saw her. Particularly on the last journey, I mean.'

'Ah, but they did! There was two little boys, brothers they were, as had been sent down to the pub. They saw Sally, and rope and all, skidding along over The Beetle and Wedge, and tore 'ome to tell their mum and dad. 'Course, all they got was a clump on the ear-'ole for being such a pair of liars, so they never said no more. And years later, when the poor ol' girl had gone, the landlord at the pub said he'd seen her picking plums two or three times, but never liked to say so.'

'I wonder why not?' I exclaimed.

Mr Willet sighed patiently. 'You a school teacher and you don't know 'uman nature yet!' he commented. 'Why, people don't mind being thought downright evil and wicked, but they fair hates to seem fools. Ain't you learned that yet, Miss Read?'

He opened the kitchen door and looked out into the windy darkness.

'That coke'll have to wait till morning now. Good-bye, miss, and thanks for the tea. See you bright and early.'

And he vanished into the night.

3. JINGLE BELLS

Mr Willet was as good as his word, and next morning, 'bright and early', I had my breakfast to the accompaniment of the brushing up of coke in the distance. He was still at it when I crossed to the school, wielding the broom vigorously in his capable hands, his breath wreathing his head in silvery clouds.

'Nasty cold morning,' I called to him, scurrying towards shelter.

'This keeps me warm,' he replied, pausing for a moment to rest on his broom. 'But I s'pose I shan't be doing this much longer.'

'Only three days,' I agreed. 'And then it's the lovely Christmas holidays!'

'You should be ashamed!' said Mr Willet reproachfully. 'Young woman like you, wishing your life away.'

But it was too cold to argue, and I only had time to wave to him before whisking into the shelter of the lobby.

The last day of term, particularly the Christmas term, has a splendour of its own. There is an air of excitement at the thought of pleasures and freedom to come, but there is also a feeling of relaxation from daily routine made much more acute by the deliciously empty desks. Books have been collected and stacked in neat piles in the cupboard. Papers and exercise books have been tidied away. All that remains to employ young hands in this last glorious day is a pencil and loose sheets of paper which have been saved for just such an occasion.

Of course, work will be done. There will be mental arithmetic, and some writing; perhaps some spelling lists and paper games, and stories told to each other. And today, the children knew, there would be Christmas carols, and a visit to the old grey church next door to see the crib recently set up by the vicar's wife and other ladies of the village. The very thought of it all created a glow which warmed the children despite the winter's cold.

They entered more exuberantly than ever, cherry-nosed, hair curling damply from the December air and wellingtons plastered with Fairacre mud. I began to shoo them back into the lobby before our virago of a caretaker discovered them, but I was too late.

Mrs Pringle, emerging from the infants' room where she had just deposited a scuttle of coke on an outspread sheet of *The Times Educational Supplement*, looked at them with marked dislike.

'Anyone 'ere seen fit to use the door scraper?' she asked sourly. 'Don't look like it to me. What you kids wants is an hour or two scrubbing this 'ere floor like I 'ave to. That'd make you think twice about dirtying my clean floorboards.'

She cast a malevolent glance in my direction and stumped out to the lobby. The children retreated before her, observing her marked limp, a sure sign of trouble.

The clatter of the door scraper and the bang of the heavy Gothic door announced Mrs Pringle's departure to her cottage, until midday, when she was due to return to wash up the school dinner things. The children's spirits rose again and they sang 'Away in a Manger' with rather more gusto than perhaps was necessary at prayer time.

The infants departed to their own side of the partition and my class prepared to give part of its mind to some light scholastic task. Multiplication tables are always in sore need of attention, as every teacher knows, so that a test on the scrap paper already provided seemed a useful way of passing the arithmetic lesson. It was small wonder that excitement throbbed throughout the classroom. The paper chains still rustled overhead in all their multi-coloured glory and in the corner, on the now depleted nature table, the Christmas tree glittered with tinsel and bright baubles.

But this year it carried no parcels. Usually, Fairacre school has a party on the last afternoon of the Christmas term when mothers and fathers, and friends of the school, come and eat a hearty tea and watch the children receive their presents from the tree. But this year the party was to be held in the village hall after Christmas and a conjurer had been engaged to entertain us afterwards.

However, the children guessed that they would not go home empty-handed today, I felt sure, and this touching faith, which I had no intention of destroying, gave them added happiness throughout the morning.

The weather grew steadily worse. Sleet swept across the playground and a wicked draught from the skylight buffeted the paper chains. I put the milk saucepan on the tortoise stove and the children looked pleased. Although a few hardy young-sters gulp their milk down stone-cold, even on the iciest day, most of them prefer to be cosseted a little and to see their bottles being tipped into the battered saucepan. The slow heating of the milk affords them exquisite pleasure, and it usually gets more attention than I do on cold days.

'It's steaming, miss,' one calls anxiously.

'Shall I make sure the milk's all right?' queries another.

'Can I get the cups ready?' asks a third.

One never-to-be-forgotten day we left the milk on whilst we had a rousing session in the playground as aeroplanes, gallop-ing horses, trains and other violently moving articles. On our return, breathless and much invigorated, we had discovered a sizzling seething mess on the top, and cascading down the sides, of the stove. Mrs Pringle did not let any of us forget this mishap, and the children like to pretend that they only keep reminding me to save me from incurring that lady's wrath yet again.

In between sips of their steaming milk they kept up an excited chatter.

'What d'you want for Christmas?' asked Patrick of Ernest, his desk mate.

'Boxing gloves,' replied Ernest, lifting his head briefly and speaking through a white moustache.

'Well, I'm havin' a football, and a space helmet, and some new crayons, and a signal box for my train set,' announced Patrick proudly.

Linda Moffat, neat as a new pin from glossy hair to equally glossy patent leather slippers, informed me that she was hoping for a new work-box with a pink lining. I thought of the small embroidery scissors, shaped like a stork, which I had wrapped up for her the night before, and congratulated myself.

45

'What do you want?' I asked Joseph Coggs, staring monkey-like at me over the rim of his mug.

'Football,' croaked Joseph, in his hoarse gipsy voice. 'Might get it too.'

It occurred to me that this would make an excellent exercise in writing and spelling. Milk finished, I set them to work on long strips of paper.

'Ernest wants some boxing gloves for Christmas,' was the first entry.

'Patrick hopes to get –' began the second. The children joined in this list-making with great enthusiasm.

When Mrs Crossley, who brings the dinners, arrived, she was cross-questioned about her hopes.

'Well now, I don't really know,' she confessed, balancing the tins against her wet mackintosh and peering perplexedly over the top. 'A kitchen set, I think. You know, a potato masher and fish slice and all that, in a nice little rack.'

The children obviously thought this a pretty poor present but began to write down: 'Mrs Crossley wants a kitchen set,' below the last entry, looking faintly disbelieving as they did so.

'And what do you want?' asked Linda, when Mrs Crossley had vanished.

'Let me see,' I said slowly. 'Some extra nice soap, perhaps, and bath cubes; and a book or two, and a new rose bush to plant by my back door.'

'Is that all?'

'No sweets?'

'No, no sweets,' I said. 'But I should like a very pretty little ring I saw in Caxley last Saturday.'

'You'll have to get married for that,' said Ernest soberly. 'And you're too old now.' The others nodded in agreement.

'You're probably right,' I told them, keeping a straight face. 'Put your papers away and let's set the tables for dinner.'

*

The sleet was cruelly painful on our faces as we scuttled across the churchyard to St Patrick's. Inside it was cold and shadowy. The marble memorial tablets on the wall glimmered faintly in the gloom, and the air struck chill. But the crib was aglow with rosy light, a spot of warmth and hope in the darkness. The children tip-toed towards it, awed by their surroundings.

They spent a long time gazing, whispering their admiration and pointing out particular details to each other. They were loth to leave it, and the shelter of the great church, which had defied worse weather than this for many centuries.

We pelted back to the school, for I had a secret plan to put into action, and three o'clock was the time appointed for it. St Patrick's clock chimed a quarter to, above our heads, as we hurried across the churchyard.

I had arranged with the infants' teacher to go privately into the lobby promptly at three and there shake some bells abstracted earlier from the percussion band box. We hoped that the infants would believe that an invisible Father

Christmas had driven on his sleigh and delivered the two sacks of parcels which would be found in the lobby. At the moment, these were in the hall of my house. I proposed to leave my class for a minute, shake the bells, hide them from inquisitive eyes and return again to the children.

This innocent deception could not hope to take in many of my own children, I felt sure, but the babies would enjoy it, and so too would the younger ones in my classroom. I was always surprised at the remarkable reticence which the older children showed when the subject of Father Christmas cropped up. Those that knew seemed more than willing to keep up the pretence for the sake of the younger ones, and perhaps because they feared that the presents would not be forthcoming if they let the cat out of the bag or boasted of their knowledge.

I settled the class with more paper. They could draw a picture of the crib or St Patrick's church, or a winter scene of any kind, I told them. Someone wanted to go on with his list of presents and was readily given permission. The main thing was to have a very quiet classroom at three o'clock. Our Gothic doors are of sturdy oak and the sleigh bells would have to be shaken to a frenzy in order to make themselves heard.

At two minutes to three by the wall clock Patrick looked up from drawing a church with all four sides showing at once, and surmounted by what looked like a mammoth ostrich.

'I've got muck on my hand,' he said. 'Can I go out the lobby and wash?'

Maddening child! What a moment to choose!

'Not now,' I said, as calmly as I could. 'Just wipe it on your hanky.'

He produced a dark grey rag from his pocket and rubbed the offending hand, sighing in a martyred way. He was one of the younger children and I wondered if he might possibly half-believe in the sleigh bells.

'I'm just going across to the house,' I told them, squaring my conscience. 'Be very quiet while I'm away. The infants are listening to a story.'

All went according to plan. I struggled back through the sleet with the two sacks, deposited one outside the infants' door into the lobby, and the other outside our own.

The lobby was as quiet as the grave. I withdrew the bells from behind a stack of bars of yellow soap which Mrs Pringle stores on a lofty shelf, and crept to the outside door to begin shaking. Santa Claus in the distance, and fast approaching, I told myself. Would they be heard, I wondered, waggling frantically in the open doorway?

I closed the door gently against the driving sleet and now shook with all my might by the two inner doors. Heaven help me if one of my children burst out to see what was happening!

There was an uncanny silence from inside both rooms. I gave a last magnificent agitation and then crept along the lobby to the bars of soap and tucked the bells securely out of sight. Then I returned briskly to the classroom. You could have heard a pin drop.

'There was bells outside,' said Joseph huskily.

'The clock's just struck three,' I pointed out, busying myself at the blackboard.

'No. *Little* bells!' said someone.

At this point the dividing door between the infants' room and ours burst open to reveal a bright-eyed mob lugging a sack.

'Father Christmas has been!'

'We heard him!'

'We heard bells, didn't we?'

'That's right. Sleigh bells.'

Ernest, by this time, had opened our door into the lobby and was returning with the sack. A cheer went up and the whole class converged upon him.

'Into your desks,' I bellowed, 'and Ernest can give them out.'

Ernest upended the sack and spilt the contents into a glorious heap of pink and blue parcels, as the children scampered to their desks and hung over them squeaking with excitement.

The babies sat on the floor receiving their presents with

awed delight. There was no doubt about it, for them Father Christmas was as real as ever.

I became conscious of Patrick's gaze upon me.

'Did you see him?' he asked.

'Not a sign,' I said truthfully.

Patrick's brow was furrowed with perplexity.

'If you'd let me wash my hand I reckon I'd just about've seen him,' he said at length.

I made no reply. Patrick's gaze remained fixed on my face, and then a slow lovely smile curved his countenance. Together, amidst the hubbub of parcel-opening around us, we shared the unspoken, immortal secret of Christmas.

Later with the presents unwrapped, and the floor a sea of paper, Mrs Pringle arrived to start clearing up. Her face expressed considerable disapproval and her limp was very severe.

The children thronged around her showing her their toys.

'Ain't mine lovely?'

'Look, it's a dust cart!'

'This is a *magic* painting book! It says so!'

Mrs Pringle unbent a little among so much happiness, and gave a cramped smile.

Ernest raised his voice as she limped her way slowly across the room. 'Mrs Pringle, Mrs Pringle!'

The lady turned, a massive figure ankle deep in pink and blue wrappings.

'What do you want in your stocking, Mrs Pringle?' called Ernest. There was a sudden hush.

Mrs Pringle became herself again. 'In my stocking?' she asked tartly. 'A new leg! That's what I want!'

She moved majestically into the lobby, pretending to ignore the laughter of the children at this sally.

As usual, I thought wryly, Mrs Pringle had had the last word.

4. MRS NEXT-DOOR

One of the most exhilarating things about the holidays is the freedom to wander about the village at those hours which are, in term time, spent incarcerated in the class room. There is nothing I relish more than calling at the Post Office, or the village shop, in the mid-morning, or afternoon, like all my lucky neighbours who are not confined by school hours.

A few days before term began I set off to buy stamps from Mr Lamb, our postmaster. It was a sharp, sunny January morning, with thin ice cracking on the puddles, and distant sounds could be heard exceptionally clearly. A winter robin piped from a high bare elm. Cows lowed three fields away, and somewhere, high above, an airliner whined its way to a warmer land than ours.

Nearer at hand I could hear a rhythmic chugging sound. As I turned the bend towards the Post Office I saw that it came from a cement mixer, hard at work, in front of a pair of cottages which were being made into one attractive house.

A group of my school children hovered nearby, gazing at the operations. Some trailed shopping bags, and I could only hope that their mothers were not in urgent need of anything, for it was obvious that the fascination of men at work was overpowering. Patrick was among them, gyrating like a dervish, as an enormous scruffy dog on a lead tagged him round and round.

''Ello, miss,' he managed to puff on his giddy journey, and the others smiled and said 'Hullo' in an abstracted fashion. The workmen seemed to be getting far more concentrated attention than is my usual lot, I noticed.

As I waited my turn to be served, I looked through the window at the scene. I had ample time to watch, for this was Thursday, pensions day, and several elderly Fairacre worthies were collecting their money. Mr Lamb had a leisurely chat with each one, and as we all had a word with each other as well, it was a very pleasant and sociable twenty minutes, and we all felt the better for it.

The cottages had been stripped of their old rotting thatch, and the men were busy making a roof of cedar shingles. Watching them run up and down ladders I suddenly remembered that it was in one of these cottages that Mrs Next-Door had lived. Miss Clare had told me her story soon after I arrived as school mistress at Fairacre School.

It happened to be the first time I had visited Miss Clare's cottage at the neighbouring village of Beech Green. She had lived there since she was six years old. When I first met her she was in charge of the infants' class at Fairacre, a wise, patient, white-haired teacher who had taught there for half a century.

It was a gloriously hot August afternoon when I set out to walk to Miss Clare's, and I very soon found that it was much further than I realized. I toiled up a short steep hill, and leant thankfully upon a field gate near the summit. Cornfields spread before me, shimmering in the heat. Scarlet poppies dropped a petal or two, and high in the blue a hawk hovered motionless for a while, and then painted invisible circles with its wing-tip, slipping languidly and elegantly round the sky.

I resumed my travels, but determined to catch the bus home. Luckily it was market day, and a bus would leave Caxley just before six o'clock, passing Miss Clare's cottage about half past.

After one of Miss Clare's sumptuous teas, and a great deal of chatter, we walked together to her white gate. Two haw-thorn trees flank it, and have met above to form a thick archway. In its welcome shade we waited, she on her side of the gate, and I on the other, ready to dart to the edge of the road when the bus came in sight.

An old lady, very upright on an ancient bicycle, pedalled slowly past, and wished us 'Good evening'.

When she was out of earshot, Miss Clare said, 'That's Mrs Next-Door. At least, she's really Mrs Wood, and my nearest neighbour, but I think of her as Mrs Next-Door.' She began to laugh, and then noticed my puzzled air. 'Of course, I forgot. You don't know the story of Polly, who was the original Mrs Next-Door. It happened years ago in Fairacre and was as good as any serial story to us in the village.'

She leant comfortably upon her gate in the shade of the leafy archway and embarked on a gay snippet of Fairacre's history.

A few years after the Great War of 1914–1918, when Fairacre was doing its best to settle down again to peaceful village affairs, two young couples moved into the pair of thatched cottages opposite the Post Office, within a few weeks of each other.

The first pair were named Leslie and Bertha Foster. They were both big, fair and rather slow, with one boy, Billy, who was almost five years old. When they arrived, soon after Michaelmas Day, Bertha was again in an interesting condition; or, it might be more correct to say, in a condition interesting to the village. Fairacre speculated upon the possible date of the unknown's arrival, its sex, and the many vicissitudes it would cause its mother before, and during, birth.

Leslie Foster was the newly appointed cowman to Walnut Tree Farm, and as he had an aunt in Fairacre his history was fairly well known. But his wife was a Caxley girl and the village watched closely to see how she would settle down.

On the whole she was approved. She was friendly and hard-working. By the evening of the first day her house was clean and tidy, and new curtains hung at the windows. To be sure, Fairacre was not at all certain about the curtains. Most people had lace ones, a few others had flowered cretonne, and the gentry seemed to go in for damask or velvet as they had done for years. But Bertha's curtains were of plain cream cotton, and she had stitched five rows of coloured braid along the bottom. The braid was a deep blue, exactly the same colour as the one cushion in the room, which was placed squarely upon the seat of Leslie's wooden armchair. Some thought the curtains were 'a bit far-fetched and arty-crafty', but one or two younger people thought them 'real pretty and up-to-date'.

A few weeks later, the second cottage became occupied. Mike Norton was also going to work for the same employer as his neighbour, for these were tied cottages. They had not moved in earlier because a faulty chimney had needed attention. His wife Polly was thin and dark. It was noticed, by keen eyes around them, that their house was not put in order as quickly as the Fosters' had been, and that Polly's curtains were extremely shabby and obviously make-shift.

There were no children, but many a wife told another that Polly Norton looked a bit peaky and as they had been married now for six months (so they had heard) perhaps she had good cause.

The two families became friends. The men did not have the same opportunity to exchange confidences, obstetric and otherwise, which their wives had, for they only saw each other briefly on the farm and were both glad to rest indoors when they reached home in the evening. But the two women spent a great deal of time in each other's houses and often took Billy for a walk in the afternoon together.

Within a fortnight Bertha had told Polly that her second was due in January and that she wanted a girl, and Polly had coyly mentioned her hopes for the following June. She had set her heart on a boy and was already trying to decide between the names Mervyn and Clifford. Bertha's girl was to be called

Maria, after Leslie's mother, and Polly secretly thought it a very common name indeed.

Thus began a halcyon period of exchanging knitting patterns, comparing the discomforts of early and advanced pregnancy, and shopping frugally in Caxley for all those things incidental to a new baby's arrival. Despite Bertha's slowness, her greater experience and her upbringing made her the leader of the two. She had been brought up in a respectable home in Caxley, had been taught well at one of the town schools and enjoyed the advantage of a mother who was an excellent cook and dressmaker. Bertha's few shillings went a good deal further than Polly's.

Polly was one of a large and somewhat feckless family from Beech Green. This was her first home and she was anxious to make it as splendid as she could without taking too much time and trouble in doing so. As soon as Mike brought home his first week's wages she clamoured for money for new curtains.

'Can't be done this week,' said her husband ruefully. 'You'll 'ave to put a bit by regular.'

Polly saw the sense in this and reckoned that she should have enough to buy the material before Christmas. She discussed the matter eagerly with Bertha, and this was her neighbour's first shock.

'If you don't mind,' said Polly brightly, 'I'd like 'em just exactly like yourn.'

Bertha was seriously taken aback. 'Well,' she began doubtfully, in her slow voice, 'I don't truthfully know as –'

Polly cut in swiftly. 'I reckons they're the prettiest curtains as I've ever seen. And another thing, the two houses'd look much nicer with matching curtains in the front. Dales had some real nice cream material in their sale last week, and I can get the braid there too.'

It was quite apparent to Bertha that the matter was as good as settled. Nettled though she was, she did not protest. After all, there was really nothing to stop Polly from having similar curtains, she told herself, and for the sake of the coming baby she tried not to feel upset.

But for the rest of the day, resentment smouldered in Bertha's breast. When Leslie came home she poured the tale into his ears.

Leslie, cold, tired and busy with his rabbit stew, did his best to smooth things over.

'I shouldn't fret about it. Don't hurt you if the curtains are the same. My ma says: "Imitation is the best form of flattery." Come to think of it, Bertha, it's a compliment, really. Shows she likes your choice.'

Bertha was somewhat mollified by this aspect of the matter. In any case, she did not want to fall out with her neighbour, and nothing more was said. Nevertheless, the incident rankled, and when the curtains were hung at last, she felt crosser than ever when she saw that the braid was the identical width and colour, and arranged in exactly the same five rows.

'Should have thought she could've had red or green, or summat different,' exclaimed Bertha to her husband. 'I should be ashamed to be such a copycat.'

Bertha's placid countenance was quite pink with wrath and Leslie again had to act as a soothing agent. The baby was now due, and whether the curtains next door had anything to do with the arrival of a fine daughter that night, no one could tell. The birth was easy, and Leslie was able to set off to work at his usual time, leaving Bertha and Maria in the capable hands of the local midwife.

'Ain't she just lovely?' breathed Polly admiringly, when she came round to see the baby. Her sharp eyes fell upon the cradle. It had been dressed in yard upon yard of spotted muslin, by Bertha's mother, and caught at the top with a splendid pint satin bow.

'You never showed me the cradle,' she said reproachfully.

Bertha, sleepy and content, smiled upon her. 'It was at my ma's. She only brought it over yesterday. What's more, she

57

made two bows, one pink and one blue, so's we'd have the right one.'

Polly was full of admiration. United in baby-worship, the two neighbours were in happy accord.

But this blissful state of affairs was not to last long. Spring arrived, and a double row of purple crocuses bordered Bertha's path. Behind them stood a fine row of polyanthuses heavy with buds. In Polly's identical border, there were also purple crocuses, and behind hers grew an equally fine collection of polyanthus plants.

"Tis too bad!' exclaimed Bertha to Leslie, thoroughly vexed. 'She knew I'd put them in. And I wouldn't mind betting her spring flowers come out yellow, same as ourn!'

They did, and Bertha's wrath grew. The tart comments which hovered on her tongue she managed to restrain, however, although she wondered at times if a bit of plain speaking would be a good thing.

Her baby was now a few months old, a big, fair, placid child like her parents. Billy had started school and Bertha was free to attend to her neighbour when she felt the onset of birth pangs. Polly was unduly fearful, clinging to Bertha in much agitation.

'Don't 'ee leave me till Mrs Drew comes!' she begged, naming the local midwife.

'Don't fret,' answered Bertha soothingly. 'I'll stay with you, but I think you'd be better upstairs.'

'No, no,' responded Polly. 'I'll walk about down here and get Mike's dinner ready atween whiles. Keeps my mind off it a bit, to have summat to do.'

Bertha saw the sense in this and did not press the matter. She was greatly relieved, though, when the midwife came and hustled her patient upstairs.

The baby was a long time arriving. Bertha and Leslie could hear muffled activity in the bedroom next door to their own.

'I do feel downright sorry for Polly,' murmured Bertha, the memory of her own experiences still fresh in her mind. 'It must be over soon, that's one comfort.'

But the baby had not arrived when the Fosters rose next morning. Mike came round, haggard and unshaven, to ask Leslie to take a message to the farm.

'She's about all in,' he said. 'Dammit all, that's the last baby we're having. Never thought it'd be such a set-to.'

Bertha and Leslie made light of it, teasing him, but he was too tired to appreciate badinage, and returned moodily to his home.

At midday the child was born. The midwife called in to tell Bertha it was a girl.

'They're both asleep, and can do with it,' declared the old woman who had brought half Fairacre into the world.

'I'll look in tomorrow,' promised Bertha, 'when she's feeling better.'

The next morning, a posy in her hand for Polly and a freshly-made pie for Mike's supper in her basket, Bertha went next door. She called, but there was no reply. She mounted the stairs and gently pushed open the bedroom door.

What Bertha saw, before the opening had widened enough to include a view of mother and child, made her grip the posy in a furiously clenched fist. For there, beside the bed, stood a cradle which was the replica of her own, even to a splendid pink satin bow.

Bertha swallowed her rage and tip-toed into the bedroom. The creaking of the old boards awakened Polly.

'Oh, Bertha!' she said, with such affection and relief that Bertha's anger melted. ''Tis lovely to see you. Take a peep at the baby. Fancy me having a girl, just like you!'

Bertha could have said that it caused her no surprise, but this was hardly the time to be so uncharitable. In any case, the new-born infant quite won her heart with its red puckered face, cobwebby black hair and skinny fingers.

'Ain't she a real beauty!' she exclaimed with sincerity. A thought struck her. 'What are you going to call her?'

'Mildred,' replied the mother. 'It begins with M, just like yourn.'

Bertha was thankful that the child was not to be another Maria, and turning her eyes from the ribbons and flounces of the hated cradle, she settled the posy in water, made Polly some tea, reiterated her congratulations and returned next door.

Billy arrived home from school and was told the news. He took it stolidly. Babies did not mean much to Billy. If anything, he disapproved of them. They drew attention to themselves, he knew, to the detriment of their older brothers' welfare. But he brightened at the thought of telling Miss Clare, his teacher, all about it when he went to school next morning.

Miss Clare was as impressed with the news as he had hoped she would be, but Billy's eyes did not miss the flicker of amusement which crossed her kind face when he said:

'And it's a girl! Just like ourn!'

At playtime Miss Clare told the news to Mr Benson, the headmaster. In common with the rest of Fairacre, he had watched the doings of the pair of cottages with amusement and considerable sympathy for the much-tried Bertha Foster.

'Isn't that typical?' he commented. 'Poor Mrs Foster! I wonder what Polly will call it. Maria, no doubt, and it will have an identical pram.'

The village hummed with the news.

'Give Polly her due,' said one fair-minded neighbour, 'she couldn't help it being a girl. Now, could she?'

'She could help her curtains and the flowers in the front and this 'ere new cradle she's got,' answered a less charitable listener. 'Bertha must be a proper angel to stay friends with a copycat like Polly.'

Time passed. It was a long hot summer and both babies flourished. Bertha's polyanthuses were succeeded by sweet williams and then asters. So were Polly's. Bertha whitewashed two large stones and set them one each side of her doorstep as ornaments. So did Polly. Leslie bought Bertha a canary in a cage for her birthday. Mike, under pressure, did the same for Polly.

By now, relations were decidedly strained between the two women, although they maintained a surface civility. Billy, overhearing many a tart comment at home, often told a tale to Miss Clare who did her best to discourage him. She found this comparatively easy. It was not so easy to stem the flow of confidences which Bertha began to pour into her unwilling ear when she came to meet Billy from school. It was at this stage that the name 'Mrs Next-Door' began to be used in a fruitless attempt to veil Polly's identity from the young listeners milling round them.

'That Mrs Next-Door,' Bertha would whisper, 'has done it again. Pink asters, same as mine. It do fairly make my blood boil at times!'

'Ignore it,' Miss Clare used to answer. 'It really doesn't matter, you know.' But secretly she had every sympathy with poor provoked Bertha. How long, she wondered, would her patience last?

The children added fuel to the fire by teasing Billy.

'Your Mrs Next-Door's got a hat with daisies on, just like your mum's!'

'I see Mrs Next-Door's got a canary now!'

'Mrs Next-Door's got a pink bedspread on the line this morning. Looked like the one your mum had out last week!'

At last the storm broke. The immediate cause, as Fairacre had foretold, involved the two babies. Christmas was now at hand, and as usual, a teaparty for the whole village was to be held in the school. Anyone was welcome to this festivity, whether a parent or not, and it was usual for all the women, and one or two old retired men, to foregather on this village occasion. The school children, dressed in their best, looked upon themselves as hosts.

Bertha took considerable trouble with her own appearance and even more with Maria's. The child was dressed in a white silk frock, embroidered with forget-me-nots on the bodice, and over this creation wore a blue coat edged with swansdown and a bonnet to match. Bertha had seen this delicious set in a Caxley shop window and had been unable to resist it. This was the first time that Maria had put it on, and very beautiful she looked.

Bertha pushed her daughter proudly towards the school. The afternoon was cold and foggy, but Maria's face glowed from inside the becoming blue bonnet. She was much admired by the throng at the school.

About twenty minutes later Polly arrived, carrying Mildred. To the amusement of some, the resentment of others, and the speechless fury and astonishment of poor Bertha, the child had on exactly similar garments to Maria's. Bertha pointedly turned her back towards the newcomers and did her best to appear unconcerned, knowing that she was the centre of all eyes.

The party appeared to be as gay as it always was, but for Bertha it was sheer misery. She was one of the first to leave, pushing Maria in her finery, with Billy clinging to the pram, at a pace which taxed the strength of all three.

It was now dark. Maria was strapped into her high chair and Billy was told to look after her. Before Leslie came home, Bertha intended to confront her infuriating neighbour. She returned to the gate to await Polly's homecoming.

'Now she's going to have it!' Bertha told herself fiercely. 'I been too meek all along, sitting down under her impudence. I'll settle her!'

The sound of footsteps and the familiar squeak of Polly's pram wheels heralded her approach. Bertha advanced like some avenging fury.

'I'll thank you,' she began ominously, 'to step inside here a minute, Mrs Norton.'

This was the first time that Polly had been so called by her neighbour, and she was at once on her guard.

'What's up?' she inquired, trying to sound at ease, but her voice trembled.

'You knows as well as I do what's up!' breathed Bertha menacingly. 'You dare to dress up that kid of yours just like my Maria and parade it in front of all Fairacre! Trying to make me a laughing-stock! I've had enough of you and your copying ways!'

Polly tried to laugh, but she was very frightened. There is nothing more terrifying than a calm woman suddenly aroused. She had no idea that placid Bertha could feel such venom, or express it with such menace.

'No law against buying a coat and bonnet for my baby, I suppose?' queried Polly.

'No, nor curtains, nor flowers, nor hats, nor bedspreads, same as mine,' burst out Bertha, 'but you're not going to do it any longer, my girl, or you'll be in trouble! Take it from me, Polly Norton, if I ever sees any more copying from you I'll be round at your place and black your eye for you! I've just about had enough, see?'

She thrust a red furious face close to Polly's startled one and slammed the gate between them. Polly, much shaken, moved slowly towards her own.

'I'll tell –' she began truculently.

'You'll tell no one,' Bertha cut in. 'All the village is on my side. You've branded yourself as a plain copycat. I ain't saying no more to you. *Not ever*. But just you mark what I've said to you!'

Still pulsing with righteous indignation, Bertha returned indoors to attend to the children and Leslie's tea.

'I feels all the better for that,' she told herself. 'It's cleared the air. Come to think of it, I should've done it months ago.'

Now that battle was joined, Bertha found life much more straightforward. She simply ignored her neighbour. If she met her in the garden, or in the village street, she had the exquisite pleasure of looking clean through her. Polly retaliated with a toss of the head or a muttered aside. The village watched with avid interest. There were a few who maintained that Polly was not as bad as she was painted, but the majority felt she had got off lightly in the affair and that Bertha had every justification for cutting off relations with her neighbour.

The two husbands found the whole thing very trying. At work, they talked normally to each other, each being careful to leave his wife's name out of the conversation. At home, they did their best to soothe their wives and keep out of trouble's way. It was not easy. Both women were expecting again, Bertha in October and Polly a month later, and tempers were frayed all round.

However, Polly had seen reason in Bertha's tirade that dark evening, and although she would not admit that she was in the wrong, she took care not to rouse her fire again by any obvious copying. Unfortunately, much remained that had been done before the split occurred. The canaries still sang and fluttered in the two front windows. The white stones flanked the two doorsteps, the curtains, the bedspreads and the babies' coats still remained identical, for neither would give way.

Even worse was the simultaneous ripening of the two rowan trees in the front gardens. Bertha's had been planted soon after their arrival. Polly's a month or two later. This year Polly's was covered in bright red clusters of berries. Bertha's was decidedly inferior. Bertha, now near her time, a massive unwieldy figure venturing no further than the garden, watched her neighbour picking sprays to take indoors. It gave her no comfort to see that Polly was wearing a blue flowered smock over her bulk exactly like the one she had on. They had been worn during their earlier pregnancies and one could hardly expect Polly to throw hers away. Nevertheless, Bertha found the sight annoying. Would she never be free from Polly shadowing her?

A week later Bertha was brought to bed. Mrs Drew arrived in the morning confidently expecting to be back in her own cottage in time to cook her midday dinner. But the day wore on, Bertha continued her labours, Leslie ate bread and cheese for his dinner, the same for his tea, and went post-haste for the doctor at six o'clock when Mrs Drew clattered down the stairs in a state of urgent alarm.

Fairacre watched with some agitation. What could be happening to Bertha? Always had her babies as easy as shelling peas! Could Mrs Drew have bungled things? Not like her to send for the doctor! Mind you, she was getting on a bit; perhaps she was a shade past it!

So the tongues wagged. Doctor Martin was seen to enter the cottage at a quarter to seven. No one saw him leave. Of course it was dark, but the doctor's old Ford car made enough noise to rouse the dead. What could be going on?

As St Patrick's church clock struck eleven Dr Martin was drying his hands in Bertha's crowded bedroom. He was smiling broadly, but his eyes were on his patient. Her eyes were closed, her hair, damp and dishevelled, clung to her forehead. Mrs Drew was busy with baby clothes. Leslie Foster, summoned from his vigil below, had just approached the bed. He looked thunderstruck, as well he might. Beside his exhausted wife lay three tightly-wrapped snuffling bundles.

He stroked the hair back from his wife's hot forehead.

'Bertha?' he whispered questioningly.

Her eyes opened slowly. She gazed at Leslie and then at the three small faces beside her. A look of intense joy lit her face.

'Let Mrs Next-Door copy *that*!' cried Bertha triumphantly.

5. A Tale of Love

The alterations to the pair of cottages where Polly and Bertha had once lived took many weeks. The children's interest in all that went on continued unabated. The four workmen who were engaged on the job became their friends and heroes, and I became more and more annoyed as the children arrived late for school.

'You can miss your playtime,' I announced to a little knot of malefactors who entered noisily, bursting with good spirits, at a quarter past nine. 'I'm tired of telling you to be punctual.'

They looked at each other with dismay.

'But we was only givin' the workmen a hand, like,' said Richard, assuming an air of injured innocence. 'They had an ol' bucket they was pulling up to the top windows, see, on a bit of rope –'

'On a little wheel, sort of –' broke in Ernest, his eyes alight at the happy memory.

'A *pulley*, he means, miss,' said John, sniffing appallingly. 'They has cement in this 'ere bucket and it's heavy to lug up the ladders, so they has this wheel thing called a *pulley*, miss, as pulls it up. That's why it's called a *pulley*,' explained John patiently, as though to a particularly backward child.

'I daresay,' I said shortly. 'And nine o'clock is not the time to stand and watch it. Get to your desks at once, and for pity's sake blow your nose, John.'

There followed a great fuss of pocket-searching, feeling under his jersey, exploring sleeves, looking in his desk and so on, accompanied throughout by sniffs and exclamations of surprise and dismay.

'Don't seem to have one, miss,' said John at length.

'Get a Kleenex from the cupboard,' I said ominously, 'and don't let me hear another squeak, or sniff, from you for the rest of the morning!'

This sort of thing went on intermittently throughout the early part of the spring term and I should be heartily glad, I told myself, when the workmen had vanished and the new house was occupied. Mrs Pringle agreed with me.

'Bad enough sweeping up honest Fairacre mud,' boomed the lady, after school one afternoon, 'without bits of cement off their boots, and shavings and nails and that out of their pockets. And when it comes to *this*,' added Mrs Pringle opening a massive fist and thrusting it before my nose, 'it's time to *speak*!'

In her palm lay some glutinous grey matter which I recognized as putty.

'Stuck on the lobby wall, if you please,' said Mrs Pringle, disengaging the stuff with a squelch and putting it, unasked, on my desk. 'I thought it might be that chewing gum again when I first saw it, and then I thought, "Not likely. Not that sized lump. No one could get a lump that big in his mouth. Not even Eric Williams, and dear knows his mouth's big enough, on account of his poor foolish mother feeding him with a dessert-spoon at six months." So I looked closer and saw it was this 'orrible putty. Them workmen want sorting out, Miss Read, letting the children have such stuff.'

'I believe they've nearly finished,' I answered, trying to soothe the savage breast. I glanced at the clock. Amy was coming to tea and it was already past four.

Mrs Pringle grunted disbelievingly. 'I knows workmen,' she said darkly. 'Got no sense of time. I feel downright sorry for that couple waiting to move in. They'll be lucky to close their own door behind them before Easter at this rate.'

This was the first I had heard of the future occupiers and though, as any normal villager, I should dearly have loved to hear more, I did not intend to probe Mrs Pringle for details, and, in any case, it was time I put on the kettle for Amy. I made my way to the door. Mrs Pringle, who can read my thoughts much too easily for my comfort, sent a parting shot after me.

'Name of Blundell,' trumpeted Mrs Pringle. 'Could tell you more, but I can see you're not interested.'

I caught the glimpse of smug triumph on her unlovely face as I closed the door.

Amy and I were at college together many years ago. We lost touch with each other and only met again when I came to Fairacre. She had moved to Bent, a village a few miles south of Caxley, when she married, and so knew more about the Caxley neighbourhood than I did.

Amy is a dynamic person, full of good works and good ideas. I only wish I had half her energy. It is always exhilarating to have a visit from her and I looked forward to an hour or two of her company on this particular afternoon.

The car arrived as I set tea. Amy, elegant as ever in a new suit, emerged with a bunch of daffodils and a new hair style. We greeted each other warmly and I complimented her on her looks.

'Do you like it?' she asked, patting her variegated locks and preening herself.

'Very much,' I answered truthfully. 'I like all those stripes, like a humbug.'

Amy looked at me with distaste. 'Like a humbug!' she echoed disgustedly. 'What a dreadful way of putting it!'

'What's wrong with it?' I asked. 'I'm very fond of humbugs, and those auburn streaks remind me of the treacly ones.'

Amy bit delicately into a sandwich.

'It cost a fortune,' she said sadly. 'And took hours to do,

with all the strands sprouting through a bathing-cap affair. I thought James would like it, but he hasn't noticed yet.'

I inquired after James, her husband, and learnt that he was away for the night at a conference in the north. To my mind, James has a suspiciously large number of overnight engagements, but it is no affair of mine, and Amy is wise enough not to discuss the matter with me.

'You know,' said Amy, looking at me closely, 'I think you could take this high-lighting effect. It would do something for you.'

'Now, Amy,' I begged, seriously alarmed, for I have had many a battle with my old friend about my mousy appearance, 'please don't start on me again! I am a plain, shabby, middle-aged woman with no pretensions to glamour. I like being like this, so leave me alone.'

Amy waved aside my pleading and took another sandwich.

'A few glints in your hair, some decent make-up, and a good strong pair of corsets would work wonders for you,' said Amy. 'Which reminds me – I want you to come to the Charity Ball at the Corn Exchange next month!'

'Never!' I cried, with spirit. 'You know I can't keep awake after eleven o'clock. And I don't like dancing. And I haven't got a frock to wear anyway.'

Amy sighed.

'Then it's time you bought one. You simply can't waste the whole of your life in this one-eyed village. You never meet a soul –'

'I do,' I protested. 'Every day. I meet far too many souls. There are thirty-odd to be faced every morning.'

'I mean *men*,' snapped Amy with exasperation. 'There's no reason why you shouldn't get married, even at your age, and it's time someone took you in hand and made you see reason.'

'But I don't *want* to get married!' I wailed. 'I should have done it years ago if I'd intended to do.'

'And who,' said Amy coldly, 'ever asked you?'

I began to laugh.

'Well there was that neighbour of yours who was in a constant state of inebriation and wanted someone to keep him from drinking –'

'You can't count him,' said Amy firmly. 'He asked everyone.'

'I can't think of anyone else at the moment,' I said.

'I can tell you one thing,' said Amy, 'if you take up this attitude, and refuse to make the Best of Yourself, then you are doomed to be an old maid.'

'Suits me,' I said comfortably. 'Have some more tea.'

Amy stirred her second cup thoughtfully. 'There's still time,' she assured me. 'Look at Elsie Parker. Blundell, I mean. She's managed it.'

'Blundell?' I queried. 'Not the Blundells who are moving to Fairacre?'

Amy looked interested, and ceased stirring. 'It's quite likely,' she said slowly. 'They are having a pair of cottages knocked into one house somewhere or other.'

'It's here,' I assured her feelingly, 'I should know. The children spend most of their time watching the workmen. It was Mrs Pringle who mentioned the name Blundell only this afternoon.'

'That must be Elsie,' said Amy, 'and her newly-caught husband. Well, well, well! So they're settling in Fairacre!'

Amy produced a beautiful gold cigarette case, a present from James after a week away, lit a cigarette, and settled back in a cloud of blue smoke.

'Well, go on,' I urged. 'Tell me about my neighbours to be!'

And, smiling indulgently, Amy began.

It was generally agreed, in the little village of Bent, that Elsie Parker was an uncommonly pretty girl. She was the only child born to Roger and Lily Parker a year or two after the First World War. Her father returned from his arduous, if

71

undistinguished, duties as an army baker to start afresh as part-owner of a small general store on the southern outskirts of Caxley.

At first, he cycled the few miles to work on a venerable bicycle, but as the business prospered he changed to a small second-hand van with which he began to build up a modest delivery round. People liked Roger Parker. He was hard-working, honest and utterly reliable. If he said that he would bring the pickles in time for Monday's cold lunch, then you could be quite sure that the jar would be with you before the potatoes had come to the boil! He deserved to prosper, and he did.

By the time Elsie was six, the shabby delivery van had been changed for two larger new ones which spent the day touring the district and the night safely locked up in the new shed at the rear of the general stores. Roger now owned a bull-nosed Morris tourer which he drove to work each morning. At the week-ends he polished it lovingly and then took his wife and pretty little daughter for a drive.

Elsie was the apple of her parents' eyes. She had a mop of yellow curls, lively blue eyes with exquisitely long curling lashes, and a smile that disarmed even the most curmudgeonly. Needless to say, she was the belle of the infants' class at Bent village school and was accompanied to and from that establishment by a bevy of small admirers.

Her first proposal of marriage came when she was seven. It came from the shabbiest of her escorts, whose nose was constantly wet, despite a rag pinned to his dirty jersey, and whose attentions had long been deplored by Mrs Parker. Elsie turned him down promptly, but gave him one of her heart-turning smiles as she did so, for she was a kind child.

It was an experience which was to occur many times in the future, and as time went on Elsie was to learn many refinements in the art of rejecting a suitor. But, as a first attempt and for one of such tender years, the present rejection was commendable – a blend of firmness and gentleness, lit by a certain light-hearted awareness of an honour received, which many an older maiden could not have bettered. The young man ran ahead to school, and after shedding a few hot tears in the blessed privacy of the boys' lavatory, recovered his good spirits and continued to accompany his goddess as before – without hope, certainly, but also without rancour.

Hard on the heels of this proposal came another, from an urchin almost as disreputable as the first. He too was turned down, and in an unguarded moment Elsie mentioned both incidents to her mother. She was much distressed.

'I can't think why such *dirty* boys like you!' exclaimed poor genteel Mrs Parker. 'You mustn't encourage them, Elsie. It won't do! It really won't do at all!'

If Mrs Parker had been capable of giving the situation a moment's clear thought she would have realized that it was the very difference in her daughter's appearance and nature which acted as a magnet to the rough rumbustious boys. Those glossy curls, the freshly-starched voiles and the enchanting scent of Erasmic soap created a being of such sweet cleanliness that she was well-nigh irresistible to the lesser washed.

'Why don't you play with some of the other boys?' asked Mrs Parker. 'There's Jimmy Bassett and Stanley Roberts,' she went on, naming the firstborn at the flourishing new garage on the main road to Caxley, and the vicar's son who would be going on to his preparatory school next term. Mrs Parker had a nice regard for the social ladder.

'Jimmy lisps,' said Miss Parker, speaking truly. 'And Stanley Roberts dropped a dead rat in old Mrs Turner's well last week.'

'*Stanley* did?' exclaimed Mrs Parker, much shocked. 'The vicar's son? A dead rat?'

'Mrs Turner's chapel,' explained Elsie succinctly.

The matter was dropped.

At the age of ten Elsie was taken from the village school and travelled daily into Caxley to attend a larger establishment run by some charming and hard-working nuns. She wore a corn-flower blue uniform which enhanced the beauty of her colouring and very soon the schoolboys who travelled on the bus with her were jostling for the place beside her. Elsie treated them with happy impartiality, bestowing conversation, smiles and sympathy upon whichever escort had been lucky enough – or rough enough – to gain the seat next to her.

On more than one occasion during her time at the convent school Elsie was drawn quietly aside by one of the sisters and given a few words of mild reproof. It was not fitting, she was told, to be seen at the centre of a crowd of the opposite sex day after day. It gave the school a bad name. She was advised to be polite but distant, kind but not too kind. Dreadful dangers, it was hinted, could attend too great an interest in the male sex.

It was all rather hard on Elsie. She did not encourage the young men, they simply gravitated towards her as wasps to a sun-ripe pear. Her father, made aware of his daughter's attractions by a dulcet word or two from Sister Teresa, decided to take Elsie to school with him in the car and collect her again in the afternoon. But this state of affairs did not last long. It was most inconvenient for Roger to leave the business. Sometimes lacrosse or tennis kept Elsie late, sometimes a half-holiday meant that she was out early. Gradually the arrangement fell through, and Elsie returned to the bus and the adoration of her swains.

At seventeen, still unscathed by love, Elsie left school and began training to be a nurse. She was at a hospital in London but spent as many weekends as possible at Bent. By now Roger was what is known in the north as 'a warm man'. A wing had been built on to the small four-square house where Elsie had been born, and a field next door had been acquired to ensure future privacy. Roger, who as a young man had voted Liberal, bought his ready-made suits from a Caxley outfitters, and enjoyed mustard with mutton, now helped himself to mint sauce instead, had his suits made in London, and voted

Conservative. He worked, if anything, harder than ever, was much respected in Caxley, and continued to give the same never-failing service which had built up the business.

Mrs Parker, too, rose with her husband. Her hopes were centred on Elsie with more concentration than ever before. In London, she felt sure, there must be many eligible bachelors. Elsie could have whomsoever she wanted, of that she was positive, for she was now at her most beautiful and the stimulation of work and life in London had given her added gaiety and poise. At weekends Mrs Parker combed the neighbourhood for likely young men, and the field next door was transformed into a tennis court, set about with the very latest garden chairs and a dashing swing seat with a canopy and cushions covered in wisteria-entwined cretonne. Delicious snacks were eaten in the gnat-humming twilight, laughter set the tall lemonade glasses tinkling and the young men feasted their eyes on Elsie Parker, cool, adorable and completely untouched by love.

Of course, it was inevitable that when Elsie fell in love the affair would be disastrous. As might be expected, Elsie's heart was first touched by a married man. He was a doctor who visited the hospital, an unremarkable man, running to fat, and so swarthy that he needed to shave twice a day. He had occasion to speak to Elsie now and again, and had no idea of the emotion which he unwittingly aroused. His presence alone affected Elsie. Her legs trembled, her hands shook, her throat grew dry and her head grew dizzy. She found it almost impossible to take in his orders.

'That Nurse Parker,' the doctor commented to one of his colleagues, 'is practically an imbecile. Talk about a dumb blonde!'

'It's love,' said the other laconically. He was sharper-eyed than most.

'Rubbish!' snorted Elsie's hero, and dismissed the whole conversation from his mind. He had a perfectly good wife, four children, a house with a mortgage, and no intention of getting entangled with a silly chit of a nurse, even if she was as handsome as Nurse Parker.

Elsie's love grew as the months went by, although it was given no encouragement. At weekends her mother noted the abstracted air, the paler cheek, the slight, but becoming, loss of weight. She longed to be taken into her daughter's confidence, relishing her role as understanding mother, but Elsie said nothing. In an earnest desire to cheer the girl Mrs Parker began to plan a small party for her nineteenth birthday.

'Oh, mum!' protested Elsie, when the project was broached. 'Let's skip my birthday this year. Honestly, I just don't feel like a lot of fuss.'

'You'll thoroughly enjoy it,' said Mrs Parker firmly. 'You've been moping long enough – about what I can't say, though I can guess – and it's time you pulled yourself together. I'll make all the arrangements.'

'I'd much rather you did nothing,' replied Elsie shortly. She had no energy or time for anything else but her preoccupation with the adored. Her mother, however, was undeterred. Invitations went out, food and drink were ordered, the local dressmaker was summoned to take Mrs Parker's ever-increasing measurements, and a Saturday night in June was appointed as the time of celebration. Scarcely aware of what was happening, Elsie acquiesced listlessly in the plans.

Work at the hospital seemed doubly hard in the warm weather. There was too, an air of profound disquiet hanging over the whole nation, for this was 1939 and the threat of world war came closer daily.

On the day before Elsie's birthday party the weather was close and thundery. Patients complained in their hot crumpled beds, nurses' tempers were short and the doctors' were even shorter. Shortest of all, it seemed, was the temper of Elsie's beloved. He was a sorely tried man. One of his children had mumps, his wife was prostrated with a migraine which could well last a week, his mother-in-law, whom he detested, was advancing plans to make her permanent home with theirs, the cat had been sick in full and revolting view of the breakfast table, and he had had considerable difficulty in starting his car that morning.

On arrival at the hospital he found that one of his cases in the men's surgical ward had developed alarming complications, and it was this that Elsie overheard him discussing with the sister on duty. Elsie was busy sluicing rubber sheets but could hear the beloved voice above the splashing of the water.

'Keep a nurse by him for the next hour,' he was saying, his words clipped with anxiety. Sister's reply was inaudible.

'Anyone you like,' responded the doctor. 'Anyone but Nurse Parker. She gets worse as she goes on.'

Elsie dropped the sheet she was washing and ducked her head as though she had received a physical blow. She felt stunned with shock. As from a great distance, she surveyed her submerged hands resting on the bottom of the deep sink. The clear cold water acted as a magnifying glass, and every hair and pore looked gigantic. Elsie observed the tiny bubbles on the fleshy part of her thumb, uncannily like the seed pearls her father had given her on her confirmation day.

Her mind seemed to dwell, with unusual clarity, on many things long forgotten. The terrible words, uttered a second before, and all that they implied, had as yet no real meaning for her. She remembered the beads of sweat on the hairy upper lip of one of her sixth-form admirers whom she had not met, or thought of, for years. She remembered bright hundreds and thousands, scattered on plates of junket, which she used to love as a child. She dwelt with compulsive intensity on the visual memory of a spider's web spangled with drops of dew. And all the time her gaze was fixed upon the tiny bubbles clustering on her thumb.

She was roused from her trance by the sound of sister

returning. All that day she went automatically about her duties, oblivious of the world about her. Late that night, lying straight and cold in her bed at the nurses' hostel, the tears began to flow, running down the side of her temple and dripping silently into the pillow. She wept noiselessly at first, and then, as the treachery and cruelty of those dreadful words began to burn into her, the paroxysm increased in intensity until she was choking with tears, her head throbbing and her chest aching with pain.

When dawn came she was red-eyed, swollen-faced and in a state of complete exhaustion.

'A cold,' she told her fellow nurses. 'I'm going home this afternoon anyway. I'll get over it during the weekend.' She was reported sick, took the two aspirins handed to her, and fell to weeping again. In the early afternoon she rose, dressed, packed her case and went to the station. She felt like a very frail old lady just recovering from a serious illness.

The sight that met her eyes on her return home brought her almost to a state of collapse. In the long room of the new wing she found her mother. The blonde parquet floor, the pride of Mrs Parker's heart, was stripped of its rugs and shone with much polishing. Against the wall stood tables already dressed in virgin-white cloths. Flowers were banked on window sills, lamps were wreathed with garlands. The room awaited young company, music, laughter and, above all, the gay presence of the daughter of the house.

Elsie put down her case very carefully. She felt that she might overbalance or even faint dead away. Her mother looked at her with a smile. She seemed not to notice anything amiss. Her mind was too occupied with ices, cherry sticks, blanched almonds and wine glasses to register much else.

'I'm ill,' announced Elsie. Her voice seemed to sound a long way off. She tried again, intent on making herself understood. 'I'm not well,' she said a little louder. 'I can't be at the party.'

'Elsie!' breathed Mrs Parker incredulously. She advanced

towards her, her poor face creased with worry. 'Can't come to the party? But, Elsie, you must – you simply must!'

She gave a small despairing gesture with one hand indicating the preparations. Elsie leant against the wall and closed her eyes. Inside her eyelids was imprinted the face of the man she loved. She studied it intently. Her mother was speaking again. Now her voice was firmer, her resolution returning.

'A nice lay-down,' she was saying. 'Slip under the eiderdown for an hour or two. I'll bring you up your tea and an Aspro. You'll soon be as right as ninepence.'

As if in a dream, Elsie found herself being propelled upstairs, her clothes removed, and her unprotesting body thrust into her bed. Still concentrating on her beloved's swarthy face she dropped instantly into a heavy sleep.

Her mother roused her at seven. The anxiety in Mrs Parker's face brought all Elsie's misery flooding back. She longed to turn away and abandon herself again to grief, but her mother, she knew, could not be disappointed. She rose and dressed, automatically making-up that lovely face which seemed recovered from its earlier ravages, and going at last to take her place in the hall to welcome her guests. She felt as though some part of her had died, and that she dragged it with her, a cold heavy weight, draining strength from her.

To outward appearances she seemed much as usual, lovely, smiling and as desirable as ever. Halfway through the evening, the vicar's son engineered a trip into the garden with his hostess, and there poured out his heart whilst offering his dank hand. With all her habitual skill Elsie extricated herself and contrived to leave the young man tolerably resigned. During the last waltz, she received her second proposal of the evening, but was cool-headed enough to realize that claret-cup had enflamed this suitor as much as her own looks. He was thanked, refused and mollified, all within the time it took to dance from the French windows to the dining table. Grief, it seemed, had not dulled either Elsie's wits or her attractions.

She returned to work, her passion still raging. Elsie thought bitterly that those who say that unrequited love soon dies know very little of the matter. In the face of her beloved's impatience, and even dislike, despite the torturing memory of those chance-heard words, Elsie adored him more as the weeks went by. It was enough to walk the same corridors, to touch the same door handles, to read the same hospital notices. When, on September the third, war was declared and a week later she heard that he had gone into the RAF and was to be posted almost immediately as medical officer to a windswept station in Scotland, she felt that she could not live without his presence.

But work, with all its blessed urgency, drove complete despair away. There were patients to be evacuated, wards to reorganize and a hundred and one matters to attend to. Only at night, before she fell asleep, did Elsie have any time to mourn her beloved, and then the pain was almost more than she could bear.

On Christmas Eve she heard terrible news. The doctor and two other officers had been killed in a car accident as they returned to the station late one foggy night. After the first few days of shock and grief, an extraordinary change came over Elsie. It was as though released, at last, from the bondage of her infatuation, she found freedom. It was over. Nothing could hurt him now, and nothing could hurt Elsie for that reason. She could look around, begin to live again, welcome kindness, affection and admiration and, perhaps, one day, return it.

During the years of war Elsie Parker was the cause of much head-shaking in Bent.

'A fast hussy!' declared one righteous matron, with three plain unmarried daughters. 'A proper flibbertigibbet, always running after the men!'

'No better than she should be, I don't doubt, up there in London where her parents can't see her!' quoth another.

There was certainly a hard gaiety about Elsie these days.

She was now Sister Parker, conscientious and hard-working in the hospital. But off duty Elsie craved excitement. The admirers were more numerous than ever. Americans, Poles and Norwegians joined Elsie's village wooers, and she parried their advances with the same skill, if not perhaps quite the same endurance, as before.

When the war ended Elsie was twenty-five. There was a spate of weddings as the young men returned home. The villagers of Bent smiled kindly upon the newly-married couples and welcomed with genuine joy the offspring who were born into a world full of shortages, inordinately tired, but at least at peace.

And still Elsie remained unattached. The years slipped by. Roger Parker died one winter. His wife followed him two years later. Elsie, as sole heir, found herself in control of the house, a flourishing business and a comfortable sum of money in the bank. She was now thirty-eight. Her hair was untouched by greyness; in fact, its golden hue was rather brighter than it had been. Her teeth, though much-stopped, were her own. Her figure was as trim as ever, her blue eyes as devastating. Level-headedly, Elsie took stock of her position.

The business could carry on, as it was doing, under its reliable manager. She would give up nursing, return to her home at Bent, and get married. Without her parents she might well be lonely. A husband was the thing and, with luck, there might still be time for children. Elsie set about putting these practical plans into action.

Within three months she was ensconced in the house, had joined the Caxley Golf Club and the Caxley Drama Group. She gave a handsome contribution to Caxley Cottage Hospital in gratitude for the kindness extended to her parents and was made a member of the hospital board. Her garden was lent for various local functions, she visited and was visited, and generally took her place in the gentle whirligig of Caxley's social life. People were genuinely glad to see her so engaged. The

Parkers had always been liked, and Elsie deserved a break after those years of nursing, they told each other.

Unfortunately, Elsie's aims were only too apparent and soon became the object of derision by the less charitable. She had never been a very subtle person. One of her charms was her openness. Now that time was running short for Elsie, she became alarmingly direct in her hunt for a husband. Naturally, eligible men were scarce. In Caxley society, at that time, there were half a dozen elderly bachelors, about the same number of widowers, and a few middle-aged men separated from their wives for an interesting variety of reasons.

They were not a very inspiring collection, but Elsie was a realist, and did not expect to find anyone who could compare, even remotely, with her first and only love. She looked now for kindness, companionship and protection. If humour and some physical attraction were added, she would count herself lucky, she decided. Financial stability was not essential, for her own position could comfortably support a husband, if need be.

Her first choice fell upon one of the widowers, a childless man in his forties, who was a partner in one of Caxley's firms of solicitors. She had known him slightly during her years of nursing and knew him to be liked by the little town. He played golf and took leading parts in Caxley plays. Elsie pursued him resolutely and charmingly, to the surprise of the flattered man and the intense interest of the neighbourhood. But, before long, the hunt was off. Elsie, to her dismay, found that her intended had one small, but unforgivable, fault. He did not wash – at least, not enough.

After this set-back, Elsie began to wonder if *cleanliness* perhaps should take precedence over *kindness* on her list of desirable qualities. She had not reckoned to be troubled by such elementals, and was not impressed by excuses put forward by well-meaning friends who seemed to have guessed the cause of her withdrawal.

'Poor dear Oswald,' they said. 'So terribly cut up by Mary's death, you know. Seemed to go all to pieces. You can see that he really needs a woman to look after him.'

Maybe, thought Elsie privately, but not to the extent of washing his ears for him or cleaning his teeth. Personal fastidiousness, heightened by a nurse's training, did not condone greasy collars, black fingernails and the same filthy handkerchief for a week. Oswald, in his expensive, well-cut and smelly suits, was rejected.

Others, observing Elsie's aims and aware of her comfortable circumstances, made themselves pleasant. Elsie earnestly did her best to see them in the role of husband, never blinding herself to the true aim of their attentions but willing to ignore it if other less ignoble qualities were present. Too often there were none.

Time passed. Elsie continued her search, an object of pity to some and derision to others. She was still lovely, though now in her forties, and her energy seemed unimpaired. But at heart she was beginning to despair. Was marriage never to be her lot?

One bleak December afternoon she made her way to the churchyard at Bent bearing a bright-berried cross of holly for her parents' grave. She walked slowly between the mounds, reading the well-known inscriptions yet again.

'*Loved and Loving wife of John Smith,*' said one. '*A beloved wife and mother,*' said a second. '*This stone was erected by a sorrowing husband to the memory of his much beloved wife,*' said a third.

All wives, all loved, all missed, all mourned, thought Elsie bitterly. Of what use was beauty, health, a loving heart and worldly possessions, if marriage never came? What would be written on her own tombstone for others to read?

Elsie Parker, Spinster? What a hateful word that was! She hastened her steps at the very thought, and reached her parents' resting-place.

'*And Lily, his dearly-loved wife,*' read Roger's daughter. '*In death they are united.*'

Controlling an impulse to rush away from the spot, Elsie set the cross gently against the headstone, stood motionless in the biting cold and offered up a small prayer for her parents, and for their only child.

She made her way quickly to the gate, carefully averting her eyes from the inscriptions around her. There was only one other person in the churchyard, and he too was setting a holly

wreath upon a grassy mound. As she came near him he stepped forward into her path. He was a big dark man, much about her own age, and unknown to Elsie.

'Elsie Parker?' said the man gently. She nodded.

'I'm John Blundell,' said the man. 'I'd have known you anywhere. But you've forgotten me.'

Elsie felt a warm surge of recognition.

'John!' she exclaimed. 'My goodness, how many years is it since we saw each other?'

'I left Bent to join up in 1939,' he said. 'I don't think we've met since then, though I've heard about you.'

Elsie looked at him. John Blundell, the little dirty boy who had been her very first suitor! Undoubtedly he had prospered. His air was quiet and authoritative, his appearance immaculate. He had come a long way from the ragged child with the handkerchief pinned to his jersey who had been such a faithful admirer all those years ago.

She remembered, in a flash, that she had heard of his marriage during the war, but no further details. Lily Parker had risen above the station of the Blundells and had not passed on news of this family to Elsie.

'I'm still living at the old house,' said Elsie. 'Where are you now?'

'Near Southampton,' said John Blundell, falling into step beside her. 'I've a small shipping business there.'

'Alone?' asked Elsie, probing gently.

'No, I've got two sons, both married now. They help me to run it. They're good boys.'

They emerged from the yew-flanked gateway into the village square. A beautiful glossy car was waiting near the railings of the village school which they had both attended so long before.

'I'll run you back, if I may,' said the man. They drove at a sedate pace to Elsie's home.

'Do have some tea with me,' said Elsie. 'You don't have to hurry back, do you?'

He must not be too late, but he would love some tea, he said. They talked until it was half past six, and during that time Elsie learnt that he had married an Italian girl whose father was in an Italian shipping line and was a man of some substance. Their two sons were born in Italy. They had come back to England for the boys' schooling. The climate had not suited his wife but she refused to leave him during the winters to run the business alone, and had contracted Asian 'flu, five years before, which had proved fatal.

It was apparent that he had loved her dearly. His voice shook as he told the tale in the shadowy firelit room and Elsie was reminded of his early tears when she had so light-heartedly turned him down at the tender age of seven.

This was the first of many meetings. Elsie knew, before a month had gone by, that this would end happily. Despite local tales to the contrary, Elsie did not pursue John Blundell. There was no necessity. There was mutual attraction, affection and need. Before the end of February they were engaged, and the marriage was arranged to take place after Easter. To Elsie it seemed wonderfully fitting that her first suitor should also be her last.

'And so, you see,' said Amy, lighting another cigarette, 'it all ended happily. Elsie adores the boys and the first one is going to live at the old house at Bent with his wife and children. Elsie and John want something smaller, and I think they both want to be at a little distance from Bent. Everyone says they're tremendously happy, even though they are, well – somewhat *mature*.'

Amy eyed me speculatively. I returned her gaze blandly.

'Funnily enough,' I said, 'I had my first proposal at the age of seven. I was fishing for frogs' spawn at the time. Not a very glamorous pursuit, when you come to think of it.'

Amy leant forward with growing interest. 'What happened to him? Do you ever hear?' Clearly, she was hoping that history would repeat itself.

'I heard only the other day,' I told her. 'He's doing time for bigamy.'

6. BLACK WEEK

I suppose everyone encounters periods when absolutely everything goes wrong. The week after my friend Amy's visit was just such a one, and it left Fairacre village school and its suffering headmistress sorely scarred.

On Monday morning I awoke to find that there was no electricity in the house. I am not a great breakfast-eater and can face a plate of cornflakes with cold milk as bravely as any other woman on a bleak March morning. But it is very hard to go without a cheering pot of tea, and this I saw I should have to do, for the clock stood at twenty to nine – inevitably, I had overslept – and the oil stove would not boil water in time.

A wicked north-easter cut across the playground. A few wilting children huddled in the stone porch.

'Go inside!' I shouted to them, as I bore down upon them.

'Can't get in!' they shouted back. I joined the mob. Sure enough, the great iron ring which lifts the latch failed to admit us.

'Mrs Pringle's inside, miss,' said Ernest.

'Well, why didn't you knock?' I asked, mystified.

'She don't want us mucking up her floor, she says.'

'What nonsense!' I was about to exclaim, but managed to bite it back. Instead I hammered loudly with the iron ring. After some considerable time, during which icy blasts played round our legs and blew our hair all over our faces, there was the sound of shuffling footsteps, the grating of a key, and Mrs Pringle's malevolent countenance appeared in the chink of the door. I widened the crack rapidly with a furious shove and had the satisfaction of hearing a sharp bang occasioned by the door meeting Mrs Pringle's kneecap.

'Can I have a word with you?' I said with some asperity, ignoring her closed eyes and martyred expression. The children surged past us to their pegs in the lobby, and I went through to my room followed by Mrs Pringle. As I guessed, her limp was much in evidence. I hoped that this time the affliction was genuine. Judging by that crack on the kneecap, it might well be.

'I have asked you before, Mrs Pringle,' I began in my best schoolteacher manner, 'to leave the door open when you arrive so that the children can come inside. It isn't fit for them to be out in this weather.'

Mrs Pringle arranged a massive hand across her mauve cardigan and gasped slightly. She replied with an air of aggrieved dignity.

'Seeing as the lobby floor was wet I didn't want the children to catch their deaths in the damp atmosphere,' began the lady, with such brazen mendacity that I felt my ire rising.

'Mrs Pringle,' I expostulated, 'you know quite well that you locked the door because you wanted to keep the floor clean.'

Mrs Pringle's martyred expression changed suddenly to one of fury. 'And what if I did? Mighty little thanks I gets in this place for my everlasting slaving day in and day out. What's the good of me washing the floor simply to have them kids mucking it up the minute it's done, eh?' Fists on hips she thrust her face forward belligerently. 'And what's more,' she continued, in a sonorous boom audible to all Fairacre, 'you've no call to give me a vicious hit like you done with the door. My knee's almost broke! I could have you up for assault and battery, if I was so minded!'

'I'm sorry about your knee,' I said handsomely. 'Of course, if you'd left the door unlocked there would have been no need to push our way in.'

'H'm!' grunted Mrs Pringle, far from mollified. 'No doubt I'll have to lay up with this injury, and with the stoves drawing so bad as they are with the wind in this quarter *someone's* going to find a bit of trouble!'

She limped heavily from the room, wincing ostentatiously.

For the rest of the day she maintained an ominous silence. I can't say I let it worry me. Mrs Pringle and I have sparred for many a long year and I know every move by heart. Now I confidently awaited her notice, and was rather surprised when it was not forthcoming.

The wind was fiendish all day. Every time the door opened, papers whirled to the floor. The partition developed a steady squeak as the strong draught shook it, and the door to the infants' lobby made the whole building shudder every time an infant burst forth to cross to the lavatory.

During afternoon playtime, when my back was turned for three minutes, Patrick, trying to shut the windows with the window pole lost his balance and broke an upper pane, bringing down a shower of glass upon the floor and a shower of invective upon himself. Now we had an even fiercer draught among us, accompanied by banshee wailing among the pitch pine rafters. We were all glad when it was time to go home.

Mrs Pringle, black oilcloth bag swinging on her arm, stumped into the lobby as I went out. She stared stonily before her and did not deign to answer my greeting. Past caring, I fled through the wind to the haven of my little house, craving only peace and tea.

On Tuesday I woke to hear the hiss of sleet on my bedroom window. The playground was white, and the branches of the elms swayed in the same wicked north-easter. Luckily, the electricity was functioning again, and after breakfast I made my way over to the school to see if the stoves were doing well.

They were not going at all. Mrs Pringle, with devilish timing, was going to give in her notice this morning, I could see. Meanwhile, sleet and snow blew energetically through the broken pane, and the usual cross-draughts stirred the papers on the walls.

Mr Willet arrived as I was lighting the stove in the infants' room. His face was red with the wind's buffeting, and his moustache spangled with snowflakes.

'Here, I'll do that,' he said cheerfully. 'They tell me her ladyship's gone on strike again.'

'I'm not surprised,' I said, and told him about yesterday's fracas.

'She's a Tartar,' commented Mr Willet. 'But never you fear, we'll manage without her. Soon as these 'ere stoves is drawing, I'll paste a bit of brown paper over that there broken window. Best tell the Caxley folk to come and do a bit of glazing, I suppose. That's too high for me to manage this time.'

The children arrived. Ernest handed me a note. The handwriting was Mrs Pringle's.

'Am laid up with my damaged knee,' it said. 'Doctor is coming today and may say give in my notice. Will let you know. Matches is short.

Mrs Pringle.'

Matches were not short, they were non-existent, as I had discovered, but by now the stoves were going, in a sullen black mood, and little puffs of smoke occasionally escaped from them. Mrs Pringle had been correct about their dislike of a north-east wind. The stoves resented it as much as we did. As the fuel grew warm the smoke increased, and we worked throughout the morning among lightly-floating smuts and eye-watering fumes.

Mr Willet, working perilously on an inadequate ladder as he blocked up the hole in the window pane, left his lofty perch now and again to survey the stoves.

'Beats me,' he said, scratching his head. 'I'll bet Mrs P. put the evil eye on 'em before she left!'

It seemed more than likely.

In the afternoon Eileen Burton complained of a stiff neck. I was about to dismiss this as a result of the draughts, but observing her flushed appearance I took her temperature. It was over a hundred, her neck glands were painful and she had not had mumps. I surveyed her anxiously.

'My cousin's just had them,' she told me. 'And we often plays together.'

There was nothing for it but to wrap her up warmly, put her in my car and run her home at playtime. How many more, I wondered, peering through the gloom of the smoke-filled room on my return, would succumb in the next few days?

The sleet had changed to heavy snow by Wednesday morning, but mercifully the wind had dropped and the stoves behaved themselves.

The relief was tremendous, and I began to enjoy school without Mrs Pringle's presence. But the snow brought its own problems. The children were excited and fussy, quite incapable of working for more than three consecutive minutes, and standing up to look out of the windows whenever it was possible to see 'if it was laying'.

'Eggs or bricks?' I asked them tartly but, quite rightly, they did not rise to this badinage and I was forced to give an elementary grammar lesson in the middle of a spirited account of Moses in the bulrushes, knowing full well that neither would bear much fruit.

The snow was certainly 'laying'. It was coming down thick and fast, large snowflakes whirling dizzily and blotting out the landscape as effectively as a fog. It was nearly six inches deep by midday, and the dinner van was remarkably late. Surely there were no drifts yet, I thought to myself, to hold up Mrs Crossley on her travels? She was usually at Fairacre between half past eleven and twelve, then having Beech Green's dinner to deliver before returning to her depot.

At twelve the children who go home to dinner departed. There was still no sign of the van and I was beginning to wonder if I should telephone the depot when Patrick came running back to school, followed by the rest of the home-dinner children, all in a state of much agitation.

'Mrs Crossley's slipped over,' shouted Patrick.

'And spilt all the gravy,' shouted another. He seemed to think that the loss of gravy was more important than Mrs Crossley's accident.

'She's hurt her leg,' volunteered a third.

By this time all my pupils, clad and unclad, were out in the snowy waste of playground. I made a valiant attempt to restore order, banishing the unclad indoors and telling the others to accompany me to the scene.

The dinner van had pulled up just out of sight of the school, and Mrs Crossley had started to walk bearing a pile of large tins propped against her chest. When we reached her she had struggled back to the van and was sitting sideways in the driving seat, massaging an ankle. I could see by the look of pain on her face and the swelling of the joint that she had a severe sprain.

A pool of brown gravy stained the snow, but that was the only culinary casualty. Two of the bigger boys carried Fairacre's food into school while poor Mrs Crossley hobbled to my house supported by half a dozen anxious children and me. She lay on my sofa looking very woebegone.

'So silly of me,' she said, near to tears. 'I must have stepped awkwardly on a hard lump of snow. I couldn't see over the tins.'

'You stay there,' I said, 'and I'll give you first aid in two shakes. In the meantime, drink this.'

I poured out a tot of brandy. Mrs Crossley shuddered.

'Knock it back!' I said firmly, tucking a rug over her. 'I'll just see that the children aren't throwing the dinner all over each other and I'll be back.'

As is so often the case in a crisis, the children were behaving in an exemplary manner. They had served themselves, said grace, and were eating with the utmost decorum when I called in. I gave them much well-deserved praise, begged them to keep it up, and left them smug with self-righteousness.

'I simply must get Beech Green's dinner to them,' was Mrs Crossley's greeting on my return.

'I'll ring Mr Annett,' I assured her, 'and he can come and collect it. But let me see to this ankle.'

'Oh please,' begged Mrs Crossley, 'do ring Mr Annett and the depot! I shan't have an easy moment till it's done!'

You won't have an easy moment for some time with that ankle, I thought, watching it turn from red to mauve as I listened to Beech Green school's telephone bell.

Mr Annett answered promptly. Yes, he would come at once. Could he take Mrs Crossley to her doctor or her home or fetch her husband? I was full of admiration for Mr Annett's rapid grasp of the situation and practical help. But Mrs Crossley, from the sofa, preferred to rest for a little and to stay where she was.

I then rang the depot who promised to send someone to collect the van, and only when that was done would Mrs Crossley put her poor swollen ankle into my amateurish hands. By the time I had strapped it firmly, made her some tea, and promised to run her back after school, it was time to go back to school.

The classroom was beautifully quiet. The dinner things had been cleared away; but on the tortoise stove stood a dinner plate, carefully covered by another.

Ernest lifted it from the stove with the folded duster and placed it reverently before me on my desk.

'Bin keepin' it hot for you, miss,' he said. And it was only then that I realized that I had missed my meal.

I lifted the lid. The gravy had dried to a papery skin, and the slices of meat were curling with the heat. It all looked horribly daunting, but touched by the children's kindness I bravely took up fork and knife. Watched by their solicitous eyes I ate my dinner thankfully.

The snow did not cease all day, and I drove Mrs Crossley home after tea through a positive blizzard. Luckily the roads were passable and I was soon home again. There was still no word from Mrs Pringle and I could hear Mr Willet manfully filling the coke buckets as I put the car away. What would Thursday hold, I wondered, as I ploughed through the snow to my front door?

It held, I discovered next morning, three more cases of mumps and no word from Mrs Pringle. It was still bitterly cold but the snow had stopped during the night. I crunched it underfoot as I crossed the playground and could imagine the snowballing that would delight the children at playtime.

The stoves had resumed their sulky behaviour and filled the two classrooms with smoke. We tried the damper open, shut, and halfway open with exactly the same result. At length we resigned ourselves to the inevitable and resumed our interrupted work on fractions in the midst of an acrid blue haze.

The vicar called during the morning. The Reverend Gerald Partridge is as near a saint as it would be possible to find in any village. His mild sweet face usually wears a vague benign smile, but today he appeared much agitated. At the sight of the smoke, his alarm grew.

'Good heavens!' he cried aghast. 'Are you on fire?'

'I wish we were,' I replied. 'We're only smouldering. The stoves object to a north-east wind.'

'It all looks very uncomfortable,' said the vicar, approaching the tortoise stove warily, as though expecting it to explode. 'I gather that Mrs Pringle is not with you at the moment,' he added delicately. I told him why.

'Yes, yes. I heard that there had been a little upset,' nodded the vicar understandingly. He is much too wise and diplomatic to take sides and, in any case, I suspect that he thinks 'our little upsets' are six of Mrs Pringle's making and half a dozen of mine. And he is probably right.

The vicar now began to twist his leopard-skin gloves together unhappily.

'I have a really dreadful confession to make, Miss Read,' he began. 'I simply cannot put my hand on that pamphlet you lent me about religious books for the young from the Oxford University Press.'

'It doesn't matter in the least,' I assured him. 'I had quite finished with it.' But he seemed too sunk in self-mortification to hear.

'You see, I put it most carefully on the hall table, and this morning my wife and the two girls began spring-cleaning.' The two girls, incidentally, are two buxom Fairacre matrons of sixty-two and sixty-five.

'And not only had the pamphlet gone,' continued the poor man, 'but the hall table and the rugs and chairs – and to tell you the truth, every room in the house is completely upside down.'

Knowing his wife's vigour and the matching energy of 'the two girls' I could imagine the state of the vicarage only too clearly. This visit, I suspected, might be in the nature of a brief escape.

I did my best to calm his fears and accompanied him out to his car.

'Just look at that splendid bullfinch!' exclaimed Mr Partridge, his face lighting up.

'Splendidly picking off my plum buds,' I responded grimly, though I had to admit that the vivid little creature was a cheerful sight on that bleak day.

The vicar climbed into his car, and looked at me anxiously through the window. 'Don't hesitate to close the school, my dear, if the stoves prove too intractable. It can't be good for your lungs, or the dear children's, to inhale those fumes. What a pity Mrs Pringle is away! She is the *tiniest* bit difficult, I realize, but she has a wonderful way with stoves.'

Before I could reply, he gave me a disarming smile, let in the clutch and shot erratically away down the lane.

During the dinner hour I consulted Mr Willet about my little cat.

For several days he had been off his food, and I had supposed that a diet of local mice had been preferred to the delicacies offered by me. But this morning he looked wretched, sitting four-square with paws tucked under him, and his eyes half-closed.

'Fur balls,' pronounced Mr Willet.

'I'll get the vet,' I said at once.

'Ain't no need to get him out from Caxley,' said Mr Willet. 'You give ol' Tib a spoonful of liquid paraffin to oil the works. He'll be as right as rain tomorrow.'

'Are you sure?' I asked doubtfully.

'Positive!' Mr Willet assured me. 'This time of year they loses their winter coats, see, and keep all on a-licking theirselves tidy, and swallering great 'anks of 'air. It all gets twizzled up inside 'em. Liquid paraffin's the stuff.'

I thanked him and watched him return to his daily coke-sweeping. What a tower of strength and information Mr Willet was!

I poured out a dessertspoonful of liquid paraffin and approached the unsuspecting cat. It is not easy to open a cat's mouth in order to administer medicine, as everyone knows. It is harder still when you are attempting it alone, and particularly when you have been foolish enough to pour out the dose beforehand and are trying not to spill it. Somehow or other I got most of it into the side of Tibby's mouth, and was just beginning to congratulate myself, when he gave his head a violent shake and ejected at least half the oil over my beautiful new suede shoes.

I returned, growling, to afternoon school, recounting my luck to Mr Willet en route.

'I'll give you a hand after school,' he said cheerfully. 'You allus wants two to cope with a cat, and then the cat nearly allus wins.'

He looked at my stained shoes sadly.

'It do seem to be one of those weeks, don't it?' he observed. And I agreed, with feeling.

There was still no word from Mrs Pringle on Friday morning. Although it was delightful to be without her presence, the school was beginning to look a little worse for wear despite my own efforts and Mr Willet's.

The snow, luckily, was melting fast, but plenty managed to find its way into the building. With it were the usual flotsam and jetsam of school life, and plentiful sprinkling of additional matter from the workmen at the Blundells' new home.

'If anyone brings any more nails, putty or shavings into this school,' I said threateningly, 'I shall ring up the builders and tell them what is happening.'

The putty in particular was a sore trial. It seemed to be the thing to have a small lump under one's desk, or about one's person, and the children's hands had never been so filthy. By dint of constant nagging I was beginning to make a little headway against this infiltration.

We were all glad that it was Friday. It had been a trying week for everyone. By the afternoon I was beginning to feel a little more hopeful. The stoves were emitting only half as much smoke as before, only one more case of mumps had occurred overnight, Tibby appeared to be on the mend, a new pane of glass had replaced the broken one, and I had decided to find a substitute for Mrs Pringle if I did not hear from the lady during the weekend.

But Fate still had one more blow in store for us. Jimmy Waites, on returning from play, set up a wail.

'I bin and lost my half crown!'

'Where was it?' I inquired.

'Under my desk. Someone's pinched it!'

Now, if anything makes me cross, it is this kind of glib accusation. I spoke sharply.

'Rubbish! And in any case, you know you should have given it to me to mind. What was it for?'

'Half of cheddar, two boxes of matches and a pricker for the Primus,' gabbled Jimmy. Obviously he had been repeating this to himself all the afternoon.

Then began the search. We turned the whole place upside down. We shifted desks, turned out likely cupboards, and completely wrecked the room. It was not to be found.

Our Friday afternoon story had to go by the board. By now I was beginning to wonder if someone perhaps had succumbed to temptation. The half crown had been seen by Jimmy's neighbours. It was there at playtime. Jimmy had been in and out of the room himself during that time.

It was a mystery that must be solved.

'We'd better look in our clothes,' I said. It is a job that I hate doing, but things looked suspicious. Pockets were turned out, socks rolled down, children jumped up and down to see if any coins would emerge from jerseys and trousers. But nothing was forthcoming.

By now it was time to say prayers and go home. In the middle of the hubbub the door opened and in stumped Mrs Pringle, complete with black bag. She surveyed the chaos grimly. 'Seems this place wants a bit of doing-up,' she boomed, but made no move to discard her coat and hat.

'Sit down for a moment, Mrs Pringle,' I said. 'We're in rather a pickle.'

'*That*,' said the lady with emphasis, 'is plain for all to see!' She folded her arms across her capacious bosom and watched the scene majestically.

'We'll have one last look,' I said desperately to the children. 'It must be somewhere in this room. If it doesn't turn up now I shall have to think about keeping you all here until it is found.'

There was something in my tone that made them realize the seriousness of the occasion and they began to look frenziedly about them, bending under desks, running their hands along the high window sills and scrabbling in the dusty corners of the classroom. Quite rightly, they resented being suspected, and I hated, just as much, the feeling that I was suspecting them.

It was Mrs Pringle who discovered the half crown. The only calm person in the room, she had perhaps a clearer eye than the rest of us. 'If it's a *coin* you're looking for,' she shouted above the din, 'it's there!'

She pointed at the back view of Jimmy Waites himself. The child was kneeling under his desk, and cleaving to the instep of his wellington boot was a glutinous lump of the ubiquitous putty. There, embedded in it, was the missing half crown.

After we had congratulated Mrs Pringle and each other, I improved the shining hour by pointing out the absolute necessity of leaving putty severely alone, and then dismissed them.

There was genuine relief in their farewells. The dark shadow of distrust was lifted, the half crown was restored and Fairacre school could relax again.

'The vicar told me you was in trouble,' said Mrs Pringle austerely, when the children had gone. 'And though I doubt if my knee will ever be the same again, I knows where my duty lies.' She advanced, limping, towards the stove. 'Been letting it smoke, have you?' she said.

I felt that this was hardly the correct expression, but was not given time to reply. To my amazement, Mrs Pringle lifted a mighty hand and smote the pipe about a foot above the stove itself. The smoke, which had been dribbling gently from the crack in the lid, ceased emerging immediately.

'Gets a bit out of true sometimes,' observed Mrs Pringle with satisfaction. 'Well, I'll get the place to rights while I'm here, so's we can be straight for next week.'

'Thank you, Mrs Pringle,' I said meekly, bowing my head, with secret relief, to the inevitable.

7. THE FAIRACRE GHOST

The Easter holidays are probably more welcome than any other, for they mark the passing of the darkest and most dismal of the three school terms and they herald the arrival of flowers, sunshine and all the pleasures of the summer.

At this time, in Fairacre, we set about our gardens with zeal. Potatoes are put in, on Good Friday if possible, and rows of peas and carrots, and those who have been far-sighted enough to put in their broad beans in the autumn, go carefully along the rows, congratulating themselves, and hoping that the black fly will not devastate the young hopefuls in the next few months.

We admire each other's daffodils, walk down each other's garden paths observing the new growth in herbaceous borders, and gloat over the buds on plum and peach trees. We also observe the strong upthrust of nettles, couch grass and dandelions among the choicer growth, but are too besotted by the thought of summer ahead to let such things worry us unduly.

It is now that the vicar gets out his garden funiture – a motley collection ranging from Victorian ironwork to pre-war Lloyd-loom – and arranges it hopefully on the vicarage verandah. Now Mr Mawne, our local ornithologist, erects a hide at the end of his lovely garden in order to watch the birds. He weaves a bower of pea-sticks, ivy-trails and twigs upon the wood and sacking framework, as intricate as the nests of those he watches.

Now the cottage doors are propped open with a chair, or a

large stone, and striped cats wash their ears or survey the sunshine blandly through half-closed eyes. Tortoises emerge, shaky and slower than ever, from their hibernation, and sometimes a grass snake can be seen sunning itself in the dry grass.

This is the time for visiting and being visited. For months we have been confined. Bad weather, dirty roads, dark nights and winter illnesses have kept us all apart. Now we set about refurbishing our friendships, and one of my first pleasures during this Easter holiday was a visit from my godson Malcolm Annett, and his father and mother.

It was a perfect day for a tea party. The table bore a bowl of freshly-picked primroses, some lemon curd made that morning, and a plentiful supply of egg sandwiches. Mr Roberts, the farmer, has a new batch of Rhode Island Red hens who supply me with a dozen dark brown eggs weekly. These are lucky hens, let me say, garrulous and energetic, running at large in

the farmyard behind the house, scratching busily in the loose straw at the foot of the ricks, and advancing briskly to the back door whenever anyone emerges holding a plate. No wonder that their eggs are luscious compared with the product of their poor imprisoned sisters.

After tea we ambled through the village, greeting many old friends who were out enjoying the air. Mrs Annett used to teach at Fairacre before she married the headmaster at our neighbouring village Beech Green so that she knows a great many families here. Mr Annett is choirmaster at St Patrick's church at Fairacre, so that he too knows us all well.

We walked by the church and took a fork to the left. It is a lane used little these days, except by young lovers and Mr Roberts' tractors making their way to one of his larger fields. A dilapidated cottage stands alone some hundred yards from the entrance to the lane.

We stopped at its rickety gate and surveyed the outline of its ancient garden. A damson tree, its trunk riven with age, leant towards the remaining patch of roof thatch. Rough grass covered what once had been garden beds and paths, and nettles and brambles grew waist high against the walls of the ruin.

The doors and windows gaped open. Inside, on the ground floor, in what had once been the living room of the cottage, we could see hundredweight paper bags of fertilizer propped against the stained and ragged wallpaper. They belonged to Mr Roberts and were waiting to be spread upon his meadows any day now. Upstairs, the two small bedrooms lay open to the sky. The thatch had retreated before the onslaught of wind and weather, and only the frame of the roof stood, gaunt and rotting, against the evening sky.

'It must have been pretty once,' I said, looking at the triangle of garden and the rose-red of the old bricks.

'The vicar told me it was lived in during the war,' said Mr Annett. 'It housed a family of eight evacuees then. They didn't mind it being haunted, they told Mr Roberts.'

'Haunted?' we cried. I looked at Mr Annett to see if he was joking, but his face was unusually thoughtful.

'It is, you know,' he said with conviction. 'I've seen the ghost myself. That's how I came to hear the history of the place from the vicar.'

'Is that why it stays empty?' I asked. It was strange that I had never heard this tale throughout my time at Fairacre.

Mr Annett laughed. 'No, indeed! I told you people lived in it for years. The evacuees said they'd sooner be haunted than

bombed, and spent all the war years here. I think Roberts found it just wasn't worth doing up after the war, and so it is now in this state.'

We looked again at the crumbling cottage. It was too small and homely to be sinister, despite this tale of a ghost. It had the pathetic look of a wild animal, tired to death, crouching in the familiar shelter of grass and neglected vegetation for whatever Fate might have in store.

'When did you see the ghost?' I asked.

Mr Annett sighed with mock impatience. 'Persistent woman! I see I shall have no peace until I have put the whole uncomfortable proceedings before you. It was a very frightening experience indeed and, if you don't mind, I'll tell you the story as we walk. Even now my blood grows a little chilly at the memory. Brisk exercise is the right accompaniment for a ghost story.'

We continued up the lane, with young Malcolm now before and now behind us, scrambling up the banks and shouting with the sheer joy of living. With the scents of spring around us, and the soft wind lifting our hair, we listened to the tale of one strange winter night.

Every Friday night, with the exception of Good Friday, Mr Annett left the school house at Beech Green and travelled the three miles to St Patrick's church for choir practice.

Some men would have found it irksome to leave the comfort of their homes at seven in the evening and to face the windy darkness of a downland lane. Mr Annett was glad to do so. His love of music was strong enough to make this duty a positive pleasure, and although his impatient spirit chafed at times at the slow progress made by Fairacre's choir, he counted Friday evening as a highlight of the week.

At this time he had much need of comfort. He was a young widower, living alone in the school house, and ministered to by a middle-aged Scotswoman who came in daily. The death of his wife, six months after their marriage, was still too painful for him to dwell upon. She had been killed in an air raid during the early part of the war, and for Mr Annett life would never be the same again.

One moonlit Friday evening in December, some years after the war had ended, he set out as usual for Fairacre. It was so bright that he could have driven his little car without headlights. The road glimmered palely before him, barred with black shadows where trees lined the road.

He was early, for he had arranged to pick up some music from Miss Parr's house and knew that the old lady would want him to stop for a little time. However, when a maid opened the door, he was told Miss Parr had been invited to her nephew's, but the music had been looked out for him.

He drove to St Patrick's, and went inside. It was cold and gloomy. No one had yet arrived, and Mr Annett decided to use his time in taking a stroll in the brilliant moonlight. There was an unearthly beauty about the night that chimed with the young man's melancholy. He made his way slowly along a little used lane near the church, and let sad memory carry him on its flood. It was not often that he so indulged himself. After his wife's death, he had moved to Beech Green and thrown himself, almost savagely, into school life. He had filled his time with work and music, so that he fell asleep with exhaustion rather than the numbing despair which had first governed every waking hour.

He passed a broken down cottage on his left, its remnants of thatch silvered with moonlight. Just beyond it a five-barred gate afforded a view of the distant downs. Mr Annett leant upon its topmost bar and surveyed the scene.

Before him lay the freshly ploughed fields, the furrows gleaming in the rays of the moon. Further away, a dusky copse made a black patch on the lower flanks of the downs. Against the clear sky their mighty bulk looked more majestic than ever. There was something infinitely reassuring and comforting about their solidity, and the young man, gazing at them, let the tranquillity about him do its healing work.

It was very quiet. Far away, he heard a train hoot impatiently as it waited for a signal to allow its passage westward. Nearer, he was dimly conscious of the rustling of dead leaves at the foot of an old crab apple tree which stood hard by the gate. Some small nocturnal animal was foraging stealthily, wary of the silent man nearby.

Sunk in his thoughts, he was oblivious of the passage of time, and hardly surprised to notice that a strange man had appeared in the lane without any noise of approach.

He came close to Mr Annett, nodded civilly, and leant beside him on the gate. For a moment the two men rested silently side by side, elbows touching, and gazed at the silvered landscape before them. Despite the stranger's unexpected advent, Mr Annett felt little surprise. There was something gentle and companionable about the newcomer. The schoolmaster had the odd feeling that they were very much akin.

Vaguely, he wondered if they had met before somewhere. He shifted along the gate – the stranger seemed excessively cold – and turned slightly to look at him.

He was a loosely-built fellow, of about Mr Annett's age, dressed in dark country clothes which seemed a pretty poor fit. He wore an open-necked shirt and a spotted neckerchief, tied gipsy fashion, round his throat. He had a small beard, light in colour, which gleamed silver in the moonlight, and his fair hair was thick and wiry.

'Full moon tomorrow,' commented the stranger. For such a big man he had a remarkably small voice, Mr Annett noticed. It was almost falsetto, slightly husky and strained, as though he were suffering from laryngitis.

'So it is,' agreed Mr Annett.

They relapsed again into contemplation of the view. After some time, Mr Annett stirred himself long enough to find some cigarettes. He offered the packet to his companion.

'Thank 'ee,' said the man. 'Thank 'ee kindly, but I don't smoke these days.'

The schoolmaster lit his cigarette and surveyed the man. 'Haven't I seen you before somewhere?' he asked.

'Most likely. I've lived in Fairacre all my life,' answered the man huskily.

'I'm at Beech Green,' said Mr Annett.

The man drew in his breath sharply, as though in pain. 'My wife came from Beech Green,' he said. He bent his head forward suddenly. By the light of the moon Mr Annett saw that his eyes were closed. The use of the past tense was not lost upon the schoolmaster, himself still smarting with grief, and he led the conversation from the dangerous ground he had unwittingly encountered.

'Whereabouts in Fairacre do you live?' he asked.

The man raised his head and nodded briefly in the direction of the ruined cottage nearby. Mr Annett was puzzled by this, but thought that perhaps he was nodding generally in the direction of the village. Not wishing to distress him any further, and realizing that his choir must be soon arriving at St Patrick's, Mr Annett began to stir himself for departure. It was time he moved, in any case, for he had grown colder and colder since the arrival of the stranger, despite his warm over-coat. The stranger only had on a long jacket, but he seemed oblivious of the frost.

'Well, I must be off,' said Mr Annett. 'I'm due to take choir practice at seven thirty. Are you walking back to the village?'

The man straightened up and turned to face the school-master. The moonlight shone full upon his face. It was a fine face, with high cheekbones and pale blue eyes set very wide apart. There was something Nordic in his aspect, with his great height and wide shoulders.

'I'll stop here a little longer,' he said slowly. 'This is the right place for me. I come most nights, particularly around full moon.'

'I can understand It,' said Mr Annett gently, scanning the sad grave face. 'There is comfort in a lovely place like this.'

A burst of laughter broke from the stranger's lips, all the more uncanny for its cracked wheeziness. His wide-open eyes glittered in the moonlight.

'Comfort?' he echoed. 'There's no comfort for the likes of me – ever!' He began to tear savagely at the neckerchief about his throat. 'You can't expect comfort,' he gasped painfully, 'when you've done this to yourself!'

He pulled the cloth away with a jerk and tore his shirt opening away from the neck with both hands. By the light of the moon, Mr Annett saw the livid scar which encircled his neck, the mark of a strangling rope which eternity itself could never remove.

He raised his horror-filled eyes to those of the stranger. They were still wide open, but they glittered no longer. They seemed to be dark gaping holes, full of mist, through which Mr

Annett could dimly discern the outline of the crab apple tree behind him.

He tried to speak, but could not. And as he watched, still struggling for speech, the figure slowly dissolved, melting into thin air, until the schoolmaster found himself gazing at nothing at all but the old gnarled tree, and the still beauty of the night around it.

The vicar was alone in the vestry when Mr Annett arrived at St Patrick's.

'Good evening, good evening,' said the vicar boisterously, and then caught sight of his choirmaster's face.

'My dear boy, you look as though you've seen a ghost,' he said.'

'You speak more truly than you realize,' Mr Annett answered soberly. He began to walk through to the chancel and his organ, but the vicar barred his way. His kind old face was puckered with concern.

'Was it poor old Job?' he asked gently.

'I don't know who it was,' replied the schoolmaster. He explained briefly what had happened. He was more shaken by this encounter than he cared to admit. Somehow, the affinity between the stranger and himself had seemed so strong. It made the man's dreadful disclosure, and then his withdrawal, even more shocking.

The vicar put both hands on the young man's shoulders. 'Poor Job,' he said, 'is nothing to be frightened of. It is a sad tale, and it happened long ago. After choir practice, I hope you will come back to the vicarage for a drink, and I will do my best to tell you Job's story.'

The younger man managed a wan smile.

'Thank you, vicar,' he said. 'I should be glad to hear more of him. I had a strange feeling while we were together –' He faltered to a stop.

'What kind of feeling?' asked the vicar gently.

Mr Annett moved restlessly. His brow was furrowed with perplexity. 'As though – it sounds absurd – but as though we were brothers. It was as if we were akin – as if we shared something.'

The vicar nodded slowly, and sighed, dropping his hands from the young man's shoulders. 'You shared sorrow, my son,' he said as he turned away. But his tone was so low that the words were lost in a burst of country voices from the chancel.

Together the two men made their way from the vestry to the duties before them.

The vicarage drawing room was empty when the vicar and his guest entered an hour or so later. A bright fire blazed on the hearth and Mr Annett gratefully pulled up an armchair. He felt as though he would never be warm again.

He sipped the whisky and water which the vicar gave him and was glad of its comfort. He was deathly tired, and recognized this as a symptom of shock. Part of his mind longed for sleep, but part craved to hear the story which the vicar had promised.

Before long, the older man put aside his glass, lodged three stout logs upon the fire and settled back in his chair to recount his tale.

* * *

Job Carpenter, said the vicar, was a shepherd. He was born in Victoria's reign in the year of the Great Exhibition of 1851, and was the tenth child in a long family. His parents lived in a small cottage at the Beech Green end of Fairacre, and all their children were born there. They were desperately poor, for Job's father was a farm labourer and times were hard.

At ten years old Job was out at work on the downs, stone-picking, bird-scaring and helping his father to clear ditches and lay hedges, but by the time he was fifteen he had decided that it was sheep he wanted to tend.

The shepherd at that point was a surly old fellow, twisted with rheumatism and foul of tongue. Job served a cruel apprenticeship under him and in the last year or two of the old man's life virtually looked after the flock himself. This fact did not go unnoticed by the farmer.

One morning during lambing time, Job entered the little hut carrying twin lambs which were weakly. There, stretched upon the sacks stuffed with straw which made the old man's bed, lay his master, open-eyed and cold.

Within two days Job had been told that he was now shepherd, and he continued in this post for the rest of his life. He grew into a handsome fellow, tall and broad, with blond wiry hair and a curling beard. The girls of Fairacre and Beech Green found him attractive, and made the fact quite plain, but Job was shy and did not respond as readily as his fellows.

One day, however, he met a girl whom he had never seen before. Her family lived in Beech Green, but she was in service in London. Job's sister worked with her and the two girls were given a week's holiday at the same time. She walked over to see Job's sister one warm spring evening and the two girls wandered across the downs to see the lambs at play.

Job watched them approach. His sister Jane was tall and fair, as he was. Her companion was a complete contrast. She was little more than five feet in height, with long silky black hair coiled in a thick plait round her head, like a coronet. She had a small heart-shaped face, sloe-dark eyes which slanted upwards at the corners, and narrow crescents of eyebrows. Job thought her the prettiest thing he had ever seen.

Her name was Mary. To Job, who had a deep religious faith, this seemed wholly fitting. She was a queen among women. Job had no doubts this time and no shyness. Before Mary's week of holiday had ended the two young people came to an understanding.

It was Christmas time before they saw each other again, and only a few letters, written for them by better-schooled friends, passed between Mary and Job during the long months of separation. They planned to get married in the autumn of the following year. Mary would return to London and save every penny possible from her pitiful earnings, and Job would ask for a cottage of his own at Michaelmas.

He was fortunate. The farmer offered him a little thatched house not far from the church at Fairacre. It had two rooms up and two down, and a sizeable triangle of garden where a man could grow plenty of vegetables, keep a pig and a few hens, and so go more than half way towards being self-supporting. A few fruit trees shaded the garden, and a lusty young crab apple tree grew in the hedge nearby.

The couple married at Michaelmas and were as happy as larks in their new home. Mary took work at the vicarage and found it less arduous than the living-in job in London. She was a quick quiet worker in the house and the vicar's wife approved of her. She was delighted to discover that her new daily was also an excellent needlewoman, and Mary found herself carrying home bundles of shirts whose collars needed turning, sheets that needed sides to middling, and damask table linen in need of fine darning. She was particularly glad of this extra money for, by the end of the first year of their married life, a child was due, and Mary knew she would have to give up the scrubbing and heavy lifting for a few weeks at least.

The coming of the child was of intense joy to Job. He adored his wife and made no secret of it. The fact that he cleaned her shoes and took her tea in bed in the mornings was known in Fairacre and looked upon as a crying scandal, particularly by the men. What was a woman for but to wait upon her menfolk? Job Carpenter was proper daft to pander to a wife in that namby-pamby way. Only laying up a store of trouble for himself in the future, said the village wiseacres in The Beetle and Wedge. Job, more in love than ever, let such gossip flow by him.

The baby took its time in coming and as soon as Job saw it he realized that it could not possibly survive. His experience with hundreds of lambs gave him a pretty shrewd idea of 'a good do-er' or a weakling. Mary, cradling it in her arms, smiling with happiness, suspected nothing. It was all the more tragic for her when, on the third day, her little son quietly expired.

She lay in a raging fever for a fortnight, and it was months before she was herself again. Throughout the time Job nursed her with loving constancy, comforting her when she wept, encouraging any spark of recovery.

In the two years that followed, two miscarriages occurred and the young couple began to wonder if they would ever have a family. The cottage gave them great joy, and the garden was one of the prettiest in the village, but it was a child that they really wanted. Everyone liked the Carpenters and Job's demonstrative affection for his wife was looked upon with more indulgence by the villagers as time passed.

At last Mary found that she was pregnant yet again. The vicar's wife, for whom she still worked, was determined that this baby should arrive safely, and insisted on Mary being examined regularly by her own doctor. She engaged, too, a reputable midwife from Caxley to attend the birth, for the local midwife at that time, in Fairacre and Beech Green, was a slatternly creature, reeking of gin and unwashed garments, whose very presence caused revulsion rather than reassurance to her unfortunate patients.

All went well. The baby was a lusty boy, who throve from the time he entered the world. Job and Mary could hardly believe their good fortune and peered into his cot a hundred times a day to admire his fair beauty.

One early October day, when the child was a few months old, Mary was sitting at the table with a pile of mending before her. The boy lay asleep in his cradle beside her.

It was a wild windy day. The autumn equinox had stirred the weather to tempestuous conditions, and the trees in the little garden flailed their branches in the uproar. Leaves whirled by the cottage window and every now and again a spatter of hail hit the glass like scattered shot. The doors rattled, the thin curtains stirred in the draught, and the whole cottage shuddered in the force of the gale. Mary was nervous, and wondered how poor Job was faring outside in the full force of the unkind elements.

As the afternoon wore on, the gale increased. Mary had never known such violence. There was a roaring noise in the chimney which was terrifying and a banshee howling of wind round the house which woke the baby and made him cry. Mary lifted him from his cradle to comfort him, and walked back and forth with him against her shoulder.

There was a sudden increase in the noise outside – a curious drumming sound in the heart of the fury. To Mary's horror she

saw through the window the small chicken house at the end of the garden swept upward and carried, twisting bizarrely, into the field beyond. At the same time a great mass of straw, clearly torn from a nearby rick, went whirling across the garden and, as it passed, one of the apple trees, laden with golden fruit, snapped off at the base as though it were a flower stem.

Mary could scarcely believe her eyes. She stood rooted to the spot, between the table and the fireplace, her baby clutched to her. The drumming sound grew louder until it was unendurable. Mary was about to scream with panic when a terrifying rumble came near at hand. The chimney stack crashed upon the cottage roof, cracking the rafters like matchwood, and sending ceilings, furniture, bricks and rubble cascading upon the two terror-stricken occupants of the little home.

When Job arrived at the scene of the disaster, soaked to the skin and wild with anxiety, he found the whole of one end of his house had collapsed. No one was there, for the neighbours were all coping with troubles of their own, and there had been no time to see how others were faring in the catastrophe that had befallen Fairacre in the matter of minutes.

He began tearing at the beams and sagging thatch with his bare hands, shouting hoarsely to his wife and son as he struggled. There was no answer to his cries. A ghastly silence seemed to pervade the ruined house, in contrast to the fiendish noises which raged about it.

An hour later, when neighbours arrived to help, they found him there, still screaming and struggling to reach his dead. Sweat and tears poured down his ravaged face, his clothes were torn, his battered hands bleeding. When, finally, the broken bodies of his wife and child were recovered, Job had to be led away, and only the doctor's drugs brought him merciful oblivion at the end of that terrible day.

In the weeks that followed, while his house was being repaired, Job was offered hospitality throughout Fairacre, but he would have none of it. As soon as the pitiful funeral was over, he returned numbly to his work, coming back each night to his broken home and sleeping on a makeshift bed in the one remaining room.

Neighbours did their best for him, cooking him a meal, washing his linen, comforting him with friendly words and advice. He seemed scarcely to see or to hear them, and heads shook over Job's sad plight.

'There's naught can help him, but time,' said one.

''Tis best to let him get over his grief alone,' said another.

'Once he gets his house set to rights, he'll start to pick up,' said a third.

Fairacre watched poor Job anxiously.

The men who had been sent to repair the cottage worked well and quickly. Their sympathy was stirred by the sight of the gaunt young man's lonely existence in the undamaged half of his tiny house.

At length the living room was done. The bricks which had crashed on that fateful afternoon had been built again into the chimney breast. The broken rafters had been replaced, the walls plastered and whitewashed afresh.

Job met the men as he trudged home from work. They called to him with rough sympathy.

'It's ready for you now,' they shouted through the twilight. 'We've finished at last.'

A kindly neighbour had gone in to replace his furniture.

'There now,' she said, in a motherly burr, 'you can settle in here tonight.' But Job shook his head, and went into his old room.

Sad at heart, the good old soul returned home, but could not forget the sight of Job's ravaged face. 'I'll go and take a look at him,' she said to her husband later that evening. 'If the lamp's alight in the room then I'll know he's settled in, and I'll go more comfortable to bed.'

But the window was dark. She was about to turn homeward again when she heard movements inside the cottage and saw the living room door open. Job stood upon the threshold, a candle in his hand. Breathless, in the darkness of the garden, the watcher saw him make his way slowly across the room to the chimney breast. He put down the guttering candle, and rested his fair head against the brickwork. Before long, his great shoulders began to heave, and the sound of dreadful sobbing sent the onlooker stealthily homeward.

''Tis best by far to leave him be,' comforted the neighbour's husband, when she told him what she had witnessed. 'We'll go and see him in the morning. It will be all over by then.'

But there was little comfort for the woman that night, for the spectacle of Job's grief drove all hope of sleep away.

Next morning they went together to the house. Her heart was heavy with foreboding as they walked up the little brick path. Inside the silent house they found him, with a noose about his neck, hanging against the chimney breast which had crushed his wife, his child, and every hope of Job himself.

* * *

There was an uncanny silence in the sunny lane as Mr Annett finished speaking.

'And that', he said soberly, 'is the tale of poor Job, as the vicar told it to me.'

Suddenly, a blackbird called from a hazel bush, breaking the spell. Despite the sunshine, I shivered. We were alone, for Malcolm and his mother had gone ahead to pick primroses from the steep banks, and though we were surrounded by the sights and scents of spring I remained chilled by this strange winter's tale.

'You're sure it was a ghost?' I asked shakily.

'Other people have seen Job,' answered Mr Annett, 'and the vicar knew all about him. But I believe I am the only person that Job has spoken to.'

'I wonder why?' I mused aloud.

'Perhaps he felt we had much in common,' said Mr Annett quietly.

I remembered suddenly Mr Annett's own tragedy. He, too, had adored a young wife and had lost her in the face of overwhelming violence. He too had watched a broken body removed to an early grave. There was no misery, no depth of hopelessness which Job had known, which was not known too to young Mr Annett.

We were summoned abruptly from the shadowy past by the sound of young Malcolm's excited voice.

'There's a nest here,' he called, 'with eggs. Come and look!'

'Coming!' shouted Mr Annett, suddenly looking ten years younger. And he ran off, all grief forgotten, to join his wife and child.

8. MRS PRINGLE'S CHRISTMAS PUDDING

One of the pleasures of school holidays is the opportunity to join in the village affairs more fully than is possible in term time. When I was asked if I would help the Women's Institute to prepare a party I agreed with alacrity.

Once a year the members of Fairacre WI invite a coach-load of Londoners for the afternoon. Many of the visitors were evacuated to this area from the East End during the last war, and some had their schooling at our village school. Their mothers, now elderly women, lived in our midst, made friends, worshipped at St Patrick's, shared our pains and pleasures, and generally forged bonds which will last a lifetime. It is always a gay afternoon, with much reminiscing about shared memories and much gossip about new babies, marriages, good fortune and bad, which have been experienced since the last meeting.

The visitors were due to arrive at two o'clock. The custom is to greet them at the village hall with the tea urns ready. The main tea – a gargantuan meal – is prepared for five o'clock, but the two o'clock cup is considered the right welcome after their long trip from London and their lunch-time stop on the way.

At one time, we used to prepare our offerings in our own kitchens, converge upon the village hall about two and deposit sandwiches, sausage rolls, cakes and so on upon the dishes provided for the main meal. As anyone who organizes these things knows, the results could be chaotic. Four people who had offered sausage rolls would decide to provide chocolate sponge instead. The six who had promised sandwiches found that the local baker had no sliced bread, and so had opted to provide rock cakes instead, and the carefully prepared lists pinned up in the hall became covered with indescribable scribblings as the two people in charge tried to sort out the muddle.

After a few years of such crises it was decided to leave the matter in the hands of the committee, ably headed by Mrs Partridge, the vicar's wife, who is our President. These noble and efficient ladies ordered the bread, butter and fillings for the sandwiches, and every other necessity, and detailed squads of underlings to prepare the food under their vigilant surveillance in the hall. It worked much better that way, we found.

Consequently, at ten o'clock on the morning of the great day I made my way to the rendezvous, carrying my basket with a knife for buttering, a knife for cutting bread and some tea and sugar as my fool-proof contribution to the festivities.

The hall was buzzing like a beehive when I entered. The card tables which are used for local whist games had been placed at intervals round the hall and covered with bright cloths ready for the visitors. At one end, two long trestle tables were the scene of much activity. Here the noise was at its greatest for about twenty women cut and buttered bread, wielded salt and pepper pots, stacked sandwiches, arranged cakes on plates and generally made as much hubbub as my own schoolchildren.

I joined the throng and found myself between Mrs Mawne and Mrs Willet. Mrs Mawne has lived in Fairacre only a year or two and is the wife of our local ornithologist. His other claim to fame is his wonderful grasp of the church accounts which used to drive the vicar to distraction before Mr Mawne's coming. Mrs Mawne has the happy knack of upsetting everyone in the village by much forthright and tactless comment.

Her remark about the general incompetence, and probable dishonesty of the clergy in money matters, spoken directly to the vicar's wife in the presence of several speechless parishioners, has long been remembered. However, as we all have to live cheek by jowl in the village here, we push such memories to the back of our minds as best we may, and get on with day to day living.

Mrs Willet, the wife of our school caretaker, is a small mouse like creature who looks meek and frail. In fact, she is a dynamic person who gets through more work in twenty-four hours than I do in a week. Her washing line on a Monday morning flies a multiplicity of spotless linen, long before her neighbours have pegged theirs out. Her store cupboards bulge with jams, jellies, pickles and chutneys of her own making. Puddings and pies, batches of scones, roast joints, and a thousand other delicacies stream from her oven to nourish sturdy Mr Willet three times a day. Besides this, she makes her own clothes, sings in St Patrick's choir, enters all the WI competitions, knits, crochets, makes rugs and generally leaves one feeling quite useless and incorrigibly lazy.

Now her hands flew briskly back and forth from potted meat to bread and butter, working at twice the pace and with twice the deftness of my own. Mrs Willet's sandwiches were models of square exactitude. Mine gradually grew more and more rhomboid as the loaf went down. Mrs Willet's crusts sliced away cleanly. Mine broke away raggedly despite my best endeavours. The only comfort was that Mrs Mawne's were, if anything, rather more dilapidated than mine.

We shouted amicably to each other among the din.

'The new people are moving in,' Mrs Willet told me. 'The Blundells. I knew her as a girl. Very pretty, she was then.' I remembered Amy's story, and waited for more.

Mrs Mawne added her usual contribution with her usual tact. 'Looks rather a rackety type now,' was her comment. 'Hair very obviously dyed, and in trade, I hear.'

Mrs Willet began to bridle.

'A very flourishing business in Caxley,' I put in placatingly. If trade is flourishing enough, I notice, there seems to be less antagonism towards it. Mrs Mawne, however, was not particularly moved. She sucked a buttery finger and continued to arrange her sandwiches. It would have made a sanitary inspector's hair curl, but we are tough in Fairacre, and one of our favourite maxims is: 'You have to eat a peck of dirt before you die,' which we quote as we sketchily dust the tomato that has rolled on the floor, or take in the loaf that has been lodged on the outside window sill.

'I shan't bother to call,' said Mrs Mawne, filching my bread knife shamelessly, and making the handle horribly buttery, I observed.

Mrs Willet muttered something which sounded like: 'Fat lot she'll care!' but was unheard by Mrs Mawne. Mrs Willet's neck was growing rosy with suppressed anger and feeling rather nervous with so many knives flashing about, I attempted to be a little peacemaker once again.

'I believe Mrs Blundell used to sing very well,' I began.

'Oh, she sung lovely!' replied Mrs Willet, with enthusiasm. 'Used to come out here with the Operatic during the war, and we had rare old times!'

She gazed round our dingy village hall with affection. The walls are covered with sticky gingery-brown matchboarding and upon its surface hang lop-sided photographs of football teams of long ago, faded brown with age. Stern country countenances, many of them wearing fine moustaches, peer from among the clouds which the damp has drawn over the group. Here and there are pinned such notices as 'Scouts' Rules', 'The Resuscitation of the Drowned' (though we are miles from any water), and 'Suggestions for WI Programme – PLEASE HELP!' By the door there is a dilapidated piece of cardboard on which is printed: PLEASE SWITCH OF THE LIGHT and that missing F has been a thorn in my flesh ever since coming to Fairacre.

Dusty plush curtains, on a sagging wire, screen the minute stage from sight, and the wood is of splintery bare boards with here and there a knot of wood, polished by friction, projecting like a buttered brazil. There is nothing truthfully to gladden the eye in our hall, and yet Mrs Willet looked upon it now with all the doting tenderness of a mother gazing upon her firstborn. Such, I observed, is the power of association.

'A lot went on here during the war,' continued Mrs Willet. 'We used to have canning sessions in here twice each summer – soft fruit time, and then later when the apples and plums were ready. The WI used to bring the canning machine and we spent all day up here. Had some fun, I can tell you!'

'I always bottled mine,' said Mrs Mawne. 'Much more wholesome.'

'Sometimes there'd be as many as thirty of us up here canning,' continued Mrs Willet, ignoring the interruption. 'With the evacuees, and that. Some of 'em will be here this afternoon. You ask 'em, Miss Read, about this hall in the war. Fairly hummed with life it did! We had the clinic here, and First Aid classes, and no end of concerts and whist drives. And when we won the war, we had a proper beanfeast for the Welcome Home!'

'I suppose most of the evacuees had gone home by then,' I said.

'Nearly all,' agreed Mrs Willet sadly. 'We missed 'em, you know. Never really wanted 'em to begin with, as you can guess, but somehow, sharing everything, we got fond of one another – and then, well, they was a larky lot, real mischieful, some of 'em! You couldn't help laughing! There was one – her name was Mrs Jarman – she'll be coming this afternoon, she was a caution. We all reckoned she was the larkiest of the lot. And I'll take my oath,' said Mrs Willet solemnly, turning earnestly towards me, 'that she was at the bottom of that Christmas pudding affair.'

'The Christmas Pudding Affair?' I echoed. 'It sounds like a detective story.'

'Well, it was one what never got explained,' said Mrs Willet. 'I'll tell you what happened – some time.'

And she returned to her sandwich stacking.

When our preparations were completed, we all trooped home to a midday meal and to exchange our pinafores and working attire for more elegant *ensembles* in honour of the visitors.

Efficient and hardworking married women, like Mrs Willet, returned to their kitchens to dish up such succulent dishes as beef casserole or steak and kidney pudding which had been cooking themselves gently since nine or ten o'clock that morning. Scatter-brained spinsters, like me, with no hungry husbands to consider, had a piece of cheese, three biscuits and a cup of coffee, while they propped up their aching feet on a kitchen chair and read the paper. It was a good thing Amy couldn't see me, I thought, as I dusted the crumbs from my lap to the floor. This was Letting Myself Go in the way which caused her such heart-burning. Amy, my censorious college friend, when she lunches alone, sets one place at the dining room table, complete with glass, side plate, table napkin and so on, and eats her meal as decorously as any memsahib.

'And just think of the washing-up!' I said to Tibby, offering him a cheese rind. The disdainful creature took one sniff, flirted his tail and walked away.

'Thousands of poor cats,' I told him severely, retrieving the cheese rind for the birds, 'would give their eye-teeth for a delicious piece of cheese rind like that!' I tossed it through the open window. It was followed immediately by Tibby who devoured it instantly, and I sipped my coffee meditating on the maddening, but absorbing, ways of cats in general.

At ten to two we were all back in the hall awaiting the arrival of the coach. Our hair was freshly brushed, our noses powdered, our handkerchiefs sending out wafts of lavender water or Chanel Number 5 according to taste and income. The sun had come out, the tea urns hissed merrily, rows of blue-banded tea cups covered the trestle tables, and the air was filled with happy expectancy. When the coach drew up in the lane the tea ladies rushed to the urns, and those with less responsibility surged out to meet the visitors.

They were a cheerful crew and dressed much more gaily than we country mice were. Little hats with eye-veils, mauve coats and pink coats, stiletto heels, lots of patent leather, green and blue eyeshadow, flashing earrings and, above all, the high-pitched rapid twang of racy Cockney voices, made us feel that a flock of some exotic birds had suddenly descended upon us, and that we were as drab and unremarkable as our Fairacre hedge sparrows.

There were hugs and kisses, and much bonhomie and badinage as they were ushered into the hall. Over their tea cups the voices rose higher and higher. The noise was deafening. Carrying cups and saucers back and forth to the trestle table I marvelled at the snippets of conversation that came my way.

'Rosie got married last May and they've got a lovely flat at Ruislip, so he's a computer.'

'And our Janice – what was born here, you remember – well, a gentleman's got a very good job for her up the West End, with a flat and all. Makes anything up to sixty pounds a week, she does.'

'Dad's retired now, of course, and all for buying a bungalow at Peacehaven, but I say: "What's wrong with Hackney? Done us all right all these years, and you do see a bit of life!"'

Mrs Willet pointed out Mrs Jarman to me. She was a tiny bird-like woman with sparkling eyes. Her face was as wrinkled as an old apple, but her lips were a vivid orange and her crêpy eyelids were thick with blue eyeshadow. A tiny black velvet hat was lodged jauntily on her yellow hair, and a cigarette dangled between her fingers. She was telling a tale with great animation, her Fairacre audience registering half-shocked delight. She certainly looked 'a larky sort', as Mrs Willet had described. She seemed to epitomize the very spirit of Cockney effervescence and one could guess at her courage and example during the dark days of war.

As I watched her, Mrs Pringle passed bearing a tray. Mrs Jarman's face lit up with devilment and she called out some quip which was drowned in the general hubbub. It was not lost upon Mrs Pringle, however, for that lady's face grew redder than ever and an expression of deep disgust curved her mouth downward. She cast a look of outraged dignity towards the gay party and continued majestically with her tray.

Mrs Willet nudged me. 'No love lost there,' she hissed behind her hand. 'There's no forgiving and forgetting about Mrs P. They fair 'ates each other – she and Mrs Jarman.'

Before long we all set out for a walk round Fairacre in the sunshine, and I had no chance to hear more. But when the massive tea was over, and the coach was packed again with visitors bearing daffodils and farm eggs and hundreds of messages to those left behind in London, and Fairacre WI had cleared up the debris, 'switched of the light,' and locked the hall door, my chance came.

Wearily, Mrs Willet and I walked down the village together and paused by my gate.

'No, I won't come in,' Mrs Willet said, shifting her basket from one arm to the other. 'I've got some flower seeds to put in before it gets dark, but I just wanted to tell you about Mrs Pringle and Mrs Jarman now you've seen 'em together.'

We propped ourselves amicably one on each side of the school house gate. A clump of nearby narcissi sent up wafts of fragrance into the evening air, and Tibby rubbed himself round my tired legs as Mrs Willet unfolded her tale of a wartime feud.

Mrs Jarman and her family arrived in Fairacre in the early summer of 1941. They had endured the air raids which had made their days and nights hideous from September 1940 onwards, sleeping most of the nights in a Tube station and doing their best to carry on a normal life during the day. In May, however, their home was demolished, Mr Jarman was killed, and Mrs Jarman brought her four children to the comparative peace of Fairacre.

The eldest, Clifford, was fifteen, a tousle-headed lad whose rubbery lips seemed constantly glued to a mouth organ. Doreen, known as Dawreen, who was twelve, already ogled the boys, and was affronted when she was made to wash off her lipstick at Fairacre school. Nigel, two years younger, spent his time machine-gunning with outstretched fingers, and Gloria, aged six, was the baby. All four had their mother's blonde hair, but none had quite the vivacity of that irrepressible widow.

The family was billeted in the cottage next door to Mrs Pringle. It was owned by an elderly woman, now dead, called Jane Morgan. Mrs Morgan's husband, like his neighbour, Fred Pringle, was serving overseas. Mrs Morgan looked upon the Jarman family as the price one has to pay in wartime, and was unhappy about their presence, but resigned to it. Mrs Jarman, for her part, thought Jane Morgan 'a stuffy old party, dead from the neck up, but never meaning no harm'. They shook down together fairly well.

It was Mrs Pringle, of course, who really caused the trouble. Her evacuees were an elderly couple who did for themselves in one room of her house. They were a self-effacing pair and were careful to give no cause for annoyance. They crept in and out like mice, giving scared little smiles to their formidable landlady and offering her such small tributes as clothing coupons or morsels of margarine in order to 'keep her sweet', as Mrs Jarman said.

Before long, the Jarman children fell foul of Mrs Pringle. It was their habit to retire to the end of the garden, climb upon the roof of the empty pig sty and there watch the activities of their next door neighbour.

They had a foreign Cockney impudence which Mrs Pringle

abhorred. Fairacre children might have called names or even thrown a clod or two of earth over the hedge. The Jarman children were much more subtle.

'You ever seen anyone what's as broad as she's high?' one would shout to the next. The result would be tempestuous giggles on one side of the hedge and much bridling on the other.

The children watched their neighbour pegging out voluminous nether garments on the line and made rude comments to each other in voices calculated to carry well. 'Never knew Fairacre'd got a barrage balloon, did you?' and so on.

To give Mrs Jarman her due, she corrected the children whenever she found them at fault, administering a brisk cuff or letting fly with a vocabulary as lively as their own. But she needed to work long hours charing at various large houses in the neighbourhood, and the children had a good deal of time on their own.

Mrs Pringle brought matters to a head one day by making a formal call next door to complain. She had donned a hat and gloves to add more dignity to the occasion, and registered majestic disapproval from the cherries nodding on her brim to the steel tips on her war-time heels. Mrs Jarman, just home from work, frying chips on an oil stove and enduring the clamour of four hungry children around her, was not in any mood to be conciliatory.

'What did you say to Mrs Pringle?' she demanded of her innocent-eyed offspring.

'Never said nothin',' said Dawreen glibly.

'Never said a word,' quoth the two younger ones, raising limpid blue eyes to their mother.

Mrs Jarman, brandishing a fish slice, turned to the massive figure in the doorway. 'That's your answer,' she said flatly. 'My kids don't tell lies. Take yourself off!'

Mrs Pringle drew in a long outraged breath. 'They not only tell lies, they're rude, pert little monkeys. And if they was mine they'd get a jolly good hiding for it.'

'Say that again!' yelled Mrs Jarman, advancing menacingly, much to the delight of the juvenile onlookers.

Mrs Pringle took a step or two backward, but did not retreat completely. 'Not that they've had any chance,' boomed the lady, 'as anyone with half an eye can see, looking at you. But if I has any more of their old buck, Mrs Jarman, I shall go to the police – and *the Caxley police*, at that!'

Mrs Jarman, eyes blazing, now rushed upon her neighbour and would have dragged the fruit-laden hat – and the hair beneath it – from her adversary's head, but Mrs Pringle, with a dexterity surprising for one of her bulk, nipped smartly down the garden path and put the gate between them. Mrs Jarman's furious shrieks, punctuated by Mrs Pringle's booms, caused several curtains to twitch in neighbouring windows. Mrs Pringle had just managed to shout something about 'East End scum!' above the din, when the four children, who had been watching the fun from the doorstep, screamed in unison: 'Fat's on fire! Mum, the fat's on fire!' and this diversion brought the ladies' immediate hostilities to a close.

From then on, a state of constant warfare existed between Mrs Pringle and the Jarman family. If the children's ball went over the hedge, Mrs Pringle impounded it with smug satisfaction. When Mrs Pringle's tea towel blew off her line into the next door garden, it ended up flying like a flag from the topmost branch of the Jarman's greengage tree, a position for which the gale was not responsible, despite the assurances of the children.

'We can't reach that, Mrs Pringle,' they said with mock regret, and dancing eyes. 'Ain't it a shame? Must have blowed there in the wind, see?'

And there it fluttered, for several weeks, before being ripped to pieces by the elements and an inquisitive pair of jackdaws who used strips for the adornment of their nest.

The two women never let the opportunity of a verbal brush pass, without making full use of it. In a way, each enjoyed the situation. They were well matched. Mrs Jarman might be quicker and more prolific of vocabulary, but Mrs Pringle had a native malice, and an incalculable capacity for taking umbrage, which stood her in good stead. She moved like a tank into battle, heavy, slow and apparently indestructible. But, now and again, a burst of deadly fire came from that implacable front to score a hit upon Mrs Jarman, the resilient sniper.

One Saturday, a jumble sale was arranged in Fairacre. It was to take place, as always, in the village hall, and on the morning of the day in question a few women went there to set up the tables and sort the jumble into the time-honoured categories of Men's, Women's, Children's, Hats and Shoes, and General Junk.

Mrs Pringle set out laden with a large bundle. All was held together with a faded mackintosh, tied securely round the bulk by the sleeves. Mrs Jarman watched her struggle up the road in a high wind before collecting her own parcel and setting forth.

'Don't want to catch up with that old Tartar,' she said to Dawreen, who was dreamily picking at the flaking paint of the mantel shelf. 'And give over that lark, will you?' she added ferociously, giving the girl a swift box on the ear. 'Don't forget,' she continued, as she whirled about the room for her possessions, 'spuds on at eleven, two large whites from the baker, tell the milkman it's six and fourpence and none of his old buck, keep the cat off the custard and expect me when you see me.'

The door slammed behind her and, despite her desire to let Mrs Pringle arrive first, she found herself entering the narrow doorway with her. Mrs Pringle drew aside with marked distaste.

'Don't mind me breathing the same air, I hope?' commented Mrs Jarman tartly, pushing in first. Mrs Pringle maintained an affronted silence.

About half a dozen women were already at work sorting a

mountain of assorted garments on the floor. Back and forth hurried another two taking the articles to the right table. Mrs Pringle, by ancient custom, was in charge of 'General Junk'. Mrs Jarman had never been forgiven for saying on an earlier occasion, 'It seemed just right, somehow, to see Mrs P. standing by that label!'

Hers was a comparatively simple task. Saucepans, chipped vases, lidless casseroles, faded pictures, lop-sided toast racks, stone hot water bottles, riding boots stuffed with beautiful boxwood trees, archaic lawn mowers, and many unidentifiable objects found their way to Mrs Pringle's table. Sometimes large pieces of furniture flanked her counter: wash stands, fire-guards, sagging wicker armchairs, and dilapidated bamboo tables. Once there was the ugliest three-piece suite in Christendom among 'General Junk'. Competition for this had been fierce, as well I knew, for on that occasion I had been Mrs Pringle's feeble assistant and had watched her masterly handling of the sale. It had gone eventually for two pounds to Mrs Fowler of Tyler's Row. She was going to present it to her mother in Caxley, and I must say I felt the greatest sympathy for that unsuspecting old lady.

Now Mrs Pringle deposited her mackintosh bundle with the other clothes and made her way to her stall. Mrs Jarman fell on her knees with the other sorters and began to work with spirit.

'Lor'!' she cried, holding up a moth-eaten moleskin waistcoat. 'Who'd buy this stuff? Talk about "Granny's little old skin rug"! Gives you the creeps, don't it?'

'My husband's,' said one of the helpers shortly. Mrs Jarman seemed not a whit abashed. She was rummaging in the bundle which Mrs Pringle had brought, making disparaging comments on her discoveries, much to the embarrassment of the Fairacre women who knew full well how important it was to guard one's tongue on such occasions.

'Look at this,' cried Mrs Jarman, 'three shirts and never a button among 'em! Who's pinched the buttons, eh?'

Mrs Pringle, wreathed in sea-grass from the unravelling footstool she was carrying, paused by the group and replied loftily. 'I took the trouble to remove those shirt buttons. They'll do for another day.'

'How's that for meanness!' commented Mrs Jarman, winking at the others. 'The poor chap who buys this will have to go about with his shirt flapping, I s'pose.'

'Some people,' began Mrs Pringle, 'knows their duty to their country in war time, and saves every possible penny, not like some I could mention, not a hundred miles from here, as buys pineapple chunks when there's rhubarb in the garden.'

This side-swipe simply had the effect of bringing Mrs Jarman's usual high spirits to bubbling point. Her blue eyes flashed with the joy of battle joined. The onlookers were half-fearful and half-delighted to see Mrs Pringle in combat with such a worthy adversary.

'Well, I never!' crowed Mrs Jarman. 'Ain't we high and mighty? But I wouldn't stoop to pinching shirt buttons and then giving the rest to the jumble. About as low as you can get, I reckon.'

'It's nothing short of *patriotism*, I tells you,' boomed Mrs Pringle, her neck flushing an ugly red. ' "Save all you can!" they keeps telling us. Well, I'm saving shirt buttons!'

She marched heavily towards her stall somewhat impeded by the strands of sea-grass trailing behind her. Mrs Jarman let out a peal of derisive laughter, and continued with the sorting. But she did not forget Mrs Pringle's last remark.

The jumble sale itself passed off without further incident between the two antagonists. In fact, Mrs Jarman covered herself with glory at the men's stall by her shrewd bargaining with customers. Her clients were kept in spasms of laughter by her barrage of raillery and Cockney patter. At the end of the sale it was discovered that her stall had taken by far the largest amount, and it was generally acknowledged that Mrs Jarman's cheeky approach to the customers was the reason.

'Not much good living near the Caledonian Market all your life, if you can't pick up a few tips!' was Mrs Jarman's reply to those who congratulated her. Needless to say, Mrs Pringle was not among them.

Some months after the sale, at the beginning of November, the good ladies of Fairacre Women's Institute decided to make their Christmas puddings together. They worked out that the whole process would be much cheaper if they made the mixture in one batch and cooked all the puddings in the large electric copper.

The recipe, cut from a daily paper, made grisly reading to those used to the normal ingredients of pre-war puddings. No brandy, stout, fresh eggs or butter appeared in the 1943 recipe. Instead, such dreadful items as grated carrot, margarine, dried-egg powder and – the final touch of horror – 'a tablespoonful of gravy browning to enrich the colour', figured on the depressing list of ingredients. But times were hard, and years of privation had blunted the sensibilities of even the most fastidious. With much cheerfulness, the ladies set about their preparations for making 'An Economical and Nutritious War-Time Christmas Pudding'.

Dozens of pudding basins, each bearing their owner's name on adhesive tape stuck on the base, waited on the long tables. Little paper bags bearing treasured ounces of currants and sultanas, mixed spices, breadcrumbs and two precious fresh lemons, jostled each other near the enormous yellow mixing bowl from the Vicarage. By ten o'clock, the ingredients were being stirred zealously by half a dozen helpers, most of them elderly women, for the majority were doing war work of some sort or other. Mrs Willet busily greased the basins with carefully-hoarded margarine papers, listening to the chatter about her.

'We'll set the copper to *Very Slow*,' said the vicar's wife, 'and then it should be perfectly safe until tea time.

Mrs Willet's staying until eleven-thirty, to make sure it's simmering properly and then the rota begins.'

It had been arranged that one or other of the WI members should look in every hour to see that all was well, and to top up the water in the copper if it was getting too low. Christmas puddings were too precious to be left entirely to themselves for such a length of time.

By eleven, the puddings were ready for immersion. Every household in Fairacre had one, and some had two or three, standing in the water. This was the Women's Institute's practical help towards Christmas, and very well planned the organization had been.

'Here's Mrs Pringle's,' said Mrs Willet, bearing a stout two-pounder to the copper. She peered underneath the basin to read the big black capitals on the tape, before letting it down gently beside the others.

'Then that's the last,' said the vicar's wife thankfully. 'Just time to have a cup of tea before we knock off.'

It was very quiet when they had gone. Mrs Willet took out her knitting and sat by the humming copper. The clock said twenty past eleven and she had promised to stay until half past. As she knitted, she read the list of names pinned on the wall by the copper. During the afternoon she saw that Mrs Pringle and Mrs Jarman were due to call in. Both worked in the mornings and had been unable to stir their own puddings this year.

'2.30 – Mrs Pringle'

'3.30 – Miss Parr' – only that would be her maid, Mrs Willet surmised, and

'4.30 – Mrs Jarman' – who would no doubt rush back to her family in time to fry the inevitable chips on which that ebullient household seemed to exist.

'5.30 – Anyone welcome.' This was when the puddings would be lifted out and handed to their lucky owners. Mrs Willet had promised to help with this chore.

At twenty-five to twelve she lifted the lid, noted with relief that the water was bubbling gently, checked all the switches, wrote a note to the next pudding-minder saying:

> '25 to 12. Everything all right.
>   Alice Willet.'

and made her way back through the village.

At five-thirty a throng of women crowded the steamy hall collecting their basins and lodging them in shopping baskets, string bags or the baskets on the front of their bicycles.

'Got the right one?' called Mrs Jarman to Mrs Pringle, as she watched that lady peering under the basins for her name. 'Bet you've got more fruit in yours than the rest of us!'

Mrs Pringle sniffed and ignored the quip. Depositing her pudding in the black depths of her oilcloth shopping bag, she passed majestically from the hall without deigning to reply.

The fantastic sequel to the pudding-making session might never have been known to Fairacre but for an unusually generous gesture of Mrs Pringle's.

As Christmas Day approached she heard that a large party of the Jarmans' friends were proposing to spend the day next door.

'My heart fair bleeds for poor Jane Morgan,' said Mrs Pringle lugubriously to her son John. 'She'll be crowded out of house and home, as far as I can see, I've a good mind to invite her round here for Christmas dinner.'

Neither Corporal Pringle nor Private Morgan were to be given Christmas leave. Mrs Pringle's sister and a schoolgirl niece, much the same age as John, were coming from Caxley for the day, and as the sister and Jane Morgan knew each other well it seemed a good idea to ask their neighbour to join the party. Jane Morgan was gratefully surprised, and accepted.

The pudding simmered all the morning, and most delightful aromas crept about the kitchen, for there was a duck roasting in the oven as well as the 'nutritious war-time' delicacy on top of the hob. Mrs Pringle and her sister had a good gossip, their children played amicably with their new presents, and except for the ear-splitting racket occasioned by the crowd next door, the benevolent spirit of Christmas hung over all. At twelve-thirty Jane Morgan appeared, thankful to be out of her noisy home, and they all sat down to dinner.

The duck was excellent. The pudding looked wonderful. Mrs Pringle plunged a knife into its gravy-darkened top and cut the first slice.

'Mum!' squeaked John excitedly. 'There's something shining!'

'Sh!' said his aunt. 'Don't give the game away! Perhaps it's a sixpence.'

Mrs Pringle looked puzzled.

'No sixpences in this pudding!' she said. 'In any case, I don't hold with metal objects in food. I always wraps up anything like that in a morsel of greaseproof.'

She put the first slice on a plate for Mrs Morgan. There was certainly a suspicious chinking sound as the pudding met the china surface.

'When I was little,' said Jane Morgan, 'we used to have dear little china dolls in our Christmas pudding. No bigger than an inch, they were! With shiny black heads. We used to put them in the dolls' house, I remember.'

But Jane Morgan's reminiscences were being ignored, for all eyes were on the pudding. There was no doubt about it, there were a great many shiny foreign objects among the other war-time ingredients. Mrs Pringle's breathing became more stertorous as the slices were cut. She sat down heavily in front of the last plate, her own, and then spoke.

'Just pick it over before you take a mouthful. I reckons someone's been playing tricks on us.'

Spoons and forks twitched the glutinous mass back and forth, amongst amazed cries from the assembled company.

When they came to count up the foreign objects they found no fewer than two dozen mother o' pearl shirt buttons.

Mrs Pringle said not a word, but opened a tin of pineapple chunks instead.

Late that night, when the Jarmans' company had roared away and the children had been chased to bed, Mrs Jarman met her landlady in the communal kitchen. Jane Morgan was in her husband's dressing gown, her wispy hair was in a small pigtail, and her teeth had been left upstairs in a glass of water. She was busy filling a hot water bottle.

'Had a good time?' asked Mrs Jarman boisterously. 'We have. Never laughed so much since I came here.'

'That'th nithe!' said Mrs Morgan politely. 'Yeth, I enjoyed it next door, but there wath thomething wrong with the Chrithtmath pudding.'

Mrs Jarman drew in her breath sharply. 'What was up with it?' she inquired.

'It wath abtholutely thruffed with thirt buttonth,' said Mrs Morgan, wide-eyed. 'Mithith Pringle wath dumbfounded.'

'Shirt buttons! echoed Mrs Jarman. She broke into peals of noisy laughter. 'Ah well,' she gasped, through her spasms, 'that should please the old trout! She told me once that she saved shirt buttons!'

Still laughing, she made her way upstairs, followed by her mystified landlady.

Mrs Willet straightened herself and patted my garden gate.

'Well, Miss Read, that's the story. Of course, it was all over Fairacre before Boxing Day sunset. Jane Morgan let it out, in all innocence, and the village was fair humming with the news.'

'Did Mrs Jarman ever admit it?' I asked.

'Never! Swore she never knew a thing about it, but it was her all right. I should know – I remember the pudding list. "2.30 Mrs Pringle". It wouldn't be her, obviously. "3.30 Miss Parr". That was her Annie that popped in then, as law-abiding as they come, and wouldn't dream of doing such a thing. "4.30 *Mrs Jarman*". And "5.30 All welcome." Don't need much working out, when you come to think of it.'

She bent to pick up her basket, and stroked Tibby affectionately. 'I will say though,' she continued, 'that Mrs Pringle minded her manners a bit more after that, when she and Mrs Jarman got together. Ah, she was real mischieful, was Mrs Jarman. You couldn't help liking her.'

Mrs Willet gazed, with unseeing eyes, down the Fairacre lane, her mind on times long past.

'I still miss them, you know, them Londoners. I liked 'em – and always shall. It was good to see them again this afternoon. Took me back to the old days. Say what you like about 'em, Miss Read, Londoners are a larky lot! A real larky lot!'

9. OUTLOOK UNSETTLED

As so often happens when term begins, the weather became idyllic. Great white clouds sailed indolently across pellucid blue skies, and warm winds from the south replaced the sneaky little easterly one which had harassed us throughout most of the Easter holidays.

One warm afternoon, in late April, we propped open the door of the schoolroom with an upturned flowerpot and did our best to turn our attention to learning Robert Bridges' poem 'Spring Goeth All In White'. It seemed an admirable choice in the circumstances, for white narcissi spilt their heady fragrance from the window sill, white daisies, gathered by the children, filled three paste pots on my desk, and an early cabbage white butterfly opened and shut its wings against the south-facing Gothic window.

Nevertheless, it was uphill work. Languor, born of unaccustomed heat, engulfed my class. Shirt necks were opened, sleeves rolled up, jerseys peeled off and stuffed in desks, and the sing-song country voices stumbled heavily through this most tripping of spring lyrics.

Sleepiest of all was young Richard, not yet five, who was spending the day with us while his mother paid a necessary visit to the hospital in our county town. It is not easy to get someone to mind a child in a small village, and I often get urgent requests asking me 'if our youngest can come along with his brother for an hour or two'. If it is possible – and it usually is – we all enjoy the newcomer's company, and it gives him an insight into school routine before he takes the plunge himself later on.

Richard lolled on the desk beside his brother Ernest, who nudged him occasionally and whispered severely to him, with no noticeable result. As we battled on, Richard amused himself by blowing large glassy bubbles from lips as red and puckered as a poppy petal. Ernest, scandalized, bent down to remonstrate.

'Leave him alone, Ernest,' I said mildly. 'He's tired. Perhaps he'll fall asleep.'

'In school?' cried Ernest, deeply shocked.

'Why not?'

Ernest, still looking affronted by my slackness, drew himself up, folded his arms and applied himself sternly to the task before him, ignoring the indolent and shameful child beside him.

Everywhere in the room were emblems of spring. The weather chart for April showed a number of umbrellas, depicting the rainy weather during the holidays, with arrows pointing fairly consistently to the north-east. But a row of triumphant suns, like yellow daisies, blossomed in the last six or seven squares, and the arrows were now happily reversed.

Across the back of the room ran a frieze of spring flowers. Crocuses, daffodils, tulips, and a large number of new species, as yet unknown to Messrs Sutton and Carter, had been cut out of gummed paper and affixed by every hand in the class. Many a fat thumb went home in the afternoon bearing an indented ring round it made by hard-worked school scissors. It was, as the seed catalogues say, 'a riot of bloom' and a very colourful addition to our dull walls.

A new spring poster to encourage savings, showing a bird and its nest, brightened the door between the two classrooms, and the nature table was laden with wood anemones, primroses, violets, sprays of young honeysuckle leaves, a few early coltsfoot and dandelions, and a splendid pot of horse chestnut twigs thrusting out green hands in all directions.

Hard by, the glass fish tank glimmered with shiny frogs' spawn, for all the world like submerged chain-mail. The tiny dots were already beginning to turn into commas, and before long the children's patience would be rewarded by the sight of a myriad thrashing tadpoles. Nothing could be more suitable, I told myself again, than 'Spring Goeth All In White' for such an afternoon.

But, there was no doubt about it, those eight exquisite lines were really more than the children could manage in the circumstances. I felt impatient and cross at their laziness, but was loth to spoil the poem for them by bad-tempered bludgeoning.

In the midst of this impasse, young Richard raised himself, stretched short arms each side of his rumpled head, and said clearly: 'Let's go out!'

There was a shocked silence. The sound of a bee droning up and down the open door could be heard distinctly as the children waited to see what my reaction would be. Sometimes a remark like this will make me fly clean off the handle, and they shivered with apprehension. Ernest's face was scarlet at the effrontery of his young brother.

I looked at the expectant children. 'What about it? Shall we?' I asked.

There was a rapturous roar of agreement, and a general stampede to the lobby.

The air outside was wonderful, heady and honeyed with hundreds of unseen flowers. The elm trees at the corner of the playground were rosy with buds, and noisy with rooks at their building.

We straggled down the village street between the beds of velvety polyanthus and the neat kitchen gardens striped with vegetable seedlings. Birds flashed across our path, dogs panted on cottage doorsteps and a cuckoo's call see-sawed across the afternoon.

All this, of course, was what had held my class in thrall – the compelling imperious spell of spring. Of what use were the frieze, the crayoned sun, the poster, the laden nature table and the captive frogs' spawn? They were but substitutes for the real thing that exploded all around them. It was the babe among us, young Richard, still in touch with the vital stuff of living, who had led us unerringly to reality.

We made our way slowly up the sunny slopes of the downs before throwing ourselves down on the dry springy turf in order to revel to the full in the glory of a warm spring day. Below us spread the village like some pictorial map. The trees were misted with young leaves, and here and there a flurry of white blossom lit up a garden. I thought of our poem left neglected, but felt no regret. Let us savour this now, and then come to Robert Bridges' poem, 'recollecting it in tranquillity', was my feeling.

A row or two of flapping washing caught the eye, and a herd of black and white Friesians, belonging to Mr Roberts, looked like toys as they grazed peacefully in the field next to the school. I gazed at it all with particular interest this afternoon, for I had a problem on my mind. Would it, I wondered, be a good thing to leave Fairacre?

I suppose that most people feel unsettled in the early spring. There must be something in the rising of the sap and the general urgency of the season that makes us long for change and movement. I read the 'Appointments Vacant' at the end of *The Times Educational Supplement* with unusual fervour during March and April, and usually find that this pastime calms the fever in my blood. What about this job in Sicily, I ask myself? Would I really be able to 'TEACH ENGLISH by Direct Method'? Come to think of it, are *any* of my teaching methods direct? Is the teaching of 'Spring Goeth All In White' direct, when one abandons the task to scramble up the springy turf of the downs, for instance?

There is a wonderful post offered in Barbados and another in New Zealand, and several in Dar-Es-Salaam (I only consider those in a warm climate, you notice) but, alas, I am not a communicant member of the Presbyterian Church, nor am I qualified to teach practical brickwork or plumbing. I browse among these delights over my cup of tea, when the children of Fairacre have run home and only the voice of Mrs Pringle, at her after-school cleaning, is heard in the land. After half an hour or so of this mental dallying, I rouse myself, take stock of my nice little school house, the fun I have in Fairacre, and decide I am better off where I am. In any case, the thought of filling up forms and asking people to give references for me, if need be, is enough to dissuade me from any serious application, as a rule. By the end of April my spring fever has usually abated. Fairacre looks more seductive than ever. I find, surprisingly, that I am in love with all the children, and even look upon Mrs Pringle with an indulgent eye. Such is the power of warm weather.

But this year my feelings were stronger. If I really wanted promotion, as headmistress of a larger school, then it was time I stirred myself before I became too decrepit to be considered at all. As Amy, my old college friend, frequently tells me, and reiterated with considerable force the other evening when I mentioned a particular post I had seen advertised, I have been in Fairacre long enough. It might be better for the school, as well as for me, to have a change.

The job which had caught my eye was the headship of a junior and infants' school in south Devon. I knew the little town fairly well from visiting it at holiday times, and because I had friends in the neighbourhood. It was a market town, rather smaller than Caxley, about five miles from the coast, and situated away from the main roads which were so busy in summer time.

I remembered the school particularly. It was a pleasant old building, with a new wing recently added, and an attractive school house adjoining it. A peach tree spread its branches fanwise over its front wall, which faced south, and at the back there was a sheltered walled garden with some fine fruit trees and lawns. One could be very happy indeed there, I had no doubt, and when my friends wrote to tell me of the vacancy and to urge me to apply for it, I fell to thinking seriously of the matter.

The biggest attraction to me was the climate. Fairacre can be bitterly cold in the winter, and the number of gnarled rheumaticky old people in our midst constitutes an awful warning to those with a tendency to rheumatism and its allied diseases. Apart from an occasional bout of influenza I didn't ail at all, but the last winter or two I had been having twinges of rheumatism which I did not like to think of as simply old age. Fairacre School, too, was renowned for its draughts and the inefficiency of its heating system, and latterly I had come to dread the winter months with their fierce blast of winter air from the skylight above my desk, concentrated on the nape of my neck, and the particularly spiteful draught that hit one round the ankles and came from the icy wastes of the outside lobby.

It would be good to work in a snug building tucked into the side of a hill, and with most of its windows facing south. The very thought of that soft mild air made me feel hopeful. I read my friend's advice. I read the advertisement a dozen times. I looked out of my school house window – it was a blustery April evening with a spatter of hail now and again – and I bravely sent for the application forms.

That had been a week ago. The forms awaited my attention still, propped behind the coffee-pot on the dresser, my usual filing place. I must get them off this week if I really intended to apply. I looked again at Fairacre, spread below me, and sighed at the difficulties of making up one's mind.

'You got the belly-ache?' asked Joseph Coggs solicitously, sitting down beside me.

'No, no,' I assured him. 'I was just thinking how pretty the village looked from here.'

A few more children left their pursuits to join us.

'It's the prettiest place in England,' declared Ernest stoutly.

''Sright!' echoed young Richard loyally.

'My auntie,' said John, 'lives at Winchelsea and she says *that's* the prettiest place.'

'Maybe she don't know Fairacre,' suggested someone reasonably. 'What's it like anyway – this ol' Winklesea?'

'*Winchelsea*!' replied John, nettled. 'Well, it's a funny place, because it used to be right by the seaside and now there's a whole lot of flat fields between the town and the sea.'

> 'Below the down the stranded town
> What may betide forlornly waits,'

I quoted, with what I thought was rather a beautiful inflection.

John looked startled. 'I dunno about that, but that's what my auntie told me. She said the sea was right up to the town once.'

'Likely, ain't it?' said Joseph Coggs scornfully. I rose to my feet. I was glad to have some interruption to my thoughts, and it was time we were getting back.

'I'll get the map out when we are in school,' I promised them, 'and you shall see for yourselves. First one to reach the lane has a sweet! Off you go!'

Shrieking and squeaking, they tumbled down the steep slope of the grassy hill leaving me to descend more circumspectly behind them.

In the lane, where the rough track ends and the tarmac begins, Dr Martin's car waited outside Laburnum Villas. As I approached the vociferous mob awaiting me – each claiming that he had arrived first – the doctor came out of one of the ugly pair of houses and watched, with some amusement, as I quelled the riot.

'Playing truant?' he asked.

I said we were.

'Very sensible too. We none of us get enough fresh air these days. When I first came to Fairacre it was lack of decent food which gave me most of my patients. Now it's too much food, and not enough air and exercise.'

He climbed into his car with a grunt of exertion, then leant from the window and laughed. 'I need more myself,' he said. 'How's my old friend Mrs Pringle? Still suffering with her leg?'

'When it suits her,' I replied. There are no secrets to hide from Dr Martin. He has known us all in Fairacre much too long to be hoodwinked. Forty or fifty years, I thought suddenly, Dr Martin has lived and worked in Fairacre! I had a sudden desire to ask him if he had ever felt like moving, but restrained myself.

'Are you feeling quite fit?' he asked, an observant eye cocked quizzically upon me.

'Yes, thank you,' I said hastily. 'Just thinking about something, that's all.'

'You look a trifle pale to me,' said the doctor, twinkling. 'Is it love?'

'No, indeed!' I said, with spirit. 'I'm too old for such capers. More likely to be advancing senility. I'm beginning to suspect that rheumatism's trying to infiltrate my old bones.'

'You aren't the only one in Fairacre,' said the doctor, starting his car. 'Let me know if it gets any worse, that's all. We get such plaguey cold winters here, that's the trouble.'

He waved cheerfully and drove off, hooting to shoo my children to the side of the narrow lane.

The memory of that south-facing Devon school returned to me with overwhelming intensity, as I made my way back to Fairacre School amongst my clamorous pupils.

'Can I get it out now?' asked John as we clanged across the door-scraper.

'Get what out?' I asked bemused.

'Why, the map! You said as you was going to show us Winchelsea, and all that!' He sounded aggrieved. I pulled myself together, and approached the map cupboard.

It is called the map cupboard, and does indeed house the maps, but that is not all. Somehow, everything that has no proper home gets thrown in the map cupboard. There are cricket stumps, old tennis shoes, a pile of china paint palettes which have not been used for years, some dilapidated *Rainbow Annuals* adored by the children during wet dinner hours, part of a train set, a large tin full of assorted pieces of Meccano, and a rusty hurricane lamp which, we tell each other, 'might come in handy'.

The maps jostle together in one corner, and ever since I came to Fairacre I have meant to label them properly and hang them in some sort of order. In practice, I go through *Muscles of the Human Body*, *The Disposition of the Tribes of Israel*, *The Resuscitation of those Suffering from Electrocution*, the tonic sol-fa modulator and a number of maps, ranging from Greenland's icy mountains to India's coral strand, until I find the one I am searching for.

This afternoon was no exception. At length, however, the map of the British Isles was hung over the blackboard and I began my lesson on coastal erosion. Refreshed by their outing the children gave me quite flattering attention.

John bustled out to the map, full of importance, and pointed to Romney Marsh with his yellow ruler, and I did my best to explain the cause of the sea's retreat here. There are times when I wish fervently that I had more geographical knowledge. This was one of them. Mercifully, the children seemed to understand my halting explanations, and I was fired to go further.

'Sometimes,' I said, 'the opposite thing happens. The sea encroaches on the land, and then the bottom of the cliffs gets washed away.' I remembered childhood holidays at Walton-on-Naze, and gave a dramatic account of a garden, and then, finally, the house belonging to it, sliding down the cliffs into the hungry sea. Perhaps I overdid the drama. There was an awed silence when I finished.

John raised his ruler and put it shakily across the Wash. 'It's eaten in there all right,' he commented.

Patrick and Ernest now walked out, unbidden, to take a closer look at the map.

'Look how it's busted its way up here!' exclaimed Patrick, his eyes on the Bristol Channel.

'And here!' echoed Ernest, peering closely at the Thames estuary. 'Looks as though they could meet, real easy, and chop us in half.'

'How quick,' asked Joseph Coggs nervously, 'do the water come?'

'You remember at Barrisford!' queried John. 'It came in as quick as lightning, and terrible strong it was. Fair sucked us off our feet when we was paddlin' and I got my best trousers absolutely soppin'.'

I did my best to calm their fears. If I weren't careful, I could see that I should have some very cross parents coming to see me on the morrow, complaining that their children had been having nightmares.

'Good heavens,' I said robustly, 'it only manages a few inches in a year, at the most. You've nothing to fear here, living in Fairacre. Why, we're safely in the middle,' I assured them, appropriating John's ruler, and pointing out *Caxley* printed in unflatteringly small letters.

These downland children see very little water, and the sea but rarely. There is a very healthy respect for it when they visit the coast, and their apprehension about inundation was understandable. Even today, some of their grandparents have never seen the sea.

St Patrick's chimes began to ring out through the warm limpid afternoon.

'Time to go home,' I said. 'Don't forget, there are miles of dry land between you and the sea, here in Fairacre. Stand for grace!'

Within five minutes the classroom was empty. I returned the

map to the shameful cupboard and made my way across the hot playground. To my surprise, Joseph Coggs was swinging on the school gate. His face was thoughtful, his dark eyes fixed upon the horizon.

'What are you doing?' I asked.

He nodded towards the vast bulk of the downs, quivering in a blue haze of heat. 'I was thinking,' he said huskily, in his hoarse gipsy croak, 'it'd take a tidy long time for the sea to get through all that lot, wouldn't it, miss?'

'It would,' I agreed.

He sighed with relief, clambered down from the gate, and set off along the sunny lane towards his home.

The long envelope, containing the application form, was horribly noticeable, sticking out from behind the coffee pot. I resolved to tackle it later that evening, but first of all I made some tea.

Mr Willet was busy at the bottom of my garden, erecting a fine row of bean poles. He cannot bear to see a few yards of untilled soil, and had insisted on turning a miniature jungle of old gooseberry bushes, draped in dead grass, into a flourishing vegetable patch. The fact that I should never be able to consume a quarter of the crops he was so generously planting did not seem to occur to him, and I was too touched by his kindness to point it out.

I took two hefty blue and white striped mugs of tea down the garden path. Balanced on top of one was a plate bearing a large hunk of fruit cake for my gardener. The heat shimmered everywhere, and some of the polyanthuses were wilting slightly already. My spirits rose at the thought of a possible fine spell.

'Well now, that do be real welcome,' said Mr Willet, grasping the mug in a mud-caked hand. He upturned a wooden box and motioned me politely towards it. I sat down, with a sigh, and let the sunshine soak into my bones. Little rainbows played round my half-shut eyes. This was the weather! They probably had it like this all the time in Devon, I thought.

The sound of steady champing told me that Mr Willet had found the cake.

'You makes a very good fruit cake,' he said indistinctly. 'Moist without being too heavy. And got your cherries well spaced. Takes a bit of doing that. My wife has a rare job with cherries. Flours 'em, or summat, to keep 'em up. You done real well with this, miss.'

I wished I deserved his compliments but truth will out, so I replied dreamily, my eyes still closed, 'Marks and Spencer's!'

'Is that so?' said Mr Willet. 'Well, they does a good job then.'

There was silence except for the sound of mastication and the birds' singing around us.

'You feeling all right?' asked Mr Willet. 'You looks a bit peaky to me, and you ain't drinking your tea!'

I sat up hastily. He was the third person this afternoon to comment on my frail looks. 'I'm fine,' I assured him.

'Don't look yourself to me,' persisted Mr Willet. 'Got a sort of bilious look. You ever had the jaundice?'

'I probably need a change,' I said briskly. 'When we get some sunshine I begin to realize what I've been missing. Perhaps I'd better take a job in France or Italy,' I added lightly.

Mr Willet looked concerned. 'Don't you go flinging off to no foreign parts now!' he warned me. 'Full of mosquitoes and malaria, they tells me, and not a decent drop of water to drink, even if it do come out of a tap. And the food's a proper mess – oily and that – wouldn't do your biliousness any good, you can take my word for it!'

At this moment, Mrs Pringle appeared at the side of the house, and bore down upon us in all her black-clothed majesty. Her oilcloth bag swung upon her arm, and from it poked a corner of the flowered cretonne overall in which she performs her cleaning duties. Obviously, these were now ended and she was on her way homeward.

'Cup of tea?' I asked.

Mrs Pringle shook her head magisterially. 'I never drinks between meals,' she said. 'And I shall be dishing up our high tea in an hour's time.'

Mr Willet whipped a sack from the wheelbarrow and spread it, with a Raleigh-like flourish, on the grass. Mrs Pringle lowered her bulk cautiously upon it, and smiled graciously.

'Ah! Nice to have a set-down! Sometimes I wonder if this cleanin' job's too much for me.'

I wondered what was coming.

'Well, not so much the *cleaning*,' continued Mrs Pringle heavily, 'as the *danger*!'

This was mystifying, but was obviously leading to a grievance.

'Sweeping, I expect. Scrubbing, I expect. A certain amount of back-breaking bending and lifting, I expect,' said Mrs Pringle, rising to heights of rhythmic peroration which made me suspect Welsh blood somewhere among her forebears. 'But *when*,' continued the lady, turning and fixing me with a glittering eye, 'I gets hit over the head through other people's carelessness, then I thinks it's time to *complain*.'

I was about to speak, but was overborne by Mrs Pringle in full spate. Mr Willet and I exchanged martyred looks, and resigned ourselves to more.

'I don't say a word about slatternly goings-on, in the ordinary way. Some are born sluts, no matter how much schooling they've had, and if they cares to muddle along with dust under their beds and the same saucepan for soup as milk, not to mention a bread crock with mildewed crumbs in the cracks, then all I says is: "Well, let them wallow in their muck", and be forbearing. But when those slatternly ways bring damage to *others*, then plain speaking has to be done!'

'Cough it up then,' I said inelegantly. I could recognize the wallower-in-muck all right. 'What hit you?'

'Nelson's Column, by the sound of it,' commented Mr Willet, unimpressed. He dusted some grass from his corduroy trousers, and began to resume his tasks.

'I was sweeping gentle-like by the map cupboard,' said Mrs Pringle with dignity, 'when the broom knocked against the door. It flew open –' here Mrs Pringle flung her arms dramatically apart – 'it flew open, I says, and down crashed a good dozen maps. Gave me a cruel blow on the side of the head – most dangerous place, that is, near the temple!'

'I'm sorry,' I said. 'That catch isn't very reliable.'

'If the maps was hung up properly,' continued Mrs Pringle severely, 'as they always was in Mr Hope's time – and after – we shouldn't get accidents like this. Might have had Concussion. Might have been Disabled. Might have been Laid Out!' intoned Mrs Pringle.

'Pity you weren't,' said Mr Willet shortly. I looked away hastily.

'You're quite right,' I said nobly to the old harridan, 'I really must tidy that cupboard. Do you want something put on your head? Witch hazel, perhaps?'

'Very suitable,' muttered Mr Willet, who was beginning to enjoy himself.

Mrs Pringle gave him a cold glance. 'Nothing, thank you,' replied the lady, with crushing dignity. 'I shall let Nature take its course.'

She began the herculean task of getting to her feet, swaying backwards and forwards and breathing heavily. I put both arms round one of hers and gave a mighty heave. Suddenly, she was erect, red in the face, but triumphant.

'Thank you, Miss Read,' she puffed.

'Here, you don't want to lift great weights like that!' cried Mr Willet, who had only just seen this manoeuvre. 'And you not very well!'

Mrs Pringle looked at me suspiciously. 'Not well?' she echoed truculently.

'I'm perfectly well,' I said.

Mr Willet, no doubt seeing a means of paying out his old enemy, shook his head vehemently. 'She's just been talking about having a change. Can't blame her, either, with folks like you to plague her!'

'A change does us all good,' conceded Mrs Pringle. She looked at me warily as though remembering something. 'As long as it don't last too long. I wouldn't think about a *permanent* change, if I was you. Taking it all in all, you could jump from the frying pan into the fire, and Fairacre ain't a bad place, when all's said and done.' She fished inside her oilcloth bag and produced a brown paper one. 'Six eggs,' said Mrs Pringle, thrusting them upon me. 'I brought 'em up when I come, expecting you'd still be in school, but seems you packed up before time today. Good job the Office don't know what goes on!'

'It's very good of you,' I said, with sincerity. 'Especially after your accident.'

Mrs Pringle grunted and set off up the garden path.

'I'll do my best to put these away tidily,' I promised, patting the paper bag.

'Hm!' commented Mrs Pringle, with one hand on the latch of the gate, 'there's some – no matter how much schooling they've had – what never learns!'

Triumphant as ever, she continued on her way.

Back in the solitude of my house I found myself putting off the task of filling in the application form. I sorted the laundry, cleaned the dining-room windows, shown up in all their squalor by the bright sunshine, and generally fiddled about in a procrastinating mood.

Should I apply or not? Now that the sun shone again, I began to shilly-shally. I remembered the peaceful view from the top of the downs. Mrs Pringle was right when she said that Fairacre took some beating. She seemed to know an astonishing amount about my present proposals, I thought, remembering her advice about making a change. There was little doubt, in my mind, that the lady had been snooping at the contents of the long envelope in the course of her dusting. I had suspected this before. Looking at it in one way, I mused, it was really rather flattering that she advised me to stay. Perhaps she enjoyed my slatternly ways after all!

I paused in my window-cleaning and gazed at Tibby basking on the top of the rainwater butt, one of his favourite spots. How would he react to a move, I wondered?

The chances of getting the job were one in a hundred, I well knew. There would be a host of applicants for such a tempting post, and a house with it meant that there would be double the number, at least. Why not send in my application form, and let the gods decide? After all, if I were lucky enough to be called up for interview, I could make up my mind then.

I groaned in turmoil of spirit. How truly dreadful it is to have to make a decision! No, I was sure that I could not leave this to the gods. This was something I must settle for myself, here and now. Either I applied because I really wanted the post, or I would decide to stay on in Fairacre. Having got thus far, I went over the reasons for and against, all over again. It was a wearing business.

I should simply hate to leave the Fairacre children and all the friends in the village. There would be more children, and friends, in Devon, I answered myself. And this little house is extremely attractive! The Devon one is even better, said my second self. I should be leaving a job which I knew I could manage fairly competently. All the more reason for trying something more ambitious, commented my nagging half.

Perhaps this was the secret. Perhaps I should be more adventurous, stretch myself a little, climb out of my rut. I was too fond of clinging to the present, to the things I knew, the friends about me. Amy was possibly right to urge me to make a change. Fairacre was not the only place in the world. It was time I uprooted myself.

Now or never! I took out the application form from the envelope and spread it on the table. I must say it looked rather daunting. I whipped out my fountain pen before I weakened again, and at that moment the telephone bell rang.

It was Amy. I was glad to hear her voice. Now I should get some much-needed moral support, I felt sure.

'I'm just filling in that application form,' I told her, rather proudly, after the first civilities were over.

'Only just?' asked Amy. She sounded incredulous.

'It doesn't have to be in for a few days yet,' I answered defensively.

'But you've had it there over a week,' answered Amy severely. 'I quite thought it had been sent off long ago.'

I began to feel rather hurt. 'I had to think about it,' I said, in an injured tone.

'Stuff and nonsense!' snorted Amy. 'We worked it all out together last week. In any case, it is your move that I've rung up about.'

'What do you mean – my move?' I asked. 'Aren't you counting my chickens for me rather prematurely?'

Amy brushed my tartness aside. 'I met Lucy Colgate at a party yesterday,' she said, 'and told her about your plans. She's interested in Fairacre School, and I'm pretty sure she'll apply when you leave.'

Lucy Colgate! I was speechless. As if it wasn't bad enough to have Amy busying herself about my affairs, and bullying me into action, without adding the insult of Lucy Colgate. She had been at college with Amy and me, and try as I might – and I must admit I did not try very hard – I could not take to her. I found her domineering, utterly self-centred, and

painfully affected. No doubt she considered me equally un-pleasant. In any case, we met as little as possible, but Amy kept in touch.

The very thought of Lucy teaching in my school and living in my house was enough to make me bristle.

'Amy,' I said firmly, 'you take too much upon yourself. At times like this you strain the bonds of friendship to snapping point.'

'Are you trying to tell me that you are *still* trying to make up your mind?' demanded Amy shrilly.

'No!' I said grimly. 'It's made up now!' And I slammed down the receiver.

Lucy Colgate, I fumed, pacing round the dining-room table. Lucy Colgate living in this house! I could well imagine its transformation, tricked out with the frilly lampshades, Regency stripes and Redouté roses beloved by my old fellow student. As for Mr Willet's vegetable patch, that would be turned into a lawn, sprouting a cretonne garden umbrella with gold fringe, before the first term was over!

The idea of Lucy Colgate queening it in my little school was even more distasteful. Fancy leaving Patrick and Ernest, and Joseph, and Linda – all the adorable and maddening hustle of them, in fact – to the mercies of Lucy! It simply could not be done.

I had a sudden vision of Mrs Pringle's face. How would the two get on?

'The meeting of the dinosaurs,' I told myself, with some relish, my fury beginning to abate. 'What a battle that would be!' I could see Lucy facing Mrs Pringle over the tortoise stoves. Lucy spilling coke, and as yet ignorant of the consequences. Lucy would face many a hazard if she ever found herself in Fairacre School. Why, with any luck, I thought suddenly, the map cupboard door might burst open again and project the contents painfully upon her!

At this uncharitable flight of fancy, I began to laugh. Lucy Colgate and Amy could connive until they were blue in the face! My mind was now made up. I advanced upon the unsullied form.

I hesitated for one moment. This news of Lucy was not the main reason for my decision. It was simply the final straw which weighted the scale in favour of staying. It had made me realize, with devastating clarity, how much Fairacre really meant to me. For that I should be grateful to Lucy always.

With infinite joy, I began to tear the application form into small pieces. Then – slattern to the last – I flung them in the direction of the waste paper basket, unmindful of whether they went in or not. I felt wonderful.

I bounded into the sunlit garden – *my* garden – and positively skipped down the path. As I passed the water butt I let out a joyous shout to the sleeping cat.

'Fairacre for ever!'

For two pins I would have run up the school's Union Jack.

10. THE WAYFARER

Strangers are rare birds in the village of Fairacre and cause us as much interest as any hoopoes. We have our annual migrants, of course, and are always eager to see them each year, but they are only half-strangers.

These half-strangers come mainly in the summer. One really can't blame them. Winter comes with a vengeance here, with great roaring winds, cruel frosts and plenty of snow. As most of the visitors are townsfolk, they wisely remain where pavements, buses, indoor entertainment and central heating are available during the worst of the weather. But once spring begins, Mr Lamb, at the Post Office, recognizes the handwriting of friends and relatives of Fairacre natives and looks at the postmarks of London, Birmingham, Bristol and Leeds, and nods his head wisely.

'Asking to come again, no doubt,' he surmises. And, usually, he is right.

As well as these people, we look forward to seeing half a dozen or so regular tradesmen. In May, a small flat cart pulled by an ancient donkey appears in Fairacre. On board are dozens of boxes of seedlings. Alyssum and lobelia for neat border edgings, tagetes and African marigold, snapdragons and stocks, and best of all, velvety pansies already a-blowing in every colour imaginable. Sometimes there is a box or two of rosy double daisies. These I can never resist, and each year they are drawn to my notice by the two dark-eyed gipsies who do the selling.

'Lovely daisies, dear. Better than ever this year. We got new seeds, see. They was more expensive, but we'll let you have 'em the same price as last year, dear, as we knows you so well.' And so I have a dozen or so, as they knew I would, and probably pay more, for I can't possibly remember what I paid the year before. And this they know, too.

While the transaction goes on, the children cluster round the donkey, stroking his plushy nose and murmuring endearments. Somehow, the donkey cart always manages to call on a sunny day, at about one-fifteen, when the school dinner is over and the children are free to enjoy the fun.

'Miss, have you got a lump of sugar?' they plead.

'Miss, the donkey likes carrots, the man says!' cries another.

'Miss, have you got a bit of ol' bread to spare?'

It always ends the same way. Bearing my damp little newspaper parcels, and my much lighter purse, I return to the school house followed by the children and the gipsy woman. I hand over sugar lumps, old apples, the end of a loaf and anything else which, at a cursory glance round my larder, will make acceptable donkey-fodder, and watch the children tearing across the playground with their largesse. But the gipsy woman remains. Her eyes have grown very large and sad, her voice pathetic. She speaks quietly, as one woman to another, on intimate matters.

'I'm not one to beg, miss, as you well know, but the fact is I'm expecting again and hardly a decent rag to fit me. I'm carrying low this time, and not a skirt will go round me.' I wonder, inconsequently, if 'carrying high' would mean that her upper garments would be too tight, but hastily dismiss the idea.

She shuffles a little closer, and looks furtively about her. The whisper becomes a whine. 'Don't matter how old, dear. Or a coat, now. Say you had a coat. Don't matter if it's torn or grubby. Do us a good turn, lady, and see what you can find, if it's only for the sake of the baby.'

I tell her to wait, whisk upstairs, collect a dear faithful old flannel skirt, which I know I shall mourn later, a tartan jacket which Amy unkindly but truthfully told me made me look 'like mutton dressed as lamb', and return.

The skinny dark hands grab them quickly and turn them inside out. The sharp eyes, I notice, are bright with approval.

'Thank you, dearie. God bless you! I've got no money to give you, with all we've got to feed, but I'd like you to have a pot plant off the cart.'

'No, really –' I protest. 'Just take the clothes.'

'You come on!' insists my caller. Meekly, I accompany her to the cart. The donkey, surfeited, is scraping the road with one neat little hoof. The scrunching of sugar lumps can be heard, but not from the donkey.

I choose a handsome pink geranium. We exchange civilities. The couple mount the cart. My skirt and jacket are stuffed under the wooden board that serves as a seat, in company with an assortment of other garments, I notice. We all wave until they are out of sight.

'Ring the bell, Ernest,' I say. 'It's time we were back to work!'

We install the geranium on my desk, as a happy reminder of one of our visitors. It will be a year before we see them again.

Later, the scissor-grinder comes, and we rush out to his Heath Robinson machine with shears and scissors, knives and bill-hooks. Sometime in June, a stocky figure appears pushing a light barrow full of assorted materials and tools. This is the chair-mender and mat-mender. He does rushing, caning and a certain amount of simple carpentry. Doormats are the things be likes mending best, and I remember the pride with which he told me one day that my back-door mat was 'one of the finest ever made in one of Her Majesty's prisons'. I have no way of testing the truth of this statement, but I like to think that I wipe the garden mud from my shoes on a decent bit of British workmanship.

Then, in high summer, more gipsies come, bearing gaudy flowers made of woodshavings and dyed all the colours of the rainbow. Sometimes they bring clothes pegs, clamped together in rows on long twigs, still green and damp from the hazel bushes where the wands were cut and peeled. All these people are known and welcomed. They are as much part of the season as the daffodils or the Canterbury bells.

In addition, we sometimes have a visitor of more exotic caste. Once a tall turbaned stranger, with dusky skin and flashing eyes, called at our cottages. When we appeared, startled, at our doors he chanted: 'You lucky lady! Me, holy man from Pakistan!' And after these opening civilities he displayed the contents of a large suitcase for our delectation. Writing paper, soap, bright ties, hair ribbons, toothpaste – all jostled together to tempt the money from our purses. But I don't think he sold a great deal in Fairacre, for he never came again. Nor did 'the antique dealer' who offered Mrs Pringle ten shillings for her grandfather clock and Mr Willet a pound for the silver teapot left him by a former employer.

But it was another stranger, who called but once, who was perhaps the most haunting of all our visitors. I see his face more clearly than many of my children's, and often wonder what happened to that shabby little figure who visited my house, long ago, and never returned.

It was a still, hot May morning when he arrived. The lilacs, tulips and forget-me-nots shimmered in a blue haze. It was a Saturday, and I had done my weekly washing. It hung motionless upon the line, but was drying rapidly, nevertheless, in the great heat.

I had dragged the wooden garden seat into the shade and was resting there, glorying in the weather, when I heard the click of the gate. A small man, carrying a battered suitcase slung over his shoulder with a leather strap, shuffled up the path. My heart sank. Must I rouse myself to face a jumble of assorted objects, none of which I really wanted, which no doubt awaited my inspection inside the case?

He did not stop at the door, but made his way across the grass towards me, slipped the heavy case from his back, with a sigh of relief, and spoke. 'Mind if I sit down, miss?' he asked. His voice had a Cockney twang and he sounded tired. I nodded and he sat abruptly on the grass, as though his legs would carry him no further.

We sat in silence for a few minutes, he too tired, I suspected, and I too bemused with the sunshine, to make conversation. A bumblebee buzzed busily about the daisies on the grass. It seemed to be the only thing that moved in the garden. At length, I roused myself enough to speak.

'Don't bother to undo your case,' I said.

The man looked faintly surprised. 'I weren't going to. Why should I?'

'I thought, maybe, you were selling things,' I replied apologetically.

'Got nothin' to sell,' he said laconically. He lay back on the grass with his eyes shut, and I studied him.

He was quite old. He was a man in his seventies, I guessed, looking at the grey stubbly hair and his wrinkled forehead. A red band ran round his damp brow, where his cap had been, and a little trickle of sweat crept down his temple. He had a humorous look, and I guessed that he was a cheerful sparrow of a man, in the normal way. At the moment he looked utterly exhausted, and my heart smote me.

'Would you like a drink?' I asked. 'I haven't any beer, but there's cider or lemonade.'

He sat up slowly, his face creasing into a smile. 'I'd like a drop of lemon, miss, thank you,' he replied. He took a red and white spotted handkerchief from his pocket, and I left him wiping his face and neck, as I went towards the kitchen for refreshment.

It was a relief to leave the dazzling garden for the cool shade indoors. I loaded the tray with a jug of lemonade, two glasses and the biscuit tin, and returned.

The stranger struggled up at my approach, and took the tray from me. He poured one glassful of lemonade straight down his throat, sighed, and put it back on the tray.

'I could do with that,' he said, thankfully, watching me refill it. 'I bin on the road since 'arpars six.'

'Have you far to go?' I asked him.

'Making for Weymouth,' he said.

'For a holiday?'

'For good!' he said shortly. He looked away into the distance, turning his glass round and round in his rough hands. There was sadness in his face, but a determination about the set of his mouth that made me wonder what lay behind his journey. I was soon to know.

'I got an ol' friend in Weymouth. We was in the army together. Went all through the war – Ypres, retreat from Mons, the lot. Name of Miller – Dusty Miller, of course.' He gave me a quick sidelong smile. 'We 'ad some good times together. And some narrer squeaks too. "You come down anytime you like," Dusty says to me, whenever we met. "Always a welcome at Weymouth," he says, "for an old comrade!" So I'm going!'

He scrunched a biscuit fiercely. He looked a little defiant, I thought.

"Course, I shouldn't say this,' he said, swallowing noisily, 'but poor ol' Dusty picked the wrong girl when he got wed. Worst day's work he ever done, in my 'umble opinion! Can't think what come over 'im!'

He ruminated for a moment, crossing one leg over the other, and contemplated his battered boots. His spirits were rising with rest and refreshment, and his natural loquacity became apparent.

'Ol' Dusty,' he assured me with emphasis, 'could 'ave 'ad 'is pick of the girls. Fine set-up feller always. Curly hair, good moustache, biceps like footballs. Always ready for a lark. Why, in France –' He stopped suddenly, coughed with some delicacy, and started again. 'After the war 'e 'ad a nice little packet of money saved up. His dad run a little confectioner-tobacco shop down the Mile End Road, and when the old boy conked out in 1920 Dusty sold up and put the money into this caffy at Weymouth. Always bin fond of the sea, 'as Dusty, and I thought that's where 'e'd end up.'

'And so he's been there for a long time,' I observed.

'Ever since. Married a local girl, too. Great pity really.' He sighed, and helped himself to another biscuit. ''Course, you can understand it,' he continued. 'With this 'ere caffy to run, and that, you need a woman to lend a hand. And I must say, she could make two pennies go as far as three. A real 'ead for figures. It's thanks to Edie the place 'as done so well, but she weren't the woman for Dusty. No fun. Never one for a laugh. One of them stringy women, with a sharp nose. A bit white and spiteful, if you know what I mean.'

I said I did. St Patrick's clock began to strike eleven, and my visitor cocked an eye at me.

'Suppose I'd best be getting along,' he said, but with a questioning inflection. 'You must be busy.'

This was the opportunity which I should have seized, but it was so warm that I dallied. I knew that I ought to take my basket and go shopping. There were bedrooms to dust, and a salad to prepare. There were two telephone calls to make and the laundry to sort out. Let all these things wait, I decided.

'I'm not particularly busy,' I replied.

'Well, I'll have another five minutes, if you're sure,' said my visitor, propping himself against a handy tree. 'It's good to 'ave a bit of a chin-wag. I must say I've been a bit lonely since Thursday.' He checked suddenly, and then resumed in a quieter vein.

'Thursday!' he said slowly, as if talking to himself. 'It seems weeks ago! A different life – that's what it seems! Eh, a lot's happened to me since this time last week. Funny, ain't it, the way you go on, year after year, in the same ol' rut, and then, suddenly – phut? Everything's changed. You find yourself starting all over again. Queer, how things 'appen. If you're sure you're not busy, miss, I'll tell you about it.'

I assured him that I had all the time in the world, stretched my legs into the sunshine, and gave him my attention.

The year that Dusty Miller went to Weymouth, it appeared his old brother-in-arms, Alf, got married and set up home near the Elephant and Castle in south London. He and his wife

occupied a ground floor flat consisting of a kitchen-living room, a bedroom, and a parlour, known as the front room. The front room was only used on Sundays, or when guests were invited, and housed most of their wedding presents on a large sideboard.

Alf had a steady job as a butcher's roundsman. He was at work at seven-thirty each morning, cutting up the joints for the orders and loading his van. This was his employer's first motor vehicle, and the pride of both men's hearts.

He enjoyed his work. He was quick and friendly, a favourite with his customers who liked his badinage and unfailing cheerfulness. At Christmas time he carried home as much in Christmas boxes from kindly clients as he did in his wage packet.

His wife, Jessie, was a round pink girl with a frizzy fringe and pearl earrings. She liked satin blouses, an evening at the music hall, or a lively sing-song with her friends in the front room. Alf adored her.

They had three children, Frank, Norman and Ursula. The first two were named after relatives, but Ursula derived her name from the pages of a novelette which her mother had been reading a few hours before the baby arrived. The heroine of the novelette had had a particularly affecting experience, at a château somewhere well behind the lines in the First World War, involving a wounded officer of unsurpassed valour and passion, and a great deal of heart-searching on Ursula's part before the final renunciation.

It was all excessively moving, and the baby was to be either Jocelyn – the hero's name – or Ursula. And, eventually, after a prolonged and painful labour, Ursula arrived.

The family thrived, despite cramped conditions. The children ran round the corner to the gaunt Board School as soon as they were old enough. The classes were enormous, the classrooms dark, but the teachers were well-trained and energetic, and the children got on famously.

Occasionally, Alf met Dusty at a British Legion function in London. The families exchanged Christmas cards, and one summer the London family was invited by Dusty to spend a holiday at Weymouth. This was a real treat and the children looked forward to it for weeks. But disappointment was in store. It was quite apparent, when they arrived, that though Dusty was pleased to see them, Edie was not.

'Miserable ol' faggot!' was Jessie's comment, in the privacy of the tiny back bedroom to which they had been shown. 'Some holiday this is going to be, Alf! You should've had more sense than to accept Dusty's invitation. He's properly under her thumb, poor soul!'

It was indeed a most uncomfortable time. The children were scolded if they brought in sand on their shoes, or shells in their pockets. Jessie, bridling, did her utmost to keep silent for the sake of poor shame-faced Dusty, as much as for her own family. But everyone was relieved when Saturday came and they could return home.

The two women pecked at each other's cheeks through their veils. The men shook hands a shade too heartily, and avoided each other's eyes. The children smiled more freely than they had done all the week as they hung out of the train window.

'Never again!' exclaimed Jessie, as the train left Weymouth station. She withdrew two long hatpins from her straw hat, threw it on the rack, fussed up her fringe, and leant back with a sigh.

'That's the last I want to see of Edie Miller!' said Jessie flatly.

It was, in fact, the last that she did see of Edie, or Dusty. For before the year was out, jolly lively Jessie was operated on for cancer, and died under the anaesthetic. Alf was inconsolable.

Ursula was ten at the time of her mother's death. The boys were twelve and thirteen. Jessie's mother, a widow who lived nearby, took over the running of the house and the upbringing of the children. For Alf, it seemed as if the sun had gone for ever. For months he went about, looking like a shadow of his usual jaunty self, but gradually he recovered. His customers were glad to see his return to cheerfulness. He threw himself with renewed fervour into his work and into such activities as the British Legion's affairs. He and Dusty met often, but never spoke of the holiday which had been Jessie's last.

Years passed, and the two boys went out to work in New Zealand, where they married and settled. Ursula took over the housekeeping when their grandmother died, and Alf and his daughter rubbed along fairly well together.

She was nothing like her mother, Alf used to think, watching her at the other side of the hearth. She was thin and angular, with a sharp tongue and a way of tossing her head when crossed, which Alf recognized as a danger signal. He was secretly relieved when she became engaged to a young man from Northampton, and he gave her away without a pang.

Then began for Alf some of the happiest years of his life. He was free to do as he pleased. His work ran smoothly, his health was good, his spirits remarkably gay now that he had the house to himself. A neighbour cleaned the flat once a week, and for the rest of the time the dust gathered gently, the oven remained cold, and only the frying pan and kettle were in general use. Life was very simple.

He began to see more of Dusty Miller. Both men were now in their sixties and had plenty of reminiscences to share. During the Second War Dusty had been to the forefront in Civil Defence at Weymouth. Alf had been in the Fire Service, and both had experienced hair-raising episodes. Somehow, they did not talk of these. It was always the First World War which engrossed their attention. They relived the flight from Mons, the tedium and terror of trench life and the horror of that day when L Battery was wiped out beside them. They reminded each other, too, of lighter moments. Did Alf remember the time when his horse wheeled smartly into the pub yard as was its wont, leaving the colonel, whom he was accompanying, looking thunderstruck on the highway? Did Dusty recall the occasion when he played the piano in the pub, and generous comrades filled his tumbler with Benedictine so that he began to think that he was playing a two-manual organ?

Time passed all too quickly when the old soldiers met. Dusty now ran a small car and frequently took Alf out. Sometimes, Alf stayed a day or two at Weymouth. Edie was civilly welcoming, but it was Dusty who did the real entertaining. The Millers had no family, and all Edie's energy seemed to go into the running of the flourishing business. The two men seemed to see very little of her.

'Don't forget, old boy,' said Dusty on many occasions, 'there's always a home here for you, if you get tired of your own company. Just say the word. Plenty of room for one more.'

Alf was grateful, and failed to notice that on these occasions Edie was either absent, or silent.

When Alf was seventy he had the first real illness of his life. It had been a miserable December, cold and foggy. Mists from the Thames hung over the area where Alf lived and worked, making life doubly difficult at the busy time before Christmas. Handling frozen meat, his hands numb and aching, Alf began to feel his age. The round seemed to take twice as long as usual, hampered as he was with fog and extra orders. Customers were short-tempered, the traffic was frustrating, and Alf looked forward to the Christmas break with more fervour than he had ever felt before.

One night, a few days before Christmas, he returned home late and tired. His chest was unusually painful. To breathe was difficult; to cough was agonizing. Reluctantly, after a night of wakefulness, he dragged himself to the local doctor's surgery.

'Bed for you,' was the verdict. 'Who is there to look after you?'

'No one,' said Alf. 'Well, I've a daughter, but she's in Northampton.'

'See if she can come down,' said the doctor, handing him a prescription. 'I'll be in tomorrow morning.'

Ursula, with a martyred expression, arrived the next evening. She made it quite clear that her duty really lay with her husband and children, that it was most inconvenient to leave home with so much to do, and that only her filial devotion had brought her so swiftly to her father's bedside. Alf thought, yet again, how different she was from her warm-hearted mother. If only his Jessie had still been alive! A tear, born of weakness, crept down his cheek, and Ursula, noticing it, was glad to see how grateful the old fellow was to her.

Two wretchedly uncomfortable days followed, while Ursula grew steadily more dictatorial and her father grew steadily weaker. The doctor, summing up the situation, removed Alf to hospital, warning Ursula that he might not be fit to live alone when he was well enough to be discharged.

'I don't need to be reminded of my duty,' said Ursula, bridling. 'Dad's got a home with us at Northampton whenever he wants it.'

'He'll want it very soon,' the doctor assured her.

It was a sad day for Alf, some weeks later, when he left the flat which had been his home for so long. A few treasured pieces of furniture travelled ahead to Northampton, the rest went to local auction rooms.

One windy March day of blinding rain, Alf took the train to the Midlands, with a very heavy heart.

He knew, as soon as he crossed the threshold, that it would never work. There was something about the angular light wood hat-stand in the hall, and the overpowering aroma of floor polish that met him, which seemed to epitomize the unwelcoming quality of Ursula's abode.

He had been allotted the front room, a bleak, north-facing apartment, sparsely furnished. An iron bedstead, with a thin mattress and frosty white counterpane, took up the space by the window. The lino, printed to look like parquet blocks, shone like a mirror. A skimpy rug slid about the polished surface whenever anyone was rash enough to step on it. A small one-bar electric fire did its best to cast a little warmth into the room, but failed miserably.

Alf's two grandchildren came into the room to greet him. They were an unprepossessing pair. Sandra was a lumpy, sandy-haired eight-year-old, and Roger a skinny, rabbit-toothed boy of eleven. Both had adenoids and breathed habitually through their mouths. As they ate almost without cessation, the spectacle of his grandchildren did not encourage Alf's affection for them.

Their father was a lorry driver, a man of few words, but enormous appetite. It seemed to Alf, in the months that followed, that Ursula spent most of her time peeling great saucepans full of potatoes to assuage his hunger. He did not see much of his son-in-law, as he worked long hours, and Alf regretted this. It would have been nice to have a man to talk to, now and again. With every week that passed, Alf realized, with increasing despair, how bitter it is not to have a home of one's own.

He did his best to remain equable. Indeed, with his unquenchable Cockney spirit, 'cheerfulness kept breaking in', whether he would or no. Ursula resented this. She would have liked to see a proper humility, an appreciation of all her hard work. The gay quip, the sardonic aside, any sort of ironic levity, beloved of Alf, smacked of insurrection to Ursula. It was obvious that the old man would rebel one day and, before long, things came to the boil between Ursula and her father.

The row began, as might be expected, over the children. It was a hot May day, so hot, in fact, that for once Alf was grateful for his cold room. He sat, reading a letter which had come from Weymouth that morning, and looking forward to his tea when the children returned from school.

Dusty wrote as affectionately as ever. He knew, well

enough, that his old friend was unhappy although he had not said so in black and white.

'Don't forget, what I've said before,' wrote Dusty, 'that you are welcome here any time you like to come.'

Alf found great comfort in that sentence. He read it several times before returning the letter to its envelope on the table, and then settled back for a doze.

Before long he awoke. The two children were in the room, the boy gazing out of the window, and Sandra – Alf's anger rose as his senses returned – Sandra was reading Dusty's letter.

He struggled to his feet and made towards the table. 'Don't you dare meddle with my things!' stormed the old man.

The child looked sideways at him and contorted her face, by the lift of one nostril, into a contemptuous sneer. Just so, many years before, Ursula had looked at him, and received a resounding box on the ear.

Without thinking further, Alf repeated the process, and had one moment of unalloyed pleasure as his palm clouted the sandy head. The piercing shrieks that followed brought Ursula hurrying from the kitchen.

''E 'it me, mum! I wasn't doing nothin', mum! 'E just 'it me!'

Ursula's face and neck grew red with wrath. 'You keep your hands to yourself,' she yelled. 'I can remember your bullying ways when I was her age! Don't you think you can knock my kids about the way you knocked us!'

'She was reading my letter –' began Alf, but was brushed aside.

'As though it's not bad enough having you here all the time, burning the firing and the lights, eating us out of house and home –'

'I pay my own way!'

Ursula gave a derisive snort. 'Pay your way?' she echoed. 'And how far do you reckon your bit of pension goes these days?'

Sandra, seeing attention slipping from her, set up a further bout of snivelling. 'Mum, I believe I've got mastoid. I do, really! My ear 'urts somethin' awful where 'e 'it me!'

Ursula threw an arm protectively round her daughter. 'We'll take you down to the hospital after tea.' She rounded again on the old man. 'And if she's got a broken ear drum and is deaf for the rest of her days, she'll have you to thank! The ingratitude! That's what gets me – the ingratitude! Here I am, slaving day in, day out, with never a word of thanks for my trouble, and how am I repaid?'

'Stop play-acting –' began Alf.

'Play-acting!' screamed Ursula. 'Don't you dare insult me after all the harm you've done. I've just about had enough of you and your ways!'

She flung out of the room, dragging Sandra with her. The boy, who had watched the proceedings with sly enjoyment, slid after them. At the door he turned, poked out an impudent tongue, and vanished. Alf was left alone.

He was more shaken than he cared to admit. He shouldn't have hit the girl, he told himself. He was enveloped in a hot wave of guilt and shame. It receded, leaving him shivering with shock. God, what a hole, he thought, looking round the room! To think of spending the rest of his days in this place, with the added misery of Ursula and the children!

His eye fell upon Dusty's letter. In all that bleak room it was the only spot of comfort. Why should he stay? Why should he endure the humiliation of living with Ursula? He had his pension. He had a true old friend – a friend, moreover, who offered him a real home.

With growing purpose he went to his bed, reached beneath it for his battered suitcase, and set it open upon the white counterpane.

Methodically, with the exactitude of an old soldier, he began to pack his possessions. He was off.

*

'That was Thursday,' said the old man, reaching for his glass. He sounded bemused. 'And now it's Saturday. Seems a lifetime ago, miss – a lifetime.'

He gazed into the distance towards the towering downs, but I guessed that he was looking beyond them to the life that he had left behind in Northampton. He looked very old, very vulnerable, to be alone and with no home. I felt uneasy.

'And your daughter?' I inquired. 'You told her where you were going?'

I could imagine the remorse which might well be gnawing at any woman in her position, despite the portrait of flinty-hearted indifference the old man had drawn of her.

'Left a note,' said the stranger perfunctorily. 'Just told her I'd had an invitation from Dusty, and this seemed a good time to go down there.'

'So she'll expect you back some time?' I said. It was a relief to know that he had not burnt his boats completely.

'Never!' he shouted, sitting bolt upright. 'Not if she begged and prayed of me! I've had more'n I can take there. Never again!'

He scrambled to his feet, still looking belligerent. His gaze flickered over the sunny garden as though he saw it for the first time, and he turned to look directly at me. The anger faded into a smile.

'You bin good to me, miss, letting me run on like I have. I must be getting along.'

He fished inside his jacket and brought out a small creased map. He unfolded it carefully, and I noticed that his fingers shook. Across its grubby surface a thick ruled line ran from Northampton to Weymouth.

'There's my route,' he said proudly, holding up the map. 'Always like a bit of map work ever since my Army days. I'm a bit off true here, but no matter. Reckon if I make for Salisbury Plain I shan't be far off.'

He stuffed the map back in his pocket and began to hoist the case across his shoulders again.

'You're not walking all the way?' I asked anxiously.

'Not me!' he said. 'I've hitch-hiked most of it so far, but took a fancy to a walk this morning. Haven't seen the country on a summer day – not to notice it, I mean – ever since Jessie died. Brought her back to me somehow, being alone and peaceful, out in the fresh air.'

'Make for Caxley,' I said. 'But wait here a minute.'

I returned to the house and looked in my purse. As usual it was remarkably light, but there was a pound note. Why, I wondered, was it always the end of the month when such emergencies arose? I hastened out again and pressed it upon him.

'No, miss,' he protested. 'I got a bit by, you know.'

'If you don't get a lift, go by train,' I urged him. 'You don't want to arrive absolutely knocked up.'

He pocketed the note and we walked together to the gate. He was smiling now, as though at some pleasurable secret.

'Can't wait to see ol' Dusty's face when I turn up,' he said, over the gate.

'You haven't told them?' I asked, my heart sinking.

'Why should I?' he replied reasonably. 'I know ol' Dusty means it when he says I can go any time.' His tone was warm and affectionate. His wrinkled old face glowed at the thought of the welcome ahead. He straightened himself up and gave me a smart salute. 'Thanks for everything, miss, bless you! Think of me paddlin' in a day or two!'

Two minutes later, I watched the little figure disappear round the bend of the lane. Despite the sunshine, I shivered, for I could not help thinking of the woman that Dusty should never have married, the stringy one with the sharp nose, who was 'white and spiteful'.

Poor Alf, I mourned, poor Alf!

*

Yes, some of our Fairacre visitors are lively birds. The gipsies, in their clashing colours, look as exotic and gay as any parrot from the East. But I remember Alf as a wren, perky and completely English but somehow infinitely pathetic in his smallness.

I think of him often, the stranger who called but once. Will he ever return?

I can't be certain, but I have a feeling that Alf was on his last flight that summer day.

11. THE OLD MAN OF THE SEA

'It's my belief,' announced Mrs Pringle, as she baled boiling water from the electric copper into the washing-up bowl, 'that they over-ate themselves.'

'I thought they were rather more abstemious than usual,' I replied. 'Usually they start eating as we reach the end of the lane, and continue until we get to Barrisford.'

'Shameful!' ejaculated Mrs Pringle, flinging a trayful of sticky cutlery into the water. The noise was deafening.

'Then it's a quick dash into the sea, out again, and time for a solid lunch. This time they didn't appear to eat so much on the journey. Unless I'm getting used to it,' I added.

We were trying to probe the mystery of the many absences from school on this particular Monday morning. Almost a third of the desks were empty, and I suspected that general inertia was the common complaint after a long day at the sea on Saturday. Mrs Pringle argued for gluttony alone, but I have never found Fairacre children suffering from delicate digestions. Their appetites, quickened by the winds which sweep the downs, are enormous, and their digestive tracts are quite accustomed to coping with a steady supply of ices, sweets, fruit, fizzy drinks, as well as four hefty meals a day.

'Could be typhoid, of course,' said Mrs Pringle chattily. 'There was a bit on the telly about the sewage going into the sea. Fair gives you the creeps! I said to Pringle: "The way folks live! Thank God we've got a nice wholesome cess-pit!"'

She plunged her hands into the steaming water and

withdrew a fistful of dripping dessert-spoons, lately used for gooseberry pie.

'But can't do you no good, say what you will, to go bathing when that sort of thing's goin' on. As well as dumpin' this atomic rubbish they don't know what to do with. The sea must be proper un'ealthy these days. Me heart bleeds for those poor fish, it do indeed!'

She was now drying the spoons and setting them rapidly in rows. She counted them hissingly, stopped, scrabbled again in the cloudy water, drew blank, and turned to me. Her unlovely face was made even unlovelier by dark suspicion.

''Ere!' said Mrs Pringle truculently. 'You bin featherin' your nest again?'

This charitable remark referred to an unfortunate incident a few weeks earlier when Mrs Pringle had come across a school dessert-spoon in the kitchen drawer at the school house. I had not been allowed to forget this lapse. Mrs Pringle guards the school cutlery – as battered and dingy a collection of plate as one could find anywhere – as if it were the Crown Jewels.

'I find that remark offensive,' I said coldly, moving off to ring the school bell.

'So's stealing!' shouted Mrs Pringle after me, above the clatter. With what dignity I could muster, I pulled the school bell-rope to summon my depleted pupils to afternoon school.

The outing on Saturday had started in brilliant sunshine. By ancient custom, the Fairacre Sunday School and Church Choir Combined Outing takes place on the first Saturday in July. Evidently, many years ago, the schools in this area used to have a fortnight's holiday at the end of June to enable the children to pick the soft fruit crop. At the end of that time, their wages were paid and there was money, as well as the longing, for a jollification. Somehow, the first Saturday in July still remains as the only acceptable day for the annual outing.

Two coachloads set off at eight o'clock, packed with

parents and friends as well as the vociferous children. It was a sparkling morning. Bright drops glittered on the fresh hedges, sunshine glinted on cottage windows, the village pond, and the glossy backs of Mr Roberts' herd of Friesians as they ambled back from being milked. It was most exhilarating.

'Won't last,' said Mr Willet morosely, following his wife into the coach.

He was dressed in his best blue suit, and his boots shone like jet. No gaudy beachwear for Mr Willet when he accompanies us to the sea! He is sexton of St Patrick's, a public figure, and he shows himself to the world as a man worthy of the dignity of his office. He now rammed a small case containing their lunch upon the rack and then bent down to whisper conspiratorially in my ear.

'Where's old misery sitting?'

'Right at the front,' I whispered back, knowing at once to whom this referred.

'Thanks, miss. I'll make for the back,' said Mr Willet, pulling the case from the rack, and departing. I heard him settle with a satisfied sigh, as Mrs Pringle entered, took her place in the front and intimated to the driver that it was now in order for him to proceed.

'Old 'ard, ma,' said the driver irreverently. 'Just gotter check we're all 'ere.'

He hoisted himself from the wheel and turned round to count us.

'All aboard?' he cried at length.

'All aboard!' we echoed cheerfully, and set off for Barrisford.

Mr Willet, as a weather prophet, is usually right, and by the time we had driven through Caxley, the sky was overcast, and remained so for most of the day. Not that this dimmed the spirits of the Fairacre children. They tore along the famous sands, rushed into the waves – but not too deeply, I noticed, for the sea is not really trusted by us landlubbers – and wielded buckets and spades energetically for most of the exciting day.

Their elders enjoyed themselves more sedately, walking along the short pier, scanning the distant horizon through the penny-in-the-slot telescope, and studying the photographs outside the miniature theatre at the very end of the pier. It was a pity, we told each other, that we had to set off for home so early, otherwise we could have seen the variety show. Twelve acts – and all spectacular – it said so!

The air was wonderful, despite the lack of sunshine, tangy and salt upon our faces, and we all had prodigious appetites when we foregathered for high tea at Bunce's, the famous restaurant on the front.

The vicar counted heads earnestly. Were we all assembled? Would someone else check the numbers with him? Thereupon half the company rose to count the other half, and confusion reigned. Order was eventually restored, but we were, it was agreed, one missing.

'Joseph Coggs!' shouted Patrick. 'I saw him mucking about under the pier. Shall I run and fetch him?'

'I think,' said Mr Partridge, the vicar, in his gentle voice, 'we'll wait for five minutes and then send out a search party if he hasn't arrived. No doubt he will be along.'

At that moment, Joseph wandered through the brown and gold swing doors. He was excessively grubby and looked pale and bewildered. No adult from the Coggs' family was present so I took charge of him. He was remarkably quiet during tea, but ate his way steadily through a plate of ham and salad, three iced cakes, a butterscotch sundae and two cups of tea. I was not perturbed by his taciturnity as I watched his eating prowess. He obviously had enough to engross him at the time, and was, in any case, a somewhat uncommunicative child.

Just before six we said a sad farewell to lovely Barrisford for another year, and mounted the coach. Still the skies were sullen. At nine we were back in Fairacre, and at ten o'clock I, for one, was in bed.

Now, on Monday afternoon, it all seemed a very long time ago. Confronting my depleted class I mentally rearranged the timetable. The song, which I had proposed to teach them, must wait until the others returned. A spelling test, and then some revived memories of Barrisford, in words and pictures, should fill our afternoon very usefully and happily.

The spelling test was greeted with groans. Perhaps because they are unbookish children, as a whole, and do not see the printed word as often as I should like, spelling is a weak point at Fairacre. Even their names, when they are first in my class, at the age of seven or so, give some of them trouble, and I silently curse the parents who saddle their poor spellers with 'Penelope', 'Francesca' or 'Reginald'. Perhaps the worst one is 'Ronald'. It has been my lot, for many years, to wrestle with 'Ronlads', 'Rondals' and even 'Ronslads' and very exhausting I have found it.

This afternoon I bullied them through such necessary exercises as the days of the week – 'Wednesday', of course, is the stumbling-block – the months of the year – all, with the possible exception of 'March' and 'June', fearfully hazardous – and a brisk revision of local place names which are invariably written awry. They tottered out to play, quite done up.

Ten minutes in the boisterous air of the school playground soon restored them to their usual vivacity, however, and they settled down to write and draw their impressions of the day at Barrisford. I wandered round the busy classroom, admiring their efforts.

They were much as I expected. Sandcastles topped with flags, sailing boats, rowing boats – even a steamer, though I am positive no steamers come to Barrisford – and unflattering portraits of fellow pupils paddling in zig-zag waves. But Joseph Coggs' picture roused my curiosity.

Beneath a framework of black-crayoned girders stood two figures. One, from the blue striped tee-shirt, I recognized as a self-portrait. The other, about half the size, wore scarlet bathing trunks and a crown on its head. A certain amount of scrawling with a pale blue crayon indicated that water was nearby, and in the distance it looked as though there were a fairytale palace with the conventional spiky towers. I began to wonder if Joseph was remembering the pantomime rather than the trip to the sea.

'Who's this little boy with you?' I asked.

''S'man!' said Joseph.

'But he's only half your size,' I protested. Our art at Fairacre is pretty pedestrian. We make the sun circular, and grown-ups are usually twice the size of children in our pictures.

'So he was!' persisted Joseph. 'But he were a man all the same.'

I was about to pass on and let him enjoy his fantasy, when he pointed out one or two other features.

'This 'ere's the pier, see, I met this man under there. He was only up to my shoulder.'

'Sounds likely, don't it!' scoffed Ernest who had come to see the picture, and was rapidly joined by half a dozen others, who felt like stretching their legs.

'Bet you dreamt it, Joe!' said John.

Joseph's dusky face grew red with anger. His dark eyes smouldered.

'He was a man,' he repeated mulishly. 'He told me. He said he was The Old Man of the Sea and he lived in a palace. That's it there!'

He thrust a black forefinger upon the spiky towers. There was a burst of derisive laughter from the onlookers which I hastily quelled. Joseph was very near to tears and I was not going to see him taunted, inexplicable though his garbled story sounded.

'Ten minutes to finish!' I announced, 'and we'll have a quiet ten minutes, please. I'm looking for someone sensible to help me clear up at home time.'

This, as usual, worked like magic, and peace descended while they finished their scribbling. Partly to keep Joseph from being teased on the way home, and partly because I was intrigued with what lay behind his account of the stranger, I

chose him to remain behind after school. The rest of the children ran off, their voices dying away in the distance.

The classroom seemed unnaturally quiet. We could hear the birds cheeping on the guttering, and the whispering of the leaves outside the Gothic window.

Joseph stacked the papers carefully. His own, I noticed, was placed lovingly on top. He brought them to my desk, put them down, and remained gazing at me.

'I ain't lying,' he said abruptly.

'I know you're not,' I answered.

There was silence for a moment, a silence which I did not intend to break first.

'I really did see him under the pier,' said Joseph slowly. 'That's why I was late for tea. That's why –'

He faltered, took a deep breath, and began again. In bits and pieces, fits and starts, the astonishing story came out. To an adult it was both pathetic and comic. To a small boy, it was quite apparent, the encounter had been terrifying and miraculous.

As far as I can gather, Joseph stayed with his younger twin sisters, as he had been bidden to do by his mother, until they had eaten their sandwiches at midday.

The three children had played blissfully with the sand and the shells for which Barrisford is famous, but in the afternoon Joseph began to get restless. The two little girls had started a mammoth earthworks, with which they were entranced. Joseph found the business of digging remarkably boring. After all, he could dig any time in Fairacre. What Joseph wanted to do was to explore.

Mr and Mrs Willet, propped comfortably in the shelter of a breakwater nearby, saw his predicament.

'You go and 'ave a look round, Joe,' said Mr Willet. 'We'll be 'ere for a bit, reading the paper. We'll keep an eye on your sisters.'

Joseph scrambled eagerly to his feet, his dark eyes sparkling, and set off in the direction of the pier.

'Don't forget tea's at half past four,' bellowed Mr Willet, in the voice that carries across the mighty winds of Fairacre. 'Keep your eye on your gold wrist-watch!'

Mr Willet gave a mighty chuckle at his own wit. Mrs Willet smiled wanly, and the two little girls looked at him open-mouthed.

''E ain't gotter wrist-watch!' explained one slowly.

'Tch! Tch!' said Mr Willet testily, and shook out the newspaper.

Joseph made his way diagonally across the sand towards the sea. His feet were bare, and he gloried in the feel of the wet ribs of sand under his insteps. The tide was out, leaving pools of every imaginable shape. Here and there were outcrops of slaty black rock. These Joseph found particularly fascinating. Slimy bladder-wrack covered many of them, and he squatted happily on the rubbery mounds popping the salty blisters one after another. There were limpets too, grey, ribbed and conical that he tried in vain to prise from the rock. He was intrigued by the way he could move them a trifle, and then no more, as they put out their defences.

He wandered nearer and nearer to the pier. Here the pools were deeper, and he discovered, for the first time, the brown jelly-like anemones that waved their tentacles and sucked at his finger.

There were a number of people walking along the pier, hanging over the railings, gazing at the sea. Joseph recognized some of the Fairacre party among them. But he was not particularly interested in what went on aloft. It was the great sub-structure of criss-crossed iron girders which Joseph intended to explore.

They were very cold, wet and rusty, he discovered. Brown streaks and green slime coloured their gaunt shapes, and where the water lapped the legs, green fringes swayed to and fro rhythmically.

Joseph made an attempt to climb up one of the girders, but

the iron-work was cruelly hard to hands and feet. Little flakes of metal came off at a touch, and the salty roughness made his finger-tips sore. He abandoned the attempt and stood listening to the strange noises around him.

Above his head came the thudding of people's feet as they walked the planks of the pier. Around him came the constant sound of trickling water as it ran down the girders, or dripped into the rock pools. The wind made a little whistling sound in the iron lattice-work, and always, as a bass accompaniment, there was the rushing and booming of the swirling sea.

It was particularly rocky under the pier. Great flat plateaus of rock overlapped, forming wide irregular steps. At their edge were deep pools, almost black in the dim light beneath the pier. Joseph, stepping into one caught his breath as the water came high above his knees. He scrambled out of the slippery hole, and walked in a more gingerly fashion, peering at this strange and frightening element.

He was now almost at the end of the pier. Above him he could hear people walking round the little theatre. There was a distant sound of tea cups, for a small refreshment room adjoined the theatre. Sometimes a child called. Sometimes a gull wheeled and cried. It was difficult to tell which was the human voice. Joseph found it all wonderful and strange.

At length he came to a large pool. It was overhung by an outcrop of rock and was as dark as ink. Something large, coloured red and white seemed to be floating in it. Cautiously, Joseph approached, knelt upon the slippery rock and peered over.

To his horror he saw that it was the motionless body of a boy. Surely he must be dead! His eyes were closed. His legs and arms floated gently away from the body and his hair moved as rhythmically in the water as the tentacles of the anemones had done.

Fearfully, his throat aching with suppressed screams, Joseph put out a shaking finger and prodded the body.

'Give over!' said the corpse, opening its eyes suddenly.

Joseph flinched away, startled, scraping his knee painfully on the sharp rock. There was a wild thrashing in the pool, the red trunks and legs were submerged and only the top half of the body confronted Joseph.

'Whatcher think you're up to?' demanded the bather. 'Poking people about like that?'

Joseph, never very voluble, found communication more difficult than usual. For one thing, he was in a state of shock. And for another thing, he was extremely puzzled. The stranger was very small. He had believed him to be a boy, possibly two or three years younger than himself, but as soon as he spoke he realized that, despite his small stature, the bather was a grown man.

Somehow it all seemed part of the fantastic world immediately around Joseph. Anything could happen here, among the faintly menacing shapes of the girders and rocks. The cold, salty air was as far removed as it could be from the pollen-laden winds that blew around Joseph's native village. The music of birdsong and rustling trees was exchanged for the queer atonal sound of dripping water and surging sea. He felt as though he had strayed into an unknown world, where colours, shapes, sounds, and now people themselves, were strange and sinister.

Despite his aching throat he managed to swallow and find his voice.

'I'm sorry, sir,' he said tremulously.

Immediately he was glad that he had added that last word to his apology. The little man's face softened. A look of gratification passed over the pudgy countenance, and he wiped the wet hair away from his forehead.

'That's all right, boy,' he said grandly. 'Now you're here you can give me a hand out.'

He presented a cold wet hand to Joseph. It was as small as those of Joseph's little sisters', but on the back were the hairs of a grown man. Joseph tugged with all his strength. There was a good deal of puffing and blowing and then the little man bounced from the pool on to the rocks.

'Get my towel, boy, will you?' asked the stranger, waving towards the direction of a nearby girder at the outside edge of the pier. Joseph saw a bundle propped between the angle of two girders, out of the wet, and made his way carefully across the slimy rocks to do as he was bidden. There was something imperious about the man which awed Joseph. He was glad to be of service to him.

When he came to withdraw the rolled-up towel from its resting place, Joseph was surprised to see that a few yards of rope ladder were tucked in with it. One end was obviously fixed aloft, and Joseph stepped out beyond the pier to see where it went. He could see it lashed securely to the bottom stay of the pier railings. From there it hung down against the girders, flapping gently in the breeze. Joseph guessed that at its full length it would easily reach the sand. Tucked up as it was, a little higher than his head, it was unnoticeable at a cursory glance.

'Come on! I'm damn near freezing!' shouted the man.

Joseph hurried back with the towel. The stranger, jumping up and down with remarkable agility, was covered with goose-pimples. He snatched the towel from Joseph's arms and began to rub himself energetically. Joseph surveyed him with interest.

Now that the water had drained from his hair, Joseph could see that the man was fair. He was thickset and very muscular. His chest and legs were faintly hairy and he had the suspicion of a moustache. His eyes were very blue, his ears very red. Joseph wondered how old he was. It seemed strange to think that he might be as old as his father, and yet he was no bigger than one of his twin sisters!

The man gave his head a final rub, threw the towel round his waist, and turned to look at Joseph.

'Perishin' cold under here,' he said. 'Let's sit outside for a bit.' He indicated the sand beyond the pier. A little faint sunlight was struggling through the clouds, and chasing the shadows across the bay.

The two picked their way across the rocks. At the edge of the pier the man stopped.

'Anyone about?' he asked. Joseph looked up and down the beach. There were a number of people further along, but no one at hand. The most popular beach, where the Willets were already beginning to think of packing up and making their way to Bunce's, lay behind them.

'Can't see anyone,' said Joseph, wondering at the man's sudden desire for privacy. They emerged into the open. It was a relief to feel flat sand again underfoot.

'I'll show you how to warm up after a bathe!' cried the little man, whose spirits seemed to have risen rapidly. He flung off the towel, and did a backward somersault before Joseph could draw breath.

'Cor!' said Joseph, full of admiration. 'Who learnt you that?'

'Never you mind!' answered the man. 'Watch out now!'

He flexed his muscles, stood on his toes, took a deep breath, and then turned three backward somersaults in a row. After the last he stretched his arms above his head, looking this way and that, as though acknowledging applause. Joseph thought he looked just like the acrobat he had seen in the pantomime last Christmas. If anything, he was better, because he was so small and neat. Joseph was entranced.

'That's chicken feed,' said the man. He swaggered slightly, thrusting his thumbs into the top of his red trunks. 'Look at this!'

He stretched his arms again and began to turn cartwheels, with extreme dexterity and rapidity. He wheeled so steadily, that his red trunks and white torso seemed to blur before Joseph's admiring eyes. He must have turned almost twenty times before he ceased and became upright again.

'Ain't you a marvel!' breathed Joseph, awed.

The little man laughed, but was obviously pleased with the boy's admiration. He smote him cheerfully across the shoulders and they sat down together in the shelter of a rock. Joseph compared their outstretched legs. His own were thin and brown, marked with many an ancient scar on the shins, and the fresh scrape across one sore knee. The stranger's were several inches shorter than his own, but twice the thickness, and bulging with muscles.

'D'you live in Barrisford?' asked the stranger.

'No,' said Joseph. 'Do you?'

'Not likely! Not in this one-eyed dump! Do I look as though I live here?'

He cocked a blue eye upon Joseph. Anxious to please this superman, Joseph hastened to apologize, although he himself could see nothing wrong with Barrisford. Indeed, to someone whose home was in the modest confines of Fairacre, Barrisford seemed a splendidly sophisticated place.

'What's your name, sir?' ventured Joseph.

'Ah now! That's telling!' said the little man teasingly. He leant back against the rock, clasping his hands behind his head, and gazed quizzically at the boy with half-closed eyes. 'I think you'd better call me "The Old Man of the Sea",' he said lazily. 'That's where you found me, wasn't it?'

'The Old Man of the Sea,' echoed Joseph, not completely understanding. 'Do you mean you live there?'

The man nodded, grinning at the boy's mystification.

'That's right,' he said. 'I live in the sea. In a palace, in fact. I'm a sort of King, you know, got a crown and that when I'm at home.'

Joseph pondered this. It sounded a bit far-fetched, but why should a grown-up man want to lie? And the whole affair was odd – the queer, dark, under-pier world, the tiny man, the cartwheels! He wanted to know more.

'Where is this palace?' he asked suspiciously.

'If you're not going to believe me,' said the man, suddenly looking sulky, 'I shan't waste my time telling you.'

'Oh, but I do!' cried Joseph, aghast at upsetting this god-like creature yet again.

The stranger appeared mollified. 'Well, if you must know, it's way out beyond the end of the pier, on the sea-bed.'

'What's it made of?' asked Joseph.

'Oh, rocks and stones, and that!' said the man airily. There was a short silence, as though he were thinking heavily, and then he began again. 'Sea shells, too, of course. It's sort of decorated with shells. And we have sea-weed trees in the garden. It's a pretty place. Fish swim in and out the windows. We always keep the windows open. I like a bit of fresh sea-water in the rooms myself.'

Joseph sat contemplating this picture of royal life beneath the waves. He found it wholly enchanting, and only a fragment of his former doubt remained.

'What d'you eat?' he enquired.

'Fish, of course,' replied the little man, opening his blue eyes very wide. 'What fool questions you ask! We've got nets from the garden, straight through the kitchen window, to the larder where we keep 'em.'

'I like fried fish,' said Joseph warmly. This talk of food was beginning to make him hungry.

'Oh, we don't fry ours,' answered the man casually. 'Too wet, you know. Makes it difficult to keep the stove alight.'

'Ah! It would!' agreed Joseph. Somehow, the difficulty of keeping the stove going underwater seemed to make sense of the whole, slightly improbable, situation.

'No, we eat 'em raw,' said the man. 'Very nutritious too.' He suddenly gave a gigantic yawn. 'Ah well, my boy, wish I could stay longer with you, but I'd best be getting along.'

'Back to the palace?' asked Joseph. He half-hoped that he would be invited to accompany him.

The man rose to his feet and began to shake out the sand from his towel.

'Not just yet,' he said, smiling. 'I've got some friends to call on first.' He wrapped the towel round his shoulders.

A distant yelling caused the two to look round. Leaning over the pier railings, just where the rope ladder was fastened, was a small figure. To Joseph it looked like a little girl.

'Come on, Bill!' she shouted. 'It's half past four. Your tea's ready!'

'Coming, Katy!' the little man shouted back, and set off towards the rope ladder with incredible speed. Joseph ran beside him.

He watched him untangle the lower rungs and begin to mount aloft. The strong little arms and legs twinkled over the criss-cross rope, like a monkey in a ship's rigging. Halfway up he stopped and looked down at Joseph's upturned face.

'Hey, boy,' he said, grinning. 'You cut off to your own folk. And don't believe all you hear, son!'

He nipped smartly up the rest of the ladder and through the railings. Joseph watched him untie the rope, his face suddenly solemn and intent. He slung it across his towelled shoulders, with never a backward glance at the boy below, and vanished towards the theatre.

Disconsolately, with the words of his hero echoing in his ears, Joseph obediently retraced his steps, seeking – tardily and reluctantly – his own folk, who were already ensconced amidst the solid worldliness of Bunce's restaurant.

'And you knows the rest, miss,' said Joseph, fiddling with the brass lid of the Victorian ink stand which dominates the teacher's desk at Fairacre school. His dark eyes were downcast, crescents of thick lashes brushing his dusky cheeks.

'And I 'ad my tea with you, and then we come 'ome,' he continued.

'I remember,' I said. I also remembered Mr and Mrs Willet's

conversation at the tea table, of which Joseph was obviously unaware.

'A pity we have to go back so soon,' Mr Willet had said. 'They say there's a good show on at the end of the pier.'

'Someone told me there's a juggler that keeps six bottles moving,' said Mrs Willet, 'and a dog, dressed up like a nurse-maid, pushing a monkey in a pram!'

'There's twelve acts altogether,' said someone further down the table. 'I looked at the posters. Top of the bill is the midgets. Acrobats they are – six of 'em. Call themselves The Mighty Atoms, or some such name. "Appeared before all the crowned heads in Europe," the poster said. I bet they'd have been worth seeing!'

'I'm partial to midgets myself,' Mr Willet had agreed, before the conversation took a different turn.

I looked at the little gipsy boy before me. What was going on under that black thatch of tousled hair, I wondered? Did he really believe the yarn spun him by the fanciful midget? Or did he merely want to believe it?

And what should be my reaction to Joseph's disclosures? I doubted whether this was the time to tell him the cold truth – whether, in fact, he would ever want to know the truth. It seemed wiser, I decided, to say as little as possible at this stage. Joseph's feelings were still too raw to stand rough handling. If he ever wanted to know more, I felt that he would ask me, and then I should answer him with the truth.

At this moment, the problem was settled, or at least shelved, by the appearance in the doorway of Mrs Pringle. In one hand she held an upturned broom, in the other a dustbin lid. She looked, at first glance, like some squat Britannia, with trident and shield.

'You done?' she inquired glumly.

'Yes, indeed,' I said. Under the present trying circum-stances, Mrs Pringle's appearance was almost welcome. I put the stack of papers on top of the ancient walnut piano, anchored them safely from the cross-draughts with *Hymns Ancient and Modern,* locked the drawers of my desk, and made my way out into the playground.

Joseph followed me, still looking thoughtful. Outside, by the doorway, Mr Willet was perched on a pair of rickety steps. He was drawing a bent stick along the guttering, collecting dead leaves, an old nest or two, twigs and odd slivers of slate, all of which impeded the flow of rainwater to the butt behind the school.

I stopped to hail him.

'Run home now, Joseph,' I said to my shadow. 'You shall pin your picture on the wall tomorrow morning. It's one of the best.'

His countenance became more animated, and he began to move off. Suddenly, as though remembering something, he turned again to confront us.

'And there *was* a little man!' he said earnestly. 'Honest, there was!'

'I know,' I assured him. We looked at each other for a moment. Then he smiled, and he set off at a brisk trot through the school gates.

'What's up with young Joe, then?' inquired Mr Willet, when the child was out of earshot. 'He bin in trouble?'

'Not trouble exactly,' I answered. 'I'll tell you all about it some day. Let's say he's finding life a bit of a puzzle at the moment.'

Mr Willet snorted, and dropped a noisome handful of muck into the bucket at the foot of the steps.

'Who don't?' he demanded.

12. Harvest Festival

There are a number of people in Fairacre who maintain that far too much importance is given to Harvest Festival in our village. Mrs Mawne, our local ornithologist's wife, is one.

'I find something abhorrently bucolic about Harvest Festival,' she announced one day, looking round the chancel of St Patrick's church where the ladies of the village were busy festooning ledges and pillars with the fruits of the earth.

Miss Jackson too, I remember, voiced much the same sentiments. She came among us – mercifully for a short time – as infants' teacher at the school, and had a very poor idea of rural festivals, church or secular.

'Simply a survival of primitive superstitions,' was her comment. 'An act of propitiation to malevolent tribal gods, bound up with fertility rites and other ceremonials of earlier civilizations.' Miss Jackson's dicta were always couched in high-flown language of this sort, and very tedious it became.

Luckily, such people are in the minority. For most of us in Fairacre, our Harvest Festival is a well-loved and well-supported institution. It is, after all, a public thanksgiving for the fulfilment of a year's hard work in the fields and gardens, and a brief breathing space before tackling the next year's labours.

Mr Roberts, the local farmer, gives a mammoth Harvest Home supper in his biggest barn at this season, but naturally it is the farm workers and their friends who attend this jollification. The service at St Patrick's caters for the whole village, for

chapel-goers join church-goers on this occasion, and the church is always crowded.

'Far more crowded, in fact,' sighs the vicar, 'than for any other of our church festivals. I sometimes wonder why.'

I think I could tell him. Here is something tangible, something vital, the fruits of the earth – in turn, the fruits of man's labour – lying in splendid array, as living witness of God's and man's work together. A good harvest means food, security, life itself. A poor one, not that many years ago, could mean starvation – and memories are long in the country. It is easier to comprehend the things of the flesh than the spirit, and although one can sympathize with the good vicar's attitude, it does not mean that the praise and honour rendered to the Almighty at Harvest Thanksgiving are any less meritorious.

On the Friday afternoon before Harvest Festival Sunday, I took the schoolchildren across to St Patrick's as usual. Every year we decorate the pews and other allotted portions of the church, and we guard this privilege jealously. On Saturday the ladies of the village come with armfuls of flowers and greenery to do their share, but they always find that the Fairacre children have done their part first.

Usually we tie little bunches of corn to the pew heads, and arrange marrows, shiny apples, onions, giant potatoes, and any other contributions which will not wither or fade, along the ledges and window sills which we know by ancient custom are 'ours'.

It was a bright windy afternoon as we made our way across to the church. Somewhere in the village an energetic gardener was having an autumn bonfire, and great billows of blue smoke hung gauzy veils between us and the distant downs. The smell of the burning leaves had that whiff of sadness which an autumn bonfire always brings; a reminder that summer is over and that soon we shall be head-bent against the gales of winter. I thought briefly of that Devon school, but this time with no regrets. This, I thought, looking at my straggling flock bearing their harvest tributes, is the place for me!

On the south side of St Patrick's, the creeper was glowing scarlet and bronze against the grey flints. On the graves chrysanthemums and Michaelmas daisies made a brave show, and over the lych-gate, where Mr Willet began his story of Sally Gray last winter, a many-berried bryony trailed its bright loops and coils. In the vicarage garden, adjoining the church-yard, I could see dahlias, pink and yellow, as big as soup plates; and on the telephone wire, which stretched from the lane to the chimney stack of the vicar's study, a row of swallows chattered together – no doubt of the journey so soon to be undertaken.

St Patrick's was very peaceful after the wind outside, and soon the children had decked the pews, the steps of the font, and the allotted window-sills. They wandered about admiring their efforts.

'I reckons it looks real good,' said John, squatting down at the foot of the font. 'Tidy and careful!' He gazed with appraisal at the neatly-spaced apples before him.

''Twould look better with a marrer in the middle,' said Ernest, surveying it.

'A marrer!' echoed John, shocked. 'Much too big! Them apples is *exactly* the same size, and four inches apart!' He whipped from his sock a yellow school ruler to prove his point. His expression was scandalized.

'A marrer!' he repeated, with infinite disgust. 'That'd prop-erly put the kibosh on it!' He gave Ernest a withering glance, replaced the ruler in his sock, and moved away in high dudgeon, every inch an outraged artist.

We returned to the school, wind-blown and much refreshed. Mrs Pringle had already arrived to clear up the mess. To give her a surprise we had already swept the floor clean of bits of straw and other debris from our harvest preparations. If we expected praise from our curmudgeonly cleaner we were to be disappointed.

'Hm! And so I should think!' was Mrs Pringle's comment, when an innocent infant drew her attention to the unusually clean floor. 'Pity it ain't done every day!'

She limped heavily across the room towards the infants' class room, and did not hear Ernest's regrettable, but justified, remark to his neighbour.

I did. But I don't mind confessing that I turned a deaf ear.

On Saturday afternoon I made my way across the church-yard again. This time I was carrying an armful of foliage for the ladies of the village to use in their part of the church decorations. Luckily, I am not required to assist on this occasion. It is considered that I have done my share with the schoolchildren the day before, so that my visit is usually brief.

Mrs Partridge, the vicar's wife, and Mrs Mawne were standing back, surveying two large stone vases which flanked the altar. Doubt was writ large upon both faces.

'It isn't so much the *form*, dear, as the *colour*,' said Mrs Partridge earnestly. 'That mass of peony leaves near the base looks far too dominant, to my mind.'

'Rubbish!' retorted Mrs Mawne, who had obviously put the peony leaves there. 'It's just a good splash of colour, repeated, if you notice, in the left-hand top of the set. Personally, I feel it is perfect for *form*. I just rather wondered if that spray of yellow golden rod which you've just added, isn't the tiniest bit jarring.'

Mrs Partridge looked hurt. She is one of the keenest members of the Caxley Floral Society, and has won several diplomas for flower arrangements of a somewhat sparse and austere nature. A few spiky leaves, and one or two tulip heads, balanced in five stones from the vicarage rockery, were much admired last year by those who know about such things.

'Such economy of line!' breathed the judge, making a little box of his fingers and peering at the arrangement through the gap. And Amy, who was present on that occasion, said that it well deserved first prize for 'inspired asymmetry'.

'She deserves first prize for keeping the thing upright,' I said. 'One good cross-draught and the lot'd capsize.'

Amy informed me coldly that I lacked the right approach to flower arrangements, and regretted my mundane outlook on Beauty and Higher Things. I was unrepentant.

Mrs Partridge, on this occasion, rose to the defence of the golden rod.

'It is freely acknowledged,' she told Mrs Mawne, 'by both Eastern and Western authorities on Floral Art, that a touch of yellow, in any arrangement, adds the vital spark of life and sunshine to the whole. It is closely connected with the fact that yellow is one of the primary colours – and the most dominant one at that!'

She advanced militantly upon the stone vase with yet another spray of the offending plant. Mrs Mawne's mouth took on a grim line, and I deposited my armful thankfully on the chancel floor and fled outside.

I get quite enough sparring with Mrs Pringle from Monday to Friday. On Saturdays and Sundays I like a little peace.

Mr Willet was working in the churchyard. He was armed with a bill-hook and was taking vigorous swipes at the long grass which grew beneath the hawthorn hedge dividing the graveyard from the vicarage garden.

He straightened up as I approached, resting one horny hand on the small of his back.

'Not so young as I was,' he said, puffing out his stained walrus moustache. 'Bending double, after three helpings of my wife's treacle pudden, don't seem as easy as it used to.'

The sun was warm. It was a mellow September day, with the elm trees turning a pale gold against a pellucid blue sky. Mr Willet's ruddy face was beaded with sweat. He had rolled up his shirt sleeves, and his muscular hairy arms were smudged with grass stains and blotched with pink where the nettles had stung him. Nevertheless, he appeared unperturbed.

He seated himself on the low flat lid of a tomb, and I sat down beside him. It was comfortable and warm with the sunshine which had been pouring on it since daybreak. Among the moss and lichens which covered the stone was the inscription; 'Jno Jeremy – Gent of this Parifh.' I felt sure that he would have no objection to our presence.

'Fred Hurst's grave's coming on a treat,' said Mr Willet approvingly. He had put the bill-hook on the stone beside him, and his two tired hands drooped between his knees. His eyes, however, were bright as they surveyed his domain.

I followed his gaze. Certainly, a fine strong growth of green grass, neatly clipped, covered poor Fred's resting place. But it was the older grave beside it that caught my eye.

'What's that on Sally Gray's mound?' I asked.

Mr Willet looked a trifle shame-faced. 'Well, to tell you the truth, it's a little rose-bush – one I took as a cutting from ourn in the garden. Seemed a pity for it to go to waste, and the poor old dear hasn't got nothing growing along her. I put it in soon after I told you the tale about her. Remember?'

I nodded. The tale of Fairacre's flying woman had certainly intrigued me.

'Funny how we all likes a story,' ruminated Mr Willet, watching a red admiral butterfly settle on some Michaelmas daisies. 'Don't matter if you really believes it or not – as far as I can see. I mean, half of you believes, let's say, but the other half doubts, and in the end it's the half that wants to believe in the story that wins.'

'What's put this in your mind?' I asked lazily. A pigeon cooed from a tree nearby, and the air was so soft that I found the two together peculiarly soporific. If Mr Willet's sturdy bulk had not been beside me, I should like to have stretched out flat upon Jno Jeremy's warm stone, and had a gentle doze.

'That business of Joe Coggs,' answered Mr Willet. 'I bet he really knew that little chap under the pier was a midget. Yet you see, he sticks to it it was the Lord of the Seas, or some such.'

'It's difficult to know,' I murmured.

'When you're that age,' continued Mr Willet, 'these 'ere fairytale ideas get hold of you real strong. Witches and that.'

He stopped suddenly and there was a pause. I felt myself slipping from reality to the world of sleep. The pigeon's cooing sounded fainter and fainter.

'We 'ad one in Fairacre,' said Mr Willet's voice, startlingly close at hand.

'A pigeon?' I asked, struggling to sit upright.

'Tch! Tch!' tutted Mr Willet. 'A pigeon! Who was talking about pigeons? What I said was – we 'ad a witch once in Fairacre. At least they said she was.'

'And when was this?' I asked, now fully awake.

'When I was a nipper. Same age as young Joe, come to think of it. Proves what I was saying. You want to believe anything out of the ordinary when you're a kid. Take me, for instance.'

'Did you believe she was?' I queried, scenting a story.

'Me? I was positive. And I went out to prove it, what's more.'

He took out a short-stemmed pipe from his trouser pocket, and a small tin of tobacco.

'May as well 'ave one as I tell you the tale,' said Mr Willet, with mischievous sidelong glance. 'You ain't busy, I suppose?'

'Never too busy for a story,' I assured him, watching him fill his pipe.

Within two minutes, with the fragrant blue smoke wreathing his head, Mr Willet began.

Mr Willet was about seven at the time, he told me. He and his brothers and sisters lived in a cottage on the way to Springbourne, and walked daily to school at Fairacre.

There were four children of school age, and a baby of two at home. The four Willet children carried a rush basket with them, containing a substantial midday meal. A large proportion of it was bread and butter, but a finger of cheese apiece, a hard-boiled egg, or a slice or two of cold fat bacon, added relish and nourishment and old Mrs Willet made sure that fruit in season and a mammoth bottle of buttermilk accompanied her little family daily.

The schoolmaster at that time was Mr Hope. He was a clever, rather sad fellow, who wrote poetry, and occasionally

read it, too, to his pupils. They were not, it seemed, particularly appreciative and, in fact, looked upon their headmaster as 'a bit loopy'. Tragedy touched the Hope family
when their only daughter, much the same age as young Willet,
died at the age of twelve. After that, Mr Hope found con-
solation in drink, and before long was asked to leave the
district.

But while young Willet was in his class, Mr Hope taught
well. He read many stories to them, chiefly the classic tales of
adventure, the myths of Greece and Rome, some stirring
passages from Scott or Henty, and so on. But now and again,
conscious that the younger members of his class were finding
difficulty in following some of the excerpts chosen, he took
down the fairy books of Andrew Lang and read them a tale of
enchantment and fantasy.

It was thus that young Willet – Bob to his family – became
acquainted with the supernatural. He had heard of ogres and
giants, of wizards and witches before, but now they became
much more real to him. He entered, it seemed, into a knowledge of their ways, became conscious of their powers and of
the infringement of such powers upon an ordinary mortal's
life. He began to look at grown-ups with a slightly suspicious
eye. Could it be that among them was a wizard? Or a witch?
Circumstances combined to persuade him that there was such
a one – and very near at hand.

About a quarter of a mile from the Willets' cottage, the road
to Springbourne dropped suddenly downhill into a hollow.
The ground here was marshy, and trees and flowers, foreign to
the surrounding downland, made it seem a strange and slightly
eerie place. Here, at the foot of the hill, was a small ramshackle
cottage known as 'Lucy's'.

Lucy had lived there for many years. At the time of the
story, she was a bent old woman in her eighties, a fearsome
sight with sparse grey locks and one formidable eye-tooth
which had grown so long that Lucy had difficulty in

accommodating it comfortably in her mouth. It protruded over her lower lip and gave the poor old crone a most sinister appearance.

Fairacre was not at all sure about Lucy, and never had been. She and her husband, Seamus Kelly, had been brought from Ireland by Sir Francis Hurley who lived at Springbourne Manor. The Kellys had been brought to his notice one day when he was visiting friends in Ireland. He had mentioned that he was in need of a coachman with a real understanding of horses, and Seamus Kelly was warmly recommended.

The couple were duly installed in rooms above the coach house at Springbourne and gave great satisfaction until one sad day when Seamus was involved in an accident. He had taken the carriage and pair to Caxley Station to meet Sir Francis who was returning from London, when one of the magnificent bays took fright as the train drew in, and bolted. Seamus was thrown, the wheels passed over his back, and his spine was permanently damaged.

Everyone agreed that Sir Francis behaved with the utmost generosity. All medical care was lavished upon the unfortunate man and he spent many months in a convalescent home by the sea, at his employer's expense. Finally, he was given a pension and the small cottage in the hollow for the rest of his days.

Lucy, who had been a somewhat scatter-brained lady's maid, also had to retire from service to look after her crippled husband. Luckily, she was a strong woman, more than able to tend the garden and look after hens and two goats, as well as running the house and acting as nurse.

Seamus's temper, always violent, grew worse as he grew older. Lucy gave as good as she got, her Irish tongue uttering the most blood-curdling oaths, which scandalized the Fairacre worthies whose swearing was limited to a paucity of curses of Anglo-Saxon origin. Lucy, they agreed, was a wild one! To hear the way she went on made you wonder if she was right in the head! I mean, they said, we know she's *Irish*, but even so!

One winter's day, when the mist from the hollow shrouded the little house, Seamus gave a great cry from his bed. Lucy, milking the goat in the nearby shed, set down her pail and ran in. There, his face tipped towards the smoky ceiling, lay her husband, his blue eyes wide open in death.

After that dreadful day, Lucy had lived alone, with only her pets for company. Three cats had lived inside the cottage, and their numerous progeny had been dealt with by Seamus, keeping the numbers within bounds. Many a Fairacre cat had started life at Lucy's, and very fine specimens they were.

Now, with Seamus gone, Lucy did nothing about the kittens, and the number grew to a score in no time. It was true that she still gave one away, now and again, to anyone in need of a cat, and gratefully received the basket of plums or bowl of chitterlings which might be given in return, but the fact remained that there were far too many cats in the house.

Lucy did not seem to worry. She did not seem to worry about anything after Seamus's death. It was as though, with her sparring partner gone, she lacked the will to live. She neglected the house and her person, and Fairacre tongues wagged even more feverishly about Lucy's feckless ways.

'A dirty ol' saucepan on the kitchen table, as large as life, and her eating out of it with a wooden spoon! It's the truth, my dear! I saw it with my own eyes!'

'And it's my belief she hasn't had a good wash since her poor husband went. She don't waste much on soap, I'll be bound!'

'As for that black skirt she wears, it's time it was burnt. She bought it up the Jumble a good eight years ago, that I do know, and she's had it on, day in and day out, ever since!'

So spoke the good wives of the village, and among them was young Mrs Willet. As Lucy's closest neighbour she particularly felt the shame of such a slut in the neighbourhood. Newly married, with a cottage as spruce as endless scrubbing and polishing could make it, Mrs Willet was already spoken of as a paragon of cleanliness. She was to be honoured as such all her days.

Time passed. Lucy continued to exist on the pension granted by Sir Francis, and now administered by his heir, Sir Edmund. Only the minimum repairs were done to the cottage to keep it weatherproof. Lucy neglected the property to such an extent that it was hopeless to do more.

She was seen very little in the village. She now began to mutter to herself and her animals, emerging when dusk began to fall and when she would not be bothered by the sight of any neighbours or casual passers. It was at this stage of Lucy's decline that young Bob Willet became convinced that she was, without any doubt, a witch.

He had said as much to his older brother Sidney as they walked home from school one summer's day. Mr Hope had read them a Russian folk tale with a description of Baba Yaga, the witch, which seemed to young Bob a faithful portrait of Lucy Kelly who lived so perilously near them.

Perhaps he half-hoped for a decisive denial from his brother. If so, he was disappointed.

'Might be,' was Sidney's perfunctory comment. At that moment he was engaged in swishing the heads from a bed of stinging nettles, and was clearly too engrossed to give the matter of Lucy Kelly much attention. Bob did not press the point, but it seemed to him that Sid too considered it a possibility. It was alarming, to say the least of it.

In the days and nights that followed, Bob listened with growing terror to any conversation about their elderly neighbour. He did not like to speak of his fears to Sid, but he did mention it, as casually as he could manage, to another boy of his own age.

Ted Pickett, Bob was relieved to find, took his remarks quite seriously.

'She might be,' said Ted slowly. 'You see, you can't tell, unless you know she flies on a broomstick.'

'Well, she don't do that,' said Bob flatly.

'Or has a black cat.'

'She's plenty of they,' said Bob, feeling a little shaky.

They sat in silence for a little while. Then Ted began again. 'The way to find out is to go down her place when the moon's full. That's when witches fly. I know that for a fact, Bob. I read it in a school book.'

'What time?' asked Bob practically.

'Any time it's real bright,' replied Ted. 'On the night it's true full moon.'

'Come with me?' asked Bob.

'Not likely!' answered his friend. 'I'm real frightened of anything like that,' he added with disarming honesty. A playfellow rushed up at this point, carrying the limp body of a long-dead grass snake. In the pleasurable few minutes following, Ted forgot the witch for ever.

Not so Bob. He could think of nothing else. He was frightened of the idea, but none the less fascinated. In school, when his mind should have been on the intricacies of punctuation or the problems of fractions, it roved instead to Lucy Kelly's cottage. What spells could she weave? Could she really fly? How could he find out if she really were a witch or not? Was Ted's test the true one?

As the month wore on towards the night of the full moon, the boy's tension mounted. He had made up his mind that he would go alone, if the night were fine and bright, to see for himself just what went on at Lucy Kelly's cottage.

Full moon, according to the almanac pinned on the kitchen wall, was on September 17th. The day was cloudless and still. From the hot schoolroom, young Bob could hear the harvesters working away under ideal conditions. Already many of the corn fields bore rows of stooks, the sheaves sagging together with the weight of a fine harvest.

The boy half-hoped that the weather would change, and that nightfall would bring such rain or tempest as would mean a postponement of his plans. But the weather held. At half past eight, he mounted the creaking stairs to the bedroom under the thatch, which he shared with his brother Sidney. Outside, the world was still bathed in golden light, and the swallows dived joyously through the air, snatching the flying insects that hung in the sunshine.

Bob had intended to stay awake until all the household was abed, but fresh air had made him drowsy and he was asleep before he knew it. Luckily, he was roused by the sound of his father and mother going to bed. It was nearly dark, but a great golden moon, low on the horizon, gave promise of a bright moonlit night.

Bob's heart thumped at the thought of the adventure ahead. He was not quite sure what he was going to look for. Certainly a broomstick, and perhaps evidence of actual flight by old Lucy. If she did fly, as Ted Pickett had said, then this was just the sort of night for her jaunting.

He listened to the sounds of the household. Sidney lay on his back, as always, snoring slightly. Bob knew that he had nothing to fear there. Once Sid was asleep, nothing – short of screaming in his ear – would wake him. The two girls, in the tiny slip room at the back of the cottage, slept as heavily as his brother. Only the youngest child roused occasionally. He slept in his parents' room, and if he should wake up, it was reasonable to suppose that his parents would calm him without having to leave the bedroom. Bob reckoned that he could leave the house and return without much trouble.

He heard the clock at St Patrick's, across the fields, strike eleven, and waited a little longer. Midnight was supposed to be the time that witches chose for their flying operations, as Bob well knew. Then he slipped from his warm bed, dressed with shaking fingers, and crept fearfully downstairs.

The creaks and groans from the ancient staircase brought his heart into his mouth, but no one stirred. He made his way through the kitchen and let himself out by the back door.

The night was mysteriously beautiful. It was scented with corn, warm earth and garden flowers. The moonlight was so bright that young Bob could have read by it, had he been of such a mind.

He slipped through a gap in the back hedge, out of sight of his parents' bedroom window, and gained the lane. It was white in the moonlight, and dropped away to the hollow which was his destination.

His boots seemed to make a dreadful amount of noise on the gritty road. A cat shot across his path – one of Lucy's, he guessed – and frightened the wits out of him. By the time he reached Lucy's, he was bathed in sweat.

There was no gate. Bob crept on tip-toe up the overgrown path with one wary eye upon the upstairs window. It was tightly shut, as indeed were all the others downstairs, Bob noticed. It was as quiet as the grave, and in the light of the moon, the little grey cottage seemed to merge into the crepuscular background of the silvery willows and dead grass surrounding it.

At the side of the house was a lean-to shed made of wood, which had once been tarred, but was now weathered to a ghostly grey. If Lucy really had a mount then this would be its stable, Bob decided. He crept quietly towards it, intending to enter, but froze in his tracks long before he gained the lean-to. For there, propped outside the door, as large as life, was a stout broom, or besom, made of birch twigs.

Bob was almost sick with fright. Was it waiting there for Lucy to ride shortly? Or was it simply an innocent garden besom, such as his mother used to sweep their garden path? Who could tell?

He decided to creep right round the cottage, listening for any movement of Lucy within. He passed by the broomstick, almost expecting to see it pulsing with hidden life, and was relieved to gain the shelter of the side wall. Here was crouched a tabby cat, sitting sphinx-like and motionless – only the glittering of its moonstone eyes showing that it was alert and wakeful.

The boy padded along the back of the house where the shabby thatch was so low that it pricked him through his jersey as he grazed by the edge. Stinging nettles and docks made a rank and painful jungle here, and he was glad to reach the side of the house where the hens had pecked a bare patch. A little window looked out on this side and Bob peered within.

As far as he could see, it was Lucy's primitive larder. A dish or two stood on the shelves, and some onions were hanging from a hook. There seemed to be little more, except for cobwebs.

The front of the house was in full moonlight. Two small windows, cracked and grimy, glinted in the moon's brilliance. Through one Bob could see little, for a tattered curtain obscured his view, but he heard the sound of a cat jumping to the floor, as though he had been observed, and the cat was making for cover.

All around him was silence. His heart had ceased to thump so dreadfully, but he still sweated with fright and the nape of his neck felt tight with terror. As he edged along to look into the remaining window, the clock of St Patrick's struck twelve, and the boy froze with renewed horror. Now was the witch's hour!

As the last clear note died away into the warm stillness, Bob looked into Lucy's living room. Moonlight lit the dishevelled apartment, and at first sight it appeared empty. Then suddenly, in the shadow beneath the window, Bob saw a dark figure roll from a low couch or mattress hard against the wall. He shrank back, out of sight, his mouth dry with fear.

Lucy was clad in her daytime black, her grey hair looked wilder than ever in the light of the moon. Her crazy eyes and one long tooth glinted from the shadows as she stumbled, muttering, about the room.

She snatched a black shawl from the tumbled bed and flung it round her shoulders. From a peg on the door she clawed an old black trilby hat of the long-dead Seamus's, and clapped it on her eldritch locks. Then, with purposeful haste, she emerged from her door and made her way towards the lean-to.

But before she reached the broomstick, Bob Willet had fled.

'So you never found out,' I commented, as Mr Willet finished.

'I found out one thing,' said Mr Willet grimly. 'And that was not to go scaring folk at night. My dad heard me coming in and caught me on the stairs. I got a cuff on the ear as made me see stars as well as moon that night, I can tell 'ee.'

He paused for a moment, contemplating that distant night encounter.

'Looking back now, I'd lay a wager the poor ol' gal was making for her privy in the lean-to, but that warn't in my mind at the time, as you can guess.'

He rose stiffly from the gravestone and picked up the bill-hook.

'Well, best get back to work, I s'pose. But it makes you think, don't it? You see, I reckons I was as keen to believe in my witch, as little ol' Joe is to believe in his King of the Sea. It's a sort of *hunger*, if you takes my meaning.'

' "More things in heaven and earth, Horatio",' I quoted.

Mr Willet looked a little startled. 'I wouldn't know about Horatio,' he said reasonably. 'I'm only telling you my opinion.' And he resumed his onslaught on the long grass.

The next day Amy came to tea. She was elegant in a new brown and white dog-tooth check suit which I much admired.

'You could have bought it for yourself,' said Amy. 'It's been in the window of Bakers in Caxley High Street for over a week.'

'I haven't been to Caxley for three weeks,' I said. 'Nor anywhere else, come to think of it.'

Amy pursed her lips impatiently. 'Are you ever going to get yourself out of this rut?' she demanded. 'You were excessively naughty about that Devon job, and all because you didn't want poor little Lucy Colgate to come here.'

'Poor little Lucy Colgate,' I pointed out with some warmth, 'weighs over eleven stone, and is the last person on this earth needing anyone's pity – great, smug, insensitive lump of self-congratulation that she is!'

'Now, now!' warned Amy. 'You see what I mean? You are getting positively *warped* living alone here – a mass of neuroses – coveting my suit, and now picking poor Lucy to bits.'

'Let's have some tea,' I said. 'It might sweeten me.'

She followed me into the kitchen, and watched me stack a tray.

'My cousin tells me,' she said, 'that there is an excellent post going at a comprehensive school in her town. I think she said there are four thousand pupils and two swimming pools.'

'Good luck to them!' I said. 'But I prefer thirty-six pupils and two buckets of drinking water. And who knows? I may live long enough in Fairacre to see water laid on to the school! No, Amy, "I won't be druv!"'

Later, we walked across to our Harvest Festival. It was a perfect evening of mellow September sunshine. Through the west window, the golden sun lit the nave and burnished the sheaves of corn and all our offerings of fruit and flower.

Mrs Pratt was bumbling happily at the organ, improvising a voluntary until such time as the vicar and choir entered. As this was an important festal day in Fairacre, and the church was suitably crammed, there would be a procession from the west door down the nave.

Suddenly there was a scuffling noise behind us, the west doors were thrown open, and the sunlight streamed in. Bathed in its golden light the choir and the vicar slowly made their way eastward while we scrambled to our feet.

> Come, ye thankful people, come!
> Raise the song of harvest home!

we sang fortissimo.

Mrs Pringle, foremost among the contraltos, swayed past me, lowing powerfully. Mr Willet was not far behind, holding his own among the basses. Ahead, several of my pupils, unnaturally clean and holy, raised their voices in song.

It was good, I thought suddenly, to be taking part in something which had happened in this church for many years, without fail, an act of thanksgiving for the harvest which surrounded this ancient building on every side. Just so did Sally Gray, Fred Hurst, poor Job the Fairacre ghost, Mrs Next-Door and a host of others who now lay so quietly outside these walls, rejoice together, as we did, for mercies received. I looked about me. Amy, friend of many years, stood by my side. In front of me I could see Elsie Blundell and her husband. Two pews ahead was Isobel Annett with Malcolm, my godchild; sitting with them was dear Miss Clare. My eye roamed to the chancel where the choir was now in place and still singing lustily under the attentive eye of George Annett, their choir-master. Mr Willet's honest face was red with his exertions, and I remembered, with affection, the story of his midnight adventure.

How right he was, I thought! We do all need a story, as he said. There is a hunger in us which needs to be assuaged. With what avidity I have listened to my neighbours' accounts of tales of long ago, and with what unfailing curiosity I observe the happenings of today!

Here, around me, are all the folk of Fairacre, both the quick and the dead. The story of the village goes back a long, long time; and it still goes on. Every hour that we live, the story unfolds, now tragic, now comical, but always and everlastingly absorbing.

Can you wonder that we are never dull in Fairacre?

The Fairacre Festival

For Anne,
with love from her godmother

On the first night of October a mighty wind arose and smote the countryside around Fairacre. The violence of that wild night took almost all by surprise. Only the exceptionally weatherwise, such as Mr Willet, had any inkling of the devastation which lay in store, and even they admitted, as they surveyed the wreckage the next morning, that it was 'a durn sight worse'n they'd thought it would be'.

We had enjoyed a week of mellow sunshine at the end of September. Butterflies clung decoratively to the Michaelmas daisies, wasps lurched drunkenly from ripe pears to ripe plums, and the schoolchildren at Fairacre School were more comfortable in their cotton frocks and thin shirts than they had been on many other occasions during a changeable summer.

Harvest Festival was celebrated on the last day of September and, as usual, we helped to deck the ancient church of St Patrick's with 'all things bright and beautiful'. Coral-berried bryony from the school hedge wreathed the font. At the foot lay mounds of apples, pears and marrows. Carrots, parsnips and onions lined the ledges, and two fine sheaves of corn gleamed and rustled in their time-honoured place, one on each side of the chancel steps. The ladies of the parish had put their natural talents, and the expertise learnt at the local floral society, into the handsome flower arrangements, and it was generally maintained by the congregation that the church had never looked so magnificent.

Monday morning dawned as benignly as ever. I watched the

children, summer-clad and relaxed, as they drank their morning milk, and congratulated myself on postponing the lighting of the two tortoise stoves. Far too often, in the autumn term, I have asked my curmudgeonly school cleaner, Mrs Pringle, to light these monsters, only to experience a spell of humid weather in which we have all sweltered in the classrooms. Mrs Pringle never lets me forget these unfortunate errors.

'Remember last year?' she demands belligerently, massive jaw out-thrust. 'You would have it. Said the children was cold, and up I come with paper, with sticks, with matches, although my leg was not what it should be –'

'But it *was* cold,' I begin, but am swept aside.

'I fetches the coal, fetches the coke, goes down on me hands and knees for a full quarter of an hour to get the stoves to draw – and what happens?'

I don't bother to answer. This, I know from experience, is a rhetorical question. Sometimes I think what a wonderful actress the stage has lost in Mrs Pringle. Her looks are definitely a

drawback, but she has a fine sense of drama and puts plenty of punch into her lines.

'We gets a hot spell. All my work's for nothing, and the coke's got to come out of us ratepayers' pockets. What's more, the children's pores are left hanging open for all the germs to get in as soon as they goes out into the cold playground!'

This year, I told myself, on that fair Monday morning, I had behaved in an exemplary manner. Tomorrow would be October the second, and after that the lighting of the stoves must surely be considered acceptable by my task mistress.

But, by midday, I was beginning to have doubts. The sun went in, the temperature dropped sharply, and the children began to rub their goose-pimpled arms. By the time they ran home in the afternoon, a cold wind had sprung up, snatching the yellow leaves from the plum tree in my garden and sending me scuttling to light my sitting-room fire.

As darkness fell, the force of the wind increased. It roared in the elm trees towering above the school. It screamed round the school house, spattering leaves against the window and sending the dustbin lid clanging across the garden. The little house shuddered at its onslaught. Safe by the leaping fire, with a pile of exercise books to mark and the cat asleep by my feet, I gave the elements scant attention.

But later, in bed, I became anxious. Never before had I heard the wind quite so violent in Fairacre. I remembered the doleful tales about elm trees which Mr Willet never tired of telling me. If one of those hefty branches fell across my roof it could be pretty damaging. And what about the roof tiles? It seemed incredible that anything could withstand the fury of the wind tonight. Strange creaks and groans seemed to come from the loft above me and an ill-fitting window let in a piercing draught accompanied by an ear-splitting whistle.

I pulled the bedclothes up round my ears, thanked heaven that I was a schoolteacher and not a sailor, and slept amidst the uproar.

*

Throughout the night the wind wreaked destruction. In the streets of Caxley it wrenched slates from roofs and toppled a dozen chimney-pots into the gutters. A flying tile broke the plate-glass window of Howard's Restaurant in the market square, and a poor unfortunate man, cycling head down against the onslaught on his way to night shift, was blown from the towpath into the cold waters of the Cax, and there drowned.

Just outside Caxley station a telegraph pole fell across the line, throwing all into confusion, and on the road to Beech Green a tree had crashed, tearing down the telephone wires in its fall. But Caxley, tucked in its hollow, came off comparatively lightly. It was the windswept villages on the downs which bore the full brunt of the wind's savagery and it was Fairacre which suffered the most shattering blow.

On a little knoll of high ground between the vicarage and St Patrick's a cluster of ancient elms stands, cradling a rookery in the topmost boughs. We, in Fairacre, admire the way that these lovely old trees form a background to the church. Rosy-purple in spring as the buds swell, providing dense shade in full summer, turning to clear gold in the autumn and spreading a black lacy tracery against the winter skies, they are a constant pleasure to the eye.

But Mr Willet has never been one of their admirers.

'One of these days,' he has said, on many occasions, 'them dratted elms is going to cause trouble. Got no proper root growth, has elms. All spread out too near the surface for my liking. A good wind up top and over they goes.' And he was to be proved right.

About two o'clock the fury of the wind was at its height. Its screaming woke me. The loose window shuddered and thudded, and the roaring outside was terrifying. It must have been this particular gust which caught the tallest of the elms nearest the church and sent it toppling. The topmost branches swept St Patrick's stubby spire, and bent the proud weather-cock until it drooped head-down from its twisted stay. The heavy branches came to rest across the nave, scattering tiles and damaging the roof for which the church is famed. The massive trunk lay athwart the graveyard and the old roots, torn from the turf, writhed above a huge gaping hole.

I did not hear the crash; nor do I think anyone else did. The noise was so continuous that it was impossible to pick out any particular incident. But the vicar said later that he awoke at that time and was conscious of some extraordinary commotion at the heart of the storm, and confessed frankly that he had felt frightened.

When light returned, the damage was discovered, and in no time at all a bevy of villagers came to survey the wreckage. Mr Willet was first on the scene, and with commendable magnanimity forebore to say: 'I told you so!' It was he who broke the news to Mr Partridge, the vicar, who was shaving when the bell of the back door rang.

'Bad news, sir,' Mr Willet shouted up to the frothy face which appeared at the bathroom window.

'The greenhouse?' queried the vicar, holding the window against the wind.

'No, sir. The church. Tree across it, sir.'

'Oh, my dear Willet!' cried the vicar, his face puckering in distress. 'What a terrible thing! I will be with you directly.'

The window slammed, and within five minutes the vicar and his wife joined Mr Willet at the scene of the disaster. Several workmen, on their way to their labours, had propped their bicycles against the flint churchyard wall, and stood shaking their heads at the confusion.

'We must get help from Caxley,' said Mrs Partridge decisively. 'There's no one in Fairacre with the equipment to shift that enormous thing.'

'We must indeed, my dear,' agreed the vicar distractedly. There were tears in his blue eyes as he paced from one position to another assessing the appalling damage to his beloved St Patrick's. 'I suppose a crane or some such piece of machinery will be necessary, Willet? I can't bear to think of the wreckage we shall discover when the tree is lifted. I must go inside at once and make sure that everything is safe.'

'I'll come inside with you,' said Mr Willet. 'You wants to watch out that none of them timbers is busted.'

They entered the church while more villagers arrived to inspect the night's work. Here was drama in plenty! The schoolchildren were pleasurably excited by it all, and to a certain extent so were their elders, but there was in addition a shocked solemnity in the face of this tragedy, and thin-lipped Mrs Fowler from Tyler's Row put into words the unspoken thoughts of all when she asked of the villagers at large:

'And who's going to pay for this lot, may I ask?'

It was a question which was to perplex Fairacre for many a long month.

Meanwhile, the work of clearing up the mess began. It was impossible to telephone to Caxley as the Post Office men were busy all the morning repairing the line at Beech Green, but Mr Mawne, churchwarden and member of the Parochial Church Council, set off for Caxley at the vicar's behest.

Henry Mawne is a comparative newcomer to Fairacre, a retired schoolmaster and a keen ornithologist. He and his wife take their fair share of responsibilities in village matters and the vicar, in particular, relishes the friendship and support of this quiet man. His competent handling of church accounts is a source of great comfort to the vicar whose grasp of financial details is hopelessly vague. Mrs Partridge confided once to me that her devout and erudite husband is under the impression that ten pennies make a shilling, and that this fundamental misapprehension is at the root of his difficulties. Certainly parochial affairs have been much more businesslike under Henry Mawne's administration.

As Mr Mawne expected, the plant hire firm had most of its

equipment spread about the country that morning, but a crane was promised for the afternoon and two men set off at once from Caxley to start cutting away branches and to clear the site for the rescue operation. He returned to find the vicar in conversation with his Bishop at the county town, the telephone lines in that direction having miraculously escaped damage. He had already been in touch with the Rural Dean, he told Henry Mawne, when he replaced the receiver, and the diocesan architect would be along as soon as possible to look at the damage.

'But the best news of all, my dear Henry,' cried the vicar, 'is from Jock Graham, who arrived just after you had gone, to say that he will act as our architect without any payment. Isn't that a magnificent gesture?'

'It is indeed,' agreed Mr Mawne. He did not care for this elderly Scot, recently retired, but realized how much this generous offer would mean to the parish.

'You see,' went on the vicar. 'I gather that all the expenses will have to be found by Fairacre. The diocesan people have just made it clear that there can be no money forthcoming from them. It's a parish responsibility. I suppose we must expect a bill of a hundred pounds or so?'

'I should prefer to wait until the diocesan architect has had his look,' said Mr Mawne cautiously, 'but from what I saw this morning, I should say we'd be lucky to get away with anything less than two thousand.'

'*Two thousand?*' quavered the vicar. Horror and stupefaction showed in his face. 'It's impossible, Henry!'

Henry Mawne rose from his seat and patted the vicar's shoulder kindly. 'Cheer up, Gerald,' he said. 'I'm probably hopelessly wrong, but I don't want you to get a shock later on. I think you'll find the bill is going to be a great deal more than a few hundred pounds, that's all.'

'But we can't pay it,' protested the vicar helplessly. 'Fairacre can't possibly raise anything more than a hundred at the outside!'

'I'm aware of that,' said his friend.

'And even that amount,' went on the vicar despairingly, 'means a succession of whist drives, fêtes, jumble sales, coffee mornings and all those terrible, terrible affairs. You realize that, Henry?'

'Only too well, Gerald,' replied Henry Mawne, doing his best to suppress a shudder.

The vicar rose from his chair and began to pace distractedly round his desk, his hands clasped behind his back and his brow furrowed. Mr Mawne watched him sympathetically from the doorway. It seemed hard to leave his stricken friend in his present distress, but there was much to be done.

Gerald Partridge stopped suddenly and faced him.

'It is a challenge, Henry! This is something sent by Providence to test us, to strengthen our faith. We must, and shall, restore St Patrick's!'

'That's the way to take it,' agreed Mr Mawne, touched by this brave display of resolution. Closing the study door gently behind him, he returned home through the wind.

When school dinner was over, I made my way to the church to see the extent of the damage. The men were busy clearing the worst of the mess from the churchyard, and I went inside by the west door.

Several people had volunteered to tidy up. Mr and Mrs Willet were there, the two sisters, Margaret and Mary Waters, and various other women.

'Got my washing on the line and come straight up,' said one.

'Had to find my poor hens first,' said another. 'The hen house blew clean off their backs, and they was everywhere from the fir tree to the coal-hole.'

Tales of the night's wrecking flew back and forth as they plied brooms and dustpans.

'The top half of Mr Roberts's hay stack went whirling by our roof.'

'Our Nelly lost three tea towels off the line. And the cat! He *would* go out and it's her belief he's been blown out of the parish.'

Somehow, I suspected, listening to these exchanges, the damages grew at each recital. We enjoy a bit of excitement in Fairacre, and the drama of this wild night would certainly go down, suitably embellished, in local history.

There was a great deal of plaster on the floor of the nave, and the pews were white with dust. Mr Willet was collecting the rubble in a wheelbarrow in the aisle. A dark patch gaped above, in the beautiful hammer-beam roof, but no daylight showed through. Hopes were running high that the damage was only superficial, but more would be known when the surveyor had inspected it.

The pulpit was badly scratched and one of the chandeliers had bounced from its hook, at the time of impact, and lay shattered on the floor.

'No loss!' remarked Mrs Mawne to me in an aside audible

to all. 'Hideous Victoriana! Pity the rest didn't come down too!'

Afternoon school was a somewhat distracted affair. The children are always excitable in windy weather, and this fascinating disaster added to their general fidgetiness. Hoping to channel their feelings into some positive and useful work – as exhorted to do by all good educationists – I set them to write an essay on the night's storm.

'And you can illustrate it too,' I added, hoping for a prolonged period of peace in the classroom.

'With crayons?'

'Yes, with crayons.'

'Won't be much good. 'Twas all dark. Shan't want no colours.'

'Then you can simply use your lead pencil,' I retorted loftily. Disgruntled muttering from the malcontent's desk I ignored pointedly.

An unusual quietness fell upon the room, broken only by laboured breathing as the pangs of composition gripped them, and the stutter of crayons depicting rain. I wandered to the window and gazed out. A drift of dead leaves rustled against the foot of the school wall, and a mat of ivy flapped loosely above it, wrenched from its anchorage by the gale.

The vicarage garden seemed bare of leaves, and through the gaps in the denuded shrubbery I could see several of the helpers making their way home. This, I told myself, certainly brings people together – nothing like a common foe to unite a community.

At that moment, young Tom in the front row raised his hand. His parents are fiercely evangelical, and he is uncomfortably well behaved and a trifle smug.

'How do you spell "Wrath-of-God"?' he inquired earnestly.

'How do you intend to use the phrase?' I asked guardedly.

He turned his attention to the paper before him and read slowly. ' "Our chapel was not hit in the night, but the church

232

was. My mum said it was—"' He paused and looked up hopefully.

I spelt out the desired phrase. My sympathy went out to those working for Christian unity, and I made a mental note to have a lesson on 'loving thy neighbour as thyself', before the end of the week.

It looked as though Fairacre might profit from it.

2

Before Monday came round again, much had happened in the village.

In the first place, Fairacre had put itself to rights as best it could. Broken branches were sawn up into neat logs and stacked inside wood-sheds. Shrubs and standard roses were lashed to new stakes. Slates and tiles were hung again, thatch patched and hen-house roofs replaced and weighted with sizeable flint stones, in case of future gales.

Nelly Potter's cat returned, none the worse for a night out. Mr Roberts, the farmer, retrieved some of his scattered hay, and Mrs Pringle, discovering a child's apron blowing on the hedge, recognized it as one of little Vanessa Emery's and returned it graciously to the child's scatter-brained mother.

'Nearly tore to shreds it was by the time the wind had done with it,' said Mrs Pringle to me, before school one morning, 'but I don't suppose it'll ever see needle and thread in that house. Proper muddler that woman is! Half-past nine when I called in, and she still in her dressing-gown!' Mrs Pringle drew an outraged breath at the very thought, and picked up a cinder which was marring the glossy jet of the stove's surround.

'Still, I will say,' she conceded, as she straightened up with an ominous creaking of whalebone stays, 'that she give me a very nice smile and thanked me for my trouble.'

'Good,' I said absently, rummaging in my drawer for a paperclip.

'*Which*,' boomed Mrs Pringle pointedly, 'is a lot more than some people do!'

And with a pronounced limp she made her way to the lobby.

Mr Willet had cleared up the mess in the school playground, and had continued the good work, in his capacity of church sexton, in the graveyard next door. Luckily, the ancient headstones had escaped injury, for the tree which caused most of the trouble had lodged against the roof of the church, and had been lifted clear by the crane without much difficulty.

The damage to the fabric of the church was Fairacre's most serious problem. Providentially, it was less than had been feared at first. The stout ancient roof beams had stood the blow well, and only three or four would need to be replaced. But much retiling needed to be done to the spire and the nave, and the belfry wanted a stonemason's attention.

'And can you give us any idea of the expense?' asked the vicar anxiously as he, Mr Mawne and Jock Graham accompanied the diocesan architect and his young assistant on the tour of inspection.

The architect peered over his half-glasses and looked solemn.

'Mr Graham will go into figures of course, but I should say, at a rough estimate –'

'A *very* rough estimate,' chimed in the assistant, speaking as one who has often been caught out and hoped to miss the unpleasant experience this time.

'As a *very rough* estimate,' agreed the architect, looking coldly at his colleague, 'somewhere in the region –'

'Only *in the region*,' interjected the assistant sternly.

'Of about one thousand eight hundred pounds to two thousand.'

'*About*, of course, *just about*,' echoed his companion. 'One can never be sure what one will find once the work is in hand, as I am sure Mr Graham will agree. One doesn't want to be too hasty in suggesting a figure.'

'So I noticed,' observed Mr Mawne drily.

His face wore a small satisfied smile. This was the sum he had suggested in the first place to his friend, the vicar, and it was some comfort in this bleak hour to know that he was not far out in his estimation.

The vicar's rosy face, however, showed no sign of pleasure, simply stupefaction and distress. He was quite beyond speech.

'We'll go back and report our findings,' said the architect kindly, tucking his half-glasses into a splendid gold-tooled case. 'And, if Mr Graham wishes, I'll send you the names of some reputable contractors who specialize in church repairs who will, of course, give you a detailed estimate when they have had a look at your little bit of trouble here.'

The vicar opened his mouth as though stung into speech, thought better of it, and said nothing. They crossed the church-yard to the black Humber at the gate.

'I shouldn't worry too much, my dear sir,' said the architect with misplaced heartiness. 'Could have been much worse, you know. Think of Coventry Cathedral. Now there *was* some damage!'

The car drove off, watched by Mr Mawne, Mr Graham and their stricken friend. As it rounded the bend to the village street, the vicar found his voice.

'I don't like to seem uncharitable, but I hope that I may never see that man again! "Our little bit of trouble" indeed!'

'Take no heed of his havering,' rumbled Jock Graham.

The vicar's lips quivered suddenly. 'But what are we to do? What are we to do?'

Henry Mawne rose to the occasion. 'We will call an emergency meeting of the Parochial Church Council and put on our thinking caps,' he replied firmly. Together they shepherded Gerald Partridge to the haven of his vicarage, and a much-needed cup of coffee.

The Parochial Church Council, all twelve of us, turned up in full force on Friday evening. We met in the vicarage dining-room which was still faintly redolent of the curried lamb and baked apples on which Mr and Mrs Partridge had recently dined.

There were present the vicar, in the chair, Mr Mawne and his wife, Mr Roberts, the other churchwarden and our local farmer, Mr Graham as honorary architect, Mr Willet and myself, all from the village. Mr Basil Bradley and Major Gunning represented Springbourne, which is also in the living of Fairacre's vicar, along with three rather prosperous younger men, who commute daily to the City, thus making up our full complement.

Basil Bradley produces a novel each year and is much thought of in the district. He is called upon to open bazaars and fêtes, and is much in demand as a speaker at various functions, twice rising to the dizzy heights of chief speaker at local Women's Institute group meetings. Since the death of his formidable mother, who guarded his goings-out and comings-in zealously, he has lived alone in a pretty cottage enjoying his freedom. He is a remarkably handsome man, with the ashen fair hair which slips imperceptibly over the years into silver, and the gentle manners born of many years of willing servitude to his tyrant. Men dislike him. Women dote on him, and do their best to get him married. Somehow, I do not think that they will ever be successful.

Major Gunning is as martial as his name, and has a garden full of well-disciplined plants as upright as himself. His paths are straight. His standard roses line them like a guard of honour. A row of poplars stands sentinel upon his skyline. No daisies spangle Major Gunning's lawns, no groundsel mars the beds. And should any pink or poppy droop its pretty head out of its appointed place, then summary execution must be expected.

It was he who spoke first after the vicar had explained the dilemma.

'Open an Appeal Fund. Stick up a good bold board outside the Church, and send notices to every man-jack in the parish.'

'Humph!' snorted Mrs Mawne beside him. 'That won't bring in much!'

'And have you any suggestions?' asked Major Gunning, bristling.

'Plenty,' snapped Mrs Mawne, slapping her gloves down on the table challengingly. 'First of all –'

'Address the chair,' put in Mr Mawne.

His wife twitched round exasperatedly and faced the vicar. 'Mr Chairman, I think determined and regular money-raising efforts should be started at once. A weekly whist drive, a weekly dance, a weekly raffle, a weekly coffee morning –'

'But, my dear Mrs Mawne,' pleaded the vicar, 'where is the money to come from?'

'I'm telling you. From all these activities!'

Basil Bradley took upon himself the thankless task of explanation. 'But where, I think our Chairman means, will *the people* get the money? Their wages will remain at the same level. They can't afford to go to so many weekly functions.'

'Thank you,' said the vicar simply. 'That is the position exactly. We must try to think of attracting outside help. The parish itself has no riches.'

A gloomy silence fell while we all pondered this sad fact.

'D'you mean that there is no help at all from some body or other?' demanded Mr Roberts at length. 'You know – Ecclesiastical Commissioners or the Diocese, or Friends of Friendless Churches? Something o' that?'

'St Patrick's isn't a *friendless* church,' said the vicar defensively. 'It's a very much-loved church.'

'Yes, indeed. Yes, indeed,' agreed Mr Willet warmly.

'But I'm afraid we have only ourselves to rely on,' went on the vicar. 'The Bishop was deeply sympathetic, but made it quite plain that the parish is solely responsible for these repairs.'

'I think Mrs Mawne's suggestions are on the right lines,' I volunteered. 'If all the village organizations make a particular effort it means that we shall raise quite a decent part of the whole by our own exertions.'

'We could map out a programme,' said Mr Roberts. 'What about a traction engine rally in my big meadow?'

'And a folk-dancing display by the village school?' said Mrs Mawne. I could have made a tart retort, but forbore.

'And a bumper Fur and Feather Whist Drive this autumn?' said Mr Willet.

'I should be very pleased to open my garden next summer,' offered Basil Bradley. 'And provide tea. I've just mastered Chelsea buns.'

'How very clever!' cried Mrs Mawne turning towards him. 'Now they are things which I simply *cannot* manage. Cream horns, almond slices, Victoria sandwiches, gingerbread – I flatter myself I can cope with anything like that, but yeast cookery is my Waterloo. How much sugar do you put in with your yeast?'

The chairman, seeing his meeting dissolve, as is so often the case in village affairs, banged loudly on the table.

'Please, please, ladies and gentlemen! Miss Read and Mrs Mawne have both made the suggestion that we see how much can be raised by superhuman efforts in the village by traditional methods. Can anyone add to this idea?'

A rumbling noise from under Mr Willet's tobacco stained moustache gave warning of wise words to follow. Little did we think, as we waited, that we were witnessing the birth of a momentous brainchild.

'What's wrong with having all these things – or most of 'em, say – in one week next summer? A festival, like. We hears a lot about the Edinburgh Festival and all their goings-on up there. And there's that chap, Britten, at the Aldwych –'

'Aldeburgh,' put in Basil Bradley.

'Same thing,' said Mr Willet airily. 'He has a festival by the

seaside. Mr Annett's been. He said 'twas a real slap-up affair. Well, what I'm getting at is this. Why can't we have a Fairacre Festival?'

We all gazed at Mr Willet with respect.

'It's a wonderful idea, Willet,' said the vicar. 'Quite wonderful! But do you think people would come?'

'Why not?' demanded Mrs Mawne. 'If they go to Edinburgh, to that perishing cold climate, not to mention the reeking smoke which they admit themselves, then why on earth shouldn't they come here?'

'Perhaps not quite in the same numbers,' said Basil Bradley. 'After all, Edinburgh has wonderful concerts and ballets and what-have-you – but I'm sure we could have a Fairacre Festival which would be successful on a more modest scale.'

'Damn good idea,' announced Mr Roberts. 'One great glorious burst of fête, jumble sale, concert, whist-drive, bingo, dancing and everything else. If we advertise it well, the money will come rolling in.'

'We might have *Son et Lumière*,' said Major Gunning, 'with St Patrick's as the background. Tell the parish story, you know.'

'Not all of it,' said Mr Willet cautiously. 'There's some things best kept quiet. Take that affair of Ted Grimble's grand-dad now –'

'Yes, well –' the vicar broke in hastily. 'Perhaps we are getting away from the point. Could we have a show of hands for Mr Willet's excellent proposal?'

We were all agreed. It was decided to meet again to plan not only the Fairacre Festival for next summer, but also to arrange other money-making efforts, starting immediately.

It was while we were congratulating ourselves, and Mr Willet in particular, on our cleverness, that Henry Mawne spoke up.

'Before we go, I think we should be realistic about these ideas. They will raise a few hundred, I feel sure, and we might raise a few more by donations. But I don't think we can hope to raise even half by these methods.'

'But what else can we do?' pleaded the vicar.

Mr Mawne screwed his propelling pencil slowly, making the lead emerge further and further. He studied it intently as he spoke.

'You said earlier that the parish had no riches. It's not quite true. I hardly like to suggest this but I'm going to. We have, as you all know, locked in the bank and used only at the great church festivals, a valuable old chalice of solid silver and impeccable workmanship. One recently fetched over two thousand pounds. It was not as fine as ours.'

We gazed at Henry Mawne in silence. We were all, I think, a little shocked by his suggestion. To tell the truth, I had not realized the value of the chalice, and had certainly forgotten its existence whilst we had been debating ways and means. The vicar looked horrified and Mrs Mawne surveyed her husband with as much disgust as she would have displayed had he suggested slaughtering her dachshund for lunch.

'Impossible!' she exclaimed.

'Unthinkable!' cried Major Gunning.

'That's not ours to give away,' observed Mr Willet austerely. ''Twas given to the church to celebrate Queen Anne's reign. Some relation of old Miss Parr's, so they told us at school, gave it over two hundred and fifty years ago. It belongs to the parish.'

The vicar found his voice. 'Willet is quite right, Henry. The chalice is beyond price, and is in any case only ours on trust. It belongs to St Patrick's.'

'So did its roof,' said Henry Mawne. 'I know the idea is distasteful, but there you are. Is it right to keep such a valuable object locked away, while rain comes through the roof and the church deteriorates? St Patrick's also belongs to the parish. Which is of more use?'

Surprisingly, it was Basil Bradley who came to Henry Mawne's support.

'It has been done before. My uncle's church in Cumberland sold a most beautiful silver paten some years ago. It went to a new church somewhere in Massachusetts where it is very much prized, I can assure you.'

'I daresay,' replied the vicar, a shade frostily. 'But I cannot entertain the thought of selling our own silver.'

'I'm only suggesting,' said Basil Bradley steadily, 'that it may be some comfort to know that if the appeal and the Festival do not raise the money then at least we have the chalice behind us, as it were.'

'Quite wrong!' said Mrs Mawne forcefully, jamming on her gloves. 'The chalice must remain here for future generations.'

'Absolutely!' growled Major Gunning.

'Let's hope it won't come to that,' said Mr Roberts. 'We'll do our best to get the cash in every other way possible.'

And on that note, the meeting ended.

Later that night, the vicar lay sleepless, watching the moonlight wavering upon the ceiling above his head. Somewhere, far away, a stoat yelped shrilly. The leaves of the Virginia creeper rustled by the open window, and near at hand his big silver watch ticked companionably from the bedside table.

All was as usual in the peaceful room, but still sleep evaded him.

His thoughts turned again and again to Henry's appalling suggestion. How could he have conceived such an idea? It amounted almost to betrayal. The whole idea was monstrous. He simply could not think what Henry meant by putting forward such an outrageous scheme. It was bad enough to have had such thoughts. To put them into words made the matter even worse! The poor vicar tossed restlessly, and remembered the beauty of the ancient chalice with piercing clarity.

How heavy and smooth it was to handle! How comforting

was the sturdy stem, the beautiful moulded base! How warm and glowing the red wine looked in its polished depths! To the vicar, and to his flock, Queen Anne's chalice, as it was known, was a precious part of the Christmas and Easter communion service. And had been, the vicar reminded himself, for generation upon generation of Fairacre folk. Lips, dusty-dead two hundred years and more, had sipped the wine from this cup. Squire and servant, man and maid, the virtuous and the villainous had knelt beside each other awaiting pardon and peace from the chalice.

And they would do so still, the vicar told himself resolutely. They would do so still!

He turned over his pillow, thumped it soundly as though he trounced the Devil himself, and was asleep in three minutes.

3

The autumn was wet, windy and unseasonably warm. The children squelched into school from muddy lanes and the puddle-filled playground, incurring the wrath of Mrs Pringle daily.

Scaffolding was beginning to shroud the stumpy spire of St Patrick's and the damaged area of the nave, and the Appeal Fund board made a new feature in the village. So far the hand of the clock on the board stood only at one hundred and twenty-three pounds, but as we all pointed out to each other, it was a wonderful beginning.

The weathervane had been removed and the cock awaited regilding. On the day it was brought down to ground level Mr Willet put his head round the school door.

'If you've got a minute to spare,' he said deferentially, 'you might like a close look at the 'ol weathercock. He's come to roost in the churchyard, afore he gets a new lick of paint.'

The children began clamouring at once, only too glad to leave their English exercises.

'We'll come straight away,' I told Mr Willet, rising in readiness to quell the stampede to the door. When we had attained some semblance of order we made our way decorously to the churchyard. Near the south door, propped against a convenient flat tombstone, stood St Patrick's weathercock. It was surprisingly large with an expression of great ferocity.

'It's bigger'n our baby,' breathed Joseph Coggs with awe, stroking its cold head with a grimy hand.

'Weighs a fair bit, too,' said one of the workmen. 'Plenty of good metal in him.'

The children surveyed it admiringly and a few of them seated themselves on the damp tombstone beside it.

'Get up! Don't sit there!' I said a trifle sharply, more concerned with internal chills than irreverence, I must confess.

'Old Tom wouldn't mind, miss,' said Mr Willet peaceably. 'A loving sort of man by all accounts, specially to children – or so his stone do say.'

I stood rebuked in the face of such tolerance. A few yellow leaves fluttered down upon the sodden grass, and a wren skittered up and down the hawthorn hedge by the lych gate. Sunshine, so seldom seen in the last few drenching weeks, flooded the scene with amber light.

'We'll go for a walk before going back to school,' I announced, amidst general rejoicing. Thanks were given to Mr Willet and the workmen, affectionate pats to the weathercock, and then we set off to profit from sweet country air and exercise, in the forlorn hope that they would sharpen our wits for the work awaiting us in the schoolroom.

As Christmas approached, the money-raising activities increased in the village. The Fur and Feather Whist Drive was well attended, and the usual display of turkeys, ducks, hens, pheasants and hares adorned the platform in the village hall. Almost thirty pounds was raised by this mammoth effort, and only the collapse of the trestle table bearing the coffee cups marred the success of the evening.

'And it's my belief,' Mrs Pringle told me the next morning, 'that Mrs Emery's ugly great dog pushed the legs along. No business to let an animal into the hall at all. Nothing but a bag of fleas and smelling worse than Mr Roberts's pigs! As I told her straight.'

Mrs Pringle is a great one for 'telling people straight' and makes much trouble in doing so. Sometimes I feel like quoting to her a prayer learned in childhood which says: 'Let me not mistake bluntness for frankness,' but I doubt if such a frail dart would penetrate my school cleaner's rhinoceros' hide. And as she herself is so fond of saying: 'You can't teach an old dog new tricks.' I have learnt to leave well alone whenever possible, for Mrs Pringle makes a formidable foe, and I have to meet her daily.

We spent the latter weeks of the term preparing a school play, in which every child from the smallest five-year-old to

Ernest, a hefty eleven-year-old, had a part. Miss Clare, who once taught the infants' class at Fairacre, emerged from her retirement at Beech Green to help to dress the children and to play the accompaniment to their songs. The parents packed the school to overflowing, and apart from such expected crises as a measles suspect, two sore throats, a burst knicker elastic and a hitch in the curtain-pulling equipment, it all went splendidly. Two performances of our masterpiece netted ten pounds for the fund, and we were well content.

'A Gigantic Christmas Bazaar' widely advertised by posters on barns, trees and gateposts, as well as a notice in the *Caxley Chronicle*, was perhaps a trifle larger than the usual Christmas Bazaar which Fairacre organizes, and we all bought knitted tea-cosies and gingham aprons for each other's Christmas presents, and little boxes of homemade fudge which we fully intended to give away too, but ate ourselves as it was quite irresistible and, as we told ourselves, might not keep. The Appeal Fund was larger by twenty-six pounds at the end of the afternoon.

Nevertheless, the hand moved very slowly towards the target of two thousand pounds. After morning service on Christmas Day, a little knot of us stood outside the church, in the bleak east wind, exchanging Christmas greetings and discussing the progress of the Appeal. The hand pointed to a little under four hundred pounds, and with the best will in the world it was hard to be very optimistic.

'I suppose it's not too bad for a beginning,' said Miss Margaret Waters to her sister Mary. 'After all, it's only a few weeks since it happened.'

'I'd like to see it nearer the thousand,' said Mr Willet, standing next to her. 'We've had in the best part of the donations, from all accounts. Once we gets into the New Year, somehow it won't seem so urgent. People soon forgets, you know.'

Mrs Pringle, emerging after her stentorian boomings in the choir, heard the last part of Mr Willet's remarks.

' "Forgets" is the word, Mr Willet. Why, in the old days, this money would've been found in next to no time. The gentry – who *was* gentry then, let me say – would have put their hands in their pockets and settled it at once.'

'There ain't the money about,' agreed Mr Willet. 'At least, not to the same extent. It's spread over a few more, that's all, and them as earns it sticks to it. You can't blame the gentry. The tax man gets it off of them, and there's nothing left for things like the church spire.'

We gazed dolefully aloft at the roof, now bristling with scaffolding. No bells had rung a Christmas peal this year, because of the damage in the belfry. St Patrick's wore a forlorn and battered air. Without its golden weathercock the little spire looked unusually truncated.

'Ah well!' said Mr Willet, turning up his coat collar against the wind, 'mustn't lose heart, you know, specially on Christmas Day! Maybe the New Year will bring us all a bit of luck. And there's always the Festival to look forward to!'

'Yes, indeed,' said Mary Waters, snatching at this comfort. 'There's always the Festival!'

We set off on our several ways determined to be of good cheer, despite the nagging little doubts which pierced our defences as keenly as the bleak east wind about us.

The Christmas holidays slipped away with their usual speed and the spring term began in a flurry of snow. The children, of course, greeted it with rapture. Mrs Pringle looked upon it as yet another cross to bear. She went about her duties tight-lipped and with the limp which becomes more marked when she feels more than usually 'put upon'.

Luckily, the snow was light, nothing more than a shower here and there, powdering the black branches of the elms and the roofs in the village. But the weather was bitterly cold and even I, a poor weather prophet, knew that we should get more snow before long.

On one freezing evening, the Festival Committee met in my sitting-room. Thanks to Mrs Pringle's administrations, it presented an unusually tidy appearance. Piles of exercise books, test papers, infant apparatus and the general flotsam and jetsam found in a schoolmistress's room had been carted up to the spare bedroom, and although I despaired of ever finding any of it in order again, it was wonderful to entertain my guests in such immaculate splendour.

The Committee was formed by most of the Parochial Church Council and one or two other energetic people who had some organizing ability and bright ideas. I must confess that I had envisaged an evening making a list of the usual entertainments known only too well to Fairacre, and possibly deciding on the days on which to present them. It was exciting therefore to have Basil Bradley's bombshell exploded at the outset.

'This is really Major Gunning's idea,' he began, glancing across at that upright figure. 'You remember that he suggested that we might have *Son et Lumière* with St Patrick's as the background. Well, I've been talking to a friend of mine who has helped to produce this sort of thing, and he's willing to stage it and produce it for us.'

Congratulatory murmurs broke out on all sides.

'And if you would allow me,' went on Basil Bradley, looking modestly at his fingers, 'I should really love to write the story and er – record it for you.'

'That is indeed most generous,' said the vicar. 'Most generous.'

We all agreed warmly.

It was Mrs Mawne who rushed in where angels feared to tread, and said, 'But all that wiring and amplifiers, and setting up seats and things in the churchyard – surely that's going to be horribly expensive?'

'I thought, if the vicar agreed, it would be much more practical to have it inside the church, with the lights changing on the chancel and altar. Then, of course, we should be independent of the weather.'

'And have seats,' cried Mrs Mawne, seeing the light.

'And have seats,' agreed Basil Bradley gravely.

'I can see no objection to having the performances inside,' said the vicar. 'After all, the churches were always used for the early miracle plays, and it seems fitting that the story of our parish should be told in the building which has seen almost all its history. I think it is a splendid idea.'

'The only thing is,' said Basil Bradley, warming to his theme in the midst of such general approval, 'it is hardly worth setting up all the paraphernalia for less than a week. Do you think we can expect enough support?'

'Why not?' asked Mr Mawne. 'We'll advertise it well. People can bring parties from miles away. They're much more likely to come if they know it will be inside the building.'

'Oh, I do agree,' said his wife firmly. 'What with gnats, and the wind, not to mention the odd thunderstorm, outdoor evenings are more of a penance than a pleasure.'

It was at last agreed that the *Son et Lumière* arrangements would be for every evening of the Festival Week, and would, in fact, be the major part of the whole project which would take place in July.

'And do you really think we shall cover our expenses?' persisted Mrs Mawne.

'There will be no expenses,' said Basil Bradley. 'My friend John is giving his services, and the electrician's bills and so on will be my own contribution to the Fund.'

'It is uncommonly generous,' repeated the vicar. 'A really wonderful gesture. I am sure we are most deeply grateful.' And with this we all concurred.

Major Gunning cleared his throat so martially that we all jumped to attention, or as nearly as we could in a sitting posture.

'I've taken the liberty of speaking to a young cousin of mine . . . by way of being a singer. You may have heard of her. Jean Cole.'

'Jean Cole!' exclaimed Mrs Mawne, looking at Major Gunning with new respect.

'Jean Cole!' echoed Basil Bradley, turning pink with excitement. 'I'd no idea she was related to you. The most beautiful contralto voice in existence today! She was superb in *Aïda* at Covent Garden last year.'

'I have all her records,' said the vicar. 'The Bach arias are my particular favourites.'

Major Gunning bowed his head politely in acknowledgement of the adulation, but his tobacco-stained fingers, drumming on the edge of the table, showed his impatience.

'Yes, well . . . top and bottom of it is that she would be willing to give us a tune—'

Basil Bradley winced.

'To come here? To Fairacre?' breathed Mrs Mawne incredulously.

'As I was saying,' continued Major Gunning with a touch of asperity, 'Jean said that she could come and sing in the church during, or after, the *Son et Lumière* performance, if it would help. Not the Monday, though. She's flying back from Berlin that day, after a tour.'

There were delighted cries from the company. The vicar broached the delicate subject which was in all our minds.

'It is indeed the most generous offer. It would mean a great deal to our efforts. But your cousin is – er – much in demand. We must offer her some – er – recompense for the honour she is doing us. Can we . . .?'

'She'll come,' said the major briefly, 'for nothing. I'll see to that.'

If this sounded a trifle ominous, it was soon forgotten in the general delight.

'It's too good to be true,' cried Mrs Mawne. 'The most encouraging news of the evening!'

And with that we all agreed.

The rest of the programme was settled provisionally. The *Son et Lumière* would take place after dark each evening, beginning about nine. The Festival would begin with a splendid service in the church on the Sunday, at which the Bishop had promised to come and bless our endeavours.

'And all denominations in the area will be invited,' said the vicar.

'Bet they don't all come!' whispered Mr Roberts to me in a horribly penetrating whisper.

'They will be invited,' repeated the vicar reprovingly.

Various functions would take place during the week, a mammoth jumble sale, a gargantuan whist drive and so on, organized by various bodies in the village, and the week would culminate with a magnificent fête in the vicarage garden on Saturday afternoon, to be opened by someone who would be 'a real draw', as Mr Willet said, followed by a dance in the evening.

'Shall we have enough going on to warrant a *whole week*?' asked Mr Willet doubtfully.

'The *Son et Lumière* will be the main thread,' explained the vicar, 'and our other festivities will be hung like jewels, as it were, upon this chain.'

'Very nicely put,' commented Mr Mawne, a trifle drily.

'Yes, it turned out rather more poetically than I intended,' replied the vicar, rather surprised and pleased with his flight of fancy. 'I really should make a note of it for a future sermon.'

By this time the hands of the clock stood at ten o'clock. I went into the kitchen to prepare coffee, and the meeting ended with much animation and hope, on the part of the Fairacre Festival Committee, before they set off to face the wintry night.

4

'No, I never!'

'Yes, you did then!'

'I never, I tell you! I never done it!'

'We knows you done it all right, don't us?'

A chorus of self-righteous voices greeted this ungrammatical exchange which floated through the schoolroom window one bright morning. Sometimes I wonder why I trouble to correct the children in the classroom, knowing full well that they will relapse into their mother tongue as soon as they escape from my clutches.

The accused appeared to be Joseph Coggs. I could recognize his hoarse, husky croak easily above the manifold sounds from the playground. He is fairly popular with the other children who do not seem to be bothered by his poor clothes and his gipsy background. What he had done to deserve their united attack I was soon to know.

''Twas there all right yesterday,' said one, belligerently.

'Funny thing you havin' a wooden dagger the same evenin',' shouted another, mockingly.

'My cousin from Caxley give it to me,' growled Joseph. 'He got it off of some kid up the street.'

'Likely, ennit?'

'What, same colour an' all?'

The voices grew shriller, and I was in half a mind to leave my marking to investigate when I heard Mr Willet's hearty voice.

'What's going on then?'

A dozen voices clamoured together, and the gist of the story was that the hand of the clock had vanished from the Appeal Fund and Joseph Coggs 'had bin and pinched it'.

'You want to watch your tongues,' announced Mr Willet sternly. 'And stop picking on Joe. I took the hand away, if you must know, to put another coat o' paint on it. Put that in your pipes and smoke it, you young know-alls.'

His heavy footsteps passed on, leaving an uneasy silence.

'See?' cried Joseph triumphantly.

'Well, how was we to know?' muttered one of the crowd. 'Your dagger was the spittin' image of that hand.'

'Always on at us to look out for folks breakin' the law,' grumbled another, 'and what thanks do us get for trying?'

'Come on up the coke-heap,' shouted someone cheerfully. 'The bell'll be going before we've had a game.'

And the drama ended in a wild confusion of yells and scrunching coke, enjoyed by accusers and accused alike.

The hand of the clock which had been the cause of this fracas was moving far too slowly towards the target for Fairacre's peace of mind.

The most dramatic leap forward, in these last months, had been caused by an anonymous gift of one hundred pounds. Naturally, rumours as to the identity of this generous benefactor were legion.

'I wouldn't put it past the vicar himself,' said one.

'Or Mr Mawne?' queried another.

'That'll be the day,' said Mrs Pringle sourly, when she heard this suggestion. 'Them Mawnes don't part with money that easy. Best end of neck served up as chops in their house, so my niece Minnie tells me.'

One of the infants thought it might be 'a fairy'. This pretty fancy was soon dispelled by the realists who were slightly older.

'Don't talk soft!' implored her brother Ernest, shamed before his fellows in the playground.

'No such thing as fairies,' added Patrick scornfully. 'And if there was, how d'you think they'd lug a hundred pounds up to the vicar's? They ain't no bigger'n my thumb.'

This irrefutable argument settled the matter in this instance, but the anonymous donor still remained a fascinating mystery. It was one which was never solved.

Even more exciting than the anonymous gift was that Peter Martin, the pop star and idol of the young, had agreed to open the fête on the Saturday and to sing at the dance in the evening, accompanying himself on the famous guitar. He was going to prove a tremendous draw.

'The weather really won't matter,' said the vicar, beaming. 'People will come from miles around just to see him. A very *personable* young fellow, I believe.'

Mrs Pringle's niece Minnie expressed the general reaction to the news. 'Ain't it just wonderful? We'll be breathing *the very same air*! To think of him coming to this place! All Caxley'll be there. You ever seen him, miss?'

I said that I had not had that pleasure yet.

'Beautiful hair, he's got. Long and that, all thick down to his shoulders. And his clothes costs a fortune, and he don't drink nothin' but champagne!'

She sighed ecstatically. A visitation from the entire heavenly host, I thought somewhat tartly to myself, could not occasion more reverent adoration than this one glamorous star. Nevertheless, I too rejoiced. Think how it would swell the funds!

Work on the roof progressed steadily, and the sound of hammers and saws formed the background to our own school activities. These included now, in the last weeks of the spring term, preparations for the entertainment which was to be our contribution to the Fairacre Festival.

Only teachers who have dealt with these affairs can truly assess the heart-burnings and headaches which accompany something which the outsider considers a simple, and even a pleasurable, undertaking.

The only other member of the staff is the infants' teacher. For years Miss Clare, now retired and living at Beech Green, ruled the infants, and most of the adults in the village learnt to read, write and calculate under her benevolent eye. Miss Gray followed Miss Clare, but left to marry our neighbouring schoolmaster, Mr Annett, who also acts as choirmaster at Fairacre. Then came Miss Jackson, a stormy young woman straight from college whose departure I viewed with relief.

Since then we have had a succession of 'supply' teachers, some good, some ghastly but, for the last year, the infants have been in the charge of Mrs Bonny, a buxom widow, who manages them very well. All goes swimmingly if she is able to work in her own way, and I interfere as little as possible. Unfortunately, any sort of mild suggestion throws the lady into a defensive and resentful mood, as if one were casting a slur on her abilities. Coming to an amicable arrangement about the concert was an operation fraught with hazards, I found.

My first idea of a play in which the whole school could take part fell upon stony ground.

'Why can't the babies sing their nursery rhymes?' demanded Mrs Bonny plaintively. 'I've spent hours teaching them, and their mothers would love to hear them.'

Both facts were true. The daily chorus – one might be forgiven for saying 'caterwauling' – had penetrated the partition between our classrooms with painful clarity. And the

mothers of these young choristers would dote on Mrs Bonny's efforts with them. I agreed resignedly.

'But nursery rhymes won't take very long,' I said, trying not to sound too relieved. 'We'd better have some other items.'

Mrs Bonny promised to consider the matter, and within two days the floorboards of the infants' room were reverberating with one of those galumphing folk dances from mid-Europe which involve much clapping and stamping. The clapping and stamping are no doubt performed in unison in the country of the dance's origin, but it certainly was not in Fairacre's infant room. Next door we were sorely tried. It was almost a relief to return to the nursery rhymes, and to listen, wincing, to:

> 'Ickory, dickory dock
> The mou-house run up the clock
> The clock struck ONE
> The mouse run down –

Here there followed a succession of claps as each child took its time to register the need for action, and then, triumphantly they would bellow:

'Ickory, dickory, dock.

Mrs Bonny would then praise them loudly, point out the aspirate at the beginning of 'Hickory' and the necessity of singing 'ran' instead of 'run', and the same thing would be repeated *ad nauseam*.

Our own efforts were little better. I had dramatized *The Princess and the Swineherd*, which gave everyone a chance of appearing on the stage, but doubted if the words would ever be learnt. Ernest, the only possible swineherd-cum-prince, became so sheepish about performing a chivalrous bow that I threatened to demote him to a courtier, although we both knew that there was no one else really capable of taking the part. Sometimes I despaired of ever getting Fairacre School to take part in the Festival, and wondered gloomily if the sale of Queen Anne's chalice might not, after all, be a better way of raising the money.

I did not, of course, voice these treacherous sentiments, but Mr Lamb, our village postmaster, spoke about it when I went to buy the school's savings' stamps one afternoon some weeks later.

'Of course, it's not plain sailing, this selling the church silver. Has to be a Faculty or something, the vicar tells me. A lot of chit-chat goes on evidently before permission's given. I can't see us being allowed to part with it. And, to tell the truth, I don't think anyone in Fairacre wants to see it go.'

He handed me the stamps and with them three or four photographs in colour.

'Your brother's family?' I asked, looking at them. Mr Lamb's brother George left Fairacre for New York after the war and runs a catering business there. He left before I took over the school but regularly corresponds with our Mr Lamb who shows us the photographs, and tells us all about his brother's successes when we visit the Post Office. He is very proud indeed of this younger brother, now the father of three husky boys who beamed from the photographs.

'Just a chance he may be over,' said Mr Lamb, taking back the photographs and inserting them carefully into his wallet. 'Some business trip, he says. They're chartering a plane, it seems, and if he can manage it, he'll be over here for a fortnight.'

This was good news. As I sauntered down the village street, enjoying the sunshine, I hoped, for Mr Lamb's sake, that his brother would be able to return to Fairacre. It was my guess that he would not find it much changed even though he had been absent now for over twenty years.

The question of the sale of the chalice was in everyone's mind. None worried quite as deeply as the vicar. He woke, on these bright summer mornings, to the chorus of the birds in his garden and then, after the first few moments of pleasure, the familiar little cloud cooled the sunshine of his waking moments and was with him for the rest of the day. He refused to do anything about negotiations for the sale of the precious chalice. He steadfastly hoped and prayed that enough would be raised by the Festival, and that this step, so repugnant to him, might never be necessary.

Mr Mawne did his best to make his friend change his mind, but he remained obdurate.

'I refuse to discuss it,' said the vicar one evening, pink with rare impatience.

'But, my dear Gerald, you simply can't bury your head in the sand like an ostrich. At least, find out the facts. Let's see if we can try for permission. Time's running out, you know. The bills are going to be pretty formidable, and can you honestly believe that the Festival will raise enough to pay them?'

'I have no doubt that the Lord will provide,' repeated

the vicar stubbornly. His friend raised his eyebrows, looked helplessly at Mrs Partridge, but forbore to reply.

The chalice had last been used at Whitsun, and not one touching the ancient mellow silver and gazing into its gleaming depths failed to feel a pang. Would this be the last time that Fairacre's treasure, with its blessed contents, would be offered to them? The service was a paean of praise. Red and white roses nodded on the altar. Sunshine poured through the windows, gilding the arum lilies at the chancel steps. Country voices had made the glittering brass vibrate with Whitsun hymns and Mrs Pratt, at the organ, had pulled out all the stops and flooded the church with mighty splendour. The thought of the possible loss of the chalice was the one touch of frost among the bursting glory of Whit Sunday.

As the Festival drew closer, our fears for the chalice became sharper. Somehow we simply must make the Fairacre Festival a success, we told each other! We did not say, in so many words, that Queen Anne's chalice was at stake, but the unspoken thought was constantly with us.

It was Mrs Pringle, usually the harbinger of doom, who brought a rare touch of comfort to Mr Partridge at about this time. He had called at the school with the list of hymns which he hoped I would teach the children, when Mrs Pringle clattered in bearing a battered pail in one hand and a scrubbing brush in the other.

'Bit late leavin', ain't you?' she remarked sourly. 'Clock wrong then? I was going to give the lobby a scrub out but no use doing it till the children have cleared off. Love's labour lost, that'd be!'

The vicar, who is used to this sort of thing, smiled benignly.

'You're going to have a churchful on the Tuesday, then. You was lucky to get that Miss Cole to sing,' she continued conversationally, setting down the bucket with a clang. 'My sister's girl, what works at the coach station in Caxley, says there's three coach loads booked already to come over.'

The vicar's smile grew wider. 'What splendid news, Mrs Pringle!'

'And no end of Women's Institutes have rung up about it, and the Mothers' Union and some Young Farmers.'

'A really *wide* audience!' commented the vicar rapturously.

'It takes all sorts to make a world,' conceded Mrs Pringle graciously. 'But it do look hopeful, I must say.'

'It does indeed,' replied the vicar, gazing affectionately upon my school cleaner. 'It does indeed.'

She bent to pick up the bucket and then took up her customary militant stance. 'Well,' she demanded, with a return to her usual truculence, 'do them children go now or not? This 'ere water's getting cold.'

'I'll send them through the other way,' I said meekly. 'We won't hold up your scrubbing any longer.'

This was no time for petty warfare, I felt. Mrs Pringle, messenger of hope, should have her way.

5

The posters were up everywhere in the countryside. They blazed from barn doors, from gateposts, from tree trunks and in the windows of many a village shop. One made a bright blue corner on the Appeals' board. Across the village street, between The Beetle and Wedge and the Emerys' house, a banner fluttered, bearing the words:

FAIRACRE FESTIVAL
JULY 9–15

Bunting was draped across our house fronts, and those of us who owned a flag had it in readiness to hoist on the Sunday which was to be the first day of the Festival. The cross of St George, freshly laundered by Mrs Willet, would soon be flaunting itself above the church spire upon which the regilded weathercock perched again.

Inside the church the electricians were putting the final touches to the wiring and lighting. Jock Graham, the retired architect who had so nobly offered his services, became extremely agitated by the ladders lodged among the timbers of the hammer-beam roof. He was unduly sharp with Mr Mawne who had dropped in one morning to see how things were progressing.

'I'll not be responsible,' he rumbled, rolling his r's in Doric splendour, 'for any damage to that historic roof. A lot of tomfoolery to rig up lights so near the timbers. Those men have no idea of the pricelessness of the work around them.'

'Oh, come now,' protested Mr Mawne. 'They are used to this sort of thing. I believe they were employed at Winchester Cathedral. Or was it Salisbury?'

'It wouldn't be allowed in Scotland,' Mr Graham assured him.

'That I can well imagine,' remarked his companion drily. The hint of sarcasm inflamed Jock Graham still further.

'A decent God-fearing kirk would be ashamed to turn itself into something no better than a theatre. I'd no idea, when I offered my sairvices, that this sort of thing would be countenanced.'

'I see nothing offensive about it,' retorted Mr Mawne. 'It is an act of praise.'

'It's commaircial!' boomed Mr Graham, his sandy eyebrows bristling. 'It wouldn't happen in Scotland, I tell ye!'

'I really can't think,' replied Mr Mawne, with maddening detachment, 'why so many of you Scotsmen bother to come south if you dislike it so much. Personally, I'm all for Scottish nationalism, and I'd rebuild Hadrian's Wall for good measure, once I'd got all you immigrants back on the right side of it.'

'Ye'd no get far without a stiffening of good Scots' blood among ye,' thundered Jock Graham. 'A weakly unprincipled set of shilly-shallyers, lacking pairpose and integrity!'

The workmen, high above, had ceased their labours and were watching this passage of arms with intense interest.

The two men faced each other. Mr Mawne's pale face wore a supercilious smile. Mr Graham's, suffused to an unbecoming shade of purple, was thrust close to his antagonist's. At this dramatic moment, Basil Bradley arrived on the scene.

'I can't tell you how relieved I am that I've already recorded the script,' he croaked huskily. 'My tonsils are absolutely aflame. I can't think why I've succumbed so easily at this time of year. I swear by orange juice for breakfast – nothing more – just fresh orange juice!'

'Ye'd do better on a braw fresh herring and a plate of salted porridge,' thundered Jock Graham. He brushed past the two men and marched, head erect, down the aisle to the west door.

'Whatever's got into him?' asked Basil Bradley, bewildered.

'Scotch blood,' said Mr Mawne cryptically. ' "Scotland for ever!" I mean "Scotland for aye!" '

'Oh dear,' croaked Basil Bradley, extracting a small tin from his pocket. 'Ah well, it makes one quite glad to have been born in humble Bayswater, doesn't it? Have a black-currant lozenge, Henry.'

Jock Graham was not the only Fairacre resident to be in a state of tension at this time. The vicar, facing the Bishop's visit, was anxious about the service, and also about the safety of the church fabric. What a terrible thing it would be if something should fall upon that stately figure! Despite reassurances, the vicar was not wholly at ease.

Mrs Partridge, whose privilege it was to entertain the Bishop to lunch, and possibly to tea, was busy planning a meal which would do honour to their distinguished visitor and yet be simple enough to prepare and serve single-handed. Cold salmon and salad had seemed a good choice until she remembered that the Bishop was extremely short-sighted and far too handsome a man to relish wearing glasses at lunch time. And just suppose that a fish-bone appeared? It would, without fail, be on the guest's plate. Perhaps cold beef? Or leg of lamb left in a slow oven during the service and mint sauce made beforehand? Mrs Partridge continued to cudgel her brains, and to long for the days when the vicarage had a resident cook and two kitchen maids.

Mr Annett, the choirmaster, was worrying about the new anthem. The choir of St Patrick's had left him in no doubt that he had bitten off more than they could chew.

'This 'ere modern stuff ain't got no tune to it,' protested Mr Willet. 'What's wrong with a bit of Bach or Handel?'

'It's a very good thing to make a change,' Mr Annett snapped back, secretly conscious that the new anthem was beyond their powers, but too proud to admit it. 'As Browning said: "A man's reach should exceed his grasp."'

'Browning never 'ad to tackle this lot,' pointed out Mr Willet, peering closely at the sheet of music. 'If there's anything I 'ates it's five flats.'

They had struggled on with their unfamiliar burden, but no matter how often they practised, Mr Annett realized that the anthem would turn out to be a hesitant dirge rather than the outpouring of praise which the composer had intended. Too late to do anything now, he told himself, as the great Sunday approached. But the thought gave him little comfort.

Basil Bradley, afflicted with his feverish cold, was suffering agonies of self-consciousness about the script which he had written, and his recording of it. He had checked all his facts most carefully, but there was always the possibility of a mistake. How dreadful if he had made some blunder! There was that episode about the nun being given shelter in the vestry during the eighteenth century. Should he have omitted it, perhaps? There were some very dubious rumours about the incumbent at that date, and the Bishop might take exception to the publicity, guarded though Basil's account had been of the affair. Really, creative work was terribly exhausting, thought poor Basil, as he gargled hopelessly before the final rehearsal.

A spell of unbroken sunshine preceded Festival week and we in Fairacre prayed that it might continue. It grew so hot that the children took many of their lessons outside, in the shade of the elm trees. Rehearsals of the infants' contributions also took place in the playground, which afforded some relief to our class, when it was working inside, and considerable interest to proud mothers who clustered at the gate to watch their offspring bounding around in the folk dance.

The Princess and the Swineherd still had many faults. Ernest had overcome his shyness with such success – terrified of handing over the part to someone else – that he now played the Prince with a swashbuckling impudence which was, to my mind, quite as offensive as his former interpretation of the part. However, I was now resigned to the shortcomings of my production and simply concentrated on getting the cast word-perfect, which was no light matter.

Mr Willet, as sexton, was concerned about the tidiness of the church and the churchyard.

'Slummocky lot, them builders,' he told me. 'Drops their paper bags everywhere. Bread crusts and cheese rinds and old potato crisps scattered all over the churchyard. Them mice are getting as big as foxes.'

'It will look splendid on Sunday,' I assured him. 'Especially if this weather lasts.'

We looked across my garden to the meadows at the base of the downs. A heat haze veiled the distance, but nearer at hand a herd of black and white Friesian cows, the pride of Mr Roberts, stood knee-deep in tall grass. Not one moved. They might have been painted there, against the hot motionless beauty of hills and empty sky, so still they stood.

'Well, let's hope it does,' agreed Mr Willet. 'Don't want it to break yet awhile. It'll end in thunder, or my name's not Willet.'

He turned to look at St Patrick's. The scaffolding had been

removed from the spire but still clad the square tower containing the belfry and part of the nave.

'Wish we could have rung in the Bishop with a fine peal,' he said regretfully. 'But there it is. All six o' they bells is up against the church wall waiting to go aloft again as soon as it's safe for 'em. I likes to go and look 'em over now and again. I've got a soft spot for them bells, particularly Old Bess. They say she was cast in the field behind The Beetle and Wedge, sometime in the 1560s.'

'The children don't want the bells to go back again. They've been over to see them – under my eagle eye, let me say – lots of times, and they've copied the inscriptions.'

' "*Sanctus, sanctus, sanctus*",' gabbled Mr Willet, swatting a gnat on his freckled forearm. ' "*In piam memoriam Caroli Fowler. Requiescat in pace*". Fowler, notice? Still a good few Fowlers in Fairacre. Wonder if any of them cast Old Bess?'

He bent to pull up a dandelion from my border, and straightened up with a sigh.

'I do truly hope this Festival puts the old church on its feet. There's a lot at stake, Miss Read. A lot at stake!'

Sunday dawned bright and beautiful. I took my breakfast tray into the garden among the dewy pinks and roses. A robin perched hopefully on the lilac bush nearby, a beady eye cocked for crumbs.

The Union Jack hung motionless from the school flag pole. High above it, on St Patrick's church the cross of St George waited for a breeze to spread it out in its full red and white magnificence.

It was already blissfully hot although the clock said only nine. By ten to eleven, when I made my way to church, the heat was almost oppressive. We were all in our best summer finery and I felt quite sorry for the Bishop, magnificently accoutred in a splendid gold and white cope which must have been uncomfortably warm.

We sang the most exultant hymns, beginning with 'Praise my soul the King of Heaven' as the choir processed from the west door up to the chancel, with their choirmaster, George Annett, at their head. Several of my pupils had undergone their weekly metamorphosis from scruffy urchins to well-scrubbed cherubs, and with hair plastered down with a wet brush and their eyes modestly downcast upon the polished boots peeping demurely from beneath their cassocks, they gave an impression of youthful sanctity which did not deceive those of us who knew them during the rest of the week.

The new anthem was tackled with dogged effort and Mr Annett gave noble support with a resonant voice which led his struggling choir valiantly. When it was over, I noticed Mr Willet mopping his brow and moustache with obvious relief.

The Bishop gave the sermon and spoke of the part the church played in parish life, the disaster which had befallen it, and praised the efforts of our small community to repair the damage.

'God will bless your work,' he promised us. 'This is a festival in every sense. It is an expression of praise for past mercies and a re-dedication of ourselves to service.'

He made a brave and unforgettable figure in our ancient pulpit, and his words were as inspiring as his presence. When the benediction had been said, and Mrs Pratt broke into a triumphant voluntary on the organ, we all felt that Fairacre was embarked upon a venture which was bound to succeed.

We emerged into the hot sunshine, blinking like owls in the dazzling light. Around us the rose bushes gave out a voluptuous fragrance. Above us an aeroplane left a white trail in the cloudless sky. Bumblebees lumbered from clover-head to clover-head on the grassy mounds of our Fairacre forefathers. It was indeed high summer.

'And real Festival weather!' said Miss Margaret Waters, gazing happily about her, beneath the brim of her old-fashioned straw hat.

'After all this looking forward,' said her sister, 'it's hard to believe that it's actually started.'

It was a thought we all shared as we made our various ways homeward to Sunday dinner.

At last, the Festival had begun!

6

Amy my old college friend, drove over from Bent to the first performance of the *Son et Lumière*.

It was to be a very grand affair. Several local landowners were bringing parties of guests and we humbler folk were busy looking out our best evening attire. It was not easy to find something splendid enough for the occasion, decorous enough for churchgoing and warm enough to counteract the chill of an evening in St Patrick's draughty pews. I had plumped for safety in my plain black frock, and had looked out my one fur piece, a useful stole, for despite the heat of the last few days, which had degenerated into an ominously still stuffiness, the age-long coolness of the church's interior would take some combating.

Amy, *soignée* in a most beautiful frock of blue silk, looked me over critically.

'You really *shouldn't* wear black, my dear, with your skin. It kills any sort of glow you have. Why not wear a deep red dress, or a brown?'

'Because I haven't got one,' I said flatly.

Her eye travelled, without relish, down my full length and lingered sadly at my feet.

'Those heels are definitely out,' she pronounced.

'Not in Fairacre,' I replied with spirit. 'In fact, they've only just *come in*! I paid a great deal of money for these shoes, my girl, and I intend to get plenty of wear out of them.'

Amy shuddered delicately, and fingered her one splendid adornment, a glittering diamond brooch on her shoulder. It was, I knew, a present from James, her husband, and marked his return from a particularly protracted business trip to the Bahamas. There are many such absences from home, about which I have my private suspicions, as no doubt Amy has too,

but they certainly result in the most beautiful presents for his wife, and she has enough sense not to cross-question James too closely.

We sat down to my carefully prepared meal of cold chicken and salad. I was secretly rather proud of the salad for I had remembered to cut the radishes into water-lily shapes in the dinner hour and had left them soaking all the afternoon. The tomatoes and cucumber had come from Mr Willet's green-house, and the lettuce from my own garden. The hard-boiled eggs, winking goldenly from among the greenery, had come from Mrs Pringle's hens and the fine chicken was lately one of the members of her flock.

Amy ate heartily, I was glad to see.

'All so deliciously fresh,' she commented, and I preened myself at this unaccustomed compliment – prematurely, as I might have known. 'But I really think the latest way of dishing up a salad is better. Just a bowl of green stuff tossed in the very best olive oil and vinegar, and tomatoes freshly sliced in a separate dish salted and peppered and with a *soupçon* of chopped chives or parsley, of course – for those who like *coloured* salad mixed with green. I find that most people these days consider radishes rather too coarse a flavour, and there's so much medical argument about hard-boiled eggs that I don't serve them, I must admit.'

'You'd better bring your own nose-bag next time you come,' I told her. I've known Amy too long to worry about her criticisms and can well recall the hearty relish with which she attacked college bread and margarine spread with thick-cut Scottish marmalade, not to mention a truly repellent dish of minced meat in a suet crust which, with juvenile flippancy, we christened 'Boiled Baby'.

However, she approved graciously of my coffee, and as soon as we had finished we set off to the church.

'Looks like thunder,' commented Amy, eyeing the

darkening sky. There was a sullen coppery look about the piled clouds, and not a leaf stirred in the airless heat.

'Let's hope it waits until we're safely home again,' I answered, as we joined the queue at the south door.

It was good to see St Patrick's so full. Seldom had the ancient hammer-beam roof looked down upon such a glittering assembly. We had all done our best to make this a splendid occasion. I studied the attire and coiffures around me. There were several new hats, worn by those who felt unable to attend church unless so crowned, and among them was one upon Mrs Pringle's locks. It was entirely new to me. Where was the faithful old number adorned with dangling cherries? Where was the navy-blue, decorated with white feathers, which had first seen the light at her niece Minnie's wedding? No doubt safely lodged on top of the wardrobe at home. I hoped so. I missed those two old friends, but studied the new creation with interest. It was of green straw, formidably brimmed, and garlanded with plastic anemones which looked suspiciously like those given away recently with packets of soap powder. It was exceedingly handsome, I thought, and proof of Mrs Pringle's support of the Festival.

In the front pews sat our local gentry, elegant in silks and velvets, their hair blue-rinsed, silver-streaked, or discreetly tinted. Occasionally, wafts of delicious perfume floated back to us, as a stole was rearranged or a handbag was opened.

The nave was shadowy, but a shaft of golden light illuminated the chancel and altar. Mrs Pratt, at the organ, played some gentle melody, vaguely familiar, which I guessed must be by Haydn or Mozart.

St Patrick's clock struck nine. The music stopped and the vicar appeared at the chancel steps.

'You are about to hear the story of Fairacre,' he told us, 'and in particular the story of this lovely old church. But before it begins, let us pray that we may see it restored to its former beauty, so that those who come after us may cherish it as we have done.'

We slipped to our knees and listened to the simple prayer. Then, with a susurration of silks and satins, we resumed our seats, eager for what might come.

The golden light which suffused the chancel changed to a dim blue. The cross glimmered upon the altar amidst the ghostly shadows. We shivered in awe. It was very quiet. Only, far away, a faint rumbling could be heard. It could have been distant thunder, or a farm vehicle out late upon its lawful business.

There was a faint crackling sound and then Basil Bradley's voice echoed strongly through the church.

'Long, long ago, so learned men tell us, the Romans may have passed this way. They did not settle here as far as we know. Among our downs water is scarce, and there are few natural defences against the elements or the enemy. The Romans left no signs of occupation here.

'But centuries later, when the next invaders came to Britain, they left their mark upon this place. Upon this spot, where now we are gathered, the Normans built a small, strong church of which parts still remain.'

At this point the chancel arch was thrown into prominence, a mellow golden light illuminating the angular stone carving. Few of Fairacre's parishioners had realized until this dramatic moment what unsuspected richness had lain in the shadowy chancel arch so high above them.

'The work was begun probably about the middle of the twelfth century –' A crackling noise interrupted the mellifluous voice, and was immediately followed by a burst of thunder which broke around us like machine-gun fire. We ducked involuntarily at the report, then, remembering ourselves, sat up and looked polite and attentive.

The church was plunged into darkness and the voice had

ceased. A little agitated whispering rustled round the congregation.

'Lord Almighty!' boomed Mr Roberts whose voice is as large as his generous heart. 'We've been and got struck!'

At this, commotion broke out on all sides. There was nothing panic-stricken about us. We are all used to storms, which can occur with horrifying ferocity but are soon over in Fairacre. What really worried us was the breakdown of the performance and the bitter disappointment of all those who had spent so long in preparing it.

The vicar, rising from his seat to direct and comfort his flock, suddenly saw, with amazing clarity, in his mind's eye Queen Anne's chalice. It seemed to float in mid-air, brilliantly clear at first, but gradually fading, as if it were passing away from him to distances unknown. The vicar's heart beat uncomfortably loudly, his throat grew constricted, but he put his fears from him and addressed his flock.

'Please remain seated, dear people. Candles will be lit at once, and would Mr Roberts be so kind as to step across to the vicarage and telephone the Electricity Board to see what can be done?'

'I'm on my way, sir,' called Mr Roberts, and the crash of strong footsteps confirmed this.

'Mark my words,' said Amy beside me. 'The *Caxley Chronicle* will tell us that this power cut was caused by a swan flying into the cable.'

'Perhaps it was,' I replied.

'Fiddlesticks!' snapped Amy. 'It was the storm!'

A jagged flash split the sky, to be followed by another reverberating thunder clap.

'It's farther off,' said someone hopefully.

'You wants to count, one, two, three, four, see? As soon as the lightning comes you starts counting and sees how many you gets to afore the thunder bangs out. That'll tell you how many miles off the storm be!'

I recognized the voice of this young know-all as Ernest, my Swineherd-Prince.

'You speak when you're spoken to,' said his mother, in a scandalized whisper. 'Piping up like that, and in church, too!'

A few scurrying figures flitted about the shadows bearing candles. There was a medieval beauty about their downbent heads and their curved hands sheltering the precious tiny flames from any draught, which was poignantly in keeping with the ancient building.

'Mrs Pratt,' announced the vicar, 'will play some music by Bach while we wait.'

We settled again against the hard pew-backs and let the sonorous chords flow over us. How many of our Fairacre forebears, I wondered, had listened to Bach by candlelight, as we were doing now? My mind began to wander. There was something wonderfully comforting in the thought that we shared so much in this building with those long-dead and those yet unborn. We were, after all, simply a link in a long chain stretching back for centuries and forward into eternity.

The candle flames stretched and wavered in the draught. A rumble of thunder rattled over the roof.

'I told you so,' whispered Ernest defensively. 'It's going away.'

At that moment, Mr Roberts reappeared. 'The power will be back at any minute,' he announced. 'A swan has flown into the cable, they say.'

Amy nudged me with such vigour that my side was quite sore.

'Thank you, Mr Roberts,' said the vicar. 'Let us sing a hymn together while we wait.'

After some whispering with Mr Annett, the vicar proclaimed: 'Pleasant are thy courts above', and we all dutifully stood in the twilit church and raised our voices. As we reached the last line, the lights came on again, and we sang 'Amen' with undue fervour.

We resumed our seats expectantly and Basil Bradley, looking slightly careworn, appeared at the chancel steps.

'I think we had better begin again from the beginning, ladies and gentlemen. We are so very sorry for this breakdown. Please bear with us, and let us hope that all is now plain sailing.'

There were sympathetic murmurs from the congregation, the lights went out and the blue spotlight lit up the altar once more. There was a preliminary crackle and then Basil Bradley's voice as before.

'Long, long ago, so learned men tell us, the Romans may have passed this way.'

We settled back, like children hungry for a story, and gave ourselves up to enjoyment.

It took a little over an hour for the tale to unfold, and so well had Basil Bradley told it and so beautiful had the lighting been, that we emerged from the experience filled with unbounded admiration tinged with awe.

Even Amy was impressed. '*Remarkably* good,' she said as we walked home. 'Really *outstandingly* good! It ought to bring hundreds of visitors.'

'Let's hope it does,' I replied. 'Two thousand pounds takes some finding.'

'I wonder if the national press will write it up,' mused Amy. 'It deserves it. You'll get people from all over the place if it's widely advertised.'

'We've done our best,' I assured her. 'It's been in all the local papers, I know.'

'I think I shall send a letter to *The Times*,' said Amy, climbing elegantly into her car. 'We want to cast the net *really wide*.'

She drove off and I returned to the school house. Distant voices in the lane and the sound of cars starting on their home-ward journeys formed the epilogue to Basil Bradley's moving production.

A star, bright as a jewel, hung beside St Patrick's spire. It looked hopeful, I thought, as I prepared for bed. If the rest of the Fairacre contributions matched this evening's in splendour, our Festival must surely succeed, and more important still, Queen Anne's chalice would remain among those who loved it so well.

7

Next morning I began to realize just how far-flung the news of our Fairacre Festival had been.

There was a hearty banging on the classroom door during our history lesson and in walked a thickset man wearing a crewcut and a broad smile. The likeness to our Mr Lamb at the Post Office was unmistakable.

'Miss Read?' he began.

'George Lamb,' I said. 'How nice of you to look in!'

'Well, you see, I was raised in this place and I felt I just had to take another peek at this old schoolroom. Don't appear to have changed much since my time. Bit cleaner, perhaps.'

'You'd better repeat that to Mrs Pringle,' I told him. 'It'll make her day.'

I turned to the class. 'Stand up and say "Good morning" to Mr Lamb, who was once a pupil here.'

There were welcoming cries and smiles, all the warmer because any interruption to lessons is a pleasurable one.

'That's a Coggs,' exclaimed our visitor, pointing delightedly at Joseph in the front row.

'Quite right,' I said. 'He's Arthur Coggs's son.'

'Oh, I know *Arthur*,' replied George Lamb with some emphasis. I had no doubt that he knew a great deal about his old schoolmate's fondness for liquor and the resultant shindies in our village.

I settled the children to some work and accompanied our guest on a tour of the room.

'Not the same piano! Sakes alive, that must be going on for a century.'

'Eighty, anyway,' I agreed, fingering the walnut fretwork front, and the ivory keys, yellow with age.

'And still the same gaps in the partition,' he went on, bending down to squint through a crack into the infants' room. 'The things we poked through there you'd just never credit, Miss Read.'

'Mr Willet's told me,' I assured him. 'Stinging nettles, knitting needles, dozens of notes – yes, I can well imagine. It happens still, you know. Children don't change much.'

He ambled appreciatively round the room, touching the walls, peering from the windows, and ruffling the children's hair as he passed.

'I hear Miss Clare's still at Beech Green. I'm paying her a visit before I fly home.'

'She'll be so pleased,' I said truthfully.

'I owe a lot to her,' he said, suddenly grave. 'Taught us all proper manners and to think of others. She used to say grace before we went home at night. It went: "Bless us this night and make us ever mindful of the wants of others." I always liked that. "Mindful of the wants of others." Good words those.'

He gazed through the window as he spoke, his eyes fixed upon the men working upon St Patrick's belfry.

'They're getting on very well. They've almost finished,' I said, intending to release the tension a little.

George Lamb shook himself into the present again. 'Ah! Looks pretty tidy now. You been to the show there yet?'

I said that I had.

'I'm taking some of the chaps who flew over with me tomorrow night. All helps the funds. I owe a lot to Fairacre, and it'll give the fellows no end of a kick to see a building that's over eight hundred years old, and to hear Jean Cole too.'

He glanced at the square gold watch upon his wrist and grimaced. 'Best get back to the Post Office for my lunch, or I'll catch it,' he said. 'Goodbye, Miss Read. Goodbye children.

Hope you'll look back on your days at Fairacre School with as much pleasure as I do.'

I accompanied him to the gate. Above the elm trees the rooks were circling high.

'Sign of rain, eh?' he said. ' "Winding up the water", we used to say as kids. You know one thing, Miss Read? Everything seems a lot smaller in Fairacre than I remember it except St Patrick's spire and them old elm trees! Maybe they've both been growing since I left here.'

Chuckling at his own fancies, he made his way back to the village.

On Tuesday evening came the eagerly awaited visit of Jean Cole.

Halfway through the recorded story of Fairacre there was an interval. A spotlight lit the chancel arch and the vicar led in the majestic figure of Major Gunning's cousin. She was resplendent in a long glittering black gown, and her appearance alone was enough to awe her country admirers, but when that glorious voice wrapped us in its warmth and beauty we were touched as never before.

She sang the aria from Handel's *Judas Maccabaeus*, to Mr Annett's accompaniment on the organ. It was a felicitous choice for it celebrated the restoration of the Sanctuary of Jerusalem. We sat in wonderment as the lovely voice soared and fell, and when finally she bowed and left us, we still sat silent and spellbound, whilst through my mind ran Shelley's lines:

> Music, when soft voices die,
> Vibrates in the memory –

I heard later that George Lamb was as good as his word, and that eight of his business friends had been among that evening's congregation.

After the performance was over, it appears, the vicar found them looking round the church in the company of the honorary architect, Mr Graham. He was busy pointing out the particular beauties of the building, and had a fascinated audience. The vicar joined the party and was moved to see the awed admiration with which the strangers viewed the ancient building.

'Back home,' said one, 'we reckon two hundred years as mighty old. It takes your breath away to touch a wall or a doorway this ancient.'

They wandered from vestry to belfry, from altar to side-chapel, and finally emerged from the west door and accepted the vicar's invitation to coffee at the vicarage.

'I can offer you Drambuie with it,' said the vicar with pleasure, as he handed round the steaming cups, 'or a liqueur called aurum, distilled from oranges, and brought from Italy as a present by some friends in the village.'

'Not for me,' said Jock Graham austerely, 'but I'll no refuse a good Scots liqueur like Drambuie.'

He was in a remarkably mellow mood. To have such an attentive audience was a joy to him. The villagers of Fairacre took their church very much for granted, but these strangers were perceptive and appreciative. Jock Graham's tongue wagged all the faster, as the Drambuie diminished sip by sip, and he extolled the unique attributes of the building he loved so well.

It was almost half-past eleven when at last the party broke up.

'I'd no idea it was so late,' said the vicar. 'Have you far to go?'

'We're booked in at Caxley,' said one. 'Two of us have business there tomorrow. The others are off to London on the early train, rustling up some more customers we hope.'

Farewells were made, and the vicar and Mrs Partridge turned back into the hall.

'What very nice fellows!' exclaimed Mr Partridge. 'George Lamb seems to have found some good companions.'

'And a wife who's interested in cooking,' added Mrs Partridge. 'He's going to ask her to send me a recipe for almond cookies.'

'Cookies?' repeated the vicar, his brow furrowed with perplexity.

'*Cookies!*' said his wife firmly. 'Biscuits to us. Really, Gerald, at times you are hopelessly insular.'

'I suppose so,' agreed the vicar rather sadly. Then his face brightened. 'But we've broadened our horizons tonight, my dear, haven't we? With our American friends, and prima donnas!'

Amicably, they mounted the stairs to bed.

The day came when Fairacre School presented its contribution to the Festival. We had decided to give two performances, one in the afternoon when mothers with young children could come, and one in the evening when fathers could attend.

We chose Wednesday for the simple reason that it is early closing day in Caxley and that the people of Fairacre would not be tempted to go there to spend their money. Thursday is market day, and three buses run from our village into Caxley on that busy day. We could not hope to compete with Caxley's magnetic pull on a Thursday. Besides, as Mrs Bonny pointed out reasonably, they would have more money to put in the silver collection *before* market day.

Excitement had mounted steadily during the Festival week and by the time Wednesday came it was at fever-pitch. The costumes and simple properties had been stacked on desks at the side of my room and Mrs Bonny's, for want of any other place to put them, and mighty little work had been done by the children with such attractions lying near by. Pens in hand, arithmetic exercises neglected before them, the children's bemused gaze turned constantly to the glamorous heaps of clothes. Here was a glimpse of another world. Our country children rarely go to the theatre. An annual visit to the pantomime is about all that comes their way. Here, close at hand, were all the trappings of magic, the means of slipping from the everyday world of school to one of enchanting fantasy. It was little wonder that I had very few sums to mark each day. But a wise teacher knows when she is beaten, and I forbore to scold.

As soon as school dinner was demolished we set about arranging the seating. The partition was pushed back, the desks removed either to the playground or to one end to form the basis of the stage. Mr Willet, Mr Roberts the farmer, and Jim Farrow his shepherd, arranged the long planks across the desks, tried the curtains we had rigged up, and pronounced the stage ready.

Meanwhile, the children were putting the chairs in rows for the audience. These were new stackable beauties from the village hall, and we had been threatened with all sorts of penalties if any damage were done.

The din was appalling. The metal frames of the chairs clanged like an iron foundry. The men's voices, raised above the racket, were thunderous. The thud of their mallets as they knocked the planks into place reverberated among the pitch-pine rafters above. When at last the work was done, and the men had departed, Mrs Bonny and I took an aspirin and a cup of tea apiece in the hope of curing our headaches.

At two-thirty the schoolroom was packed tight. In the front seats were the vicar and the managers and a number of illustrious friends of the school. Parents, aunts and uncles, little brothers and sisters and numerous distant relations, whom I had never seen before, kept up a cheerful hum of conversation while panic grew steadily behind the stage curtain.

The first item was a collection of folksongs sung by the whole school. It was a tight squash to get all sixty-odd children on to the stage, and one scaremonger among the infants told everyone that 'them planks ain't safe', thus causing widespread terror.

'Anyone who wants to get off the stage can do so,' I said fiercely. 'But don't forget your mothers have come to see you.'

This quelled the riot a trifle, but Mrs Bonny and I had the usual fears to calm.

'S'pose us forgets the words?'

'S'pose there's a fire. Which door does we go for?'

'I feels a bit sick.'

'I forgets how the tune goes.'

'John Todd shoved me!'

'I never then!'

'Miss, there ain't enough room for us up this end. The wall's all coming off on my sleeve, miss. My *best* sleeve.'

At this moment, Mrs Bonny was obliged to take three of her youngest to the lavatory – an inevitable hold-up at any school function – whilst I applied my eye to the crack of the curtain to watch the audience. It really was a wonderful house, kindly and enthusiastic, and I only hoped we should not disappoint all those present.

At last all was ready. Mrs Bonny took her seat at the piano. United in the face of their common ordeal, the children grew suddenly silent. I hauled on the curtain rope, and we were off to a flying start.

The deafening applause which greeted every item was most gratifying. The infants, naturally, won the palm, and every time the curtain rose upon them there were loving cries of: 'Oh, aren't they sweet?' 'Look at our Billy!' 'The pretty dears!' 'Don't they sing lovely?' and the like. They certainly went through their paces magnificently, after initial bashfulness, and the folk dance nearly brought the roof – and the stage – down with energetic clapping and stamping.

This number ended the first half and we could hear the infants hard at it as my class prepared for *The Princess and the Swineherd* in the lobby. Ernest, usually so stolid, had become

hilariously excited and was clowning about in his finery,
reducing the girls to a state of helpless giggling.

The princess's skirt had been trodden on, and given
way drastically at the gathers, so that I was obliged to do
last-minute repairs with safety pins, with my hand inside her
waist-band.

'Oh, miss, you tickles!' giggled Elizabeth, wriggling about
like an eel. 'Oh, miss, your hands is cold!' Then a squeal. 'Oh,
miss, you've bin and *pricked* me!'

'Stand still then,' I begged, snapping the last pin home.
'There, now you'll do!'

'It's pinned to my vest, miss.'

'And that's how it will have to stay,' I assured her flatly.
'We're on in five minutes.'

These words had a dual effect. Some children were, mercifully, struck dumb. Others became panic-stricken and fussed
even more vociferously. Luckily, applause and cheers broke
out from the schoolroom at this stage, the infants came

trooping back, flushed with success, and we were obliged to collect our senses ready for our big moment after the brief interval.

'The magic saucepan's bin and gone!' exclaimed Patrick dramatically. This was the highly necessary property round which the Princess and her ladies gathered to discover the meals being cooked all over the town. There was a frenzied scattering of costumes, searching under chairs and general confusion until one of the infants, flown with success, was discovered with it on his head from whence it was wrenched by one of his enraged elders.

'You might have had his ears off,' observed an onlooker dispassionately, but relief was so general that no one took much notice of this true statement.

After all the excitement I was prepared to find the cast both agitated and wordless, but all went well. Ernest's courtly bows were marvels of grace, and the only slight slip was the addition of 's' now and again, in true Fairacre fashion.

'We knows who's going to have sweet soup and pancakes! We knows who's going to have porridge and chops!' chanted the ladies exultantly. At least, I told myself philosophically, they did not say: 'Us knows', as they might so easily have done.

The applause at the end of the performance was deafening, and augured well for the repeat programme in the evening.

By the time the children and their parents had gone home, Mrs Bonny and I were dog tired. We tottered across to my house, and revived our strength with tea, tomato sandwiches and shortbread.

'Mr Willet says we've taken over seven pounds this afternoon, and it should be as much again this evening,' said Mrs Bonny, surveying her stockinged feet at the other end of the sofa. 'It should help the funds quite a lot.'

'It should,' I agreed. We lapsed into exhausted silence, and I guessed that her thoughts were running on the same lines as mine. Should we ever, in this small village, even with the herculean efforts we were making, ever come anywhere near the target we had so hopefully and bravely set ourselves?

Three hours later, much refreshed, we crossed the play-ground for our second house. Against a ravishing blue sky, the newly gilded weathercock flamed triumphantly on the pinnacle of St Patrick's spire. It was a heartening sight.

Resolutely we thrust our doubts from us, pushed open the heavy school door, and were engulfed once again by our teeming mob.

8

Our School Concert, which finally netted sixteen pounds for the funds, was one of the more modest efforts in Festival Week. It was on a par with the Mammoth Whist Drive, the Giant Draw and the Fabulous Flower Show. The *Son et Lumière*, with the added attraction of Jean Cole, was the backbone of the week, of course, and was so successful that it was decided to carry on for the next week as well, much to everyone's joy.

It was fortunate that it had done so well, for calamity hit Fairacre the day before the fête. The pop star Peter Martin, whose advent we had all awaited so eagerly, was involved in a car crash on Thursday evening, and was taken to hospital with two broken ribs and concussion.

We heard the news on radio and television that evening and were plunged into gloom. The vicar, good Christian that he is, forbore to express what was in most of our minds, simply saying: 'Poor young fellow! It is a mercy that his injuries are no worse!'

Jock Graham was more outspoken. 'This'll make a differ-ence to the takings,' he observed dourly, reading the headlines in Friday's *Guardian*.

'He won't die, will he, miss?' asked a bevy of little girls round my desk. Peter Martin's injuries and the cruelty of Fate in thus snatching him from us were the playground topics of the day, and in fact, of the whole neighbourhood.

Lady Sawston, who lives locally, nobly agreed to step into the breach and to open the fête, but it was quite apparent that fewer people would attend now that our star attraction had gone. It was a sore blow indeed to our efforts.

The final item in the Festival's programme was the Gala Dance which was held in the Village Hall on Saturday evening and at which Peter Martin was to have sung. It was the culmination of our efforts, and the ladies of the Floral Society excelled themselves with shower arrangements on every wall bracket and a bank of massed flowers, contributed from Fairacre cottage gardens, across the width of the stage.

Homemade refreshments had been billed as one of the chief attractions, my own modest contribution consisting of two dozen sausage rolls and a rather handsome set of small savouries in aspic jelly, so ravishingly pretty – at least, in my own eyes – that I hoped that Amy might drop in unexpectedly and be impressed. Needless to say, she did not, and the only comment which I heard on their appearance came from Mrs Mawne, who remarked disparagingly to one of her helpers: 'Probably sent by the vicar's wife. She dabbles in aspic.' *Dabbles in aspic indeed*, I thought, smarting in silence. It is hardly surprising that Mrs Mawne is so generally detested.

I looked in during the last hour of the event. Faces were flushed, skirts whirling, you could have cut the air with a knife, and 'The Dizzy Beat' from Caxley lived up to its name, with enough tympani to drown the other three instruments.

It was a huge success, and I joined with zest the great circle for 'Auld Lang Syne', and wrenched other people's arms from their sockets with enthusiasm matching my neighbour's. After 'God Save The Queen', the company drifted away to the sound of car engines, roaring motor bikes and farewell cries, and I helped to wash up the debris.

Mrs Willet accompanied me home. It was lovely to be out in the cool night air. Someone had night-scented stocks growing in his front garden, and the fragrance was delicious. A half-moon lay on its back, cradled in the tree-tops, and an owl hooted from the vicarage cedar tree.

'A beautiful night,' said Mrs Willet. 'And a successful one. Do you think the vicar will know the result of the Festival Week tomorrow? Everyone's praying we'll have made enough to save the chalice, though they don't say much.'

'We'll live in hope,' I replied, opening my gate. 'We couldn't have done more anyway. That's one comfort.'

The vicar did not make an announcement the next day, but the hand on the Appeals' board shot round to one thousand and seven hundred pounds.

'Getting along now!' said the parishioners excitedly, as they made their way past the board. 'It's coming on, isn't it?'

'But not fast enough,' was Mr Mawne's comment to the vicar, after the service.

'I agree with you there,' said Jock Graham soberly. 'I've kept a tight eye on the money all the way along the line, and give Christie's their due, they've done a fine job at a reasonable price.'

'What is still outstanding?' inquired the vicar, leading the two to the vicarage for a glass of sherry.

'My estimate, a generous one, was two thousand. Christie's have had two lots of four hundred so far, the rest to be paid when the job is finished. That's twelve hundred to find. With luck we'll find the total is something under two thousand, and the rest can go into the Fabric Fund. We must have something behind us in case of further disaster.'

'God forbid!' exclaimed the vicar, his mouth working

piteously. He poured a sherry with a shaking hand, and they sipped in silence.

Mr Mawne broke it at last. 'It's no good, Gerald. You must go into this business of the sale of the chalice. It's all very well to be sentimental –'

'*Sentimental!*' cried the vicar, but his friend swept on.

'But the fact is that the chalice could be our salvation. Not only now, but as a hedge against future crises. After all, we could always have a replica made.'

'*A replica?*' echoed the vicar in anguish. 'But it wouldn't be the same!'

'Of course not,' agreed Mr Mawne soothingly, as though addressing a fractious child, 'but it would do as well.'

The vicar, too stunned to explain, shook his grey head sadly.

Jock Graham, unusually perceptive, spoke gently. 'It's a sore blow, I know, vicar, but it would be prudent to find out the possibilities. With any luck, it may never be needed, but it's only fair that the parish should know the position. We need another five or six hundred pounds to pay for this damage and to put the Fabric Fund on a sound footing. The Festival may bring in another sixty to seventy. There are the sums from the guarantors and the covenantors which will bring in another hundred or so, over a period of time. But it just isn't enough.'

The vicar put down his sherry glass carefully and looked from one to the other. 'Let me sleep on it,' he said. 'I'll give you an answer, one way or the other, early next week. It's a step I can hardly bear to contemplate.'

'Good man!' said Mr Mawne encouragingly, slapping his old friend painfully on the back, and the two men left the vicar to his own troubled thoughts.

'Simply pecking at your food, Gerald,' commented his wife, briskly removing the plates at lunch time. 'You worry far too much. You'll have another of your dizzy spells, if you're not sensible.'

'I'll have a walk this afternoon,' said the vicar meekly. 'Fresh air always calms me.'

The road to the downs above Fairacre peters out into a grassy track. Birds darted across the vicar's path, with cries of alarm. Rabbits bounded away with a flourish of white scuts, and at least four larks vied with each other high against the blue and white dappled sky. It looked so peaceful, so unchanging, much as it looked, thought the vicar with a pang, when the silversmith had finished his masterpiece, in the reign of Queen Anne over two hundred and fifty years ago.

He sat himself heavily on the springy turf and plucked a nearby harebell, twisting its wiry stem this way and that as he gazed at the village spread out below.

What should he do? He had had faith that his prayers would be answered, but God in His wisdom had seemed to withhold the easy way. There, below him, the villagers rested after their wholehearted efforts in Festival Week. The response had been wonderful, the village united as never before. There could be very little more expected from them. Henry Mawne was right. More help must come from another source, and the

only possibility was the chalice. He must bring himself to approach the Bishop and to seek his advice. He owed it to his church and to his villagers. He had been selfish and weak in refusing to face the facts.

He sighed heavily, and the view below him grew suddenly blurred. Sad at heart, he struggled to his feet and made his way home.

The vicar slept little in the nights that followed. He had met Mr Mawne and Jock Graham and agreed reluctantly to consult the Bishop. It had taken him a week to compose a letter, and now he awaited a reply in an agony of spirit.

One morning he sat leaden-eyed before his breakfast egg, surveying the pile of letters. There was no word yet from the Bishop, but among the bills, receipts and circulars was a long blue air mail envelope, as gaudy as a peacock among sparrows. The vicar took it up first, savouring this rare foreign treasure.

'George Washington had a fine face,' he observed, studying the stamps closely. 'And what a good idea these little address tickets are! So much more legible than some unknown hand-writing at the head of a letter.'

'Who's it from?' asked Mrs Partridge, cutting to the heart of the matter.

'Oh, now let me see. "G. D. Lamb," it says, Lamb,' said the vicar ruminatively. 'Do we know a Mr Lamb in America, my dear?'

'Of course we do!' exclaimed his wife impatiently. 'George Lamb who was here during the Festival. That's probably the recipe for almond cookies he promised me. Do open it, dear, and *please* eat your breakfast. I want to clear the table. I'm having a coffee morning here today to raise more funds.'

The vicar obediently took a bite of toast and then slit the envelope. The letter was written in a firm hand in good copper-plate which owed its beginnings to Miss Clare's guidance, many years earlier.

Mrs Partridge watched her husband's eyes widen and his face grow pinker as he perused the paper in his hand. At last, bemused, he put it down, and rummaging in the envelope produced a cheque which he studied with stupefaction.

'Is my recipe there?' asked Mrs Partridge.

The vicar shook his head slowly, as if to clear it, rather than in answer to his wife's query. He seemed beyond speech.

'Has he sent something to the Fund?' asked Mrs Partridge, her glance falling on the cheque. 'How very, very kind of him!'

The vicar opened his mouth, and shut it again. He took a sip of coffee, and then found his voice.

'He has sent us a cheque for two thousand dollars.'

'*No!*' said his wife, thunderstruck. 'He *can't* have done! Not even Americans are as rich as that, and George only has a catering business which he built up himself!'

Without a word, the vicar handed the cheque across the table.

'It must be two thousand, because it's got it in words as well as figures,' said Mrs Partridge, studying the cheque earnestly,

and speaking with great care as though she were explaining matters to herself. 'I simply can't take this in, Gerald.'

'It's not George alone, my dear. It appears that his good friends on the trip were most concerned to hear of our plight, and contributed very generously, and also got other people to do so. George says in his letter that two old ladies, whose parents came from these parts originally, gave a considerable part of the money, and so did some relatives of George's wife. Can you believe it, my dear? We have been gloriously blest.'

'It is absolutely wonderful!' said his wife huskily. 'In the face of such generosity one hardly knows whether to laugh or cry. Oh, Gerald, this will save the chalice, won't it?'

'It was my first thought,' confessed the vicar. 'I must telephone Henry immediately, and Jock, and then we must get in touch with the Rural Dean and the Bishop.'

He pushed back his chair and came round the table to kiss his wife. He looked, she thought, as though twenty years had fallen from him in the last five minutes. She watched him affectionately as he gazed once again at the cheque.

'How does one translate it into pounds?' he asked.

'Divide by three,' said Mrs Partridge promptly. 'That's somewhere near. Henry will know exactly.'

'But that means this is worth almost seven hundred pounds! It is quite incredible! To think that people who have never seen us or our little church should be so overwhelmingly generous! It does one's heart good.'

'The same sort of thing happened at Dorchester Abbey,' his wife reminded him. 'And there was a simply lovely service of thanksgiving with lots of Americans there. Remember?'

'Yes, indeed,' nodded the vicar. 'And there will be one here in Fairacre before very long, I can promise you.' He picked up George Lamb's letter and put it carefully, with the cheque, into his wallet. 'I shall do my telephoning, and write this morning to George and all his kind friends,' he said. 'But what I shall say, I really don't know. My heart is too full.'

The joyous news flashed round the Fairacre grapevine within hours, helped considerably by the partakers of coffee at Mrs Partridge's morning meeting. Villagers were incredulous at first, and then genuinely touched by the unexpected benefaction. Even Mrs Pringle seemed moved by the magnificence of the present, though she was grudging in her first pronouncements to me.

'That George Lamb must've done well for himself in New York. Been fleecing the customers, I shouldn't wonder.'

I was roused to wrath and told her that the idea may certainly have been George's, but the bulk of the money was from Americans who had never even seen St Patrick's, which made the gesture even more wonderful. Mrs Pringle had the grace to look a little sheepish as she spread a tea towel over the hot boiler to dry.

'Yes, that's true,' she conceded. 'I've always understood the Americans – for all their funny ways – had a feeling heart. And say what you like, Miss Read, it's a feeling heart that matters when you're in trouble. They tell me the vicar's already planning a thanksgiving service as soon as the repairs is done.'

'We'll all be there,' I promised her.

EPILOGUE

Exactly a year after the fateful night which wrecked the roof of St Patrick's, the bells were rehung in the repaired belfry.

Now all was completed. The spire and the roof presented their usual tidy aspect to the village. At last the scaffolding had gone. The workmen's huts had vanished, and the trodden grass of the churchyard was fast returning to its velvety greenness under Mr Willet's tending. The hand on the Appeal Fund board stood triumphantly at well over two thousand pounds thanks to the efforts of the folk of Fairacre and their friends near and far.

In his study, the vicar was composing the sermon he would be giving the next Sunday at the great thanksgiving service. On his desk stood Queen Anne's silver chalice reflecting the autumn sunshine in its mellow curves. The vicar touched its ancient beauty with loving fingers. In a few minutes it would be in the kitchen being cleaned by Mrs Partridge in readiness for its part in the festivities of the great day.

What hopes and fears had centred round this lovely thing during the past year, he thought! What a year it had been for them all in Fairacre!

He pushed aside his papers and went into the garden for a breath of air. It was a quiet, gentle day with no breath of wind, a contrast indeed with the fury of the first of October last year when disaster had struck.

He thought, with gratitude, of all the blessings which had followed – the united efforts of all in the village, the bravery, the generosity of everybody, particularly of those American friends who had forged an unforgettable link with this small unknown village, as a result of last year's storm. What friends Fairacre had made! What fun it had been!

He stooped to pick up a shred of paper which was lodged among the button chrysanthemums in the border. He smoothed it out and surveyed the lettering with a smile of intense happiness. Crumpled, rain-washed and faded, it was the final triumphant scrap of

THE FAIRACRE FESTIVAL
EVERY EV

Farther Afield

For Audrey and Jack
with love

CONTENTS

* * *

PART THREE

Return to Fairacre

PART ONE

A Visit to Bent

* * * *

1. END OF TERM

'When do we come back?' said Joseph Coggs.

He stood close by my chair, rubbing the crepe sole of his sandal up and down the leg. A rhythmic squeaking, as of mice being tortured, had already turned my teeth to chalk. I turned to answer the child, anxious to put us both at ease, but again I was interrupted.

In the midst of the hubbub caused by end-of-term clearing up, Patrick and Ernest had come to grips, and were fighting a silent, but vicious, battle.

Without a word, I left Joseph, moved swiftly into the arena, and plucked the two opponents apart with a practised hand. With a counter-movement I flung them into their desk seats where they sat panting and glowering at each other.

Despite all the modern advice by the pundits about irreparable damage to the child's ego, I continue to use out-dated but practical methods on an occasion like this, and find they work excellently. Sweet reasoning will not be any more effective with two young males in conflict than it will with a dog-fight on one's hands. The first objective is to part them; the second to find out why it happened.

In this case, a revoltingly dirty lump of bubblegum had been prised from under a desk, and both boys laid claim to it. Both are well-nourished children, from decent homes, whose mothers would have been as disgusted as I was by this filthy and aged sweetmeat finding its way into their hands, let alone their mouths.

3

I held out my hand, and Patrick put the clammy object into it. For once, it landed in the waste-paper basket without mishap, and the incident was closed.

Patrick and Ernest returned to their desk-polishing, much refreshed by the tussle, and at last I found time to answer Joseph Coggs.

'Term begins on 5 September,' I told him.

He sighed. 'It's a long time,' he said mournfully.

'A *very* long time,' I agreed, beaming upon him.

No matter how devoted, dedicated, conscientious and altogether *noble*, a teacher is, I feel pretty sure that each and everyone feels the same sense of freedom and relief from her chains when the end of term arrives.

And of all end of terms, the most blissful is the end of the summer term, when six weeks or more stretch ahead, free of timetables, bells, children and their parents. Six weeks in which to call your soul your own, to enjoy the garden, to think about next year's border plants, and of stocking up the log shed; even, perhaps, a little house decoration and tidying cupboards, although the thought of Mrs Pringle over-seeing the latter operation cast a cloud upon the sunny scene.

Mrs Pringle, school cleaner and general factotum to Fairacre School, sometimes obliges by giving me an extra hour or two on Wednesdays. I greet her offers with mixed feelings. On the one hand, the house certainly benefits from her ministrations, but her gloomy forebodings and her eloquent dissertations on the deplorable way I manage my house-keeping affairs are enough to dash the stoutest heart.

I had already determined to assist Mrs Pringle in her 'bottoming', as she terms a thorough cleaning, and to behave in as kind and Christian a manner as was possible under extreme provocation. If, as I knew from experience, Mrs Pringle's needling became intolerable, I could always put some cheese, biscuits and fruit in the car, with the current book and that day's crossword puzzle to solve, and drive to one of the nearby peaceful spots, far from Mrs Pringle's nagging tongue and the reek of unnecessarily strong disinfectant.

'After all,' I told myself, 'I can take quite a lot of Mrs P. It's when Mrs Hope is dragged up and flaunted before me that I crack.'

Mrs Hope was the wife of a former headmaster, and had lived in the school house as I do now. She must have had a dog's life, for her husband drank, and she found solace in unceasing work in the little house.

'From dawn to dusk, from morning till night,' Mrs Pringle has told me, far too often, 'Mrs Hope kept at it. Never without a duster in her hand, and anybody invited to tea was met on the doorstep, and offered a clothes brush and a pair of slippers so as not to soil the place.'

'I shouldn't think many returned.'

'No, that's true,' said Mrs Pringle thoughtfully. 'But then Mrs Hope was *very* particular who came to the house.'

This was a side-swipe at me whose door stands open for all to enter.

Mrs Hope, so I am told, was always at the wash-tub before seven, twice a week, and even scrubbed out the laundry basket each time. Like Mrs Tiggywinkle, she was 'an excellent clear-starcher', and naturally *nothing*, not even heavy bedspreads and curtains, was ever sent to the laundry.

'Mrs Hope would have scorned such a thing, and anyway laundries don't get the linen really clean. And, what's more they use *chemicals*!'

If she had said that the dirty linen was prodded by devils with pitchforks, she could not have sounded more scandalized.

The introduction of Mrs Hope into any conversation was usually breaking point for me, and I could foresee many alfresco meals whilst Mrs Pringle was obliging.

There are many places within a quarter of an hour's drive from Fairacre which make glorious picnic spots. There are hollows in the downs, sheltered from the winds, where the views are breathtaking, and the clouds throw little shadows like scurrying sheep on to the green flanks of the hills.

There are copses murmurous with cooing wood pigeons, and fragrant with damp moss and aromatic woodland flowers. But my favourite spot is by the upper reaches of the River Cax, before it wanders into Caxley, and threads between the rosy houses to find its way eastward into the Thames.

Here the wild cresses grow in the shallows, their white flowers dazzling against the darker water. Little water-voles splash from the bank into the stream, stopping occasionally to nibble a succulent shoot, or to chase another of their kind. And here too a heron can be seen upstream, standing like some shabby furled umbrella, dark, gaunt and motionless upon the bank.

It is here, particularly on a sunny day, that its magic works most strongly. It is the 'balm of hurt minds'. No human being is in sight. No human habitation distracts the eye. The slow-moving water flows at the same pace as it has always done, sheltering and giving life to fish, plants and insects. Thirsty bees cling to the muddy brink. Dragonflies dart, shimmering, across the surface, and the swallows swoop to drink. Below, in the murk, among the drifting water weeds, the dappled trout lie motionless. Life, in its infinite forms, pursues its unchanging course, timeless and unhurried, and a man's cares fall from him as the things that matter – sunshine, moving water, birds and small beasts – combine to cast their spell upon him.

I was snatched from my reverie by Linda Moffat's voice.

Where, she was demanding, should she put the two dozen or so fish-paste jars she had just collected and washed 'off of the nature table'?

'Never use "off of",' I replied mechanically, for the two thousandth time that term. A losing battle this, I thought resignedly, but one must soldier on. 'Having a lend of' or 'a borrow of' is a similar enemy, while 'she never learnt me

6

nothing' or 'I never got teached proper', pose particular problems to those attempting to explain the niceties of English usage.

'Try the map cupboard,' I suggested, watching the child transferring a black smear from her hand to a freshly-starched linen skirt. Poor Mrs Moffat, I thought compassionately, and the child at home for six weeks!

'Miss,' shouted Ernest, above the din, 'it's home time.'

'Two minutes to finish clearing up,' I directed, fortissimo.

Within three, they rose for prayers. The class-room was bare, ready for Mrs Pringle's ministrations during the coming week, and the waste-paper basket was overflowing.

'Hands together, eyes closed.'

I waited until the seats had stopped banging upright, and the fidgeting had stopped.

> Lord, keep us safe this night,
> Secure from all our fears,
> May angels guard us while we sleep,
> Till morning light appears.
> > *Amen.*

If this was taken at a more spanking pace than usual, why not? Ahead stretched freedom, fresh air, bathing and fishing in the infant Cax, wrestling and jumping, rejoicing in growing strength and, no doubt, eating all day long – ice-cream, potato crisps, biscuits and loathsome bubblegum, in an endless stream.

'Make sure you take *everything* home, and enjoy your holidays. When do you come back?'

'September the fifth, miss,' they chanted.

'Very well. Good afternoon, children.'

'Good afternoon, miss.'

And then began the stampede to get out into the real world which was theirs for six whole weeks.

I remained behind for a few minutes, locking drawers and cupboards, and retrieving a few stray papers to add to the load in the waste-paper basket.

I locked the Victorian piano. How much longer would it hang together, I wondered? The tortoise stove stood cold and dusty now, but Mrs Pringle's hand and plenty of blacklead would prepare it for the autumn term. There would be the familiar battle I supposed, about '*the right day*' to light it, Mrs Pringle playing for time, whilst I pleaded, cajoled, and finally ordered, the stove to be lit.

But what did that matter now? 'Seize the moments as they pass,' said the poet, I intended to follow his sound advice and, locking the school door, emerged into the sunshine.

There was a welcoming chirrup from Tibby as I entered the front door of the school house. She was at the top of the stairs,

yawning widely, her claws gripping the carpet rhythmically as she stretched.

Plain Wilton carpet costs an enormous amount of money, as I discovered when I was driven to replace the threadbare stair carpet last year. Tibby has seen to it that the top and bottom stair are generously tufted, much to the horror of Mrs Pringle, and to my lesser sorrow.

It is sad, I know, to see such maltreatment of one's furnishings, but one must look realistically at life. Either one has no cat and plain Wilton, or one has a cat and tufted Wilton. I prefer the latter.

Tibby, I knew, had just arisen from her resting place on my eiderdown – another habit which Mrs Pringle deplores.

'Cats' fleas cause cholera', she told me once with such conviction that I almost believed her. She followed up the attack with a vivid account of someone she knew who had allowed their child – or maybe it was their second cousin's child – to bite the skin of a banana. The result was a rash, diagnosed on the spot by the doctor as leprosy, and the child was never seen again by the family.

Although I did not believe a word of this cautionary tale at the time, so downright was Mrs Pringle's manner whilst telling it, that I still find myself opening a banana with careful fingers and making sure that the children do the same. The cholera I have decided to ignore. A school teacher's life is too busy to follow up every precaution suggested, and in any case, Tibby, I tell Mrs P. robustly, has no fleas.

The cat sprang down the stairs and accompanied me into the kitchen, watching the kettle being filled, the tray being set, and all the familiar routine leading to a few drops of milk in a saucer for her, as I drank my tea.

A quarter of an hour later, my second cup steaming beside me, I watched her as she lapped. Eyes half-closed in bliss, her pink tongue made short work of the milk.

'We've broken up, Tib,' I told her. 'Broken up at last.'

I leant back and thought idly about the hundred and one domestic affairs I must see to. There was Mr Willet to consult about a load of logs. And then I had promised the vicar I would play the organ whilst the regular organist, Mrs Pratt, had her annual holiday. I must check the dates. And the sitting room curtains were in need of attention. Ever since their return from the cleaners, the lining had hung down a good three inches, so that even I had been irritated by their slip-shod appearance.

Then I really ought to tidy all the drawers in the house. The kitchen table drawer jammed itself stubbornly on the fish-slice every time it was opened. But where could the fish-slice go? And the paper-bag drawer had so many stuffed into it that half of them had fallen over the back into the bottling jar cupboard below.

Never mind, I told myself bravely, with all this time before me the place would soon be in apple-pie order. Why, I might even get round to labelling all those holiday prints of yesteryear before I clean forgot the names of the places.

It was pleasant lying back in the armchair reviewing all the jobs waiting to be done, confident that all would be accomplished in the golden weeks that lay ahead. I should tackle them methodically and fairly soon, I told myself, stretching as luxuriously as Tibby. No need to rush. And later on I should take myself for a short holiday somewhere pleasant – Wales, perhaps, or Northumberland, or the Peak District. Or what about Dorset? Very attractive, Dorset, they said . . .

Near to slumber, I basked in my complacency. The tea-pot cooled, the cat purred and a bumblebee meandered murmurously up and down the lavender hedge outside.

Months later, looking back, I realized that that blissful hour was the highlight of the entire summer holiday.

2. STRUCK DOWN

Dawn breaks with particular beauty on the first day of the holidays, no matter what the weather. On this occasion, the sun fairly gilded the lily, rousing me with its beams, and dappling the dewy garden with light and shade.

I took my coffee cup outside, and sniffed the pinks in the border. This was the life! Even the thought of Mrs Pringle, due to arrive at 9.30 for a 'bottoming' session, failed to quench my spirits.

Across the empty playground stood the silent school. No bell would toll today in that little bell-tower. No jarring foot would jangle the metal door scraper. No yells, no screams, no infant wailings would make the air hideous. Fairacre School was as peaceful as the graveyard nearby – a place of hushed rest, of garnering dust, given over to the little lives of spiders and curious field mice.

Not for long, of course. Within a few days Mrs Pringle would begin her onslaught. Buckets, scrubbing brushes, sacking aprons, kneelers, and a lump of tough yellow soap prised from the long bar with a shovel, with an array of bottles containing disinfectant, linseed oil and vinegar, and other potions of cleanliness, would assault the peaceful building under the whirlwind direction of Mrs Pringle herself. Woe betide any stray beetle or ladybird lurking behind cupboards or skirting boards! By the time Mrs Pringle's ministrations were over, the place would be as antiseptic as a newly-scrubbed hospital ward.

In the far distance I could hear sheep bleating and a tractor chugging about its business. A car hooted, a man shouted, a dog barked. The life of the village went on as usual. The baker set out his new loaves, the butcher festooned his window with sausages, the housewife banged her mats against the wall, and the liberated children beset them all.

Only I, it seemed, was idle, glorying in my inactivity as happily as the small ruffled robin who sat sunning himself on a hawthorn twig nearby. But such pleasant detachment could not last.

St Patrick's had long ago struck nine o'clock, and the crunch of gravel under foot now told of Mrs Pringle's arrival.

I sighed and went to greet her.

Mrs Pringle's black oil-cloth bag, in which she carries her cretonne apron and any shopping she has done on the way, was topped this morning by a magnificent crisp lettuce, the size of a football.

'Thought you could do with it,' she said, presenting it to me. 'I know you don't bother to cook in the holidays, and I noticed all yourn had bolted. Willet said you was to pull 'em up unless you wanted to be over run with earrywigs.'

I thanked her sincerely for the present, and the secondhand advice.

'Tell you what,' went on the lady, struggling into her over-all, 'if you pull them up just before I go, I can throw them to my chickens. They can always do with a bit of fresh green.'

I promised to do so.

'Well, now,' said Mrs Pringle, rolling up her sleeves for battle, 'what about them kitchen cupboards?'

'Very well,' I replied meekly. 'Which shall we start on?'

Mrs Pringle cast a malevolent eye upon the cupboards under the sink, those on the wall holding food, and the truly dreadful one which houses casseroles, pie dishes, lemon squeezers and ovenware of every shape and size, liable to cascade from their confines every time the door opens.

'We start at the top,' Mrs Pringle told me, 'and work down.' She sounded like a competent general issuing orders for the day to a remarkably inefficient lieutenant.

I watched her mount the kitchen chair, fortunately a well-built piece of furniture capable of carrying Mrs Pringle's fourteen stone.

'Get a tray,' directed the lady, 'and pack it with all this rubbish as I hand it down. We'll have to have a proper sort-out of this lot.'

Obediently, I stacked packets of gravy powder, gelatine, haricot beans, semolina and a collection of other cereals and dry goods which I had no idea I was housing.

'Now, why should I have three packets of arrowroot?' I wondered aloud.

'Bad management,' snorted Mrs P. There seemed no answer to that.

'And half this stuff,' she continued, 'should have been used months ago. It's a wonder to me you haven't got Weevils or Mice. I wouldn't care to use this curry myself. That firm went out of business just after the war.'

I threw the offending packet into the rubbish box – a sop to Cerberus.

'Ah!' said Mrs Pringle darkly, 'there'll be plenty more to add to that by the time we've done.'

It took us almost an hour to clear all three shelves. Mrs Pringle was in her element, wrestling with dirt and disorder, and glorying in the fact that she had me there, under her thumb, to crow over. I can't say that I minded very much. Mrs Pringle's slings and arrows hardly dented my armour at all, and it was pleasant to come across long lost commodities again.

'I've been looking everywhere for those vanilla pods,' I cried, snatching the long glass tube from Mrs Pringle's hand. 'And that bottle of anchovy essence.'

'It's as dry as a bone,' replied Mrs Pringle with satisfaction, 'and so's this almond essence bottle, and the capers. What a wicked waste! If my mother could see this she would turn in her grave! Every week the cupboards were turned out regular, and everything in use brought forward and the new put at the back. "Method!" she used to say. "That's all that's needed, my girl. Method!" and it's thanks to her that I'm as tidy as I am today,' said my slave-driver smugly.

'My mother,' I replied, 'died when I was in my late teens.'

But if I imagined that this body blow would affect my sparring partner, I was to be disappointed.

'It's the early years that count,' snapped Mrs Pringle, throwing a box of chocolate vermicelli at my head.

I gave up, and we continued in silence until the cupboard was bare. Then I was allowed to retreat upstairs to dust the bedrooms whilst Mrs Pringle attacked the shelves with the most efficacious detergent known to man.

A little later, over coffee, Mrs Pringle gave me up-to-date news of the village.

'You've heard about the Flower Show, I suppose?' she began.

I confessed that I had not attended this Fairacre event on the previous Saturday.

'A good thing. There's trouble brewing. Mr Willet says he's writing to the paper about it.'

'Why? What happened?'

'You may well ask. Mr Roberts won first prize for the best-kept garden.'

This did not seem surprising to me. Our local farmer always keeps a fine display of flowers and vegetables.

'What about it?'

Mrs Pringle took such a deep breath that her corsets creaked. 'Mr Roberts,' she said, with dreadful emphasis, 'has Tom Banks working in that garden three days a week – if working you can call it. And, what's more, he had all the farmyard manure at his beck and call. How can us cottagers compete with that?'

I saw her point.

'The Flower Show's never been the same,' said Mrs Pringle, 'since that fellow that worked up the Atomic got on the committee. Good thing he's been posted elsewhere, but the trouble still remains. All this Jack's-as-good-as-his-master nonsense! Don't you remember the outcry when he wiped out the cottager classes? Said it was degrading to have two types of entry. As though we bothered! If you does your own digging and planting, you're a cottager. If you gets help, you're not. I never could see why that man was allowed to question the ways of the Almighty. "The rich man in his castle, the poor man at his gate", says the hymn. And what's wrong with that, I'd like to know? If there'd been a cottagers' class, as there always used to be, then Mr Willet would have come first, and rightly so. He's drafting a fair knock-out of a letter to the *Caxley*.'

I said I should look forward to reading it in next week's *Caxley Chronicle*.

'Oh, I don't say it will be in that early,' said Mrs Pringle, stacking our cups. 'So far, it's only got as far as the first draft on a page of Alice Willet's laundry book. But he's keeping at it.'

She replaced the lid of the biscuit tin.

'Mrs Partridge's niece goes back to London today. I should think she and the vicar will be downright thankful. As far as I can hear, the girl's done nothing but wash her hair and walk about with one of those horrible transistors all day.'

'She's supposed to be a very clever girl,' I said, rising to the absent one's defence.

'Being clever don't get you far,' sniffed Mrs Pringle. 'There's some, not a hundred miles from here, who's passed examinations and that, but don't know no more than that cat what's in their cupboards.'

Reminded of her duties, she rose and removed the tray from the kitchen table to the draining board.

'You'd be least bother to me,' she told me, 'if you made yourself scarce while I tackle that china cupboard. I don't trust myself to keep a civil tongue in my head while that's being bottomed, and I've never been one to speak out of place, I hope.' She glanced at me sharply. 'I suppose you wouldn't have such a thing as some good white paper for lining the shelves when I've washed them?'

'As a matter of fact,' I told her with some pride, 'there's a roll of lining paper upstairs. I'll run up and get it.'

It was pleasant to dazzle Mrs Pringle with my efficiency for once, and I rooted about in the landing cupboard among boxes of stationery, stored Christmas tree decorations, and a mound of yellowing cuttings from magazines which I tried to deceive myself into calling 'Reference Material' although, in my honest moments, I knew full well I should never refer to them.

The roll of lining paper had managed to work its way to the very bottom of the cupboard, and right to the back behind a pile of box files dusty with age, and bearing such labels as 'Infant Handiwork Ideas', 'Historical Costumes', and the like. I wouldn't mind betting that most teachers have just such a collection of junk tucked away, carefully garnered as an insurance against the future, and looked at only once in a blue moon, or else forgotten completely.

The cupboard was a deep one and by the time I had wriggled the slippery roll from behind the boxes, I was hot and dusty and had laddered one stocking. I struggled to my feet feeling quite giddy with my exertions.

I hoisted one of the dusty files under one arm. It contained, if I remembered rightly, some patterns for making simple lamp shades, and these might prove useful for handiwork next term. I would go through the box at my leisure.

Mrs Pringle's lining paper began to behave like a telescope, the inside sliding out at remarkable speed. From being eighteen inches in length, the roll rapidly became thirty, and caught itself in the banisters as I took the first unsteady step downwards.

Everything happened at once. The heavy file slipped, the lining paper jammed, my ankle turned over with a crack, and the hall carpet rushed upwards to meet me amidst whirling darkness lit with stars. The latter moved into a circle, as though about to embark on 'Gathering Peascods'. Suddenly they vanished altogether, and I wondered why so many bells were ringing.

When I came round I was sitting on the bottom stair with my face against Mrs Pringle's bosom.

It was enough to bring me rapidly to full consciousness.

'You bin and fell down,' said that lady reproachfully.

There seemed nothing to add.

Five minutes later, on the sofa, I found myself trying to control my chattering teeth and to assess the damage done.

Mrs Pringle, who had collected the papers strewn all over the hall, now surveyed me lugubriously.

'Well, you've made a proper job of it,' she told me, with some satisfaction. 'If you don't have a black eye by morning, I'll eat my hat. And something's not right with that ankle.'

'Sprained,' I said. 'Nothing more, but my arm feels strange.'

It hung down at approximately its usual angle, but felt queerly heavy.

'Could be broken,' Mrs Pringle suggested, about to investigate.

'Don't touch it,' I squealed. I lifted it carefully. 'I don't think it can be broken,' I said. 'I mean there aren't any bones sticking through the flesh, and it isn't a funny shape, is it?'

'Could still be broken,' replied Mrs Pringle, with conviction. 'You don't know much about it, do you?'

I admitted that I was entirely ignorant when it came to anatomy. All I knew was that I was shaking and cold and for two pins would have howled like a dog.

'I should like some brandy,' I said. 'It's in the sideboard.'

Leaning back, I closed my eyes and gave myself over to being a casualty. Hell, how that ankle hurt! It would be swollen to twice the size in an hour, that was sure, and heaven alone knew what was the matter with my right arm.

I took the proffered glass in my left hand and sipped the fire-water.

'Where's Dr Martin this morning?' I asked. 'He'd better look me over, I suppose.'

'Wednesday,' said Mrs Pringle, seating herself heavily on the end of the sofa, far too close to my damaged ankle for my peace of mind. 'Wednesdays he's in Fairacre. He'll be at Margaret Waters sometime this morning, having a look at her bad leg. What a bit of luck!'

'Who for?' I said crossly. 'Oh, never mind, never mind, I'll ring there and leave a message.'

I struggled to my feet, screamed, and fell back on to the sofa again.

'It's The Drink,' said Mrs Pringle, in a voice of doom. I remembered that the blood of dozens of Blue-Ribboners beat in her veins, and regretted that I had allowed her to administer brandy to me, even for purely restorative reasons.

'No,' I managed to say, 'it's the ankle. Perhaps you would ring Miss Waters and ask her to see if Dr Martin could call.'

She went into the hall, and I swallowed the rest of the brandy. It was such a solace in the midst of my increasing discomfort that, for the first time in my life, I began to understand why people took to the bottle.

I lay back and surveyed the room through half-closed eyes. A bump over my right eye was coming up at an alarming rate. Would it be the size of a pigeon's egg by the time the doctor arrived, I wondered? And why a *pigeon's* egg? Why not a hen's or a bantam's egg?

Objects in the room had a tendency to shift to the left when I looked at them, and the curtains swayed in a highly distracting fashion. The clock on the mantelpiece grew large and then small in a rhythmic manner, and I began to feel as though the sofa had floated out to sea and we had run into a heavy swell.

Above the rushing noise in my head, I heard Mrs Pringle's boom from the hall.

'I'll tell her, Miss Waters. We'll be glad to see him. She looks very poorly to me – very poorly indeed. Oh, no doubt it'll be hospital with these injuries! Yes, I'll let you know.'

'*I'm not going to hospital!*' I shouted to the open door. Something crashed inside my head and, groaning, I turned my face into the sofa, giving the bump a second wallop.

Mrs Pringle appeared in the doorway. 'It's a good thing it's the first day of the holidays,' she said smugly. 'Give you plenty of time to get over it, won't it, dear?'

I drew in my breath painfully.

'Mrs Pringle,' I said, very quietly and carefully, 'I could do with a little more brandy.'

3. MEDICAL MATTERS

Extreme pain, it seems, has a curiously numbing effect on one's normal reactions. Preoccupied as I was with my afflictions, Mrs Pringle's deplorable remark, which ordinarily would have aroused my fury, now simply appeared to be unhappy but true.

It certainly looked as though a week at least would be needed to put me back into fighting trim. Nursing my arm I began to mourn those blissfully planned picnics, the efficient tidying-up, and the trips to distant places.

'Can't see you doing much in the next week or two,' announced Mrs Pringle, as if divining my melancholy thoughts. 'When my John sprained his ankle at football it was all of three months before he could put his weight on it – and him a *young* man, of course.'

Still cocooned, in my pain, from these barbs, I nodded agreement.

'Tell you what,' said the lady. 'I could come in each morning for an hour or so, seeing as it's holiday time. Get you an egg, say, or some soup to keep you going.'

This was a kind thought and I did my best to register gratitude. By now the arm was beginning to swell, and hurt badly. Would Dr Martin be able to get my sleeve rolled up? Would it have to be cut from the frock?

Alarmed now, I sat up and begged Mrs Pringle to help in my undressing.

'Before the doctor comes?' she asked scandalized.

I explained my fears.

'If that's all, I can slit it up now with the kitchen scissors,' she volunteered, making for the door.

'But I don't want it slit,' I wailed. 'I like this frock! If we can get it off now before this blasted arm gets more and more like a bolster, I can put on my dressing gown.'

'That would look decent enough,' conceded Mrs Pringle, 'and of course I'll stay in the room while he's here. It's only proper.'

She went stumping up the stairs, leaving me to wonder if Dr Martin, now somewhere around seventy, was in any great danger from a plain middle-aged school teacher temporarily one-legged and one-armed.

I could hear Mrs Pringle opening doors above. The room still pitched about, though the swell was not quite as severe as at first.

Closing my eyes, I let myself float gently out to sea upon the sofa.

'Well,' said a man's voice, 'you lost that fight, as far as I can see.'

I opened my eyes and saw Dr Martin surveying me. Mrs Pringle stood beside him. He pulled up a chair and began to examine the bump on my temple.

'Any pain?'

'Of course there is,' I said, wincing from the pressure of his ice-cold fingers. I explained the symptoms of rocking motions and the movement of furniture in the room.

'Humph!' He felt my skull gently.

'Any pain in the ox-foot?'

'In the *what*?'

'The ox-foot.'

I looked blankly at him.

'The *occiput*, girl,' he explained.

I continued to look at him dumbly.

'The *occiput*, the back of the head, woman!'

'Oh, no, no! None at all,' I assured him. 'Just this bang on the forehead.'

I began to feel rather cross. Why do medical men expect people to know all the Latin terms? Most patients, I suspect, are as ignorant of anatomy as I am. My doctor gets a plain statement in basic English from me, and I can't think why his reply cannot be expressed in the same vein.

If I tell him that the bony bump on my wrist hurts, what sort of answer do I get? It is usually some glib explanation about the action of the lower lobelia on the gloxinia, which may well affect the ageratum and so lead to total tormentilla. Bewildered by all this mumbo-jumbo the patient's normal reaction is to go straight home, apply witch hazel and make a cup of tea.

Dr Martin opened his black bag, moistened some cotton wool and dabbed my forehead.

'You'll survive,' he assured me, as I flinched. He looked across at the brandy bottle.

'Been drinking?'

'Purely for medicinal purposes,' I told him with dignity.

There was a sniff from Mrs Pringle.

'No need to keep you from your work,' said Dr Martin.

Mrs Pringle left the room reluctantly.

'Now, let's look at the arm.' He felt it and I screamed. 'Can you bend it here?'

'*No!*' I shouted fortissimo.

He nodded with evident satisfaction. 'Radial trouble, I think,' he said. 'Have to get it X-rayed.'

At that moment the telephone shrilled, and I heard Mrs Pringle lift the receiver.

By this time, the doctor had produced a calico sling from his bag and was folding it deftly. It smelt horribly of dog biscuits and was very rough when tied round my neck.

23

'Must keep it still and supported,' he told me. 'You're bound to have a good deal of pain with an elbow injury.'

No one could be kinder than dear Dr Martin, and normally I count him among my most respected friends at Fairacre, but the evident relish with which he imparted this information was hard to bear.

I lay back, exhausted, on the sofa. The pain had frightened me, and I was very careful to keep the arm quite still.

Dr Martin now turned his attention to the ankle. I had taken off my stockings and shoes, and looked morosely at the swelling of my left ankle. As he began to wriggle the toes this way and that, Mrs Pringle came into the room.

'Mrs Garfield on the phone,' she told us. This was Amy, my old college friend, and it was welcome news. Perhaps she could come to my aid?

'I must speak to her,' I told Dr Martin. 'She might be able to take me into Caxley if I have to go to be X-rayed.'

'Caxley? That's no good to you, my girl. There's no casualty department there now.'

I looked at him in horror. 'Do you mean I've got to be jogged all the way to Norchester?'

'That's right, my dear. And if your friend can take you, the sooner the better.'

The thought of travelling over fifteen miles to our county town appalled me. I lowered my bare legs gingerly to the ground, clutching my wounded arm tenderly the while.

Dr Martin came to my aid, and leaning heavily on his shoulder I hopped to the telephone.

'I've told her you're suffering from an accident,' Mrs Pringle said importantly, as I stood on one foot holding the receiver.

'What's happened?' asked Amy.

I told her.

'I'll be over in half an hour,' she promised. 'Get ready for the hospital and I'll take you straight there.'

My cries of gratitude were cut short by a click and the line going dead.

Amy had gone into action.

By the time she arrived, Dr Martin had departed on his rounds, and I was lying on the sofa, dressed by Mrs Pringle ready for the journey.

It had not been an easy preparation. Fastening stockings to suspenders I now found quite impossible with one hand, and I was obliged to Mrs Pringle for her assistance.

It was equally impossible to put on a coat, and this was draped round my shoulders insecurely. The sling was like emery paper round the back of my neck until Mrs Pringle managed to insert a silk scarf between it and my scarlet flesh. The ankle had been wrapped in yards of crepe bandage, and I felt as swaddled as an Egyptian mummy.

'You'll be a lot worse before you're better,' Mrs Pringle warned me.

The cupboards had been abandoned since my fall, and I could see she was torn between returning to her duties and tending the fractious sick.

'I'll be all right,' I told her, 'if you'd like to get on with the work.'

Before she had time to make her decision, the door opened and in walked Amy, looking as elegant as ever in a cream silk suit.

'Poor old love,' she said in a voice of such warm sympathy that only Mrs Pringle's presence kept me from shameful weeping.

'What do you need?' she asked more briskly.

'Only this chit from Dr Martin, I think.'

'Then let's ease you into the car and trundle on our way.'

Together, they helped me to hop to Amy's waiting car.

'Take the lettuces,' I shouted to Mrs Pringle through the window, 'and your money, and a thousand thanks.'

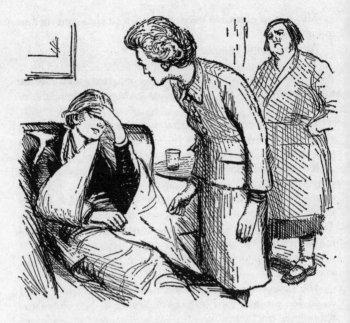

I finished on a high-pitched yelp as Amy let in the clutch and my elbow moved a millimetre.

'Sorry,' said Amy, looking anxious.

With infinite caution we began our journey.

Amy and I have known each other ever since our college days. She was one of that establishment's brighter stars, excelling in sport as well as work, and would have made a splendid head-mistress of some lucky school had she not married within three years of leaving college.

It was quite apparent that James would succeed in anything he took up. He was a dark-eyed charmer, with boundless energy and an effervescent sense of humour. He loved parties and social occasions of all kinds, going to great lengths to arrange outings which would please his friends, and always generous with his time and money.

He was, as the saying goes, 'good with children', and I know it was a blow to both of them that they had no family of their own. Nephews and nieces were frequent visitors to the house, and I think that Amy's spells of supply teaching gave her much-needed contact with children.

These spells grew more frequent as James advanced in his career and was more and more away from home. At this time he was a director of a cosmetic firm, and his work took him abroad several times a year. There were also a great many meetings in the United Kingdom to attend, and Amy was often alone at the lovely house in Bent, the village not far from Caxley and Fairacre, where they lived.

I must confess that I had my suspicions about James's fidelity. He was a warm-hearted gay fellow, as appreciative of pretty women as he was of the other attractive things in life. His frequent absences from home gave him ample opportunities for dalliance, and although I never doubted his love for Amy, some of his absences seemed unusually protracted to me. Added to that, his home-coming presents to Amy were so magnificent, that I personally should have viewed them with some suspicion, even from such a generous man as James.

Amy, however, was completely loyal and discreet. Secretly I had no doubt that she shared my feelings – she was far too astute to be deceived. Nevertheless, nothing had ever been said between us, and our affection increased over the years. Certainly, Amy tends to be bossy, and is always attempting to reform me in one way or another, but I am wonderfully resistant to pressure, as Mrs Pringle knows, and Amy's failure to improve me had not altered the very warm regard which we feel for each other.

This immediate response to my cry for help was typical of her, and I tried to tell her so as we turned into the hospital grounds.

Still clutching my piece of paper from Dr Martin, I was ushered into the waiting room of the casualty department, with Amy in attendance.

There were about fifteen of us unfortunates gathered there, some looking, to my inexperienced eye, at the point of death. There were also several children, all of whom appeared to be in excellent spirits.

'Sit down, dear,' said a nurse briskly, pushing up a wheel chair. It struck me smartly behind the knees, so that any modest refusal was cut short as I sat down abruptly.

A lively six-year-old pranced up to make my acquaintance.

'Are you very bad?'

'No,' I said bravely, 'Just my arm and leg are hurt.'

'My sister's bitten her tongue in half,' he said, indicating a screen in the middle distance. 'She won't let them put the stitches in.'

I began to hope that the child would be called away. I had quite enough to bear without all this extra harrowing.

'D'you know what that's for?' he asked, indicating a small scoop about the size of an ash tray, on the arm of my chair.

'No,' I said faintly. Hadn't this horrible child got a mother somewhere?

'It's to be sick in,' he told me.

'Here,' said Amy severely, 'you run away and find a book to read. This lady doesn't want to be bothered with you.'

'I don't want to be bothered with *her* either,' said the horror, moving towards the end of the room, where a battered cardboard box housed a collection of even more battered toys.

He selected a fiendish mechanical car which needed to be run over the tiled floor to make it work. The noise was hideous, but infinitely preferable to the child's company.

He was still at it when I was summoned to be examined by a doctor young enough to be my son. Used as I am to Dr

Martin's venerable aspect, I had some qualms, but he was quick and competent and I was despatched to the X-ray department with yet another piece of paper.

Amy waited in the first room and smiled cheerfully at me as I passed to be wheeled down a long corridor. There is nothing, I decided, as we steered an erratic course down the shiny passage, quite so demoralizing as being obliged to sit in a push chair.

By now the elbow was torturing me, and no matter how carefully the nurse arranged my arm for the camera I yelped frequently.

'One of the most painful injuries,' she told me, echoing Dr Martin, 'and of course it can't be put in plaster.'

I heard this with mixed feelings.

'The sling will be a great help,' she assured me, seeing my consternation.

'This one won't,' I told her. 'It's as rough as emery paper.'

'I'll change it,' she promised me. 'This does seem rather antique. Must be war issue.'

She set me up with one rather less scratchy, and I begged her to accept Dr Martin's.

'Dear me, no,' she replied, folding it up briskly. 'Take it home as a spare. After it's been boiled a few times it will be quite comfortable.'

We returned in the push chair to the waiting Amy. The horrible boy had been joined by another, slightly larger, and they were engaged in sticking out their tongues at each other.

'I'm glad you've found a *quieter* game,' said Amy kindly to them.

We waited yet again. At last, my X-ray photographs were displayed on a screen.

'A nasty crack across the radius,' I was told. 'Don't move it for three weeks, and we'll see you then.'

Don't move it, I thought rebelliously! What a hope!

I shuffled crossly towards the door, with Amy in attendance.

'Goodbye, Auntie Hopalong,' shouted the rude boy.

'I think you'd better come straight home with me,' said Amy, as we left the town behind us. 'You can't be alone like this. You're practically helpless, and there are some knock-out pills which I see Dr Martin left on the mantelpiece which you are supposed to take before you go to bed. Lord knows what they'll do!'

'It's terribly good of you, Amy, but I really can't be such a nuisance to you. Besides, there are all sorts of things to see to. Tibby, for instance, and the laundry hasn't been sorted, and the groceries arrive tomorrow, and I'll have to make some plans with Mrs Pringle.'

'Then I'll come and stay with you tonight,' said Amy firmly. 'James is away. There's nothing to worry about, and you're certainly not staying alone in the house. So, no arguing.'

I was deeply grateful. If only I could go to sleep, I felt that I would face anything when I woke up. Now all that I craved for was oblivion, and no doubt Dr Martin's pills would help there.

The journey seemed endless, but at last the school house was in sight. I edged my way painfully from the car, and was glad to gain the sitting room.

'Good heavens,' I said, catching sight of the clock. 'It's only half past two! I feel as if I'd been away for a fortnight.'

'I'm going to heat some soup,' said Amy, 'then make up a bed for you on the sofa here. Mrs Pringle's left you a note.'

She handed it to me and then vanished towards the kitchen.

It said: 'Have put all to rights and fed cat. Will come up this evening. Can live in if needed.'

Amy reappeared in the doorway.

'I take back all I've ever said about Mrs Pringle,' I told her, giving her the note to read.

'A handsome offer,' agreed Amy.

'Downright noble,' I said warmly.

'And how long,' said Amy, 'do you think you two could rub along together?'

'Well—' I began, and was cut short by Amy's laughter.

4. AMY TAKES COMMAND

Those of us who are lucky enough to live in a village, face the fact that our lives are an open book. Those dreadful stories of town-dwellers found dead in their beds, having been there for months, and even years sometimes, are not likely to be echoed in smaller communities.

Here, in Fairacre, villagers tardy in bringing in their milk bottles run the risk of well-meaning neighbours popping round 'to see if they are all right'. There are times when this concern for each other seems downright irritating. On the other hand, how comforting it is to know that people care about one's welfare!

Mrs Pringle, of course, had not been able to resist telling several of her friends about the drama in which she had taken part that morning.

Thanks to one of Dr Martin's pills I knew nothing from three o'clock that afternoon until I woke at ten that night, but Amy evidently had a succession of visitors during that time, and was very touched by their sympathy and their practical offers of help.

'The vicar's wife brought those roses,' she told me, waving towards a mixed bouquet which smelt heavenly on the side table. 'And she says you are not to worry about the organ on Sunday, as she is quite able to cope if she transposes everything into the key of C, and they cut out the anthem.'

I clutched my aching head with my sound hand. 'I'd forgotten all about that!'

'Well, keep on forgetting,' Amy advised me. 'You'll have to get used to the brutal fact that no one is indispensable.'

I nodded meekly, and wished I hadn't. Those pills were dynamite.

'And Mrs Willet's sent six gorgeous eggs and some tomatoes, and will do any washing while your arm's useless.'

'That woman's an angel. Luckily, her husband recognizes it.'

'Someone from the farm – I didn't catch the name—'

'Mrs Roberts.'

'That's it. She'll help in any way you like. Shopping, bringing you a midday meal. Anything!'

'People *are* kind.'

'They most certainly are,' agreed Amy, 'and I am absolutely flabbergasted at the way they're all rallying round you.'

I felt slightly nettled. Anyone would think that I am normally such a monster that I do not deserve any consideration. I was deeply grateful for all this concern, but Amy's astonishment was hard to bear.

'It isn't as though they have children at the school,' went on Amy, musing to herself.

'Even Mrs Pringle,' she continued thoughtfully, 'called this evening to see how you were.' She sighed, then jumped up to straighten the counterpane. 'Ah well! People are odd,' she said, dismissing the subject.

But by this time, my irritation was waning, for Dr Martin's blue pill was wafting me once more into oblivion.

The sun was warm upon the sofa when I awoke. It shone through the petals of the roses, and sent their fragrance through the room.

Amy was gazing at me anxiously.

'Thank God, you've woken up! I was beginning to wonder if you'd ever come to.'

'Why, what's the time?'

'Ten o'clock.'

'No! I must have had about sixteen hours' sleep.'

'How do you feel?'

'Marvellous, if I don't move.'

'Could you manage an egg?'

I sat up cautiously.

'I could manage an egg and toast and marmalade and butter and lashings of coffee and perhaps an apple.'

Amy laughed. 'You've recovered. Do you ever lose your appetite?'

'It improves in a crisis,' I assured her. 'When war broke out, I ate with enormous gusto. The more sensitive types on the staff of that school I was at then couldn't touch a morsel – or so they said – but I had the feeling each meal might be my last, so I made the most of it.'

Amy laughed, and went to the kitchen.

I could hear her moving china and saucepans, and lay back feeling one part guilty and nine parts relieved. How pleasant it was to be waited on! I tried to remember the last time I had lain back while someone else cooked my breakfast, and found it beyond my powers.

Tibby came undulating into the room, giving little chirrups of pleasure. She jumped elegantly on to the sofa, missing my damaged ankle by a millimetre. I clasped my poor arm in trepidation. Tibby's affectionate attention was a mixed blessing this morning.

Before she could do much damage, Amy appeared with the tray.

'I've cut your toast into fingers, my dear, and I'll spread your marmalade when you want it.'

'I feel about three years old,' I told her, 'and backward at that.'

Eating a boiled egg left-handed is no easy task, and I should certainly have gone without butter and marmalade if Amy had not been there to help me. Suddenly, I realized how horribly helpless I was. It was frightening.

'Now, about plans,' said Amy, putting down the knife.

'With all these offers of help from kind neighbours, I should be fine,' I said.

She looked at me quizzically. 'You haven't tried walking yet, or washing, or doing your hair or dressing.'

'No,' I agreed sadly.

'And let's face it, you can't possibly negotiate the stairs even with that ankle strapped.'

I knew this was the plain truth.

'I've thought it all out. You're coming back to Bent with me. There's plenty of room. I shall be glad of your company, and it will do you good to have a change of scene. So say no more.'

'It's more than generous of you, Amy, but—'

'It's no use arguing. I know what you are going to say. Well, Tibby can come too, or Mrs Pringle has offered to come in to feed her, so that's that. We can shut up the house and give Mrs P. the key. Mr Willet says he'll keep an eye on the garden and mow the grass.'

'But Dr Martin . . . ?'

'Dr Martin can be kept informed of your progress by telephone, and is welcome to visit you at my house.'

I looked at Amy with admiration. 'You've worked it all out to the last detail, I see.'

'I had plenty of time yesterday – and lots of offers from others, don't forget.'

I nodded in silence.

'I expect you'd like a wash. It'll have to be the kitchen sink.'

Bracing my arm stiffly, for I dreaded the pain when it was moved, I struggled to get my legs to the floor. Once they were there it was obvious that only the right one could bear any weight. Amy was quite right, I was helpless.

She was looking at me with some amusement. 'Well?'

'You win, you lovely girl. I'll come thankfully, bless you.'

One arm round her shoulders, I shimmied my way to the kitchen.

We were seen off that afternoon by a number of friends and well-wishers. I began to feel rather a fraud. After all, no one could say I was seriously ill. Nevertheless, it was delightful to receive so much sympathy and attention.

'The vicar and I will visit you next week,' promised Mrs Partridge.

'I've taken the dirty clothes,' called Mrs Willet.

'And I'll give the place a proper bottoming, cupboards and all, before you're back,' said Mrs Pringle, in a tone which sounded more like a threat than a promise.

We moved off, waving like royalty, to the accompaniment of Tibby's yowling from a cat-basket borrowed from Mr Roberts.

It is only about half an hour's run to Bent but I was mightily glad to arrive at Amy's house and to be ensconced in the spare room, which luckily was downstairs. Some wise person in the past had made sure that the window sills in the bedroom were low enough for the bed-ridden to admire the view, for which I was truly grateful.

Beyond Amy's immaculate garden, bright with lilies and roses, stretched rolling agricultural land. The crops were already ripening, and no doubt the combines would be out in the fields long before my beastly arm was fit to use. In the middle distance, a blue tractor trundled between the hedges on its way to the fields, and near at hand, on Amy's bird table, tits and starlings squabbled over food.

There would be plenty here to amuse me. How good Amy was! She had made light of taking me on, useless as I was, but I knew how much extra work I should be making, and determined to be up and about as soon as possible.

Tibby, released from the hated basket, was roaming cautiously about the room, sniffing at Amy's rose and cream decor with the greatest suspicion and dislike. She had deigned to drink a little milk, but was clearly going to take some time to settle down.

'You are an ungrateful cat,' I told her. 'You might well have been left behind with Mrs Pringle, and she would have bottomed you with the rest of the house.'

Amy entered with the tea tray.

'I imagine heaven's like this,' I said. 'Perfect surroundings, and angels wafting in with the tea.'

'But this one's going to watch you spread your own jam this time,' she warned me.

*

Later that evening, as the summer dusk fell and the scent of the lime flowers hung heavy on the air, Amy sat by the lamp in my bedroom and stitched away at her tapestry. A moth fluttered round the light, tapping a staccato tattoo on the shade, but Amy did not seem aware of it.

It was very quiet in the room. It seemed to me that Amy was unusually pensive, and although she had enough to think of, in all conscience, with me on her hands, somehow I felt her thoughts were elsewhere.

'Amy,' I began, 'you know I can't thank you enough for all you're doing, but won't I be even more of a burden when James comes home?'

'It won't be for several days,' said Amy, snipping a thread. 'It may be even longer. There was some possibility of going straight on to Scotland, if he can arrange things with somebody at the office to attend to that end and save him coming back again.'

There was something in Amy's tone which disquieted me. Despondency? Resignation? Hopelessness? I had never seen Amy in this mood, and wondered what was the cause.

'I don't think I shall need a blue pill tonight,' I said, changing the subject. 'I can hardly keep awake as it is.'

'I'm horribly sleepy too,' confessed Amy. She began to roll up her work, and glanced at the clock.

'James usually rings about eight, but something must have stopped him. No doubt there will be a letter in the post in the morning. I shan't wait up any longer.'

She rose, and came close to the bed.

'Have you got all you need? I've left this little bell to ring if you need me in the night, and I shall prop my door ajar. Tibby's settled in the kitchen, so there's nothing for you to worry about.'

She bent to give me a rare kiss on the forehead.

'Sleep well. I'll see you in the morning.'

After Amy had gone, I turned out the light and slid carefully down the bed. Tired though I was, I could not sleep.

It grieved me to see Amy so unhappy. Something more than my problems was eating at her heart. I had not known Amy for over thirty years without being able to measure her moods. That James was at the bottom of it all, I had no doubt. Was the rapscallion more than usually entangled this time? Was their marriage seriously threatened by the present philanderings?

It is at times like this that a spinster counts her blessings. Her troubles are of her own making, and can be tackled straightforwardly. She is independent, both monetarily and in spirit. Her life is wonderfully simple, compared with that of her married sister. And she cannot be hurt, quite so cruelly, as a woman can be by her husband.

Conversely, she has no one with whom to share her troubles and doubts. She must bear alone the consequence of all her actions and, coming down to brass tacks, she must be able to support herself financially, physically and emotionally.

I know all this from first-hand experience. I know too that there are some people who view my life as narrow and self-centred. Some, even, find a middle-aged single woman pitiable, if not faintly ridiculous. This, I have always felt, is to rate the value of men too highly, although I recognize that a truly happy marriage is probably the highest state of contentment attainable by either partner.

But how often something mars the partnership! Jealousy, indolence, illness, family difficulties, money troubles – so much can go wrong when two lives are joined.

Outside, in the darkness, a screech owl gave its blood-curdling cry. A shadow crept over the moon, and turning my face into the comfort of a pillow, I decided that it was time for sleep.

5. RECOVERY AT BENT

The days passed very agreeably at Amy's. Time hangs heavily, some people say, when there is nothing to do, but I found, in my enforced idleness, that the hours flew by.

The weather had changed from its earlier brilliance. The sky was overcast, the air was still. There was something curiously restful about these soft grey days. The air was mild and I sat in the garden a great deal, nursing my arm and propping my battered ankle on a foot-rest.

Amy had a small pond with a tinkling fountain in her garden, and the sound of the splashing water was often the only noise to be heard. I felt stronger daily, and began to get very clever at using my left hand. I was more and more conscious how much I owed to Amy's generosity of spirit. Without her care and companionship these early days of progress would have been much slower.

During these quiet days I had the opportunity of observing Amy as she went about her tasks. She dealt with her domestic routine with great efficiency, and I began to realize, at the end of a week, that without the method with which she approached each chore, I should have been alone far more often. As it was, she had time to sit and talk to me, or simply to sit beside me and read, or work at her tapestry. I think we grew closer together, in those few days, than we had ever been before.

Very little mention was made of James, although Amy did say one evening that he had telephoned to say that he was in Scotland and would not be returning for a week or so. The determinedly gay manner in which she told me this, confirmed my fears that Amy herself was a very worried woman. It made her kindness to me doubly dear.

One morning I was taking my cautious walk in the garden, leaning heavily upon a fine ebony stick of James's, when I was horrified to see the corpse of a hedgehog floating in the pond. Obviously, it had tried to reach the water, toppled in, and been unable to scramble out again. It was a pathetic sight, and I was wondering how I could get it out when Amy called from the house, and emerged with one of her friends, Gerard Baker.

I had met him first at one of Amy's parties, and several times since then. He had been collecting material for a book about minor Victorian poets, and visited Fairacre once or twice to learn more about our one poet Aloysius Stone.

We, in Fairacre, are rather proud of Aloysius, who lived in one of the cottages in Tyler's Row, and was somewhat of a trial at village concerts in the early part of the century. He loved the opportunity of reciting his poems, and was apt to go on for far longer than his allotted time, much to the consternation of the programme organizers and the outspokenness of his audience.

'This is a great day,' said Amy after we had exchanged greetings, and Gerard had commiserated with me about my battered condition. She held up a book.

'Not *The Book*?' I said.

'The very same,' said Gerard. 'Came out last month.'

'Well! And I didn't hear a thing.'

'I'm not surprised. I shouldn't think a book ever crept out into the world with as little notice as this one had.'

'But surely it will be reviewed? After all your hard work you're bound to have some recognition.'

'I doubt it. I'm not carping. There aren't exactly queues at the bookshop doors for *any* book, and one about Victorian poets won't set the Thames on fire. If it covers the costs I'll be content, and so will the publishers.'

By this time, Amy had walked across to the pond, and was studying the floating corpse with some distaste.

'Give me a rake,' said Gerard, approaching, 'and I'll fish the poor thing out for you.'

We surveyed the pathetic body, the shiny black snout, the brindled prickles, the scaly black legs.

Amy returned with the rake.

'It's really dead, I suppose?' she asked, bending closer to examine the corpse.

'Well, I can tell you flat,' said Gerard, casting his rake, 'that I'm not volunteering to give it the kiss of life! There are limits to the milk of human kindness.'

He fished the body to the edge and lifted it out.

'I think a distant patch of nettles, or some such rough cover, would be his best shroud. You aren't proposing burial? I'm no great shakes with a spade.'

'Good heavens, no, Gerard dear!' exclaimed Amy. 'Follow me, and we'll put him over the hedge into the ditch in the cornfield, poor little sweet.'

' "Sweet" ', said Gerard, his nose wrinkled, 'is not quite the word for it.'

He followed Amy towards the end of the garden, balancing the dripping victim precariously on the rake. I watched the funeral cortege from my chair with some amusement. The more I saw of Gerard Baker, the more I liked him.

He was clever but unaffected, sympathetic but not mawkish, and had a cheerful practical approach to problems – such as this present one – which I found wholly admirable. No wonder Amy welcomed him.

'What about a restorative?' she said when they returned. 'Gin, sherry?'

'Could it be coffee?' asked Gerard.

'Of course.' She went into the house.

'What a marvel she is!' exclaimed Gerard.

'I'll endorse that,' I said, and told him how wonderfully she had coped with me.

'Typical,' said Gerard. 'I was full of admiration for the way in which she coped with that lovelorn niece of hers, Vanessa.'

'I believe we may see something of her before long,' I told him. 'Evidently she's quite got over that infatuation. You know she's in Scotland? Working in a hotel?'

Gerard, to my surprise, looked somewhat embarrassed.

'Yes, I did know. As a matter of fact, I happened to call at the hotel a week or two ago. She seemed in great spirits.'

'Did you hear that, Amy?' I cried, as she put down the tray. 'Gerard has seen Vanessa, and she's very well.'

Amy shot a lightning glance at Gerard's face, and looked away quickly. He was endeavouring to look nonchalant, and not succeeding very well.

'I was in the district. I'm collecting material for a book about Scottish poets – a companion volume to the Victorian one, I hope – and I remembered the name of the hotel.'

'How nice! Is she flourishing?'

'In very good spirits. She said something about a holiday soon, and I gather she may come and see you.'

'That's right,' agreed Amy. She poured the coffee.

'Any news of the young Scotsman who was being so attentive?' she asked. Her tone was polite, but I detected a hint of mischief in her face.

Gerard had recovered his composure. 'I didn't hear anything about him. No doubt there are a number of attentive young Scotsmen. Vanessa's looking very attractive these days. Quite a change of aspect from the time when she was mourning the Chilean.'

'Bolivian!' said Amy and I together.

We sipped our coffee, relaxed and happy. A red admiral butterfly flitted decoratively from flower to flower in the herbaceous border, and I remembered the pale unhappy Vanessa whose passion for a four-times-married foreigner had blinded her to all summer delights on the first occasion of our meeting. She had spent a week with Amy then, and I don't think I had ever seen my normally resilient friend quite so exhausted.

'And how's Fairacre?' inquired Gerard. 'What of my friend Mr Willet?'

I gave him a brief account of village affairs to date, and conversation grew general. It was half-past eleven before he leapt to his feet, protesting that he must be off.

'I've an aunt living not far from here, and I'm taking her out to lunch. She's eighty-five and a demon for exercise. Think of me at about two-thirty, walking my legs off along some cart track.'

'Come again,' said Amy.

'I will,' he promised. 'But no corpses next time, please.'

That afternoon I broached the subject of my return home to Amy. I had been with her for well over a week, looked after as never before, and felt that I really could not impose upon her much longer.

'But I love to have you,' she assured me.

'You're too kind. There are lots of things you must be neglecting, and surely there's a holiday cropping up soon?'

I remember that she had discussed a visit to Crete earlier in the year. Nothing had been said about it while I had been staying at Bent, and it occurred to me that perhaps the plans had fallen through.

'That's nearly a fortnight away,' said Amy.

'You'll probably need to go shopping.'

'That doesn't mean that you've got to go back to Fairacre.'

I pointed out that there were a number of matters to attend to at home. There were some school forms to be filled up, and a certain amount of organization for next term. My domestic arrangements also needed some attention, though no doubt Mrs Pringle's bottoming would be almost finished.

'I'm mobile now,' I said, stretching out my lumpy ankle.

'Why, I can even dress myself if I keep to button-down-the-front things, and remember to thread the bad arm through the sleeve first!'

'You're getting above yourself,' Amy smiled. 'I really think you *are* getting better.' She surveyed me with her head on one side. 'I can see you're really bent on going. Tell you what. Let's drive over tomorrow afternoon and get the place ready, and see if you can manage the stairs and so on. If so, I'll install you the day after.'

And so it was agreed.

Amy took up her tapestry and I turned the pages of a magazine.

The thought of going home excited me. I should never cease to be grateful to my old friend, but I longed to potter about my own home, to get back to my books and my garden, to see the familiar birds on the bird table, and to smell the pinks in my border again. Tibby, too, would welcome the return.

Beyond Amy's window the rain was falling. Grey veils drifted across the fields, blotting the distant hills from view. It made the drawing-room seem doubly snug.

'I wonder how long it will be before I can do without this confounded sling,' I mused aloud. 'I can wriggle my fingers quite well. How long does a bone take to mend?'

Amy looked at me thoughtfully.

'Weeks at our age, I imagine.'

'I'm not decrepit, and I don't feel old.'

'I do now and again,' said Amy, with a vigour that belied her words. 'I find myself behaving like an old lady sometimes. You know, never walking up escalators, and not minding if young things like Vanessa stand up when I enter a room.'

'I haven't got quite to that stage yet.'

'But when I start pinning brooches on my hats,' said Amy, resuming her stitching, 'I shall know I'm *really* old.'

There was a companionable silence for a while. Outside, the rain grew heavier, and began to patter at the windows.

'Of course, I think about dying now and again,' I said.

'Who doesn't?'

'What do you do about it?'

'Well,' said Amy, snipping a thread, 'I make sure I'm wearing respectable corsets – not my comfortable ones with the elastic stretched and speckled with rubber bits – and I pay up outstanding bills and, frankly, there's not much else one can do, is there, dear?'

'But hope,' I finished for her.

'But hope,' she echoed.

She turned her gaze upon the rain-swept view through the window. There had been a dying fall in those last two words.

It was plain that it was the sadness of living, not of dying, which preoccupied my friend's thoughts.

And my heart grieved for her.

The next afternoon we drove from Bent to Fairacre. The rain had ceased, leaving everything fresh and fragrant. The sun shone, striking rainbows from the droplets on the hedge, and in its summer strength drawing steam from the damp roads. Sprays of wild roses arched towards the ground, weighted with the water which trembled in their shell-pink cups, and everywhere the scent of honeysuckle hung upon the air.

In the lush fields the cattle steamed as they fed, and birds splashed joyously in their wayside baths. Everywhere one looked there was rejoicing in the sunshine after the rain, and my spirits rose accordingly. As Fairacre drew nearer I grew happier and happier, until I broke into singing.

Amy began to laugh.

'What an incorrigible home-bird you are! You remind me of Timmy Willie.'

'When he was asked what he did when it rained in the country?' I inquired.

' "When it rains," ' quoted Amy, dodging a fat thrush in the road, ' "I sit in my little sandy burrow and shell corn and seeds." '

' "And when the sun comes out again," ' I finished for her, ' "you should see my garden and the flowers – roses and pinks and pansies." '

'I'm sorry for children who aren't brought up on Beatrix Potter,' said Amy. 'Look! There's St Patrick's spire ahead. You'll be back in your burrow in two shakes.'

The lane to the school was empty, and we arrived unseen by the neighbours. It was very quiet, the village sunk in the somnolence of early afternoon.

Inside the school house everything was unusually tidy. A few fallen petals from the geranium on the window sill made it look more like home, however, counteracting the symmetrically draped tea-cloths on the airer, and the Vim, washing up liquid and so on, which were arrayed with military precision in order of height on the draining board. Every polished surface winked with cleanliness. Never had the stove flashed so magnificently. Never had the windows been so clear. Even the doormat looked as if it had been brushed and combed.

'Well,' said Amy, gazing round. 'Mrs Pringle's had a field day here.'

Awe-struck, we went into the sitting room. Here, the same unnatural tidiness was apparent.

'I feel as though I ought to take off my shoes,' I said. 'It's positively holy with cleanliness.'

The coffee pot on the dresser, behind which I stuff all the letters needing an answer, now stood at the extreme side of the board. There was nothing – not even a single sheet of paper – behind it.

'Save us!' I cried. 'Where on earth is all my correspondence?'

'Gone to heaven on a bonfire,' Amy replied.

'But I *must* have it,' I began in bewilderment.

'Calm down,' said Amy, 'or you'll break your arm again.'

This idiotic remark had the effect of calming us both. We sat down, somewhat nervously, on the newly washed chair covers.

'She's washed every blessed thing in sight,' I said wonderingly, 'and I declare she's oiled the beams too. Look at the fire-irons! And the candlesticks! And the lamp shades! It's positively uncanny. I shall never be able to live up to this standard.'

'Don't worry,' said Amy comfortingly. 'By the time you've had twenty-four hours here, it will look as though a tornado has hit it, and it will be just like home again.'

It was one of those remarks which could have been more delicately expressed, or, better still, left unsaid. In normal circumstances I might have made some sharp retort, but Amy's kindness over the past week or so enabled me to hold my tongue.

We sat for a few minutes, resting and marvelling at Mrs Pringle's handiwork before embarking on a tour of the whole house. It was a relief to find that I could negotiate the stairs if I attacked them like a toddler, bringing both feet to one stair before essaying the next. I could have wished the banister had been placed on the left hand side instead of the right, but by assuming a crab-like motion I could get up and down very well and was suitably smug about it.

'And what about getting in and out of the bath?' asked Amy, deflating me.

'I'm going to get one of those rubber mats, so that I don't slip,' I told her. 'And I shall *kneel* down to bath, so that I can get up again easily.'

Amy laughed. 'You win, my love. If the worst comes to the worst, you can always ring me, and I'll nip over and scrub your back.'

We checked the goods in the larder, and made out a shopping list, and then went to inspect the garden. As well as Timmy Willie's roses and pinks and pansies, the purple clematis had come out, the velvety flowers glorious against the old bricks of the house.

We sat together on the rustic seat warmed by the sun, and tilted up our faces to the blaze as thankfully as the daisies on the grass.

Tomorrow, I thought, I shall be back for good. As if reading my thoughts, Amy spoke.

'No place like home, eh?' She sounded relaxed and slightly amused at my happiness.

'None,' I said fervently.

6. AMY NEEDS HELP

I woke next morning in jubilant spirits. Through the bedroom window I could see two men examining the standing corn. No doubt the farmer was hoping to start cutting later in the day when the dew had vanished. I should not be there to see it, I thought happily.

The harvest fields of Bent would be far distant. I should be watching Mr Roberts, our local farmer, trundling the combine round our Fairacre fields. But that would be a week or so later, for our uplands are colder than the southward slopes of Amy's countryside, and all our crops are a little later.

Amy and I lingered over our coffee cups. I was looking hopefully among the newspaper columns for some crumb of cheer among the warfare, murders, rapes and attacks upon old men and women for any small change they might have had upon them, without – as usual – much success. Amy was busy with her letters.

She had left until last a bulky envelope addressed in James's unmistakable hand. She slit it open, her face grave, and gave the pages her close attention. In the silence, I refilled her coffee cup and my own, and turned to an absorbing account of a woman with nine children and a tenth on the way, who had struck her husband over the head with a handy frying pan, after some little difference about methods of birth control.

She was reported as saying that 'he didn't like interfering with Nature,' and I was glad to see that her solicitor was putting up a spirited defence. I wished her luck. Really, marriage was no bed of roses for some women, I thought, congratulating myself, yet again, on my single state.

The rustling of paper brought me back to the present. Amy was stuffing the letter back into the envelope. Her mouth was set grimly, and I looked hastily at the newspaper again.

I was conscious that Amy was staring blindly across the cornfields. I finished my coffee and rose. 'If you'll excuse me,' I said, 'I'll go and finish packing.'

There was no reply from Amy. Still as a statue, she stared stonily before her, as I crept away.

An hour or so later, we packed up the car together. Amy seemed to have recovered her good humour, and we laughed about the amount of luggage I seemed to have accumulated.

Tibby's basket took up a goodly part of the back seat. An old mackintosh had been folded and placed strategically beneath it. We had had trouble before, and were determined to prevent Amy's lovely car 'smelling like a civet's paradise', to quote Mr Willet, referring to the poet Aloysius Stone's noisome house long ago.

Two cases, a pile of books, a bulky dressing gown and a basket of vegetables and flowers from Amy's garden, filled the rest of the back seat and the boot, and we still had a box of groceries to collect from Bent's village stores.

'Anyone would think we were off for a fortnight's holiday,' observed Amy, surveying the luggage.

'Well, you will be soon,' I said.

Amy's smile vanished, and I cursed myself for clumsiness.

'Let's hope so,' she said soberly.

I edged myself into the passenger seat while Amy returned to the house to lock up. How I wished I could help her! She had been so good to me, so completely selfless and welcoming, that it was doubly hard to see her unhappy.

But nothing could be done if she preferred to keep her troubles to herself. I respected her reticence. Too often I have been the unwilling recipient of confidences, knowing full well that, later, the impulsive babbler would regret her disclosures as much as I regretted hearing them. 'Least said, soonest mended' is an old adage which reflects much wisdom. I could only admire Amy's stoicism, and hope that one day, somehow, I should be able to help her.

We set off for Fairacre, stopping only once to pick up the groceries. Our pace was sedate, for the faster we went the shriller grew Tibby's wails of protest from the wicker basket. Even at thirty-five miles an hour the noise was ear-splitting.

'I meant to have told you,' shouted Amy above the racket, 'that I had a letter from Vanessa this morning. She's coming down for a day next week. She's on holiday, I gather.'

'Bring her over if she can spare the time,' I shouted back.

Amy nodded. 'Funny thing about Gerard, wasn't it?' she said at last. 'Do you smell a romance?'

'What? Between Gerard and Vanessa?'

'Yes. I thought he looked remarkably like a cat that has got at the cream when he spoke of her.'

I digested this unwillingly.

'No, I don't think so,' I said finally. 'He's years older.'

'A mature man,' began Amy, in what I recognized as her experienced-woman-of-the-world voice, 'is often *exactly* what a young thing like Vanessa *needs*. She probably knows this subconsciously. She's very intelligent really underneath all that dreadful clothing and flowing hair. I shall do my best to encourage it.'

I began to feel alarmed for both innocent parties. Amy, on match-making bent, has a flinty ruthlessness, as I know to my cost. On this occasion, however, I decided to keep silent.

An ominous pattering sound, as of water upon news-paper, distracted our attention from Vanessa and Gerard, and directed it upon Tibby.

'Thank God for the mackintosh!' exclaimed Amy, accelerating slightly.

We drew up with a flourish at the school house, and let the cat escape into the kitchen, where she stalked about, sniffing at the unusual cleanliness with much the same expression of amazement which Amy and I had worn.

We unpacked, and Amy insisted on putting a hot water bottle into my bed, despite the bright sunshine. We made coffee, and I asked Amy to stay to lunch.

'Scrambled egg,' I said. 'I can whip up eggs with my left hand beautifully.'

'I mustn't, my dear,' she said rising. 'James comes home tonight, and there's a lot to do.'

'Then I won't keep you,' I said, and went on to try and thank her once again for all she had done.

She brushed my efforts aside. 'It was good to have company,' she said.

'Well, you'll have James now.'

'Only for a day or so. We've a lot to discuss before the holiday. Some of it, I fear, not very agreeable.'

She climbed into the car and waved goodbye, leaving me to savour her last sentence.

It was, I discovered later, the biggest understatement of Amy's life.

During the afternoon, Mrs Pringle called.

I invited her in, and thanked her from my heart for all she had done.

'The house,' I told her, 'is absolutely transfigured. You must have spent hours here.'

A rare smile curved Mrs Pringle's lips. Her mouth normally turns down, giving her a somewhat reptilian look. Turned upwards, it had the strange effect as if a frog had smiled.

'Well, it needed it,' said Mrs Pringle. 'What I found in them chair covers when I pulled them out is nobody's business. Pencils, knitting needles, nuts, bits of paper, and there was even a boiled sweet.'

'No!' I cried. 'What, all sticky?'

Slattern though I am, I could not believe that a sucked sweet would turn up in the debris.

'Luckily it was wrapped in a bit of cellophane,' conceded Mrs Pringle. 'But it is not what anyone'd have found when Mrs Hope was here.'

'Have a cup of tea?' I asked, changing the subject abruptly. Mrs Hope's example leads to dangerous ground. Over the tea cups, Mrs Pringle brought me up to date with village news. The Scouts were having a mammoth jumble sale. (All our village jumble sales are 'mammoth'.) The Caxley bus was now an hour earlier on market day, and a dratted nuisance everybody found it. The new people at Tyler's Row had bought a puppy, and Mr Mawne had seen a pair of waxworks in the garden.

I must admit that this last snippet of news took me aback, until I remembered that Henry Mawne's hobby is ornithology and Mrs Pringle was probably referring to waxwings.

'I thought they came in the winter,' I hazarded.

'Maybe they do,' agreed Mrs Pringle, 'but that garden of the Mawnes is always perishing cold. It may have confused the waxworks.'

Privately, I thought that they were not the only ones to be confused, and we let the matter drop.

'While your arm's mending,' said Mrs Pringle, 'I'll be in each morning for an hour.' I thanked her.

She rose to go, looking with pride at the tidiness around her. 'Don't want to see this slide back into the usual mess,' she said, echoing Amy, and departed.

The next two or three days passed pleasurably, and I gloried in my growing accomplishments. I found that I could lift my right arm, if I held it at exactly the correct angle, and even began to comb the hair on my *occiput* with my right hand. I became quite nimble at mounting and descending the stairs, and each small triumph cheered me greatly.

One morning Amy rang me. 'Vanessa is with me. May we come over?'

I expressed my delight.

'And another thing,' said Amy, and stopped.

'Yes?'

'Perhaps I should wait until I see you.'

It was most unlike Amy to shilly-shally like this.

'What's it about?'

'Crete.'

'Crete? I don't know a thing about it! Do you want to borrow a map or something?'

'No. I want you to consider visiting it with me, as my guest, of course.'

I was struck dumb.

'Are you still there?'

'Partially.'

'Well, think about it. James can't come, but wants me to go ahead with the holiday. We'll talk about it later.'

There was a click and the line went dead.

Dazed by this thunderbolt, I wandered vaguely through the open French window, caught my poor arm on the latch and, cursing, returned to earth again.

The two arrived soon after lunch, and in the meantime I had turned over this truly wonderful invitation in my mind. Of course, I should love to go, and so much better was I that my disabilities would not hold up proceedings in any way. We should be back several days before term began. Mrs Pringle, no doubt, would be only too glad to have charge of the house again, and the local kennels would look after Tibby – not, of course, to the cat's complete satisfaction – but perfectly well.

On the other hand, I had accepted so much from Amy already that I hardly liked to take an expensive holiday as well. My bank balance would certainly not stand the expense of paying my share, which would be the right thing to do, and so I felt that I really should refuse, sad though it was.

It was good to see Vanessa again. She was dressed in a white trouser suit with a scarlet blouse, unbuttoned to the waist, under which she wore nothing. I was rather perplexed about this. Did she know that she was unbuttoned? Should she be told? I decided to say nothing, but felt rather relieved that no men were in the party.

On her feet were two bright red shoes, so clumsy and stubtoed that they might have been football boots, and in her hand was a minute bag of silver mesh of the kind that my grandmother carried at evening parties.

But her long hair was as lustrous as ever, and her looks much improved since the overthrow of the Bolivian Roderick who had so fascinated the poor child when last she was in Fairacre.

On her first visit to the school house she had said practically nothing. Today she rattled on, with much animation, about Scotland and her work at the hotel.

'And you saw Gerard?' I could not resist saying.

Her face lit up. 'Wasn't it lucky? He happened to be nearby. I can't tell you how lovely it was to see him again. We write sometimes, but it's not the same thing as meeting.'

She clapped a hand to her brow, and looked anxiously at Amy. 'The book! Did we bring it?'

'In the car,' said Amy. 'It's for Mr Willet,' she explained. 'Gerard asked Vanessa if she would deliver it as he knew we were coming to Fairacre.'

'I'll walk down,' said Vanessa, scrambling to her feet. She surveyed the red football boots proudly. 'These are real walking shoes, the girl in the shop told me. But, of course, I mustn't get them wet.'

'Why not?' I asked. 'Surely shoes are worn for the purpose of keeping the feet dry.'

'Not these days,' Vanessa assured me pityingly. 'That's a very old-fashioned idea. Today the shoes have a label on saying that they mustn't be used in the wet.'

She smiled upon me kindly, and went off for the book.

Now that we were alone, Amy turned directly to the subject which was uppermost in our minds.

'Well? What do you think? Would you like to see Crete?

'I'd love to—' I began.

'It won't be quite as lovely as it was when I first saw it one April. It's bound to be drier and hotter, but the air in the mountains is delicious, and there is plenty of shade at the hotel.'

'But, Amy,' I persisted. 'I really can't accept a holiday like this.'

'Why not, for heaven's sake? It's all paid for and arranged. You'd simply be taking over the plane seat and James's bed and board. Perfectly straightforward.'

'But I can't afford it, my dear.'

'No one wants you to afford it. I told you that, so put that out of your dear, upright, puritanical mind. I should be most grateful for your company. It would be a kindness from *you* to *me*. Not the other way round.'

'You've done so much already,' I said, weakening.

'Right,' said Amy briskly. 'Return the compliment, and help me out.'

She jumped up suddenly and went to the window. Her back towards me, she spoke quickly.

'Things are very rough between James and me at the moment. I'm quite used to seeing him make a minor ass of himself over a pretty face now and again, but this time I'm frightened. He's deadly serious about some young thing about Vanessa's age. I've never seen him so determined, so ruthless—'

Her voice broke, and I moved swiftly to comfort her. She shook her head violently.

'Don't be kind to me, or sympathize, or I shall sob my heart out, and have eyes like red gooseberries.' She fought for control, and then continued. 'He wants me to give him a divorce.

57

I've refused to consider such a step until we've both had time to think things over. We shall stay apart for a few weeks, and he wants me to go to Crete as arranged and have a break. Apart from this terrifying singleness of purpose about the girl, he's as considerate as ever. It makes it all the more incredible.'

She turned to face me. Her poor face was crumpled and her eyes were wet. 'Now will you come with me?' she pleaded.

'Yes, please,' I said, with no more hesitation.

7. FLYING AWAY

Fairacre's reaction to my proposed foreign jaunt was swift and varied.

The first person to be told was Mrs Pringle, of course, when she arrived the next morning to repair any havoc I might have caused overnight. Her response was typical.

'If you ask for my opinion,' she began heavily (I hadn't, but was obviously going to get it), 'then I should say you was very unwise indeed!' She folded her arms across her cretonne-clad bosom, and settled down to a good gossip. 'I take it this place is in the Mediterranean?'

I said that it was.

'Then don't touch the fish,' said Mrs Pringle, warming to her subject. 'The pollution out there's something chronic, and the fish don't stand a dog's chance, if you follow me.'

I nodded.

'And keep the water off of that arm of yours – no bathing or any of that lark, or you'll be writhing in agony from *germs*.'

'Oh really—!' I began to expostulate.

'Furthermore,' went on Mrs Pringle ruthlessly, 'lay off the fruit and veg unless they've been cooked. An aunt of mine had a very nasty rash from eating raw fruit in Malta. Disfiguring, as well as irritating. Never looked the same after, and she had been a nice looking woman when made up.'

I said that I should take all reasonable precautions, and rose, hoping that Mrs Pringle would take the hint.

'And another thing,' said she, not budging, 'you'll be flying, I take it?'

'Yes. It only takes four hours or so.'

Mrs Pringle gave a short bark of a laugh. 'If you're lucky! This aunt I told you of, spent eight hours getting to Malta. First, the aeroplane needed mending, and when they started off two hours late, they found something else wrong, no petrol or one wing off – something of that – so they landed again for another two hours.'

'There's often some delay—' I began, but was brushed aside.

'Mind you,' said Mrs Pringle fairly, 'they give 'em something to eat while they waited. Spam and sardine sandwich—'

'What? Mixed?' I exclaimed in horror.

'That I couldn't say,' responded Mrs Pringle heavily, after thought, 'but they didn't have to pay a penny for it.'

She now made a belated foray to the dresser drawer to find a duster. Her face brightened.

'It'll keep this place tidy for a bit longer, won't it, having you away?'

Happiness comes in many guises, I thought.

Mrs Partridge, the vicar's wife, was more enthusiastic, and told me not to miss Knossos on any account – she would look out a book they had about it – and would I please take plenty of pictures so that I could give a talk or, better still, a *series* of talks to the Women's Institute when I returned.

Mr Mawne said that there was a particularly rare hawk indigenous to Crete, though he doubted if I should see one, as the Cretans probably shot every bird in sight like the blasted Italians. Strange, he mused, that such warm-hearted people, positively *sloppy* about their children and so on, should be so callous in their treatment of animals. Anyway, he hoped I should enjoy myself, and if I were lucky enough to catch sight of the hawk then of course a few close-up photographs would be invaluable.

Mr Willet said it would do me the world of good to have some sea air and sunshine, although Barrisford would have been a sight nearer and less expensive. His cousin had been in Crete during the last war, but hadn't cared for it much as the Germans overran it while he was there and his foot was shot off in the upset.

'Still,' he added cheerfully, 'it should be nicer now the fighting's over. I don't doubt you'll have a very good time out there.'

'Crete,' mused Mr Lamb at the Post Office. 'Now would that be the one up in the right-hand corner, shaped like a whelk?'

'Cyprus,' I said.

'Ah, then it's the one with the famous harbour, Valetta!'

'Malta,' I said.

'That so? Well, I must be getting nearer. It's not that triangular one off the toe of Italy, is it?'

'Sicily,' I said.

'Don't tell me,' begged Mr Lamb, 'I'll get it in the end. It's not one of that lot like a hatful of crabs hanging off the bottom of Greece?'

'You're getting nearer.'

'It's the long thin one,' he shouted triumphantly. 'Am I right? With some old city a chap called Sir Arthur Evans dug up with his bare hands? Our scout master told us all about it one wet evening when the cross-country run was washed out.'

'I don't know about the bare hands,' I told him, 'but the rest is right enough.'

Mrs Coggs, who had been waiting patiently to collect her family allowance while this exchange was going on hoped I'd have a lovely time and come back sunburnt.

Joseph, who was with her, looked alarmed. 'You *are* coming back?' he asked.

'Joseph,' I assured him, 'I'll be back.'

The next few days passed in a flurry of preparations. Amy fetched me one afternoon for a last-minute shopping spree in Caxley, as I was still unable to drive my car.

She had a wan, subdued look about her, so unlike her usual energetic manner that my heart was wrung for her. She mentioned James only once, and then simply to say that they had seen each other once or twice, and now proposed to think things over and have a discussion after the holiday.

'At least, I'm supposed to think things over,' said Amy bitterly. 'As far as I can see, his mind is made up. How this chit of a girl could have managed to get such a hold on someone as intelligent as James, I simply can't imagine!'

We were flying from Heathrow at a little after eleven in the morning, so that we did not have to make one of those dreadful journeys by car in the small hours which so often add to the traveller's discomfort.

It was one of those cold grey summer days when Amy came to collect me. A chilly wind whipped round corners, scattering a few dead leaves and wreaking havoc with our newly-arranged hair.

'I've got one of those net things with little bows all over it,' confessed Amy when we had finally stowed our baggage in the boot, and checked, yet again, passports and other documents. 'But I look like a culture-vulture from the mid-west in it, and am too vain to wear it, although it does keep one's hair tidy.'

I said I had a silk scarf if the wind became too boisterous, but I looked more like little Mother Russia in my headgear.

'Besides,' I said, 'it grieves me to pay a pound to have my hair fluffed out and then to see it flattened in five minutes.'

Rain began to fall as we approached the airport.

'Won't it be marvellous to leave all this murk behind?' crowed Amy. 'Just think of the blue skies waiting for us, and all that lovely sunshine.'

Our spirits rose, and remained high throughout the leaving of the car, the taxi ride through the tunnel, and the slow shuffle through to the departure lounge.

We found a seat, disposed our hand luggage around us, and settled down to watch our fellow travellers, and to look at the magazines we had bought to pass the time. It was while we were thus engaged, that it suddenly dawned upon me that Amy was looking uncommonly nervous. It was the first inkling I had that she might suffer from the fear of flying.

'Do you mind flying?' I ventured.

'I loathe it,' replied Amy with some of her old energy. 'In the first place, it's dead against nature to have that great lump of metal suspended in mid-air, and no amount of sweet reasoning is going to budge that basic fact from my suspicious mind.'

'But think of the thousands and thousands of people who fly all over the place daily.'

'Lucky to be alive,' said Amy firmly. 'And think of all the hundreds who died in air crashes. I always do.'

'You shouldn't dwell on such things.'

'If you hate flying you can't help dwelling on such things! Then think of all the thousands of screws and bolts and rivets and so on, supposed to keep the bits together. How can you be sure every one of them is reliable? And what about all-over metal fatigue? Not to mention having so little time, or enough mechanics, to service the thing properly between flights.'

Amy, warming to her theme, was much more her usual forthright self, and I was pleased to see that, for a time anyway, James was forgotten.

'And then there's fire. I don't feel at all happy about all that petrol being pumped into the thing before you start off.'

'Better than forgetting it,' I pointed out. Amy ignored me.

'How does one know that there is not some ass with a cigarette drifting about nearby, and we won't all be burnt to a cinder on the tarmac?'

'There are fire tenders.'

'I daresay. With the crews in the canteen swilling coffee, and you frizzled before they can stick their axes in their belts.'

At this point, a confused noise came from the loud speakers. Someone with his head in a blanket was evidently honking down a drain-pipe. The message was quite incomprehensible to my ears, but an alert young man nearby spoke to us.

'Gate Nine, evidently.'

We collected our baggage and joined the queue.

'Well, here we go,' said Amy resignedly. 'I wonder if the pilot is a dipsomaniac?'

We settled into our seats, Amy insisting that I took the one by the window. Through it I had a view of the rear side of the wing, and beyond that the grey expanse of the airport with only the brightly coloured tankers and aeroplanes to enliven the scene.

'Thank heaven it's daylight,' said Amy, 'and we shan't be able to see the flames shooting out of the exhausts! I face death every time I get into a blasted plane.'

'It's a quick one, I believe.'

'I wonder. I always imagine twirling round and round like a sycamore key, with one wing off.'

'Caught in the enemy's search-lights, I suppose? Amy, you've been watching too many old war films on television. Have a barley sugar, and think of Crete.'

The engines began to roar, and the aeroplane began its interminable trundling round the airport, bumping and bumbling along like some clumsy half-blind creature looking for its home.

Amy had closed her eyes, and both hands were clenched in her lap, resting on the glossy cover of a magazine which had blazoned across its corner: 'Australia: Only A Day's Flight Away'.

Suddenly, the pace of the engines altered, the roaring was terrifying, and we started to set off along what one sincerely hoped was the correct runway, and the path to Crete. Buildings rushed past in the distance, the grass dropped away, the wing of the aeroplane dipped steeply, and far below us, tipped at an absurd angle, the streets and parks, the reservoirs and rivers of Middlesex hung like a stage backcloth.

Excitement welled in me. Amy opened her eyes and smiled.

'Well, we're off at last,' she said, with infinite relief in her voice. 'Now we can enjoy ourselves.'

The adventure had begun.

PART TWO

Farther Afield

* * * *

8. In Crete

Our first glimpse of Crete was in the golden light of early evening for we had been delayed at Athens airport. It would have given Mrs Pringle some satisfaction.

If we had known how long we should have to wait for the aeroplane to Heraklion we could have taken a taxi into Athens and enjoyed a sight-seeing tour. As it was, we were told at half-hourly intervals that the mechanical fault was almost repaired and we should be going aboard within minutes. Consequently, we were obliged to wait, while Amy and her fellow-sufferers grew more and more nervous, and even such phlegmatic travellers as myself grew heartily sick of cups of tepid coffee, and the appalling noise and dust made by a gang of workmen who were laying a marble floor. It was infuriating to be so near the cradle of western civilization and yet unable to visit it, tethered as we were by the bonds of modern technology, and a pretty imperfect technology at that.

But our view of Crete from the air dispelled our irritation. There it lay, long, green and beautiful in a sea so deeply blue that the epithet 'wine-dark', which one had accepted somewhat sceptically, was suddenly proved to be true.

Below us, like toys, small boats were crossing to and from the mainland, their white wakes echoed by the white vapour trails of an aeroplane in the blue above.

We circled lower and lower, and now we could see a white frill of waves round the bays, and white houses clustered on the green flanks of the hills. Away to the west the mountains were amethyst-coloured in the thickening light, with Mount Ida plainly to be seen.

By the time we had gone through customs and boarded a coach, it was fairly dark, and we set off eastwards along the coast road to our destination.

It was a hair-raising ride. The surface of the road – probably one of the best in the island – was remarkably rough. The coach which had met us rattled and swayed. Seats squeaked, metal jangled, windows clattered, and the driver kept up a loud conversation with our guide, only breaking off to curse any other vehicle driver foolish enough to cross his path.

We soon realized how mountainous Crete is. The main ridge of mountains runs along the central spine of the island, but the coast road too boasted some alarming ascents and descents. Part of our journey was along a newly built road, but there was still much to be done, and we followed the path used by generations of travellers from Heraklion to Aghios Nikolaos for most of the way.

The last part of the journey took place in complete darkness. The headlights lit up the white villages through which we either hurtled down or laboured up. Occasionally, we saw a tethered goat cropping busily beneath the brilliant stars, or a pony clopping along at the side of the road, its rider muffled in a rough cloak.

Every now and again the coach shuddered to a halt, and a few passengers descended, laden with luggage, to find their hotel.

'I wouldn't mind betting,' said Amy, with a yawn, 'that we are the last to be put down.'

She would have lost her bet, but only just, for we were the penultimate group to be dropped. Two middle-aged couples, and a family of five struggled from the coach with us and we made our way through a courtyard to the doorway.

We were all stiff and tired for we had been travelling since morning. A delicious aroma was floating about the entrance hall. It was as welcome as the smiles of the men behind the desk.

'Grub!' sighed one of our fellow-travellers longingly.

He echoed the feelings of us all.

School teachers do not usually stay in expensive hotels, so I was all the more impressed with the beauty and efficiency of the one we now inhabited.

The gardens were extensive and followed the curve of the bay. Evergreen trees and flowering shrubs scented the air, lilies and cannas and orange blossom adding their perfume. And everywhere water trickled, irrigating the thirsty ground, and adding its own rustling music to that of the sea which splashed only a few yards from our door.

Amy and I shared a little whitewashed stone house, comprising one large room with two beds and some simple wooden furniture, a bathroom and a spacious verandah where we had breakfast each morning. The rest of the meals were taken in the main part of the hotel to which we walked along brick paths, sniffing so rapturously at all the plants that Amy said I looked like Ferdinand the bull.

'Heavens! That dates us,' I said 'I haven't thought of Ferdinand for about thirty years!'

'Must be more than that,' said Amy. 'It was before the war. Isn't it strange how one's life is divided into before and after wars? I used to get so mad with my parents telling me about all the wonderful things they could buy for two and eleven-three before 1914 that I swore I would never do the same thing, but I do. I heard myself telling Vanessa, only the other day, what a hard-wearing winter coat I had bought for thirty shillings *before the war*. She didn't seem to believe me, I must say.'

'It's at times like Christmas that I hark back,' I confessed. 'I used to reckon to buy eight presents for college friends for a pound. Dash it all, you could get a silk scarf or a real leather purse for half a crown in those days.'

'And a swansdown powder puff sewn into a beautiful square of crêpe-de-chine,' sighed Amy. 'Ah, well! No good living in the past. I must say the present suits me very well. Do you think I'm burning?'

We were lying by the swimming pool after breakfast. Already the sun was hot. By eleven it would be too hot to sunbathe, and we would find a shady place under the trees or on our own verandah, listening to the lazy splashing of the waves on the rocks.

On the terrace above us four gardeners were tending two minute patches of coarse grass. A sprinkler played upon these tiny lawns for most of the day. Sometimes an old-fashioned lawn-mower would be run over them, with infinite care. The love which was lavished upon these two shaggy patches should have produced something as splendidly elegant as the lawns at the Backs in Cambridge, one felt, but to Cretan eyes, no doubt, the result was as satisfying.

For the first two or three days we were content to loll in the sun, to bathe in the hotel pool, and to potter about the enchanting town of Aghios Nikolaos. We were both tired. My arm was still in a sling for most of the time, and pained me occasionally if I moved it at an awkward angle. Amy's troubles were far harder to bear, and I marvelled at her courage in thrusting them out of sight. We were both anxious that the other should benefit from the holiday, and as we both liked the same things we were in perfect accord.

'We'll hire a car,' Amy said, 'for the rest of the holiday. There are so many lovely things to see. First trip to Knossos, and I think we'll make an early start on that day. It was hot enough there when I went in April. Heaven knows what it will be like in August!'

Meanwhile, we slept and ate and bathed and read, glorying in the sunshine, the shimmering heat, the blue, blue sea and the sheer joy of being somewhere different.

Now and again I felt a pang of remorse as I thought of

Tibby in her hygienic surroundings at the super-kennels to which I had taken her. No doubt she loathed the comfortable bed provided, the dried cat-food, the fresh water, and the concrete run thoughtfully washed out daily with weak disinfectant by her kind warders.

Where, she would be wondering, is the garden, and my lilac tree scratching post? Where is the grass I like to eat, and my comfortably dirty blanket, and the dishes of warm food put down by a doting owner?

It would not do Tibby any harm, I told myself, to have a little discipline for two weeks. She would appreciate her home comforts all the more keenly when we were reunited.

Our fellow guests seemed a respectable collection of folk. In the main, they were middle-aged, and enjoying themselves in much the same way as Amy and I were. There were one or two families with older children, but no babies to be seen. I assumed that there were a number of reasons for this lack of youth.

The hotel was expensive, and to take two or three children there for a fortnight or so would be beyond most families' purses. The natural bathing facilities were not ideal for youngsters. The coast was rocky, the beaches small and often shelving abruptly. The flight from England was fairly lengthy, and it was easy to see why there were very few small children about.

It suited me. I like children well enough, otherwise I should not be teaching, but enough is enough, and part of the pleasure of this particular holiday was the company of adults only.

We looked forward to a short time in the bar after dinner, talking to other guests and sometimes watching the Greek waiters who had been persuaded to dance. We loved the gravity of these local dances as, arms resting on each others' shoulders, the young men swooped in unison, legs swinging backwards and forwards, their dark faces solemn with concentration until, at last, they would finish with a neat acrobatic leap to face the other way, and their smiles would acknowledge our applause.

One of the middle-aged couples who had made the journey with us often came to sit with us in the bar. Their stone house was near our own, and we often found ourselves walking to dinner together through the scented darkness.

She was small and neat, with prematurely white silky hair, worn in soft curls. Blue-eyed and fair-skinned she must have been enchanting as a girl, and even now, in middle-age, her elegance was outstanding. She dressed in white or blue, accentuating the colour of her hair and eyes, and wore a brooch and bracelet of sapphires and pearls which even I coveted.

Her husband looked much younger, with a shock of crisp dark hair, a slim bronzed figure, and a ready flow of conversation. We found them very good company.

'The Clarks,' Amy said to me one evening, as we dressed for

dinner, 'remind me of the advertisement for pep pills. You know: "Where do they get their energy?" They seem so wonderfully in tune too. I must say, it turns the knife in the wound at times,' she added, with a tight smile.

'Well, they're not likely to parade any secret clashes before other people staying here,' I pointed out reasonably.

'True enough,' agreed Amy. 'Half the fun of hotel life is speculating about one's neighbours. What do you think of the two who bill and coo at the table on our left?'

'Embarrassing,' I said emphatically. 'Must have been married for years, and still stroking hands while they wait for their soup. Talk about washing one's clean linen in public!'

'They may have been married for years,' said Amy, in what I have come to recognize as her worldly-woman voice, 'but was it to each other?'

'Miaow!' I intoned.

Amy laughed. 'You trail the innocence of Fairacre wherever you go,' she teased. 'And not a bad thing either.'

It was the morning after this conversation that I found myself dozing alone, frying nicely, under some trees near the pool. Amy was writing cards on the verandah, and was to join me later.

I heard footsteps approach, and opened my eyes to see Mrs Clark smiling at me.

'Can I share the shade?'

'Of course.' I shifted along obligingly, and Mrs Clark spread a rug and cushion, and arranged herself elegantly upon them.

'John's in the pool, but it does mess up one's hair so, and I thought I'd miss my dip today. How is your arm?'

I assured her that I was mending fast.

'It's all this lovely fresh air and sunshine,' she said. 'It's a heavenly climate. My husband would like to live here.'

'I can understand it.'

'So can I. He has more reason than most to like the Greek

way of life. His grandmother was a Greek. She lived a few miles south of Athens, and John spent a number of holidays with her as a schoolboy.'

'Lucky fellow!'

'I suppose so.' She sounded sad, and I wondered what lay behind this disclosure.

'We visited her as often as we could manage it, right up to her death about five or six years ago. A wonderful old lady. She had been a widow for years. In fact, I never met John's grandfather. He died when John was still at Marlborough.'

She sat up and anointed one slim leg with sun tan lotion. Her expression was serious as she worked away. I began to suspect, with some misgiving, that once again I was destined to hear someone's troubles.

'You see,' she went on, 'John retires from the Army next year, and he is set on coming here to live. He's even started house-hunting.'

'And what do you feel about it?'

She turned a defiant blue gaze upon me. 'I'm dead against it. I'm moving heaven and earth to try to get him to change his mind, and I intend to succeed. It's a dream he has lived with for years – first it was to live in Athens. Then in one or other of the Greek islands, and now it's definitely whittled down to Crete. I've never seen him so ruthless.'

I thought of Amy who had used almost exactly the same words about James.

'Perhaps something will occur to make him change his mind,' I suggested.

'Never! He's thought of this kind of life wherever he's been, and I feel that he's been through so much that it is right in a way for him to have what he wants, now that he will have the leisure to enjoy it. But the thing is, I can't bear the thought of it. We should have to leave everything behind that we love, I tell him.'

She began to attack the other leg with ferocity.

'We live in Surrey. Over the years we saved enough to buy this rather nice house, with a big garden, and we've been lucky enough to live in it for the past seven years. Before that, of course, we were posted here, there and everywhere, but one expects that. I thought that John had given up the idea of settling out here. He's seemed so happy helping me in the garden, and making improvements to the house. Now I realize that he was looking upon the place as something valuable to sell to finance a home here. And the garden—'

She broke off, and bent low, ostensibly to examine her leg.

'Tell me about it,' I said.

'I've made a heavenly rockery. It slopes steeply, and you can get some very good terraces cut into the side of the hill. My gentians are doing so well, and lots of little alpines. And three years ago I planted an autumn-flowering prunus which had lots of blossom last October – so pretty. I simply *won't* leave it!'

'You could make a garden here I expect. My friend Amy tells me that when she was here last, in April, there were carnations and geraniums, and lilies of all sorts. Think of that!'

'And then there are the grandchildren,' she went on, as though she had not heard me. 'We have two girls, both married, who live quite near us, and we see the grandchildren several times a week. There are three, and a new baby due soon after we return. I'm going to keep house for Irene when she goes into hospital, and look after her husband and Bruce, the first boy.'

'You'll enjoy that, I expect,' I said, hoping to wean her from her unhappiness. I did not succeed.

'But just think of all those little things growing up miles away from us! Think of the fun we're going to miss, seeing them at all the different stages! I keep reminding John of this. And then there's Podge.'

'Podge?'

'Our spaniel. He's nearly twelve and far too old to settle overseas in a hot climate. Irene has offered to have him, but he would grieve without us, and I should grieve too, I don't deny. No, it can't be done.'

She looked at me, and smiled.

'I really shouldn't be worrying you with my problems, but you have such a sympathetic face, you know.'

This is not the first time I have been told this. I cannot help feeling that my face works independently of my inner thoughts. It certainly seems to make me the repository of all kinds of unsolicited confidences, as I know to my cost.

'I'm quite sure,' she continued, screwing on the stopper of the lotion bottle, 'that my daughters wouldn't be putting up with this situation. For one thing, of course, they could be financially independent, a thing I've never been.'

'Even if you were,' I said cautiously, 'you wouldn't part from your husband surely?'

'No, I suppose not.' She sounded doubtful. 'There's been no choice, of course. I wasn't brought up to do a job of any kind, and I married fairly young. Now I suppose I am virtually unemployable. I must stay with John, or starve.'

She laughed, rather tremulously, and hastened to skate away from this thin ice. She spoke firmly.

'No, of course, I wouldn't leave him. We really are devoted to each other, and he is a wonderful husband. It's just this terrible problem . . .'

Her voice trailed away. Sighing, she lay down again, and stretched herself, enjoying the warm air, heavy with the scent of orange blossom.

Far away a gull cried, and water slapped rhythmically against a wooden boat moored by the little stone jetty. It seemed sad to me that such an earthly paradise should be spoilt for this poor woman by the cloud of worries which surrounded her.

One's first thought was how selfish her husband was to insist on disrupting her happy domesticity. On the other hand he had served his country well presumably, had been uprooted rime and time again in the course of his duties, and surely he was entitled to spend his retirement in the place he had always loved.

A pity they were married, I thought idly. Separately, they could have been so happy – she in Surrey, he in Crete. Or would they have been? Obviously, they loved each other. She would not be suffering so if she were not concerned for his happiness.

Ah well! There was a lot to be said for being single. One might miss a great deal, but at least one's life was singularly uncomplicated.

Side by side, spinster and spouse, we both slipped into slumber, as the sun climbed the Cretan sky.

9. AT KNOSSOS

The night before our trip to Knossos we had a thunderstorm, frightening in its intensity.

Normally, I enjoy a thunderstorm at night when the black sky is cracked with silver shafts, and sheet lightning illumines the downs with an eerie flickering. Nature at her most dramatic can be very exhilarating, but a Mediterranean storm was much more alarming, I discovered, than the Fairacre variety.

The sea had become turbulent by the time we undressed for bed. The usual gentle lapping sound was transmuted to noisy crashes. Our little stone house, so solidly built, seemed to shudder in the onslaught from the sea.

But soon the noise of the waves was lost in the din of the storm. Thunder rumbled and cracked like a whip overhead. The lightning seemed continuous, turning the bay into a grotesquely coloured stage-set, against which the moored boats jostled and dipped like drunken men trying to stay upright.

The rain came down like rods. Everything glistened, roofs, walls, trees and flowers. And everywhere there was the sound of running water. It poured from gutters, rushed down slopes, turning the brick paths to rivers, and washing the carefully garnered soil down to the sea below.

'You can't wonder,' shouted Amy, above the din, from her bed, 'that the Greeks made sacrifices to propitiate the gods when they thought they were responsible for all this racket. I wouldn't mind pouring out a libation myself, to stop the noise.'

'No oil or wine available,' I shouted back, 'unless you care for a saucerful of my suntan oil.'

'We may as well put on the light and read,' said Amy, sitting up. 'Sleep's impossible.'

Propped against our pillows we studied our books. At least, Amy did. She was zealously preparing for tomorrow's trip by reading a guide to Knossos. Amy's powers of concentration far outstrip my own, and despite the ferocity of the storm outside, she was soon deeply engrossed.

Less dedicated, I turned the pages of one of the magazines we had brought with us, and wondered how Fairacre would react if, salary allowing, I appeared in some of the autumn outfits displayed. What about this rust-coloured woollen two-piece trimmed with red fox? Just the thing for writing on the blackboard. Or this elegant pearl-grey frock banded with chinchilla? The plasticine would settle in that beautifully.

'Do you imagine anyone ever buys these things?' I asked, yawning. 'Or do they all go to Marks and Spencer, and their local outfitter's as we do?'

Amy looked vaguely in my direction. One could see her mind gradually returning from 2000 BC to the present time.

'Of course someone wears them,' she replied. 'I've even had some myself when James has been feeling extra generous.'

She drew in her breath sharply. She was once again firmly in the present with all its hurts and its hopes. I cursed myself for disturbing her reading and its temporary comfort.

'Listen,' I said, 'the storm is going away.'

It was true. The rain had become a mere pattering. The thunder was a distant rumbling, the spouting of gutters diminished to a trickle.

Amy smiled and closed her book.

'That *silly* man,' she said lovingly. 'I wonder what he's doing?'

She slid down under the bedclothes and was asleep in three minutes, leaving me to marvel at the inconsistency of women.

*

The morning was brilliant. Everything glittered in its freshness after the storm, and the sea air was more than usually exhilarating.

We piled our belongings into the hired mini which was to carry us to Knossos, and a score of other places, during the rest of our stay. It was the cheapest vehicle we could hire, and privately I thought the sum asked was outrageous, but Amy did not turn a hair on being told the terms, and once again I was deeply conscious of her generosity to me.

'Let's lunch in Heraklion,' said Amy, 'and have a look at the museum first. Most of the things are of the Minoan period. I must have another look at the ivory acrobat, and spend more time looking at the jewellery which is simply lovely. Last time, we spent far too long gazing at frescoes, and to my mind, it's the small things which are so fascinating.'

Her enthusiasm was catching, and we drove westward towards Crete's capital in high spirits. The mini coped well with the rough surfaces and the steep gradients, and I felt considerably safer with Amy at the wheel than I had with our coach driver.

Heraklion teemed with traffic, but Amy found a car park, with her usual competence, not far from the museum, so that all was well.

It was a wonderful building, with the exhibits well arranged, and everything bathed in that pellucid light which blesses the Greek islands. Amy and I started our tour together, but gradually drifted apart, enjoying the exquisite workmanship of almost four thousand years ago, at our own pace. I left her studying the jewellery while I went upstairs.

I could see why she and James had spent so long admiring the frescoes on their earlier visit. There was such pride and gaiety in the processions of men and women on the walls. Sport was depicted everywhere, vaulting, leaping, running, wrestling; and the famous bulls of Crete were shown in all their powerful splendour by the Minoan artists.

We spent two hours there, dazed and awed by so much magnificence.

'What we need,' said Amy, when we met again, 'is two or three months in this place.'

'But first of all, lunch,' I said.

We crossed the road to some shops and cafés which seemed to have tables set out on the pavement under shady awnings. We were met by three or four garrulous proprietors, each rubbing and clapping his hands, pointing out the superior quality of his own establishment, and the extreme pleasure which he would have in receiving our custom. The noise was deafening, and the constant stream of traffic made it worse.

We were practically tugged into one café and settled meekly

at the paper-covered table. A large dark hand brushed the remains of someone else's lunch to the ground, and a menu was thrust before us.

'All sorts of salads,' observed Amy, studying it closely, 'or something called "Pork's Livers Roasted" and another one named "Chick's Rice Fried". Unless you fancy "Heart's Beefs Noodled".'

I said I would settle for shrimp salad. We had soon discovered that the shrimps of Crete are as succulent as prawns, and much the same size. We were fast becoming shrimp addicts.

'Me, too,' said Amy, giving our order to the beaming proprietor.

An American couple were deposited suddenly in the two empty chairs opposite us. They looked apologetic, as their captor rushed away to rescue the menu.

'I hope you two ladies don't object to us being thrust upon you,' said the man earnestly. 'We didn't intend to have lunch here, but were kinda captured.'

We said we had been, too.

'One comfort,' said Amy, 'the food looks very good.'

'I'm sure glad to hear that,' said the man. 'I can eat most anything, but Mrs Judd here has a highly sensitive stomach, and is a sufferer from gas. Ain't that so, Mother?' he said, bending solicitously towards his wife, who was studying our fellow diners' plates with the deepest suspicion.

Mother, who must have weighed fourteen stone and had a mouth like Mrs Pringle's, with the corners turned down, was understood to say she couldn't relish anything in this joint, and how about pushing on?

Her husband consulted a large square watch on a hairy wrist, and surmised time was on the short side if they wanted to take in Knossos, and get back again for shopping, before meeting the Hyams for a drink at 6 o'clock. He guessed this place was as good as the next, and at least they were at the table, no lining up like that goddam place they went to yesterday, so why not make the best of it?

Mother pouted.

Of course, said her husband swiftly, if Mother was real set on going elsewhere, why, that was fine by him! Just whatever Mother wanted.

At that moment the menu arrived.

'Beefs very good. Porks very good. Chicks very good. Salads very good,' chanted the waiter, his eyes darting this way and that in quest for yet more clients.

'What you two girls having?' asked Mother grumpily.

'Shrimp salad,' we chorused.

'That'll do me, Abe,' she said, 'the tomaytoes are certainly fine in this country. You got tomaytoes?' she added anxiously.

'Plenty tomaytoes,' nodded the waiter. 'Tomaytoes very good. You like?'

'I'll have the same,' said Abe.

The waiter vanished. Abe patted Mother's hand, and beamed upon her.

'You certainly know what you like,' he said proudly. If she had suddenly explained Einstein's theory he could not have been more respectful.

Our shrimp salads arrived, and Abe and Mother studied them as we ate. They were delicious, and soon a mound of heads and tails grew at the side of our enormous white plates.

A thin white cat weaved her way from the shop through the legs of the chairs, and sat close to us.

With thoughts of my incarcerated Tibby, I handed down a few shrimp heads. There was a rapid crunching, and the pavement was clear again. I repeated the process. So did the cat.

'Like a miniature Hoover,' commented Amy.

'Starving, poor thing,' said Mother. 'Or got some wasting disease maybe.'

'I haven't seen any animals looking hungry in Crete,' I said, coming to the defence of our hosts. 'Cats in hot climates often look thin to our eyes.'

'I was raised where cats were kept in their place,' said Mother. 'If us kids had fed our animals at the table, we'd have caught the rough side of our Pa's tongue.'

I forbore to comment.

'You ladies aiming at going to Knossos?' asked Abe, changing the subject with aplomb.

We said we were.

'You done the museum?'

We said we had.

'Some beautiful things there,' said Mother, 'but I didn't care for the ladies in the wall-paintings. Shocking to think they went topless like any disgusting modern girl. I sure was thankful our Pastor wasn't present. What did you think, Abe?'

Abe looked uncomfortable. 'Well, I thought they were proper handsome. Fine upstanding girls they looked to me.'

Mother gave him a stern look.

'After all,' said Abe pleadingly, 'it was a long time back. Maybe they didn't know any better.'

At that moment, their plates arrived, and we asked for our bill and paid it.

'See you at Knossos!' shouted Abe, as we said our farewells and walked away from the table.

'Do you take that as a threat or a promise?' asked Amy, when we were safely out of earshot.

As luck would have it, we did not come across our friends at Knossos, but Amy commented on them as we parked the car at the gates at the site of the ruined palace.

'I wonder how many English wives would be pandered to as Mother is,' she mused.

'Would they want it?'

'On the whole, no. On the other hand, it must be wonderfully encouraging to be deferred to so often. It might make one terribly selfish, of course. After all, it hasn't done Mother a lot of good – sulking like a spoilt child when things go wrong.'

'Perhaps they haven't any children,' I surmised. 'Couples without children often get over-possessive with each other.'

'Not all of them,' said Amy drily. And I remembered – too late as usual – that she and James were childless. Whoever it was called the tongue an unruly member was certainly right. Trying to control my own proves well-nigh impossible, and results in more self-reproach than I care to admit.

'Or perhaps,' I continued hastily, 'it's a case of arrested development, and Abe panders to her simply because she's so immature.'

'Immature? Mother?' snorted Amy, locking the car door with a decisive click. 'Mother's development has reached its highest peak, for what it's worth. She's got that man exactly where she wants him – under her thumb. Whether it makes her happy or not is another thing, but you see it over and over again in marriages. One must be boss; never an equal partnership.'

We made our way in the brilliant sunshine to the entrance to Knossos.

'You make marriage sound a hazardous proceeding,' I remarked. 'I don't think I could have succeeded in it.'

Amy shook her head at me. 'You don't know what you've missed, my girl. It has a bright side, believe me. I'll tell you all about it one day. I bet even Abe and Mother have a few happy times.'

'Well, let's hope they enjoyed their shrimp salads. I don't like to think of Mother suffering with gas while she's sightseeing.'

We entered the grounds, and made our way through a shady avenue which led uphill to the site of the great palace, where men and women, some two thousand years BC, had faced, no doubt, the same marital problems at large today.

I had no idea, when reading about Knossos, how vast an

area the whole concourse covered. As before, Amy and I started our tour together, but soon decided to meet, two hours hence, at the gate, for there was so much to see that one was better on one's own.

As always, it was the light that impressed me most. It was easy to see how such a happy civilization evolved. The clarity of light, the warmth of the sun and the embracing sea, combined to give an exhilaration of spirit. Fertile soil, many rivers and trees were an added blessing. Small wonder that the ancient Minoans had a spontaneous gaiety and energy which created such a wealth of superb architecture, paintings and sculpture.

They were practical people, too, I was glad to see, with sensible plumbing, spacious bathrooms and plenty of storage space for their provisions. Many a twentieth-century builder in England, I thought, could have learnt a thing or two from the workmen of Minoan Crete.

The great staircases, supported by the massive red columns, smaller at the base than the top, led from one floor to another, and on each were things to stand and marvel at. A little crowd stood looking at King Minos's throne, reckoned to be the oldest in the world. But the object which gave me most pleasure was the fresco in the Queen's room showing dolphins at sport above the entrance. There they play, some four thousand years old, still bearing that particularly endearing expression of benignity which so enchants us when we see the fish today cavorting, for our delight, in water parks and zoos.

Their gaiety was echoed in the frescoes showing processions or feats of physical skill. Many we had seen in the museum, but replicas were here, and one could not help but be impressed with the physical beauty and elegance of the men and women. The topless gowns, so frowned upon by Mother, had beautiful bell-shaped skirts, and the stiff bodices, cut away to expose the breasts, supported them and were intricately adorned with gold and precious jewels. Their hair was long and wavy, their eyes made up as lavishly as Vanessa's. They were really the most decorative creatures, and not above helping in the acrobatic pursuits, as the pictures of them assisting their men-folk in the bull-vaulting escapades showed clearly.

Perhaps, I mused, this is what northerners lack. Our climate is against flimsy clothing, sea-bathing and outdoor sports. If we took more physical exercise, should we be more blithe and energetic? Would our lives become as creative and as happy as the Minoans' most certainly were? Should we be less introspective, less prone to self-pity, less critical of others?

The secret, I decided, was simply in the sun. Given that, given warmth and light, one was more than half-way to happiness.

I rose from my staircase seat looking out to sea, and made my way reluctantly to the outside world.

'But I shall come again,' I said aloud, stroking the ancient dust from a pillar as I passed. There was so much more to learn from the Minoans about the proper way to live.

10. AMY WORKS THINGS OUT

'It is a truth universally acknowledged,' Jane Austen tells us, 'that a single man in possession of a good fortune must be in want of a wife.'

A lesser truth, universally acknowledged, is that the first week of a fortnight's holiday is twice as long as the second week. Why this should be so remains a mystery, but no doubt the theory of relativity might throw some light on the matter if one could only understand it.

'Or course,' say some people, trying to be rational, 'one *does* so much the first week. Trips here and there, friends to visit, new people to meet – it's bound to seem longer.'

But this theory did not apply to Amy and me. Apart from the trip to Knossos, and some blissful walks in the mountains after the main heat of the day had passed, we had done nothing but sleep, bathe, eat and converse in a languid fashion. True, we had roused ourselves to write a few postcards, now and again, but on the whole the first week had seemed like two days, and here we were, embarking on our second week, with dozens of places as yet unvisited.

Aghios Nikolaos itself we quartered fairly thoroughly, for we had taken to shopping for our midday picnic, collecting a hot fragrant loaf from the bakery in a cobbled side street, choosing cheese and chocolate, but learning quickly to wait until we reached the villages to buy the famous tomatoes, for here, in the town's dusty streets, their freshness soon withered. We soon knew the most welcoming cafés, the newsagent who sold English newspapers, the shoe-maker who would make you a pair of leather sandals in next to no time, and the jewellers who displayed the beautiful gold filigree work which was beyond even Amy's purse.

But it was life in the country, in the small villages among the olive groves and the carob trees, which fascinated us. Despite the splendid electric lights which hung in some of the narrow streets, most of the houses seemed to have none indoors. The interiors were dark, and the families seemed to sit on their doorsteps as long as the light lasted.

We met them, during the day, and particularly in the early evening, on their way home. The little groups usually consisted of a man and wife, and perhaps one or two children. They would be accompanied by a mule or a donkey, sometimes both, and two or three goats. Occasionally, a cow swaggered indolently with them, its full bag swaying from side to side. The animals were in fine condition, and the American, Mother, was quite wrong to accuse the Cretans of callousness. All those we saw were lovingly tended, and the sheepdogs that sometimes ran with the family were as lively as those at Fairacre.

Always there would be a great bundle of greenery, culled from the banks, for the beasts' evening fodder, and always too, a large bundle of kindling wood lodged across the front of the donkey's saddle, intended, no doubt, for cooking the evening meal.

The women were dressed in black, and the men in clothes of dark material. All acknowledged us when we met, and smiled in a friendly way, but it was quite apparent that they were busy. They were at work. They wished us well but would not dally. Here, the Biblical way of life still held – a day to day existence, charted by the hours of light and darkness, and by the swing of the seasons. There was a serenity about these people which we have lost it seems. Perhaps we have too many possessions, look too far ahead, take 'too much thought for the morrow, what we shall eat, what we shall put on'. Amy and I would not have wanted to change to this style of living, even if we could, but it was balm to our spirits to see the simplicity and dignity of another way of life, and to learn from it.

We decided to visit the monastery of Toplou at the far eastern end of the island. We had soon realized that it was impossible to attempt to see the western half of Crete, for the hilly nature of the country and the surface of many of the roads made the going slow.

'We'll come again,' promised Amy, 'and we'll stay in Heraklion next time, and push westward from there.'

Meanwhile we intended to see as much as we could with Aghios Nikolaos as our very good centre. The coast road eastward, we soon discovered, on the morning we set off for Toplou, had its own hazards, for falls of rock had crashed into the road, and gangs of workmen shook their heads and did their best to stop us.

Amy was at her most persuasive, and tried to explain that we should never be so foolhardy as to run into real danger, but surely, if they themselves were brave enough to be working on the road then our little car – driven with *infinite* care – could edge past?

They grimaced at us, poured forth a torrent of Greek to each other, held up their elbows and looked fearfully above them, miming the dangers we must expect if we persisted. We sat and smiled at them, nodding to show we understood, and at last, with a shrugging of shoulders, they beckoned us on. Their expressions showed clearly their feelings. On our own heads be it – and that might well be, literally, a ton or two of overhanging rock, made unsafe by the violent storm of a few nights before.

We survived. The sky was overcast that day, but the sea air lifted our hair, and we sat on short turf which smelt aromatically of thyme, to have our picnic.

'I wonder,' said Amy lazily, as we rested after lunch, 'what the outcome will be between the Clarks. She came round this

morning, when you were up at the hotel, to borrow the Knossos guide book. Do you know, that wretched man thinks he's found a house! She's beside herself.'

'Where is the house?'

'Malia.'

I remembered it as one of the ancient sites on the road to Heraklion. I also remembered it as a dusty, somewhat sleazy, long street full of booths selling straw hats, and bags, and some pretty fearful souvenirs. I couldn't see Mrs Clark settling there after the green and pleasant purlieus of Surrey.

'What's her reaction?' I asked.

'Unusually forceful, which I think's a good thing. He's gone a little too far a little too quickly, and while she was really doing her best to meet him halfway a week ago, now she's beginning to get much tougher.'

'What a problem! I only hope they don't fall out

permanently. They seem so fond of each other that I can't see them getting too vicious over this affair.'

'I'm sure they'll find some solution. Evidently, she now stipulates that nothing is bought outright until they have lived in the place for a few months, and can see how they like it.'

'Seems sensible. So he's agreed to rent something?'

'I don't know. The difficulty is that people move step by step into awkward positions, and then won't swallow their pride and climb down.'

'Too true.'

'Look at James. I really can't believe that he wants to spend the rest of his life with this girl. She'll bore him to tears by the end of the year.'

'You know her then?' I was taken by surprise. Amy had said so little about the girl that I had jumped to the conclusion that James had met her somewhere on his travels.

'I've met her a few times in James's office. She's one of his typists. Perfectly nice child, I imagine, but should be flirting with some cheerful young man at her local tennis club or dramatic society – not ogling her boss.' Amy stubbed out a cigarette viciously among the thymy grass. 'If this had happened twenty or thirty years ago,' she went on, 'I should have tackled it quite differently. I keep remembering my Aunt Winifred who coped with much the same situation when she was my age. Did I ever tell you about it?'

'No,' I said, settling comfortably for a domestic saga. 'Tell on.'

'Well, soon after I left college I had a couple of years at a rather nice school near Highbury. As my Aunt Winifred lived close by, my parents, after much heart-searching, asked her if I might stay there as a P.G.

'She was a game old girl, and had no children of her own, and said of course I must stay there, which I did, going home at weekends. Incidentally, she refused to take a penny in rent which made my upright parents most uncomfortable, but there it was.

'My uncle Peter was an accountant – perhaps book-keeper is nearer the mark – at one of the good London stores, Harrods or Jacksons, something of the sort. He caught the 8.10 train every morning and came into the house between 6.30 and 7 every evening. He was very sweet and gentle, and always brought us a cup of tea in bed in the mornings, and spent his spare time pottering about in his greenhouse.

'Imagine then, the horror when he calmly asked Aunt Winifred if she would kindly remove herself as he wished to bring home "*a very lady-like girl*" – I can hear my poor Aunt Win mimicking his tone to this day – whom he hoped to marry as soon as he and Aunt Winifred could get a divorce. I was not present, naturally, at this scene, but heard all about it from my aunt some time later.'

'What on earth did she do?'

'You'll be amazed. As amazed as I was, all those years ago, I expect. She told me this with a smile of such self-satisfaction on her face that I was rendered speechless at the time. It seems that she had been left a small legacy by a godfather not long before. Something in the region of two hundred pounds. When she was telling me this, I remember thinking: "Oh, what a good thing! She could make a start somewhere else!" But I realized that she was telling me that she decided to use the money "to win him back". She proposed to ignore his suggestion completely, but do you know what she did?'

'Bought him back with two hundred?'

'As near as! She blew the lot on having her hair dyed and re-styled. She bought masses of new clothes. She had a face-lift and heaven knows what else. Then she calmly waited for him to fall in love with her all over again.'

'And did he?'

'I think not. He was even more subdued after that little escapade, but she did succeed as she intended to do.'

Amy sighed. 'You can imagine my feelings on hearing this tale. I was absolutely furious. At that age I thought I should let the man have his way, and gone off myself, rejoicing in the two hundred which would keep me going until I found a suitable job. To crawl around trying to get him back was the last thing I should have done. I was so shocked by my aunt's attitude that I said nothing. Perhaps it was as well.'

'And how do you feel now about it?'

Amy looked at me steadily. 'I'm thirty years older and wiser. I know now how Aunt Winifred felt. To put it at its lowest level first – why should she give up her bed and board, and all the settled ways of a lifetime simply because he wanted to opt out of a solemn contract they had made? Why should she – the innocent party – shatter her own life simply because he wanted to be unfaithful?

'On a slightly less material plane, she realized, I know – and now that I'm facing the same problem I know how much it hurts – that one can't just destroy a shared life by walking away. The memories, the experiences, the influences one has had on the other, have simply made you what you are, and they can never be completely wiped out.'

Amy reached for a piece of grass and began to nibble it thoughtfully. Her voice was steady, her eyes dry. It seemed to me that this outpouring was the fruit of much suffering and tension. One could only hope it would give her relief, and I was glad to be able to play the role of passive friend.

'And then, of course, Aunt Winifred was a religious woman and took her marriage vows seriously. When she was told that God had joined them together and that no man, or woman, should put them asunder, then she believed it without a shadow of doubt. I'm sure she stuck to Uncle Peter because she felt sure he would be committing a mortal sin and must be saved from this truly wicked temptation. She told herself – as God knows I've told myself often enough – that this was a kind of madness which would pass if she could only hold on.'

Amy threw away her ruined grass stalk.

'And she did, and the marriage held, and I don't think she ever chided Uncle Peter about the affair. But for all that, it could never be quite the same again. You can't be hurt as much as that and get away without the scars.'

There was a little silence, broken only by the mewing of a seagull, balancing in the air nearby.

'And will you hold on?' I ventured.

Amy nodded slowly. 'I've learnt that much from Aunt Winifred. In the end, the outcome may not be the same, but I've more sense now than I had thirty years ago than to fling off in high independence and precipitate things.'

She turned to me suddenly and smiled.

'And another thing, I'm so awfully fond of the silly old man. We've shared too much and for too long to be pettish with each other. I'm not throwing that away lightly. That's the real stuff of marriage which you lucky old spinsters, with your nice uncomplicated lives, can't appreciate. It's an enrichment. It's fun. It's absorbing – more so, I imagine, if you have a family – and so you just don't destroy it, but nurture it.'

She sprang to her feet, took my one good hand in hers and heaved me upright.

'Come along, Nelson,' she said, as I adjusted my sling. 'Toplou is some way off. Think of those fortunate monks who have no such problems as mine!'

We piled the remains of our picnic into the basket, and picked our way back to the car.

Amy's spirits had recovered. She chanted as we headed eastward:

> And miles to go before I sleep
> And miles to go before I sleep.

11. TOPLOU

The monastery of Toplou stood like a fortress silhouetted against the grey sky. We approached it by a tortuous road, snaking up the hillside. The wind grew stronger as we ascended, and a fine drizzle of rain misted the windscreen. At the summit, we drove across bumpy grass into a deserted forecourt.

The wind buffeted us as we emerged from the car, and went towards the cliffs' edge. We stood on a headland, the dark sea hundreds of feet below us clawing with white foamy tentacles at the rocks below. Seabirds screamed and wheeled, floating like scraps of paper in the eddies of wind. It was too rough to talk. The wind blew into our mouths, snatching words away, making us gasp with shock.

There was no one in sight. A disused mill, sails gone, and one salt-bleached door hanging awry, stood nearby. At its footings, a dozen or so scrawny chickens scratched and pecked, scurrying away with clucks of alarm, as we struggled by them.

It was more sheltered in the courtyard, but equally deserted. A verandah ran round the four sides, at first floor level, and large rusty tins were ranged at intervals. Once they had acted as window-boxes, it would seem, but now, rust-streaked and battered, only a few dead stock plants protruded from them.

Everywhere the paint was flaking, and the walls were streaked with the rain-trickles of many seasons. This famous Christian monastery, built by the Venetians 600 years earlier to withstand the assaults of the infidel Turks across the water, presented a pathetic sight close to, in contrast with the magnificence of its aspect when viewed from afar.

We approached a door and knocked. There was no sign of life. We looked about us as we waited. Someone, somewhere, lived in this sad place. A tattered tea towel flapped from a make-shift wire line, destined never to dry whilst the misty air encompassed all.

We knocked again, louder this time, but with the same result. Disconsolate, we began to explore further. A dark archway seemed to lead to another courtyard. A broom was propped against a wall. A bucket stood nearby. Were those potato peelings in its murky depths?

We tried another door. This time we began to open it gently after our preliminary knocks had brought no answer. The handle was rough and gritty to our touch, eroded by the salt air, clammy in our palms.

'May we come in?' we cried into the twilit room.

There was a responsive rumbling, and the sound of a chair being pushed back upon stones. A monk, in his black habit, smiled a welcome. I suspect we had woken him from a nap.

He spoke little English. We had no Greek, but he nodded and smiled, and led the way across the courtyard to the chapel. He was obviously very proud of it. His face was lined and tired, I thought, although he could not have been much more than forty, but it lit up with happiness as he conducted us from one ikon to another and stood back to let us study them.

Truth to tell, the place was so dark, and the ikons so dimly lit that I am sure we saw less than half of the beauties with which he was familiar. But we admired them, and followed our guide on a further tour of inspection.

It was uncannily quiet. Our companion was the only living soul we saw. Could the other monks be away for the day, or locked somewhere in meditation or prayer? We did not like to inquire, and in any case could not possibly ask for enlightenment in the primitive sign language we were obliged to use for communication.

We followed him through a long room which reminded me so sharply of Fairacre's village hall that a pang of homesickness swept over me. Wooden chairs were ranged all round the walls. A billiard table took up the major part of the room, and photographs hung awry on the walls. Everywhere lay dust. The smell of sea-damp clung about the rooms, and the banisters and rails were sticky with the all-pervading salty air.

Our host continued to smile and to point out objects of interest – a framed text, incomprehensible of course, to us, an archway, a window. At last we came back to the door where we had met him. What, we wondered, did we do about almsgiving? We noticed a wooden platter on a low shelf, just inside the door, in which a few coins lay. We put our own upon them, looking questioningly at our guide, who nodded and smiled and bowed.

He held our hands in farewell. His were cold and bony, and with a rare maternal urge I wished suddenly that I could cook him a luscious meal and build a good fire, to keep out the desolation of the place.

We retraced our steps. I was chilled to the marrow, and would have been glad to climb back into the car, but Amy strode across to a white marble war memorial hard by the deserted mill, and I followed her.

The monastery itself had been forlorn enough, but here was the very essence of sadness. Against the foot of the cross was propped a wreath of brown dead laurel leaves. Above it, the inscription was streaked with brown stains. Dead grass shuddered in the wind from the sea, and nearby an old fruit cage, its wire broken and rusty, protected nothing but a jungle of tall grass bleached white by the salt winds, and rustling like the wings of a flock of birds.

Another chapel stood beyond it. It too was deserted, some of the windows broken and boarded. On this magnificent headland, in its proud position as one of the bastions of Christianity, it was infinitely sad to see this once-loved, splendid place, so desolate and forlorn.

We returned in silence to the car, too moved to speak, until we had wound our way down the great hill and reached the road again.

This experience had made us pensive, and I reflected, as we drove in silence, upon the life of the monk, living in chill discomfort, in that remote place high above the sea. For once, my smugness at contemplating the single life was shaken. I felt again the touch of the cold thin hand in mine, the gritty dampness of the surrounding walls, the dust, the darkness.

And, for a moment, I looked upon a lot which might well be mine and other solitary old people's in the future, where loneliness and bleakness stalked, and even the light of religious beliefs could do little to comfort.

I shivered, and Amy patted my knee with a warm hand.

Thank God for friends, I thought gratefully.

Our spirits rose as we took a roundabout route back to the hotel. The clouds lifted, and the blue Cretan sky was above us again.

We stopped in Kritsa, a village we had grown to love, a few miles from our hotel. It lay in the hills among olive and carob groves, and there were wonderful walks nearby, as we had discovered. We sat on a log on the side of the hill, our feet in the damp grass. In the distance we could see a woman on her balcony busy spinning wool on a hand spindle. Nearer at hand, another woman dragged branches of carob tree towards three splendid white goats, who strained at their chains bleating madly. Their stubby tails flickered with excitement and anticipation, and as soon as the greenstuff was near enough they fell upon it, crunching the bean pods with every appearance of delight.

We walked down the hill and revisited the church. This was

freshly whitewashed, and as spruce inside as out. Two dark-eyed children jostled each other as they rushed towards us, a bunch of wilting flowers in their hands, hoping for custom.

There were two letters for me when we returned to the hotel, which I welcomed with cries of joy. Why is it that letters when away are so much more satisfying than those that drop through one's own letter box?

One was from the kennels assuring me that Tibby had settled down well, was eating everything put before her, including the dried food which is spurned at home, and seemed well content.

How typical of a cat, I thought sourly. At home, she will reject anything from a tin, and all forms of dried cat food. Rabbit, from *China* not *Australia*, is welcomed, preferably still warm from her personal casserole, raw meat cut very small, and occasionally poached fish. Her tastes are far too extravagant for a teacher's budget, but I weakly give in. Now, it seemed, she wolfed everything in sight, and made me appear an even bigger ass than I am.

The other letter was from Mrs Partridge, the vicar's wife, and I thought how uncommonly kind she was to take time from all her commitments to cover three pages to me with all the news of Fairacre.

Mrs Pringle's bad leg had flared up again and Dr Martin had been to see her. However, she was still at work, both in the school and the school house. (I could foresee that I should have to express my gratitude and admiration to the martyr, when I returned, in terms as fulsome as my conscience would permit.) The Mawnes had held a coffee party which raised twenty-eight pounds, and would no doubt have raised more but it rained, which damped things. (Not surprising.)

Mr Mawne had high hopes of my returning with plenty of pictures of the hawk. Had I had any luck? The Coggs twins had gone down with measles, but appeared to be playing with all and sundry, as recommended by modern medical men – such a mistake; it would never have been allowed in their own nursery – so no doubt my numbers at school would be much depleted when term began.

She ended with high hopes for my complete recovery and kind regards to Amy.

'I am to pass on Mrs Partridge's kind regards,' I said, turning to her. She was engrossed in a letter of her own, and did not reply for a minute or two.

'Very sweet of her,' she remarked absently, looking up at last. She waved her own letter.

'From Vanessa. She wants a silk scarf trimmed with little gold discs. You can wear it over your head, she says, and somebody called Bobo, or maybe Baba – the child's handwriting is appalling – Dawson, brought one home from Greece recently and looks "fantastic" – spelt with a "k" – in it.'

Amy looked inquiringly at me.

'Have you seen such a thing?'

'There are lots in the hotel shop.'

'Must be white, black or a "yummy sort of raspberry pink",' said Amy, consulting the letter.

'I think I saw a black one.'

'Then we'll snap it up as soon as the shop opens,' said Amy decisively. 'I'm not trying to track down "a yummy sort of raspberry pink". By the way, Gerard's been up to Scotland again. It does look hopeful, doesn't it?'

'He's bound to be there quite a bit,' I pointed out reasonably, 'if he's doing this book on Scottish poets.'

Amy snorted. 'He's staying at Vanessa's hotel, and she sounds delighted to see him. I should say there's definitely something cooking there. Here, would you like to read her letter?'

'Read all about Fairacre in return,' I said, as we exchanged missives, and I settled back in the deep armchair to decipher Vanessa's sprawling hand. Amy certainly had the best of this bargain, I thought, remembering Mrs Partridge's immaculate copperplate.

'This Hattie May,' I said, struggling laboriously through the letter, 'she had tea with. Does she mean *the* Hattie May who was leading lady in all those musical comedies just after the war?'

'Must be, I suppose. She faded out after she married, I remember.'

'Well, Vanessa says that she is now a window – widow, presumably – and happily settled in a cottage near their hotel. I think I saw her in everything she did. What a dancer!'

'Come to think of it,' said Amy, putting down Mrs Partridge's letter, 'she mentioned her when she stayed with me last. Hattie May was living in the hotel then and looking for a

permanent home. Nice of her to invite Vanessa out. I sometimes wonder if the child is lonely up there. Scotland always
seems such an empty sort of country.'

'That's its attraction. Anyway, Gerard told you that there
were lots of young men who were being attentive, and I can't
imagine a stunning-looking female like Vanessa being short of
companions.'

'You're probably right,' agreed Amy. 'And anyway, I imagine Gerard is to the forefront of the attentive ones. I hope he
can persuade Vanessa to become a little more literate when
they are married.'

'Amy!' I cried, 'you are quite incorrigible! Let's go and
change.'

'And then,' said Amy, 'we must do Vanessa's shopping. I
have a feeling I shall never be paid for it.'

We had a splendid dinner, as usual, with lamb cooked in a
particularly succulent sauce made with the magnificent Cretan
tomatoes and a touch of garlic. Afterwards we pottered round
the shop and Amy bought a black scarf for Vanessa and some
silver pendants for presents.

My purchases were more modest and consisted of attractive
tiles which I hoped would be acceptable to Mrs Pringle and
other kind souls who had made the holiday possible. Amy was
admiring one of the beautiful gold plaited belts, and resisting
temptation with remarkable strength of will. They were certainly expensive, and I hoped that she would not weaken and
buy one, as I fully intended to get her one myself as a little
thank-offering for her generosity over the past few weeks.

She left the belts reluctantly, and we returned to our little
house with our purchases. The moon was out, and the night
was calm.

We went out and descended the steps through the sweet-
smelling night air. The scent of the lilies hung heavily about us.
We walked in amicable silence along the seashore. Little waves
splashed and sucked at the sand, and a flickering silvery

pathway lay across the sea to the moon. It was one of those moments I should remember for the rest of my life, I knew.

We were in bed early that night, and Amy was asleep long before I was. Somehow, sleep evaded me. I could not get the memory of Toplou from my mind. That deserted place, with the wind crying in its courtyards, haunted me. And the tired patient face of the monk, so gently smiling and polite, floated before me in the moonlight. He seemed to embody the spirit of his surroundings, the lost splendour and the forgotten ardour.

The experience had shaken me, for it had presented me with the stark surprising fact that single people can be lonely. My own solitary state had always been a source of some secret pride to me. I was independent. I could do as I liked. Now I had seen the other side of the coin, and I found it daunting.

All my old night-time fears came flocking back. Suppose my health gave way? Suppose I out-lived all my friends? And why didn't I set about buying a little house *now*, instead of shelving the idea? Someone else, all too soon, would need the school house when they took over my post. I must start facing things, or the bleakness of the monk's life would be echoed in mine.

Perhaps Amy was right to be so engrossed in match-making. Crippled though she was, at the moment, by the blows to her own marriage, maybe she was being true to a proper urge, something natural and normal, when she took such a keen interest in Vanessa's future. Some inner wisdom, as old as mankind itself, stirred Amy's endeavours. Maybe, in my comfortable arrogance, I was missing more than I cared to admit.

I thought how smug I had been when married friends had told me of their problems; how perfunctorily, for instance, I had disposed of Mrs Clark's dilemma. The truth was, I told myself severely, that, as in all things, celibacy has its good and bad sides. Nine times out of ten I was happy with my lot, which was as it should be. If I have to live by myself, it is as well to be on good terms with myself.

On the other hand, this salutary jolt would do me no harm.

Toplou had made me suddenly aware, not only of the sadness of the solitary, but the warmth of loving companionship, which Amy had spoken of so movingly, which marriage can bring.

The dawn was flushing the sky with rose, and the small birds were twittering among the orange trees, before I finally fell asleep.

12. THE LAST DAY

The last day of our holiday arrived much too quickly. My feelings were divided. On one side, I hated the idea of leaving this lovely place, probably for ever, for I doubted if I should be able to come again. On the other hand, the thought of going home to the waiting house and garden, to wicked Tibby and to all my Fairacre friends was wonderfully elating. I remembered Amy's amusement at my excitement on returning home from Bent. But surely wasn't that as it should be? How dreadful life would be if home were not the best place in it.

We decided to potter about the town and hotel rather than make a long excursion. We were to start at the gruelling time of five-thirty the next morning, catching an aeroplane from Heraklion a little before eight. If all went well, we should be home about tea-time.

After breakfast, Amy drove the car back to the garage from which we had hired it, and I was left to my own devices. The first thing I did was to hurry to the shop and select the finest gold belt available, taking advantage of Amy's absence.

Having secreted it among my pile of packing, I took my camera and set out on a last-minute filming expedition. A small private boatyard adjoined the hotel, and here I had been watching a young couple painting their boat in white and blue, with here and there a touch of scarlet. It was most attractive, and, with the blue sea and sky beyond it, would make a perfect colour photograph.

Then there were close-ups of some of the exotic flowers to take. I might have fallen down badly on Mr Mawne's Cretan hawk, but I intended to have something noteworthy to show the Women's Institute at some future meeting in Fairacre's village hall.

I was hailed by a voice as I passed the Clarks' house. Mrs Clark was sunning herself on the verandah.

'Are you off tomorrow?'

I said we were, unfortunately.

'We're staying another week. Do come and sit down. John has walked down to the town to get the newspapers.'

I sank into a deckchair and closed my eyes against the dazzling sunshine.

'I wonder if I shall ever feel sun as hot as this again at ten-thirty in the morning.'

'Of course you will. I've no doubt you'll come again next year, or sometime before long.'

'And what about you?'

'More hopeful, my dear. We are staying on this extra week for the express purpose of looking for something to rent, probably for a few months next winter.'

'So you are still thinking of coming here to live?'

Mrs Clark's expression became a trifle grim. 'John is. He found the most appalling house in Malia. Far too big, needing three servants at least, and crumbling into the bargain. I can't make him realize that, if I do agree to come, we simply must have something we can manage on our own. We shall be far from rich on an army pension, and John still seems to imagine we shall have batmen hovering round us. I've persuaded him to try a short period here before we do anything drastic. I must say, he's agreed very readily.'

'It seems sensible,' I said.

'Well, we have to adapt, otherwise marriage could be a very uncomfortable state.'

She shifted her chair so that her face was in the shade. Her legs, I noticed, were a far more beautiful shade of brown than my own.

'Have you read *Mansfield Park*?' she asked unexpectedly.

'Constantly.'

'Do you remember a passage near the beginning when the Crawfords discuss matrimony? Mary Crawford says something to the effect that we are all apt to expect too much, "but then, if one scheme of happiness fails, human nature turns to another – we find comfort somewhere." I often think of that. It's very true, and no marriage will work unless there is a willingness to adapt a little. I've no doubt we'll end very comfortably, one way or the other. The danger is in making long-term decisions too quickly, and I'm glad that I've made John see that.'

She sighed, and wriggled her bare toes in the sunshine.

'Why I should worry you with my affairs, I can't think. It's that sympathetic face of yours, you know.'

There was the sound of footsteps on the path, and John appeared with the newspapers.

'I must go,' I said, after we had exchanged greetings. 'I'm off to take photographs of all the things I meant to take days ago. I shall see you again before we go.'

I left them together, John in my vacated chair. They were smiling at each other.

Plenty of give-and-take there, I thought, going on my way. But I hoped she would win.

We had our last lunch at a favourite restaurant nearby. Here the shrimps seemed to be larger than ever, the salads even more delicious. Two cats attended us, and obligingly cleared up the shrimps' heads and tails. Would Tibby have been so helpful? Perhaps, after her Spartan fare at the kennels . . .

We sauntered back, replete, to the welcome shade of our little house, and lay on our beds to rest. Outside, the light and heat beat from the white walls. All was quiet, wrapped in the hush of siesta time. Only the sea moved, splashing its minute waves on the beach below us.

'Must remember to put out my air-sick pills,' yawned Amy. 'That's the thing to take shares in, you know. Wholesale chemists. When you think of the handfuls of pills the GPs hand out these days, you can't go wrong.'

'I'll remember,' I said, 'when I don't know what to do with my spare cash.'

'My Aunt Minnie,' went on Amy languidly, 'left me some hundreds of shares in something called Nicaraguan Railways or Peruvian Copper. I can't quite recall the name, but something far-flung in the general direction of South America. They bring in a dividend of about thirty-five pence every half year. James says for pity's sake sell 'em, but I don't like to. She was a dear old thing, though addicted to musical evenings, and she left me a beautiful ring.'

'The one you're wearing?'

Amy has a square-cut emerald which is my idea of a perfect ring.

'No. This is part of the product of five hideous rings my dear mother left me. She was left four of them by her older sisters, and every one was the same setting – a row of five diamonds like a tiny sparkling set of false teeth. I sold them when she died, and bought this instead, and put the rest in the Caxley Building Society. Very useful that money has been too, for this and that.'

Silence fell. It was very hot, even in our stone-built house, but I gloried in it. How long before I saw sunshine like this again, I wondered? Amy's eyes were closed, and I was beginning to plan my packing when she spoke again.

'Did you have musical evenings when you were young? Aunt Minnie's were real shockers, especially as she made me accompany the singers, who were no keener on my assistance than I was on their efforts. She had a baby grand, covered with a horrible eastern scarf thing, ornamented with bits of looking-glass, and *nothing* would persuade her to open the lid. Mind you, it would have been a day's work to clear off all the silver-framed photographs, not to mention the arrangement of dried grasses. We all just soldiered on, while Aunt Minnie nodded her head, and tapped her foot in approximate time to the music.'

'We got stuck with oratorios mainly,' I remembered. '"Penitence, Pardon and Peace", "Olivet to Calvary", "The Crucifixion". My father could sing very well. Unfortunately, I couldn't play very well. Tempers used to get rather frayed, until we fell back on something simpler, like "The Lost Chord" or "Merry Goes The Time When The Heart Is Young".'

'I sometimes think,' said Amy, 'that people of our generation who are constantly mourning "the good old days" must have forgotten such things as musical evenings and starched knickers, and washdays tackled with yellow soap and a wash-board.'

'And button-hooks that pinched your flesh, and elastic driving you mad under your chin,' I added. 'Children have such lovely clothes these days. No wonder they learn to dress themselves so much earlier than we did.'

'A case of have to, I expect, with all the mums having to rush off to work.'

Amy grunted contentedly and turned her face into the pillow. Peace descended again, and I lay listening to the gentle splashing of the waves and the chirruping of a nearby cricket until I too drifted into sleep.

We slept for over an hour and woke much refreshed.

'Let's ring for tea here,' suggested Amy, 'and remind them about early breakfast. What hopes of bread rolls, I wonder?'

It had been a standing joke. Each morning our tray had arrived with one bread roll each, a sweetish confection rather like a Bath bun without the sugar, and a slice of sultana cake.

Accompanying these things was a small dish of unidentifiable jam.

The bread rolls were excellent. The other things too cloying for our taste first thing in the morning. Marmalade we had on one unforgettable occasion. Our telephone conversation with the kitchen staff ran on the same lines each morning.

'Hello. This is room twenty-eight.'

''Ullo. Good morning. Breakfast?'

'Please, for two. Coffee for two.'

'Coffee for two.'

'Bread rolls for two. NO BUNS OR CAKE, PLEASE.'

'Blead rolls. No ozzer zings?'

'No, thanks. Just bread rolls.'

'Just blead rolls.'

'And *marmalade*, please, not jam.'

'Just marmalade. No nice jam?'

'No, thanks.'

'Bleakfast coming.'

'Thank you.'

'Okay. You're welcome.'

And within a few minutes the waiter would arrive with a beaming smile, and a few words of English, and a laden tray with exactly the same food as before.

'We might just as well save our breath,' Amy had said. But I disagreed. It was part of the fun to keep trying, and as I pointed out, we had been given marmalade *once*.

I must say it seemed odd that with oranges and lemons bowing the trees to the ground with the weight of their fruit, marmalade seemed to be looked upon as a luxury. As it was, we had been obliged to buy a jar in the town, and very poor stuff it was, reminding me of the jam manufacturer who made a fortune from his product SPINRUT, the main ingredient of which can be readily recognized by those who can read backwards.

Our tea tray arrived, and we were told that, as we had to

make such an early start, our breakfast would be delivered in the evening, with the coffee in a flask. We received the news stoically, as befitted Britishers.

'At least it will wash down the Kwells,' Amy pointed out. 'Let's go out and get some air.'

It was still too hot for much exertion, but we strolled in the shade of the trees, and watched the more energetic holiday-makers swimming in the pool. A gardener was pushing a hand mower very carefully and slowly over the two tiny lawns. The hose and sprinkler lay nearby. I wished my lawn at Fairacre received such love. It would be the showpiece of the village. It was sad to think that this time tomorrow I should not be here to see the sprinkler at work on those two thirsty patches.

Later, after dinner, we took a last walk through the streets of Aghios Nikolaos, and stopped for coffee at our favourite café. The night was velvety dark, and we sat at a table near the water's edge. The sea slapped the bottoms of the moored boats as they swayed at anchor. Out to sea, a lighted ferry boat chugged across to Piraeus, and I wished that one day I might visit Greece itself.

As though reading my thoughts, Amy said: 'We haven't seen nearly enough, of course. Next time we must stop in Athens, and then come on to Crete and see the western end. The thing to do would be to spend six months or a year in these parts.'

'I can't see our Education Committee giving me leave of absence for that time,' I observed.

'If things don't turn out well at home,' said Amy slowly, 'it's a comfort to think there's so much to do here. I shall hang on to the idea. It would be a life-line to sanity, wouldn't it? I mean, in the presence of civilizations as old as these, one's own troubles seem pretty insignificant. Or so I've found, anyway,' she added, 'during the past fortnight.'

'I'm more glad than I can say, to hear you say that,' I told her soberly.

'And I can't thank you enough for coming with me. You've been the perfect companion for an old misery like me.'

'*Thank me?*' I cried. 'Why, it's entirely—'

But Amy cut me short. 'One word of thanks from you, my dear, and I shall throw those sandals you've just kicked off, into the sea, and you'll have to walk back to the hotel barefoot!'

The threat sufficed. Amy had won, as usual. We took our time over the coffee, and lingered to look at the sea on our way home.

Sure enough, on the low table in our room the breakfast tray waited for us. It was covered with a snowy cloth.

When we came to investigate we found one bread roll, one

bun, one slice of cake and a dish of dark brown (fig?) jam apiece. Two stout flasks flanked our empty cups.

'Well, there we are,' said Amy, replacing the cloth. 'How about that at five in the morning? I don't think I'll be able to face a thing.'

'I shall,' I said robustly. 'Just think how far it is to England! Why, we may not be able to eat on the plane.'

'I shan't want to,' replied Amy, putting her Kwells on the tray with a sigh.

We undressed and climbed into our beds for the last time. I meant to lie awake for a little, savouring all the pleasures of scent and sound that came drifting from the garden at night, but I scarcely had time to arrange my pillow before sleep overcame me, and a few minutes after that, it seemed, the telephone was trilling, telling us to get up in readiness for our departure.

13. Going Home

It was still dark when we set off along the bumpy road to Heraklion, but by the time we were in the aeroplane, the sky was filled with rows of little pink clouds, made glorious by the sunrise.

We circled the island, and I wondered, with a pang, if I should ever set foot there again. The experience had opened my eyes to a larger, more beautiful world, to an ancient culture happier than our own, and had given me a glimpse of 'the glory that was Greece'.

I felt wonderfully refreshed, and my arm and ankle were so much better that I discarded my sling whenever possible. Prudence, however, made me wear it on the flight. One gets jostled quite badly enough during travel when hale and hearty. With a slowly-knitting bone, I intended to take all precautions.

We made an unscheduled stop at Athens. The workmen were still pushing screaming machines over the marble floor, and the dust was as thick as ever. However, we found a cup of good coffee and a very nasty chocolate biscuit apiece, while we waited, and then we were herded aboard the new aeroplane.

Amy had taken her Kwells, with a swig of flask coffee and much shuddering, and dozed for most of the journey. I had insisted that she sat by the window this time, so that I was in the middle seat of the three. There were a good many empty seats, so that I was somewhat surprised when a lone female came to sit by me.

'Haven't I seen you in Aghios Nikolaos?' she began.

I said indeed she might have done.

'I saw your friend had dropped off, and thought you might be glad of some company,' she said.

'How kind of you.'

'Well, I'm a schoolteacher, and I should think you are too, so I thought we might have something in common.'

Now, I am not ashamed of being a schoolteacher, rather the reverse, when I consider that I am still strong and healthy after so many years of classroom battling, but there is something depressing in being told that one wears one's profession like a brand upon one's forehead – the mark of the beast, in fact.

I said civilly that yes, I was a schoolteacher.

'There's a look, isn't there?' she prattled.

'Downtrodden? Hungry? Mad?'

'Not quite that. Shabby perhaps, and not much given to dressing well and making-up properly.'

This was really rather hard. I had visited the hairdresser at the hotel the night before, and she had given her all. Never had I looked so *bouffant*, so glossy, so truly feminine. The sunshine had produced highlights which I had never before seen in my normal mouse, and I was looking forward to dazzling Fairacre with my new glamour, and my suntan.

I was also wearing an expensive – for me – pale pink linen dress and jacket, and Aunt Clara's seed pearls, not to mention new white sandals. And here was this stranger, bursting in upon my previous solitude, and generally undermining my self-confidence.

I was catty enough to notice her own crumpled floral print frock and dirty white cardigan, and also her undistinguished coiffure, but was humane enough to forbear to comment. Really, civility puts almost too great a strain on mankind at times.

Primitive woman, I reflected, under such provocation, would have torn the greasy hair from this person's head in handfuls, and felt very much better for the exercise. Instead, I asked her where she had stayed in Aghios Nikolaos and she mentioned a hotel near our own, which we had visited for lunch once.

'If I'd had the money,' she said, 'I should have stayed where you were, but you can't do that on a teacher's salary.'

She sounded suspicious, and I wondered if she thought I had some secret source of income – heroin, perhaps, smuggled in the heels of my new shoes. Obviously, in her eyes, my age and dowdy appearance would exonerate me from any other immoral activity.

I did not rise to the bait, but asked her if she had far to go when we reached Heathrow, and she told me that she lived at Chatham near the docks, and would be met by her fiancé and his twin brother. They were *exactly* alike, and went everywhere together.

I asked when she hoped to get married, and wondered, but didn't ask, if both twins would be together on the honeymoon.

'Next Easter,' she said, and went on to ask where I lived. I told her.

'It's so pretty round there,' she said enthusiastically.

I agreed.

'You wouldn't like to exchange houses, I suppose? It sounds a lovely place for a honeymoon, and Chatham would make a nice change for you.'

'Frankly, no. I seldom leave home,' I said shortly.

I put one of my magazines firmly upon her knee, and opened my own.

She looked aggrieved, but opened it obediently, and silence fell. I glanced at comatose Amy. One eye opened and shut again in a conspiratorial wink. Amy doesn't miss much.

A few minutes later she roused herself, and sat up with a yawn. 'What a lovely nap! What's the time?'

The stranger told her, returned my magazine and stood up.

'I'll go back to my seat now,' she said, showing more tact than I imagined she had. On the other hand, it was said so primly that maybe she had taken offence at my disobliging refusal to exchange houses. Whatever the reason, it was a great relief to see her depart, after such an unnerving encounter in mid-air.

We were late arriving at Heathrow and we seemed to wait for hours around the revolving contraption that disgorges one's luggage. Why is it, I wondered, that other people's luggage always seems superior in size, quality and polish to one's own? I was somewhat cheered by watching a red-faced man, very much like our local farmer Mr Roberts, collecting his pieces of battered luggage, each securely lashed with orange binder twine.

'I've lost two good leather straps up here in my time,' he said, catching my eye. 'They won't bother with binder twine, and if they do there's plenty more where that came from.'

Amy rang the garage whilst I collected our bags, and hours later, it seemed, we settled ourselves into her car.

The air was chilly, the clouds like a grey tent, low over us. Rain lashed the tarmac, umbrellas glistened all around, and goose-pimples stood on our arms. One could almost feel the tan fading.

We were in England again.

'What an extraordinary woman that was,' commented Amy, as we drove from the airport. 'I noticed her once or twice when we were walking about the town. She seemed to be holidaying alone.'

'I'm not surprised.'

'A typical case of someone who lives alone,' continued Amy, hooting at the motorist in front of us who had signalled that he was going left for the last half-mile, then right, and eventually went straight on.

'How do you mean?'

'Well, there's a tendency for solitary people – *some* of them, I should say – to tag on to complete strangers and engage them in conversation. Lonely, of course, that's all, but a trifle disconcerting for those button-holed. And then these loners never stop talking. Most exhausting. I must say, you choked off that poor dear in a brutally efficient way.'

I began to feel qualms on two counts. 'I hope I wasn't brutal,' I said.

'Let's say *decisive*,' said Amy, 'and I really don't blame you after such cheek on her part.'

'And I hope I don't waylay people and talk too much,' I added, expressing my second fear.

Amy laughed indulgently. 'You silly old dear! You've always talked too much!'

I digested this unpalatable truth as we drove towards Bent. We had arranged to go straight to Amy's house from Heathrow, when we planned the holiday. It was nearer than Fairacre, and we both felt that a good night's sleep after our flight would enable us to face the home chores before us.

As always, Amy's house presented a calm and beautiful aspect. There were flowers in every room, no sign of dust, everything immaculate and welcoming. There was even a tray laid ready for two complete with biscuit tin, and Amy lost no time in putting on the kettle.

A pile of letters stood on the hall table, and Amy looked at it anxiously as we brought in her luggage from the car.

'I'll tackle that later,' she said.

I was in my old bedroom overlooking the corn fields. In the driving rain nothing was moving. No doubt the farmers were cursing all around, I thought, for some of the fields I could see were only half-cut.

But despite the rain, my spirits were high. We were home again, back among the wet fields, the dripping trees, the little runnels of brown rainwater chattering along the roadside. I thought of those two parched lawns at the hotel as I gazed at Amy's lush slopes before me. A thrush, head cocked on one side, was listening for a worm, and three sparrows searched among the plants in the border, with raindrops splashing on their little tabby backs. Somewhere, far away, a sheep bleated, and another answered it. The fragrance of wet earth and leaves was everywhere, and I thanked heaven for the sights and scents of home.

Later that evening, Amy read her correspondence, sorting it into piles very tidily, while I read a gardening magazine and learnt about all the things I should have done last spring in order to have a flourishing flower border next season.

'Too late,' I said aloud.

'What is?'

'Taking pipings and cuttings, and sowing seeds ready for planting out this autumn, and a hundred other things. It's an extraordinary thing, but whenever I rush to the nurseryman in autumn, fired to have some particular plant, then the right time to put it in was last spring. And, of course, when I rush there in the spring, the particular plants I'm mad for should have gone in last autumn.'

'I must remember to give you a basic gardening book for Christmas,' said Amy severely. 'You sound the most haphazard gardener. It's a wonder yours looks as well as it does. Mr Willet, I suppose?'

She patted her piles of correspondence into neat stacks.

'Friends who won't mind waiting. Friends who will mind waiting. Business and bills,' she said, surveying them.

'Well, bills could go on the won't-mind-waiting stack, I should think.'

Amy shook her head. 'I was brought up as you were, my dear, to pay as I went along. I've a perfect horror of owing money, born of a frugal upbringing. As for hire purchase, my blood runs cold at the thought. Suppose I suddenly had no money—'

She stopped, and looked out at the grey evening. When she spoke again, her voice had altered.

'A letter from James among this lot.' It was in the friends

who-will-mind-waiting pile, I noticed. 'He's still pressing for a divorce. What a hopeless situation this is! I wonder what the outcome will be? I felt so strong and sensible while we were away, but now I'm back I feel as wobbly as a jellyfish.'

'Put it out of your mind,' I advised. 'You've had a long day travelling. Things will seem saner after a night's sleep. And if I were you,' I added, 'I should transfer his letter to the friends-who-*won't*-mind-waiting pile.'

Amy laughed, and did so. It seemed to give her some comfort.

Next morning the sky was blue, and our breakfast table was bathed in sunshine. I presented Amy with the plaited gold belt, with which she was agreeably delighted. Beside my plate was a large square parcel which turned out to contain a splendid book of photographs of Crete with short accounts of the different places. It was a perfect memento of a perfect holiday.

We drove back to Fairacre by way of the kennels, where Tibby sat on top of her sleeping house, looking aloof. I stroked her head, and muttered endearments to which she responded with a yawn.

Only when she was safely in the car, secured in the cat basket, did she deign to give tongue, and then only to keep up the nerve-racking caterwauling by which she registers strong disapproval of car travel.

'I hope you've got a supply of the tenderer portions of the most expensive rabbit,' shouted Amy, above the din.

'It's "Pussi-luv" or nothing,' I shouted back. 'If she can eat it in the kennels, she can eat it at home.'

We turned into the school lane. My hedge seemed to have grown six inches in the past fortnight, and the lawn needed cutting. But the border was full of colour, despite my abortive forays to the nurseryman.

I felt under the third stone on the right of the porch, and withdrew the key. The door was difficult to open, because there was a pile of letters still on the mat. One was stuck in the letter box.

It was a note in Mrs Partridge's handwriting, and I put it aside to read later. Probably, a change of date for the W.I., I thought. We picked up the letters and put them on the hall table. Tibby was released, and bounded into the garden, giving us time to look around us.

Something was wrong. The house smelt musty. Everything was tidy, but a fine layer of dust was everywhere. Unlike Amy's house, there were no flowers. Usually, Mrs Pringle does me proud with a handful of marigolds stuffed in a mug, but today there was nothing.

'Come and sit down,' I said to Amy. 'This is all very strange. Something must have happened to Mrs P. There may be a note in the kitchen.'

But there was no note. The paint had been washed, the windows cleaned, the sink whitened with bleach, the dish-cloth draped along its edge, stiff and dry, but here too, dust lay.

I filled the kettle for coffee, remembered Mrs Partridge's note and read it while the kettle boiled.

It said:

So sorry to tell you that Mrs Pringle is in hospital – probably appendicitis, nothing very serious, but she was worried because she could not get in the last-minute provisions.

If you are not too tired, do have dinner with us tonight. Very simple. About 7.30. Longing to hear about Crete.

Cordelia Partridge

I handed it to Amy, and set about putting out the cups. I was sincerely sorry for my old sparring partner in hospital, and remembered how kind she had been to me at the beginning of the holiday when I had had my accident.

'Poor old girl,' I said, spooning instant coffee into the cups. 'I must ring the hospital later on. I suppose she'll be at Caxley.'

'I expect all this "bottoming" brought it on,' said Amy, gazing at my dazzling paintwork.

'Don't rub salt in my wounds,' I begged her. 'I'm already suffering from remorse for all the things I've said to her in my time.'

'She can take it,' said Amy robustly. 'And anyway, she gives as good as she gets, from all I hear.'

She finished her coffee, and stood up.

'Must be off. Dozens of things to do at Bent, and you have just as many here, I can see.'

I waved goodbye to her, watching until the car turned the bend in the lane, and went back to the garden.

My new rose bush had a dozen or more coppery buds on it, and the lavender hedge was in full flower. A few bumble bees buzzed lazily among the blossoms, and Tibby approached and weaved herself round my legs affectionately.

I picked up the exasperating animal and gave her a hug. 'Tibby,' I told her. 'We're really home!'

PART THREE

Return to Fairacre

* * * *

14. Mrs Pringle Falls Ill

There is no doubt about it, going away does one so much good because, for one thing, it makes one's home seem doubly desirable.

I pondered on this truth as I walked round to the vicarage under my umbrella. The hotel could not be faulted, but how much cosier the small rooms of the school house seemed, and what a blessing it was to drink cold water straight from the tap, instead of having tepid mineral water, tasting faintly of soda, from a bottle!

And how green everything was! I looked with approval at the glistening hedges, the flowers drenched with rain, and the great green flanks of the downs where the sheep were grazing. I even felt kindly towards a worm which was struggling on Mrs Partridge's doorstep, and transferred it to a luscious wet garden bed. There had been no worms in Crete.

'Come in! Come in!' cried the vicar, and to my surprise he clasped me close to his Donegal tweed jacket, and kissed me on both cheeks. I felt as though I had returned from some long exile in the salt-mines.

'My dear, she's come!' he announced, ushering me into the drawing room where Mrs Partridge sat knitting.

'Bootees,' she said, after we had exchanged greetings and I had been supplied with a glass of sherry. 'For the sale, dear, but I've made a most unfortunate mistake. Can you see?'

Certainly, there was something strangely awry with the garment.

'I think you've knitted a row or two with a piece of wool that was hanging down, and not the main line, if you follow me.'

'Oh dear, it's these glasses! I've mislaid my others. They're bound to turn up, they always do. Last time they were in the laundry book. So I'm driven to wearing these.'

'Shall I undo it for you?'

Mrs Partridge looked anguished.

'*Must you?* Shall we put it aside for a bit, and just enjoy our drinks?'

We did so, and I answered a volley of questions about the holiday, until I could ask about Mrs Pringle.

'I did try to ring the hospital,' I said. 'Three times, but the exchange didn't answer.'

'I know. What has happened to all those nice girls who used to be so obliging years ago, I simply don't know. I can remember, many a time, asking for a number and the girl would say: "If it's Mrs Henry you want, I'm afraid she's out shopping. I saw her go into Boots not five minutes ago." So friendly, and always had time to let you know about their families. Gerald used to find them such a help when people needed visiting.'

'Those days have gone,' I agreed. 'I suppose it would be all the same if one were lying with two broken legs and a fire in the house, though no doubt 999 might answer.'

Mrs Partridge nodded thoughtfully. 'Except that you would not be able to get to the phone with two broken legs and the fire might be your side of it.'

'Tell me about Mrs Pringle,' I said. One can't afford to be too literal.

It appeared that she was taken ill in Caxley on market day.

'In Woolworth's, and I must say the manager sounds a thoroughly sensible fellow and deserves promotion, for he fetched a doctor and she was taken straight to Caxley hospital.'

The vicar intervened. 'Don't tell her what they found, my dear,' he advised his wife. 'We are eating soon.'

I was grateful to him. He knows of my squeamishness.

Mrs Partridge looked disappointed, but loyally kept to generalities.

'Top and bottom of it was that they operated within an hour or two, and she'll be there for another week at least. But nothing serious. In fact, the hospital sister said she was comfortable when I inquired. It seemed a funny way to describe it when I know for a fact she was slit—'

'*Cordelia!*' said the vicar warningly.

'Sorry, sorry! Well, anyway, poor Mr Pringle had to go in, of course, taking nighties and things, and brought back the shopping, and was too upset to unpack it until next day. So the fish, my dear, from that jolly fellow in the market, was absolutely uneatable, and the cat was furious, Mrs Willet told me. You see, it *knows* it has fish on Thursdays.'

'Do you think our dinner is ready?' inquired the vicar.

'Of course it is. Come along,' said Mrs Partridge rising from the web of knitting wool criss-crossing the armchair.

'Cold chicken and salad,' she said, leading the way. 'I did warn you it would be simple, but I wish now I'd put some soup to heat. It's such a miserable evening for a cold meal. Shall I do that?'

We dissuaded her, protesting that cold chicken and salad would be splendid, and entered the dining room.

The meal was delicious, and afterwards, back in the drawing room, with the bootee growing even more grotesque, I caught up with the Fairacre news. Measles, it seemed, was now rife, and Mr Roberts' cowman had gone down with it and was in a very bad way.

'Of course, it will have its brighter side for you,' said Mrs Partridge. 'There won't be so many children next term, which will be a help with Mrs Pringle laid up.'

'I suppose I'd better look for someone else to stand in.'

'Well, Minnie Pringle won't be able to come. There's a new baby due, any minute now.'

'That's a relief. I shan't feel obliged to ask her. After ten minutes of Minnie's company, I'm nearly as demented as she is.'

'If the worst comes to the worst,' said the vicar, 'the older children must just turn to and help with the cleaning. Do-it-yourself, you know,' he added, beaming with pride at being so up-to-the-minute.

Mr and Mrs Mawne, it appeared, were in Scotland for a holiday, and I felt somewhat relieved. It would give me a breathing space before having to confess that I had no photographs of the Cretan hawk. The new people at Tyler's Row were repainting their house. Miss Waters' bad leg was responding to Dr Martin's liniment, and her sister had offered to embroider a new altar cloth.

At this stage, an enormous yawn engulfed me, which I did my best to hide, without success.

'It's time you were in bed,' said Mrs Partridge, looking over the top of the blameworthy glasses. 'You've had two busy days.'

It was true that I was almost asleep, but I did my best to look vivacious as I thanked her for a truly lovely evening, and departed into the rain.

Some poor baby, I thought, as I tottered home, was going to have a very odd bootee. Ah well, we all have to come to terms with life's imperfections, and one may as well begin young.

As might be expected, the minute I climbed into bed sleep eluded me, and I lay awake thinking about possible substitutes for Mrs Pringle, without success. I was going to visit her the next day, and hoped that she might have someone in mind. Otherwise, it looked as though the vicar's suggestion might have to be put into action.

After two hours or so of fruitless worrying, I heard St Patrick's clock chime, and then one solitary stroke. Very soon after this I must have fallen asleep, for I had a vivid dream in which the vicar was officiating at a marriage ceremony, clad in an improbable pale blue surplice. The bride was my importunate friend on the flight from Crete, and the groom was the monk from Toplou. Neither appeared to be interested in the ceremony, but were engrossed in a chess set which was lodged on the font.

I wonder what a psychiatrist would make of this?

The next morning I rang the hospital to inquire after my school cleaner. Mrs Pringle, I was not surprised to learn, was comfortable, and would be ready to receive visitors between two and four in the afternoon.

This was my first attempt at driving since the accident, and I was mightily relieved to find that I could do all that was necessary with my arm and foot.

Mrs Pringle, regal among her pillows, greeted me with unaccustomed warmth, and admired the roses I had cut for her.

'A good thing I was handy for the hospital when it happened,' she told me. 'If I'd been slaving away at your place with nobody to call upon, I doubt if I'd be alive to tell the tale.'

I expressed my concern, and took the opportunity of thanking her for all the hard work she had put in at the school house, but I don't think she heard. Her mind was too full of more recent events.

'Ready to burst!' she told me with relish. 'Ready to burst! A mercy I didn't have to be jolted all the way to the County. I'd never have lasted out.'

She looked around her. Patients in neighbouring beds had fallen silent and were presumably listening to the saga. Mrs Pringle lowered her voice to a conspiratorial whisper.

'I'll tell you all about it when I'm back home,' she promised. 'There's some things you don't like to mention in mixed company.'

'Quite, quite,' I said briskly, thanking my stars for the postponement. It seemed a good opportunity to ask when she might be back in Fairacre.

'They don't tell you nothing here,' she grumbled. 'But I heard one of the nurses say something about next week, if all goes well. It don't look as though I'll be fit for school work for a bit. I've been thinking about it, and you know our Minnie's expecting again?'

I said I had heard.

'How she does it, I don't know,' sighed Mrs Pringle. I assumed that this was a rhetorical question, and forbore to respond.

'To tell you the truth, Miss Read, I've lost count now, what with his first family, and hers out of wedlock, and then these others. Then of course his eldest two are married and having families of their own. When I visit there – which isn't often I'm glad to say – there are babies all over the place, and I'm hard put to it to say whose are whose. Sometimes I wonder if Minnie knows herself.'

'No other ideas, I suppose?'

'There's Pringle's young brother, if you're really driven to it. He's quite handy at housework, but of course he'd have to come out from Caxley on the bus, and he's a bit simple. Nothing violent, I don't mean, but you'd have to watch your handbag and the dinner money.'

'It would be better to get someone in the village,' I said hastily, 'if we can find one.'

'There's no one,' said Mrs Pringle flatly, 'and we both knows it. How many wants housework these days? And specially school cleaning! Thankless job, that is, everlasting cleaning up after dozens of muddy boots. I sometimes think I must be soft in the head to keep the job on.'

Mrs Pringle's face was assuming its usual look of disgruntled self-pity, and I felt it was time to go.

'You're a marvel,' I told her, 'and keep the school beautifully. You deserve a good rest. We'll find someone, you'll see, and if the worst comes to the worst we shall have to do as the vicar suggested.'

'What's that?' asked Mrs Pringle suspiciously, on guard at once.

'Do it ourselves'

'God help us!' cried Mrs Pringle, rolling her eyes heavenwards.

I made my farewells rapidly, before she had a total relapse.

Mr Willet turned up in the evening to cut the grass.

'I meant to have it all ship-shape for you when you got back,' he apologized, 'but what with the rain, and choir practice, and giving the Hales a hand with their outside painting when the rain let up – well, I never got round to it.'

I assured him that all was forgiven.

'That chap Hale,' he went on, 'got degrees and that, and a real nice bloke for a schoolmaster, but to see him with a paint brush is enough to make your hair curl! Paint all down the handle, paint all down his arm, drippin' off of his elbow – I tell you, he gets more on hisself than the woodwork! You could do out the Village Hall with what he wastes.'

He paused for breath.

'And how's the old girl?' he inquired, when he had recovered it. 'Still laughing fit to split?'

I said she seemed pretty bobbish, and told him about the dearth of supplementary school cleaners.

Mr Willet grew thoughtful.

'One thing, she did the place all through before she was took bad. I reckons we can keep it up together till she's fit again. After all, we shouldn't need to light them ruddy stoves she sets such store by. They're the main trouble. Won't hurt some of the bigger kids to lend a hand.'

'That's what the vicar said.'

'Ah!' nodded Mr Willet, setting off to fetch the lawn mower, 'and he said right too! Our Mr Partridge ain't such a fool as he looks.'

A minute later he wheeled out the mower. Above the clatter I heard him in full voice.

He was singing:

> God moves in a mysterious way,
> His wonders to perform.

15. Term Begins

As always, the last week of the school holidays flew by with disconcerting speed. I had time to put the garden to rights, and to do a little shopping, but a great many other things, mainly school affairs, were shelved.

Nevertheless, I found time to call on Mrs Pringle, now at home and convalescent, and discovered, as we had all thought, that it would be two or three weeks before the doctor would allow her to resume work.

There was simply no one to be found who could take on her job, even temporarily. A fine look-out, I told myself, for the future when Mrs Pringle finally retired. She obviously greeted my do-it-yourself plans with mixed feelings.

'It's a relief not to have our Minnie messing about with things,' she announced. 'Or anyone else, for that matter. I likes to know where to lay my hands on a piece of soap or a new dish-clorth, and where to hide the matches out of Bob Willet's way. I don't say he thieves. I'm not one to speak ill of anybody, but he sort of *borrers* them to light that filthy pipe of his, and pockets 'em absentminded. It's better there's no stranger trying to run the place.'

'I'm glad you like the idea,' I said. I was soon put straight.

'I *don't* like the idea!' boomed Mrs Pringle fortissimo. She spoke with such vehemence that I trembled for the safety of her operation scar. 'But what can I do?' she continued. 'Helpless, that's what I am, and I must just stand aside and watch them stoves rust, and the floor turn black, and the windows fur over with dust, while you and Bob Willet and the children turns a blind eye to it all.'

I said, humbly, that we would do our best, and that Mrs Willet had offered to oversee the washing-up at midday.

Mrs Pringle looked slightly mollified.

'Yes, well, that's something, I suppose. A drop in the ocean really, but at least Alice Willet knows what's what, and rinses out the tea clorths proper. Tell her I always hangs 'em on that little line by the elder bush to give 'em a bit of a blow, and then they finishes off draped over the copper.'

I promised to do so, and made a hasty departure.

'And tell Bob Willet not to lay a finger on them stoves,' she called after me. 'There's no need to light them for weeks yet.'

I let her have the last word.

Certainly, there was no need for the stoves on the first day of term. As so often happens, it dawned soft and warm, the morning sky as pearly as a pigeon's wing, and the children appeared in their summer clothes.

They all seemed to be in excellent spirits as I passed through the throng from my house to the school, and as far as I could see, attendance would not be appreciably lower, despite the measles epidemic.

A few were disporting themselves on the pile of coke, as usual, and came down reluctantly when so ordered. Unseasonably, a number of the girls were skipping together in the remains of someone's clothes line.

They were chanting: '*Salt, mustard, vinegar*', and then, with an excited squeal: '*Pepper!*' At which, the line twirled frenziedly, and some of the skippers were vanquished.

Three mothers waited with new children by the door, and I ushered them all in to enter the children for school. Two I knew well, for both had sisters at the school, but the third was a stranger, a well-dressed dark-eyed boy of about nine.

'We're living at the cottage opposite Miss Waters,' his mother told me. 'My husband is at the atomic energy station.'

I remembered Mrs Johnson, who had lived there before, and prayed that the present tenant would not be such a confounded nuisance. She certainly seemed a pleasant person, and it looked as though Derek would be an intelligent addition to my class.

'Show Derek where to put his things, and look after him,' I said to Ernest, who was hovering near the door, anxious not to miss anything.

His mother made her farewells to the child briskly, smiled at us all and departed – truly an exemplary mother, I thought, and the boy went willingly enough with Ernest.

The other two would be entering the infants' class, and their mothers were rather more explicit in their farewells.

'Now, don't forget to eat up all your dinner, and ask the teacher if you wants the lavatory, and play with Susie at play time, and keep off of that coke, and use your hanky for lord's sake, child, and I'll see you at home time.'

Thus adjured, the children were taken into the infants' room, and I went out to call in the rest of my flock.

By age-old custom, the children are allowed to choose the hymn on the first morning of term. Weaning Patrick from 'Now the day is over', at nine in the morning, and Linda Moffat from 'We plough the fields and scatter', as being a trifle premature, we settled for 'Eternal Father, strong to save', for although we are about as far inland at Fairacre as one can get in this island, we have a keen admiration for all sea-farers, and in any case, this majestic hymn is one of our favourites.

The new child, Derek, was standing near the piano and sang well, having a pure treble which might perhaps earn him a place at a choir school one day, I thought.

After prayers, we settled to the business of the day. Only five children were absent from my class, three with measles, one with ear-ache, and Eileen Burton for a variety of reasons supplied by her vociferous class-mates.

'Gone up her gran's,' said Patrick.

'No, she never then,' protested John. 'She's gone to Caxley with her mum about something on her foot.'

'A shoe perhaps,' commented some wag, reducing the class to giggles and much explaining of the joke to those who had been too busy chattering themselves to hear.

When order was restored, a more seemly set of reasons was offered for her absence. Someone said she was shopping, John stuck to the foot story with growing vehemence, someone else was equally positive that her mum was bad, while Joseph Coggs' contribution was that she was all right last night because she'd gone scrumping apples with him up Mr Roberts' orchard.

At this innocent disclosure, silence fell. I took advantage of it to point out, yet again, the evils of stealing and, finally, requested Ernest and Patrick to give out the school books in preparation for a term of solid work.

Temporarily chastened, they settled down to some arithmetic in their rough books, with only minor interruptions such as:

'I've busted the nib off of my pencil.'

'Patrick never give me no book,' and other ungrammatical complaints which I, and thousands of other teachers, deal with automatically, with no disturbance to the main train of thought.

Before half an hour had gone by, however, the infants' teacher, Miss Edwards, appeared at the partition door, holding one of the newcomers by the hand.

The little girl's face was pink with weeping. Tears coursed downward, and it was quite clear that the hanky, thoughtfully pinned by her mother to her frock, had not been used recently.

'Don't worry,' I said. 'Let her stay here with Margaret.' Margaret, motherly in her solicitude, did some much-needed mopping, some kissing and scolding, and took her to sit beside her in the desk. The tears stopped as if by magic.

'Perhaps she would like a sweet,' I said, nodding towards the cupboard where a large tin of boiled sweets is kept for just such emergencies.

Margaret went to get it. There was an expectant hush in the classroom as the children watched the little one select a pear drop. Would I? Wouldn't I?

'You'd better take the tin round,' I said.

One needs something to help the first day along.

The golden day crawled by, and at the end of afternoon school I sauntered through the village to the Post Office to buy National Savings' stamps before Mr Lamb put up his shutters.

This was one of the jobs I should have done during the past week, but somehow the lovely holiday with Amy had unsettled me, and getting back to the usual routine had been extremely difficult.

I found my mind roving back to that delectable island, thinking of the white goats tossing their heads up and down as they nibbled carob branches, of the bearded priests, dignified in their black Greek Orthodox robes, of the smiling peasant we had met up in the hills, carrying a curly white lamb under each arm, and the old woman sitting on her doorstep to catch the last of the light, intent upon her hand-spinning.

That dazzling light, which encompassed all out there, was unforgettable. It served, too, to make me more aware of the subtleties of gentler colour now that I was at home.

As I walked to the Post Office I saw anew how the terracotta of the old earthenware flower pot in a cottage garden matched the colour of the robin's breast nearby. The faded green paint of Margaret Waters' door was echoed in the soft green of her cabbages. The sweet chestnut tree near the Post Office was thick with fruit, as softly-bristled as young hedgehogs, and matching the lime-green tobacco flowers which are Mr Lamb's great pride.

Mrs Coggs was busy filling in a form, assisted by the postmaster. She wrote painfully and slowly, far too engrossed in the job to notice me, and I waited while Mr Lamb did his instructing.

'Now just your name, Mrs Coggs. Here, on this line.'

The pen squeaked, and I thought how patient he was, bending so kindly over his pupil. He moved, and a shaft of sunlight fell across Mrs Coggs' arms. I was disturbed to see that they were badly bruised, and so was the hand that held the pen so shakily.

'And here?' she asked, looking up.

'No, no need for you to fill that in. I can do that for you. That's all now, Mrs Coggs. I'll see to it.'

She gave a sigh of relief, and turned. I saw that one eye was black.

'Lovely day, miss. Had a nice holiday?'

'Yes, thank you. Are you all well?'

'Baby's teething, but the rest of us is doin' nicely.'

She nodded and smiled, and went out to the baby who was gnawing its fists in the pram.

'Doing nicely,' echoed Mr Lamb, when she had pushed the pram out of earshot He put Mrs Coggs' form tidily, with others, in a folder. 'Beats me why she stays with that brute,' he went on. 'Did you see her arms? And that black eye?'

I nodded.

'I bet she copped that lot last Saturday. Arthur had had a skinful down at The Beetle and Wedge, I heard. That chap drinks three parts of his wage packet – when he earns any, that is – and she's hard put to it to get the rent out of him.'

'I thought things seemed better now they were in a council house.'

Mr Lamb snorted, and began to open the folder holding savings' stamps without even asking my needs.

'Better? You'll never alter Arthur Coggs even if you was to put him in Buckingham Palace! Usual, I suppose?' he said, looking up.

'Yes, please.'

'Pity she never left him before all those children came. Now she's shackled, and he knows it. Gets her in the family way every two years or so, and there she is tied with another baby and another mouth to feed, poor devil.'

'I wonder how we can help,' I said, thinking aloud. 'It might be an idea to have a word with the district nurse.'

'If you're thinking she can help with the pill and that,' said Mr Lamb, 'you'll have to think again. If Arthur got wind of anything like that, he'd knock the living daylights out of the poor woman.'

He folded the stamps and I put them in my bag. To my

surprise, he looked rather embarrassed as he scrabbled in the drawer for my change.

'Shouldn't be talking of such things to a single lady like you, I suppose.'

I said that I had been conversant with the facts of life for some time now.

'Yes, well, no doubt. But you can take it from me, miss, you've a lot to be thankful for, being single. When I see poor souls like Mrs Coggs coming in here, I wonder women get married at all.'

'Mrs Lamb seems happy enough,' I observed. 'Not all husbands are like Arthur Coggs, you know.'

'That's true,' conceded Mr Lamb. 'But nevertheless, you count your blessings!'

I pondered on Mr Lamb's advice as I walked back to the school house through the sunshine. It reminded me again of Amy's plight, of Mrs Clark's at the hotel, and of all the complications which, it seemed, married life could bring. Somehow, in the last few months, the advantages and disadvantages of the single and the married states had been thrust before me with disconcerting sharpness.

After tea, still musing, I took a walk through the little copse at the foot of the downs. Honeysuckle was in flower in the hedges, and the wood itself was heavy with the rich smells of late summer. Yes, I supposed that I should count my blessings, as Mr Lamb had said. I was free to come and go as I pleased. Free to wander in a summer wood, when scores of other villagers were standing over stoves cooking their husbands' meals, or were struggling with children unwilling to go to bed whilst the sun still shone.

And yet, and yet . . . Was I missing something as vital as Amy insisted? I remembered the sad monk at Toplou, the garrulous schoolteacher, the victim of loneliness, on the flight home, and a dozen more single people who perhaps were slightly odd when one came to think about them. But any odder than the married ones?

I began to climb the path up the downs beside a wire fence. A poor dead rook had been hung there, as a warning, I supposed, to others. I looked at the glossy corpse with pity as it hung upside down, its beautiful wings askew, like some wind-crippled umbrella. How quickly life passed, and how easily it was extinguished!

I looked up at the downs and decided I should turn back. Moods of melancholy are rare with me, and this one had quite worn me out. What, I wondered, besides the encounter with Mrs Coggs, had brought it on? Could I, at my advanced age, be love-lorn, regretting my lost youth, pining for a state I had never known? A bit late in the day for that sort of thinking, I told myself briskly, and not the true cause of my wistfulness anyway.

It appeared much more likely to be caused by the first day of term combined with an unusually nasty school dinner.

I returned home at a rattling pace, ate two poached eggs on toast, and was myself again.

16. GERARD AND VANESSA

One afternoon, a week later, I stood at my window and watched large hailstones bouncing on the lawn like mothballs. With any luck, the children should have got home before this sudden storm had broken, and any loiterers had only themselves to blame.

I was carrying out my tea tray to the kitchen when the telephone rang. It was Amy.

'Are you free this evening?'

'Yes. Anything I can do?'

'Yes, please. Come over to dinner. Gerard and Vanessa are here, just arrived. He's on his way to town, and has a lunch appointment tomorrow. I've persuaded him to stay the night. Do say you'll come.'

I said I should love to and would be with them at seven-thirty, if that suited her.

'Knowing you,' said Amy, 'you will be on the doorstep at seven-ten, asking what's on the menu. I warn you, mighty little! It's the company you're coming for!'

She rang off, and I was left to wonder how many times Amy has upbraided me for punctuality. Personally, I cannot bear to wait about for visitors who have been asked for seven or seven-thirty, and who elect to come at eight-fifteen while the potatoes turn from brown to black, and I stand enduring a fit of the fantods.

It was good to be going out, and I put on a silk frock which Amy had not yet seen, and hoped it would please her eye. I had seen nothing of her since our return, although we had spoken briefly on the telephone once or twice. How things were going with naughty James, I had no idea.

The hailstorm was over by the time I set out – carefully not too early – but it was cold and blustery. I took the back way to Bent, enjoying the distant view of the downs with the grey clouds scudding along their tops.

Vanessa opened the door to me. She was looking very pretty in a long blue frock, and her favourite piece of jewellery without which I have never seen her. It consists of a hefty brown stone, quite unremarkable, threaded on a long silver chain which reaches to her waist. I have nicer looking pebbles in the gravel of my garden path, but obviously Vanessa sets great store by this ornament, and one can only suppose that she has sentimental reasons for wearing it.

'Lovely to see you again,' she said, kissing my cheek, much to my surprise. 'Come and see Gerard. He brought me down, as I've some leave due to me, and Aunt Amy said I could come here for a few days.'

Gerard was as pink and cheerful as ever.

'Doesn't he look well?' commented Amy, 'I'm so glad he's staying the night. He's meeting his publisher tomorrow. It sounds important, doesn't it?'

'It is to me,' said Gerard. 'They're suggesting that I attempt another book. We're meeting to see how the land lies.'

'But what about the Scottish poets?' I asked.

'Ticking over nicely. I should get them done within a month or so.'

We talked of this and that over our drinks, and I had to give him the latest news of Fairacre, with particular reference to Mr Willet and our local poet, Aloysius Stone, now long-dead, but not forgotten, in the parish.

Over dinner Amy told him about Crete with many interruptions from me. The black silk scarf had been received by Vanessa with expressions of joy and, what's more, with an offer to pay for it which had taken Amy completely off-guard.

'Of course, I couldn't possibly allow it,' she said to me privately afterwards. 'But I was very much touched by the offer. I must say Eileen's brought her up very well.'

As always, Amy's scratch meal turned out to be far more sophisticated and enjoyable than one had been led to expect.

After avocado pears stuffed with shrimps, we had a beef casserole and then fruit salad. I sat enjoying the fruit and thinking idly how typical it was of Amy to be able to produce avocado pears, not to mention everything else, at an hour or so's notice.

'This sliced banana,' said Vanessa dreamily, 'lying on my plate, is wizened to the likeness of a cat's anus.'

'*Really!*' exclaimed Amy, putting down her spoon with a clatter.

'Oh, it's only a quotation,' explained Vanessa, becoming conscious of our startled gaze upon her. 'One of our waiters is a poet, and he wrote it.'

'Well, I don't think he should be quoted at table, if that's typical of his work,' said Amy severely.

'He's really terribly gifted. He's had a book of poems published. I meant to tell you, Gerard dear. You may be able to help him. He paid three hundred pounds, he told me, to have them printed.'

'More fool him,' said Gerard.

'But couldn't you put in a word for him tomorrow when you meet your publisher?'

'I have more respect for my publisher than to lumber him with that sort of twaddle. I should say your waiter friend wants definite discouragement.'

'He's a very good waiter.'

'Then let him stick to his last,' advised Gerard. 'A good waiter's more use in the world than a poor poet.'

Vanessa sighed. 'I asked Angus if he could help. His father

runs a Scottish evening paper, but they don't print poetry, he said.'

'Angus has tact.'

'And Ian Murray too, but he was no help. In fact, he used a terrible Scotch word about my poor little poet. I didn't quite understand it, and he refused to explain.'

'Ian Murray has been properly brought up.'

'And as for Andrew Elphinstone-Kerr, he simply roared his head off!'

'Do all your friends have such very Scotch names?' inquired Amy.

Vanessa's blue eyes opened very wide. 'Well, they do *live* in Scotland, Aunt Amy, and were born and bred there, so it's hardly surprising, is it? Apart from being so horrid to my waiter,' she added, 'I love them all.'

'I'm glad to hear you've made so many friends,' said Amy. 'We were interested to hear you had met Hattie May. How is she?'

'Quite spry, really, considering she's so old.'

'So old?' we echoed in unison.

'What nonsense!' said Amy, 'she's only a year or two older than I am.'

'I'm sorry,' began Vanessa, 'I forgot that you used to see her.'

'We never missed one of her shows,' I said.

'They're reviving one,' said Gerard. 'In fact, Miss May is in town at the moment for the first night. There's to be a party afterwards.'

'And Gerard's been invited,' said Vanessa.

'Only because she heard that I would be in town,' explained Gerard. 'I knew her husband, years ago, and then we met in Scotland at Vanessa's hotel.'

'You'll have a super time,' Vanessa enthused. 'I hope your evening clothes are up to the occasion.'

'I shall do my best to appear respectable,' Gerard assured her.

'Come and have coffee,' said Amy, leading the way to the drawing room. 'Would you like a tot of rum with it, Gerard?'

'Nothing I'd like more,' he replied.

Amy began clashing bottles in the cupboard.

'I'm so sorry, there doesn't appear to be any, and I was so looking forward to some myself. James usually keeps his eye on the drinks. Have whisky instead?'

'Let me ran to the local,' said Gerard, 'and get you some rum. It would do me a world of good to get five minutes' exercise.'

After polite expostulations on Amy's side, he had his way, and set off accompanied by Vanessa.

The coffee percolator belched and burped companionably on the side table as we waited.

'I wonder,' said Amy, sounding unusually wistful, 'whether anything will ever come of this affair. She seems so fond of Gerard.'

'She's also fond of half the eligible males in Scotland, as far as we can gather.'

'That's the pity of it. I really think that Gerard should realize that she won't hang about for ever. If he is really serious, I'm sure he should tell her so. Perhaps I could have a word with him. Tactfully, of course.'

'Amy,' I begged her, '*say nothing!* They are both old enough to know what they are doing, and you will only cause everyone – including yourself – a great deal of embarrassment.'

'Perhaps you're right,' said Amy doubtfully. 'He's such a dear man, and it's time he was married. He'll start getting cranky if he waits much longer.'

'Gerard,' I said stiffly, 'is younger than I am.'

'That's what I mean,' replied Amy.

I was saved the necessity of answering by the arrival of Gerard, Vanessa and a large bottle of rum. And I was relieved to find that the rest of the evening passed without any reference to matrimony.

When the time came for me to go, Amy accompanied me to the car. A half-moon, low on the horizon and lying on its back, glowed as tawny as a ripe apricot.

'I haven't had a chance to tell you about James,' began Amy. She shivered. The night air was chilly.

'Get in the car,' I advised. 'We'll be more comfortable.'

'He came down last weekend, and we tried to have a straight talk. But oh, it's so sad! After all our years together we're becoming like strangers. I don't think I can bear it any longer. He's beginning to loathe me. I can see it in his face. Something will have to happen.'

'In what way?'

'I felt sure that I was right to give this matter time to fizzle out. Somehow I still think it will – but perhaps that's simply wishful thinking. I just don't know. All I can be sure of now, since we've been back from our holiday, is that he's getting more and more desperately unhappy.'

She fumbled for a handkerchief and blew her nose. After a moment or two, she went on.

'Now I ask myself, am I right in making three lives miserable? Has the time come to put my pride in my pocket and give in? Or am I right in thinking that one day he will give her up, and then need me? You can see how I torture myself. The position's getting more painful daily. What can I do?'

The question hung between us. A pinkish light from the rising moon warmed the front of Amy's pretty house. From the woods behind us, an owl cried.

'Amy,' I said slowly, 'I honestly don't know. I just can't think what sort of advice one could give in such a situation. I'm no help to you, and how desperately I wish I could be!'

Amy dabbed at her eyes.

'I wouldn't want my worst enemy to go through the misery I've had during these last few months. I feel torn this way and that. Whichever path I choose may be the wrong one.'

She sighed, put her damp cheek against mine, and then opened the door.

'I must go back. Thank you for coming, and for being such a prop in a tottering world. I'll give you a ring later on.'

I started the car and drove slowly down the drive. For the first time, the lonely figure I left standing in the doorway looked old and defeated, and I drove home struggling with tears of my own.

Soon after this evening with Amy, I had to keep an appointment at Caxley Hospital. This was to check that the broken arm was in good trim, and as I could do practically everything with it I had no doubt that I should be paying my last visit there.

The time of the appointment was three-thirty on a Wednesday afternoon, which meant that I should have to leave school at three, no doubt arriving at the hospital waiting room to find a score of other unfortunates called imperiously for exactly the same time.

I explained to my class that they must work on their own for the last half-hour or so, that Miss Edwards would leave the partition door ajar between the two rooms, and would keep an eye on them. They knew, of course, that I was off to hospital, and were suitably impressed, not to say ghoulish about it.

'Will they have to break it again? They did my dad's – to reset it.'

'I sincerely hope not.'

'Will you be put to bed?'

'Good heavens, no.'

'Will you come to school tomorrow?'

'Of course. Now stop fussing and get on with your work.'

Reluctantly, they took up their pens again.

After play, the new child, Derek, distributed boxes of crayons and enormous sheets of paper.

'You can draw a picture,' I told them, 'about any episode in history that you like.' This, I felt, should provide plenty of scope for the boys, who would settle, no doubt, for scenes of warfare involving a great many human figures in various attitudes both upright and prone, and for the girls who would probably decide to illustrate such events as Queen Victoria hearing of her accession, or Henry VIII meeting one of his wives, and needing a good deal of detailed work on the costumes. Such subjects should keep them busily scribbling until the end of school.

But for good measure, I wrote my old friend CONSTANTI-NOPLE on the blackboard, and supplied an extra piece of paper, to be folded long-wise into four, for lists of words made from that trusted standby.

'And you are to work quietly,' I said, 'and be a good example to the infants.'

They assumed unnatural expressions of virtue and trust-worthiness, I bade farewell to Miss Edwards, and set off.

I arrived at the hospital in good time, and followed a fellow-patient to the waiting room. She was on two sticks, and attended by an anxious daughter. The path led by a devious route to the back portions of the building and was composed of so much broken asphalt, pot-holes, manhole covers and the like, that it was a wonder that anyone arrived at the waiting room without injury, I reflected, as I picked my way cautiously between the laurel bushes.

There were quite a few of us hurt and maimed distributed on the benches. Legs in plaster casts, arms supported at shoulder level, people with slings, people with bandages – it might well have been the aftermath of just such a battle scene as those being created in Fairacre School.

I sat in the middle of an empty bench, but was joined within two minutes by a mountainous woman with a bandaged leg who told me, in hideous detail, what was concealed beneath her wrappings. I learnt more about the vascular system of the human frame, in that unfortunate ten-minute encounter, than I

wished to know, and it was a relief to hear my name called and to be ushered into the doctor's presence.

He seemed a morose young man, and he had my sympathy.

'And how is it going, Mrs Potter?' he asked. I said I was Miss Read, and he put down the photographs he was studying rather hastily, and fished out another envelope.

'Of course, Mrs Read.'

'I'm single,' I said. He appeared not to hear, and I remained Mrs Read throughout the interview.

He felt my elbow, and then directed me to put my arm into various positions. The results seemed to depress him.

'Yes. Well, you shouldn't be able to do that with your injury. It pains you, I expect, Mrs Read?'

'Not at all.'

He looked disbelieving, and took a firm grip on the upper arm with one hand and the lower with the other hand, and tried a wrenching movement.

I yelped. An expression of satisfaction spread over his dour countenance.

'Still some need for improvement,' he said smugly. 'Keep on with the exercises. No need to come again, Mrs Read.'

He shook my hand warmly. No doubt about it, I had made his day.

The mountainous woman was on her way in as I came out. 'Coming again?' she asked.

'No!' I cried triumphantly, and made my escape into the sunshine.

17. A Visit from Miss Clare

One blue and white October day, I went to Beech Green to fetch Miss Clare who was going to pay a visit to Fairacre School where she had taught the infants for so many years.

Miss Clare, now a very old lady, lived alone in a thatched cottage which had been her home since early childhood. She was always invited to school functions, and was greeted with much affection by many of the Fairacre parents who owed their own early education to her efforts.

But today's visit was somewhat different. I had long been aware of the avid interest, shown by the older children, in the accounts of life in their village as remembered by their grandparents and other folk of that generation. Mr Willet's memories frequently enliven our schoolroom and, naturally, these first-hand accounts of local history have far more impact on the children than something read in a book.

Miss Clare, who had been a pupil as well as a teacher at our school, was willing to come and talk to the children, and as soon as school dinner was cleared away, I drove to Beech Green to collect her.

As always, she looked immaculate. She wore a navy-blue suit, and a very pale blue jumper under it. I admired the colour, which matched her eyes.

'Dear Emily knitted it a few months before she died,' she said calmly, speaking of her life-long friend who had shared her cottage for the last few years of her life. 'I keep it for best. I should like it to last.'

She was carrying a basket, covered with a white cloth, which she insisted on holding herself. She nursed it carefully throughout the journey and I wondered what it contained.

She was as long-sighted as ever, and on our drive to Fairacre, she pointed out a hovering sparrowhawk, which I confess I should have missed completely, and a weasel which emerged from the grass verge for an instant before turning tail and scurrying back to cover. Her mind was as keen as her eyesight, and she regaled me with snippets of Beech Green gossip, and with future plans for her garden, and a description of some new curtains she was sewing for her bedroom, until I began to feel lazier and more inefficient than ever.

She was greeted with enthusiasm by my class when we entered. Genuine affection, I knew, inspired nine-tenths of their exuberance, but I was aware that the fact that they would not need to exert themselves in work of their own that afternoon partly contributed to their jubilation.

We set the most comfortable chair close to the front row, and the children at the back of the classroom came forward to squeeze companionably three in a desk, so that every word of Miss Clare's should be heard.

I sat at my desk and watched their intent faces. Certainly, Miss Clare had lost none of her old magic in holding children's interest.

The contents of the basket emerged one by one. The first object to be held up was a small china mug with a picture of Queen Victoria on the side.

'We all had one of these given to us,' she told the children, 'when the good Queen had reigned for sixty years. It was called her Diamond Jubilee, and you can see it written here.'

'Were you in this school then?' asked Linda Moffat.

'No, my dear, I was at Beech Green School then.' She went on to describe the junketings of that far-distant day when she was a young child, joining with her sister Ada in the sports arranged in a nearby field.

She told them how she came to Fairacre School a year or two later, carefully omitting the reason, which I knew, for the move. A weak headmaster, with views too advanced for his time, had caused so much concern among the parents that several of them had transferred their children to other local schools, despite the long walks, in every kind of weather, which this involved.

Miss Clare described those daily walks. It was almost three miles from her cottage to the school, and she told the wondering class where she found a robin's nest one spring, and where a tiny river once overflowed one February, and she and Emily Davis, her friend, took off their boots and stockings to paddle through the flood to get to school.

She showed them more treasures from her basket. A starched white pinafore, 'kept for Sundays', intrigued the girls who admired the insertion down the front as it was passed round the class for them to examine.

Her first copybook from Beech Green School with rows and rows of pot-hooks and hangers on the first few pages, and maxims of a strong moral flavour on the rest, was a source of wonder, but the object which gave them most excitement was the photograph of the whole of Fairacre School taken outside in our playground with Mr Wardle, the then headmaster, his wife, the infants' teacher Miss Taylor, and Dolly herself and Emily Davis as pupil teachers, standing meekly at one side of the rows of children. The clothes of the latter caused hilarity and a certain amount of sympathy.

'What's he doin' with that great ol' thing round his neck?' asked Patrick, gazing with bewilderment at one boy sporting an Eton collar. And the fact that nearly all the children wore lace-up boots, despite the brilliant sunshine which had caused most of them to screw up their eyes against the dazzle, puzzled my class considerably.

She described the village as she remembered it so long ago, telling of houses and barns now vanished, of splendid trees, which had towered over the roofs, felled years before, of a disused chapel now turned into a house, and a host of other changes in their environment. The questions came thick and fast, and she answered all with care and composure.

The last thing to be brought from the basket, for the children's delectation, was a fine Bible.

'I was lucky enough to win the Bishop's Bible,' she told them. 'I sat just there, where Ernest is sitting, and it rained so hard that we could hardly hear the questions, I remember.'

The Bishop's Bible is still presented annually to the child who seems best grounded in religious knowledge, so that many a child in the class had just such a Bible at home, presented to a parent or relative years before. It seemed to bring home to them the continuity of tradition in this old school, and the bond between the Victorian child and those of the present day was forged even more firmly in Miss Clare's last few minutes with the class.

Patrick, primed and rehearsed beforehand, thanked her beautifully, and the children were sent to play.

I feared that she might be tired by her efforts, but she seemed stimulated, and insisted on calling on the infants after play where she spent the rest of the school afternoon.

'D'you reckon,' said Ernest, 'that you'll live as long as Miss Clare?'

I said I doubted it.

'Why not?' chorused the class.

'Children nowadays,' I told them, with as much solemnity as I could muster, 'are not as well-behaved as those Miss Clare taught. Teachers today get worn out before their time.'

They smiled indulgently at me, and at one another.

I would have my little joke!

Miss Clare came over to the school house for tea when school was over. One last object, not shown to the children, was produced. It was a pot of her own plum jam which made a most welcome addition to my larder.

The fire crackled merrily for I had slipped across during playtime to put a match to it. Outside, the shadows were already beginning to lengthen, and the chill of autumn became apparent as evening fell.

'It's a time of year I love,' said Miss Clare, stirring her tea. 'I love to see the barns full of straw bales, and to know the grain is safely stored, and to watch them ploughing Hundred Acre Field ready for another crop. I always feel when the harvest's home, that that's the true end of one year and the beginning of the next.'

'I must admit,' I agreed, 'that there's something very satisfying in pulling up all the tatty annuals and having a gorgeous bonfire in the garden. I like to think it's simply an appreciation of good husbandry, but I know that it's partly the thought of being relieved of gardening for a few months. And it's a positive pleasure to see the lawn mower go for its annual overhaul at the end of the summer. The older I get the less I enjoy pushing a mower. Mr Willet does it quite often, but he has so much to do in the village I don't rely on him.'

Miss Clare sighed. 'A man is *useful*! I suppose, if we're honest, we miss having husbands.'

'Like most things, there are points for and against husbands.' I told her about Mrs Coggs.

'I hope she's an exception, poor woman. It isn't only as a husband that Arthur Coggs fails. He's a complete failure at everything else. He won't work, he drinks, he lies and he sponges on the rest of us. But, after all, he's not typical of most men, and personally I very much regret that I did not marry.'

'You surprise me. I've always thought of you as one of the happiest, most serene people I know, with a perfectly full and satisfying life.'

Miss Clare smiled. 'I *am* happy. And, of course, one fills one's life whether single or married. I don't say that I sit and mope about being a spinster. I'm much too aware of my good fortune in having a home of my own, in a place I love, among a host of friends. But it's natural, I think, to wish to have someone of the next generation to carry on one's traditions and work. No, I think if I had been able to marry Arnold, I should truthfully have been happier still.'

She fingered the gold locket, which she always wears, containing the photograph of her fiancé so tragically killed in the First World War.

'After Arnold, there was nobody whom I could care for enough to marry. In any case, there was a dearth of young men after those terrible four years of war, and here in Fairacre and Beech Green, of course, men were few and far between anyway, and we hardly ever went further afield than Caxley to meet others.'

This was true. When one came to think of it, those couples

of Miss Clare's generation were probably born and brought up within a very few miles of each other. More probably still, they were related, which accounted for the few names in those old registers shared by a large number of children.

'No cars, no holidays abroad,' I said, thinking aloud. 'It certainly restricted one's choice.'

'Not only that. There were so few openings for girls and boys. I could either go into domestic service, or a shop, or nursing or teaching. Really there was nothing else open to a girl from a poor home. Nowadays, the young things go all over the world, or get a grant for further education somewhere miles from their own area, where they meet scores of other young people from all walks of life. No wonder they seem so sophisticated compared with ourselves at that age!'

'But are they happier?'

'When it comes to marriage, I have my doubts. In our day, we took our marriage vows pretty seriously and divorce was difficult and expensive. You knew you must make a go of the affair. Maybe there was a lot of unhappiness which was kept hidden, but on the whole I think the young people did better when they waited for each other and got to know themselves more thoroughly.'

Tibby arrived on the window sill, mouthing her complaints. I hurried to let her in. Her fur was fresh and cold, smelling of dry grass, bruised leaves and all outdoors.

'You would make a very good wife yourself,' said Miss Clare, watching me pour some milk into a saucer for my domestic tyrant.

'The chance would be a fine thing,' I replied. 'No, I haven't the pluck to risk it, even if I did have the chance. The single state suits me very well.'

'Tell me more about Crete,' said Miss Clare, and in that moment I knew that Amy's troubles were known to her and, no doubt, to most other people in the neighbourhood. Nothing had been said, and certainly not by me, but here it was again –

that extraordinary awareness by country people of what is going on about them.

I launched enthusiastically into an account of all the wonders I had seen, and out came the photographs and maps and guide books.

It was past seven o'clock when I finally drove her home, and never once was Amy's name spoken between us. Nevertheless, I knew Amy's affairs were now common knowledge, and I was not surprised.

Mrs Pringle's return to her duties I greeted with mingled relief and apprehension. We had done our best, in the last few weeks, to keep things clean and tidy, but I doubted if our standards would please Mrs Pringle.

I did not doubt for long.

''Ere,' said the lady, issuing from the back lobby where the washing up is done. 'What's become of my mop? Alice Willet thrown it out?'

I said I did not know.

'Hardly worn, that mop. A favourite of mine. Hope nothing's become of it.'

I thought of the character in *Cold Comfort Farm* who had the same affection for his little twig mop.

'Perhaps it's been put somewhere different,' I suggested weakly.

'*Everything*, as far as I can see,' boomed Mrs Pringle, 'has been put somewhere different. And the bar soap's almost gone, and them matches is standing for all to see and help themselves to.'

This was a side-swipe at Mr Willet, luckily not present, or battle would have been joined without hesitation.

'And where's the little slatted mat I stands on at the sink?' demanded the lady.

'I think it got broken.'

'Then the office should send out another. If I have to stand on damp concrete, in my state of health, I'll be back in Caxley Hospital before you can say "knife".'

I said that I would indent for another mat without delay.

Mrs Pringle prowled around my classroom, sniffing suspiciously. 'Funny smell this place has got. You been letting the mice in?'

'Is it likely?' I responded coldly. 'Do you imagine I spread a mouse banquet of cheese crumbs and bacon rinds and then open the door and invite them in?

'There's no saying,' was Mrs Pringle's rejoinder. She ran a fat finger along the top of a door and surveyed the resulting grime.

'And not much dustin' done neither,' she commented.

'The children can't reach the tops of the doors.'

'There's others who can,' she answered.

As usual, I could see that I should lose this battle. Luckily, at this juncture, the new boy Derek appeared on the scene with a cut finger, and I was obliged to break off our exchanges and attend to him.

As I wrapped up his finger, I noticed his eyes were fixed on Mrs Pringle who still roamed the room, sniffing and making small noises of disapproval as she examined cupboard tops, window sills and even the inside of the piano.

'Off you go,' I said, when I had completed my first aid. 'Try and keep it clean.'

Mrs Pringle made her way into the infants' room. No doubt she would find plenty there to gloat over, I thought.

Through the open window I became conscious of two voices. One belonged to Derek.

'Who's that lady in there?'

'Ma Pringle.'

'What does she do? Is she a teacher?'

'Nah! Old Ma Pringle? She's the one what keeps the school clean.'

'But I thought we did that?'

'You thought wrong then, mate. We done a bit while she was ill, but I bet Ma Pringle don't reckon we've kept it clean!'

Too true, I thought, too true!

18. Autumn Pleasures

Saturday mornings are busy times for school-teachers. It is then that they usually tackle the week's washing, any outstanding household jobs and, of course, the weekend shopping.

The latter can usually be done in Fairacre, but this Saturday in question I found that I needed such haberdashery items as elastic and pearl buttons. As there were one or two garments to be collected from the cleaners as well, I faced the fact that I must get out the car and make a sortie into Caxley.

While I was choosing a piece of rock salmon for Tibby and two fillets of plaice for myself, Amy smote me on the back.

As usual, she was looking as if she had come out of a bandbox, elegant in dark green with shoes to match. I became conscious of my shabby camel car coat, heavily marked down the right sleeve with black oil from the lock of the car door, and my scuffed car shoes.

'Nearly finished?' she asked.

'Just about. A pound of sprouts, and I'm done.'

'Let's have a spot of lunch together at The Bull,' suggested Amy. 'They do some very good toasted sandwiches in the bar, and I'm famished.'

'So am I. An hour's shopping in Caxley finishes me. Partly, I think, it's the smug pleasure with which half the assistants tell you they haven't got what you want.'

'And that it's no good ordering it,' added Amy. 'I know. I've been suffering that way myself this morning.'

I bought my sprouts, and we entered The Bull. A bright fire

was welcoming and we sank gratefully into the leather arm-chairs to drink our sherry. We were the only people in the bar at that moment, for we were early. Within a short time, the place would be crowded.

'Vanessa's back at work,' said Amy.

'Did Gerard take her to Scotland?'

'Oh no, he's back in London in his little flat, putting the final touches to the book, I gather. A very personable young man picked her up. I never did catch his name. Could it have been Torquil?'

'Sounds likely. I take it he was a Scot?'

'They're *all* Scots at the moment, which makes me anxious about Gerard. He really should be a little more alert if he wants to capture Vanessa.'

'Perhaps he doesn't.'

Amy's mouth took on a determined line. 'I'm quite sure *she* is fond of him. She talks of him such a lot, and is always asking his advice. You know, she really *respects* Gerard. Such a good basis for a marriage where there is a difference in age.'

'Well, there's nothing you can do about it,' I pointed out. 'Have another sherry?'

I went to get our glasses refilled. Amy was looking thoughtful as I replaced them on the table by the sandwiches.

'James was down during the week,' she said. 'He looks worried to death. I don't know whether the girl is wavering and he is having to increase his efforts, or whether he senses that *I'm* wavering, but something's going to give before long. And I've a horrible feeling it's going to be me. It's an impossible situation for us all. What's more, I keep getting tactful expressions of sympathy from people in the village, and I'm not sure that that isn't harder to bear than James's indiscretions.'

I remembered Miss Clare.

'You can't keep any secrets in a village,' I said. 'You know that anyway. Don't let that add to your worries.'

Miss Read

'But how do people find out? I've not said a word to a soul. Even Mrs Bennet, our daily, knows nothing.'

'You'd be surprised! A lot of it's guesswork, plus putting two and two together and making five. Bush telegraph is one of the strongest factors in village life, and works for good as well as ill. Look how people rallied when I broke my arm!'

'Which reminds me,' said Amy, looking at her watch. 'I must get back to pack up the laundry. Mrs Bennet hasn't been for the last two days. She's down with this wretched measles. Caught it from her grandchild.'

'There's a lot about. Three more cases last week in the infants' room.'

'There's talk of closing Bent School,' Amy told me. 'Actually, they rang up last week to see if I could do some supply work there, but I felt I just couldn't with James coming down, and so much hanging over me. They're two staff short, and no end of children away.'

'Have you had it?'

'What, measles? Yes, luckily, at the age of six or seven, and all I can remember is a bowl of oranges permanently by the bedside, and the counterpane covered with copies of *Rainbow* and *Tiger Tim's Annual*.'

We collected our shopping and made for the door, much fortified by The Bull's hospitality.

'I wonder if I've got the stamina to go looking for a new winter coat,' I mused aloud.

Amy eyed my dirty sleeve. 'You certainly look as though you need one,' she commented.

'The thing is, should it be navy blue or brown? In a weak moment last year I bought a navy blue skirt and shoes, and I ought to make up my mind if I'm to continue with navy blue, which means a new handbag as well, or play safe with something brown which will go with everything else.'

Amy shook her head sadly. 'Well, I can't spare the time to

168

come with you, I'm afraid. What problems you set yourself! And you know why?'

I shook my head in turn.

'*No method!*' said Amy severely, waving goodbye.

She's right, I thought, watching her trim figure vanishing down the street. I decided that I could not face such a problem at the moment, collected my car and drove thankfully along the road to Fairacre.

The conker season was now in full swing. Rows of shiny beauties, carefully threaded on strings, lined the ancient desk at the side of the room, and as soon as playtime came, they were snatched up and their owners rushed outside to do battle.

There were one or two casualties understandably. Small boys, swinging heavy strings of conkers, and especially when faced with defeat, are apt to let fly at an opponent. One or two bruises needed treatment, usually to the accompaniment of heated comment.

'He done it a-purpose, miss.'

'No, I never then.'

'I saw him, miss. Oppin' mad, he was, miss.'

'Never! I saw him too, miss. They was jus' playin' quiet-like. It were an accident.'

'Cor! Look who's talking! What about yesterday, eh? You was takin' swipes at all us lot, with your mingy conkers.'

'Whose mingy conkers? They beat the daylights out of yourn anyway!'

Luckily, the conker season is a relatively short one, and the blood cools as the weather does.

Out in the fields the tractors were ploughing and drilling. We could hear the rooks, dozens of them, cawing as they followed the plough, flapping down to grab the insects turned up in the rich chocolate-brown furrows. The hedges were thinning fast, and a carpet of rustling leaves covered the school lane. Scarlet rose hips and crimson hawthorn berries splashed the hedgerows with bright colour, and garlands of bryony, studded with berries of coral, jade and gold, wreathed the hedges like jewelled necklaces.

The children brought hazel nuts and walnuts to school, cracking them with their teeth, and as bright-eyed and intent as squirrels as they examined their treasures. Their fingers were stained brown with the green husks from the walnuts, and purple with the juice from late blackberries. Plums and apples from cottage gardens joined the biscuits on the side table ready for playtime refreshment. Autumn is the time of plenty, of stocking up for the lean days ahead, and Fairacre children take full advantage of nature's bounty.

So do the adults. We were all busy making plum jam and apple jelly, and keeping a sharp eye on the wild crab apples which would not be ready until later. There are several of these trees among the copses and hedges of Fairacre, and most years there is plenty of fruit for everyone. One year, however, soon after I arrived in Fairacre, there was a particularly poor crop of these lovely little apples. A newcomer to the village, one of the 'atomic wives', living in the cottage now inhabited by young Derek and his parents, was rash enough to pick the lot, much to the fury of the other good wives of Fairacre. I remember, in my innocence, attempting to be placatory, suggesting that ignorance, rather than greed, had prompted her wholesale appropriation.

'We'll learn her!' had been the vengeful cry. And they did. Perhaps it was as well that her husband was posted elsewhere after this unfortunate incident. I can't think that she really enjoyed her crab apple jelly.

There is a very neighbourly feeling about picking these wild fruits, and very few would strip a hedge of nuts or blackberries. Leaving some for the next comer is usual. It is as though the generosity of nature communicates itself to those blessed by it, and many a time I have heard the children, and their parents, recommending this hedge or that tree as the best place to try harvesting.

One of the group of elms at the corner of the playground was considered unsafe and had to come down. The children were allowed to watch the operation at a respectful distance. The two men had the small branches off, the trunk sawn through and the giant toppled, all within the hour.

It fell with a dreadful cracking sound, and thumped into Mr Roberts' field beyond. The children raised a great shout of triumph, but one of the infants grew tearful and said, 'I don't like it falling down.'

'Neither do I,' I said. We seemed to be the only two who felt saddened at the sight. Everyone else rejoiced, but I cannot see a tree felled, particularly a majestic one such as this was, without a shock of horror at the swift killing of something which has taken a hundred years or more to grow, and has given shelter and beauty to the other lives about it.

However, I was not too shattered to be grateful for some of its logs which Mr Willet procured for me. I helped him to stand them in my wood shed one afternoon after school.

The sky was that particularly intense blue which occasionally occurs in October. Across the fields, in the clear air, the trees glowed in their russet colours. It was invigorating handling the rough-barked wood, knowing that the winter's fires would be made splendid with its burning.

But it was cold too. Mr Willet, stacking the final few, blew out his moustache. 'Have a frost tonight, you'll see. Got your dahlias up?'

I had not. Mr Willet evinced no surprise.

'Shall I do 'em for you now?' he offered.

'No need. I've kept you long enough. It's time you were home.'

'That's all right. Alice has gone gadding into Caxley to a temperance meeting.'

Gadding seemed hardly the word to use under the circumstances, I felt.

'Come and have a cup of tea with me then,' I said. We stood back to admire the stack of logs before making for the kitchen.

'That baby of Mrs Coggs has got the measles, they say,' said Mr Willet, stirring his tea. 'Them others away from school?'

'Not today. I'd better look into it. Two more infants are down with it, but we're not as badly off as Bent.'

I told him what Amy had said about the possibility of the school there having to close.

'And how is your friend?' inquired Mr Willet. 'I did hear,' he added delicately, 'that she was in a bit of trouble.'

Here we were again, I thought. I had no desire to snub dear

old Mr Willet, but equally I had no wish to betray Amy's confidences.

'Aren't we all in a bit of trouble, one way or the other?' I parried.

'That's true,' agreed Mr Willet. 'But you single ones don't have the same trouble as us married folk. Only got yourself to consider, you see. Any mistakes you make don't rebound on the other like. Take them dahlias.'

'What about them?'

I was relieved that we seemed to have skated away from the thin ice of Amy's affairs.

'Well, if my Alice'd forgot them dahlias, I should have cut up a bit rough, seeing what they cost. But you, not having no husband, gets off scot free.'

'Not entirely. I shall have to pay for any new ones.'

'Yes, but that's your affair. There ain't no *upsets*, if you see what I mean. No bad feelings. You can afford to be slap-dash and casual-like. Who's to worry?'

I laughed. 'You sound like Mrs Pringle! Am I really slap-dash and casual, Mr Willet?'

'Lor', bless you,' said Mr Willet, rising to go, 'you're the most happy-go-lucky flibbertigibbet I've ever met in all me born days! Many thanks for the tea, Miss Read. See you bright and early!'

And off he went, chuckling behind his stained moustache, leaving me dumb-founded – and with all the washing-up.

I had time to savour Mr Willet's opinion of me as I sat knitting by the fire that evening. I was amused by his matter-of-fact acceptance of my shortcomings. His remarks about the draw-backs of matrimony I also knew to be true. Any unsettled feelings I had suffered during the holidays had quite vanished, and I realized that I was back in my usual mood of thinking myself lucky to be single.

For some unknown reason I had a sudden craving for a

pancake for my supper. I had not cooked one for years, and thoroughly enjoyed beating the batter, and cutting a lemon ready for my feast. I even tossed the pancake successfully, which added to my pleasure.

If I were having to provide for a husband, I thought, tucking into my creation, a pancake would hardly be the fare to offer as a complete meal. No doubt there would be 'upsets', as Mr Willet put it. Yes, there was certainly something to be said for the simple single life. I was well content.

The fire burnt brightly. Tibby purred on the rug. At ten o'clock I stepped outside the front door before locking up. There was a touch of frost in the air, as Mr Willet had forecast, and the stars glittered above the elm trees. Somewhere in the village a dog yelped, and near at hand there was a rustling among the dry leaves as some small nocturnal animal set out upon its foraging.

With my lungs full of clear cold air I went indoors and made all fast. I was in my petticoat when the telephone rang.

It was Amy. She sounded incoherent, and quite unlike her usual composed self.

'James has had an accident. I'm not sure where. In the car, I mean, and the girl, Jane, with him, I'm just off.'

'Where is he?'

'Somewhere near Salisbury, in a hospital. I've got the address scribbled down.'

'Shall I come with you?'

'No, no, my dear. I only rang because I felt someone should know where I was. Mrs Bennet's not on the phone, and anyway, as you know, she's ill. I must go.'

'Tell me,' I said, wondering how best to put it, 'is he much damaged?'

'I don't know. They told me nothing really. The hospital people found his address on him and simply rang me to say he was there. He's unconscious – they did say that.'

I felt suddenly very cold. Was this the dreadful way that Amy's affairs were to be settled?

'Amy,' I urged, 'do let me come with you, please.'

I could hear her crying at the other end. It was unendurable.

'No. You're sweet, but I must go alone. I'll be careful, I promise. And I'll ring you first thing tomorrow morning when I know more.'

'I understand,' I said. 'Good luck, my love, and call on me if there's anything I can do to help.'

We hung up. Mechanically, I got ready for the night and climbed into bed, but there was no hope of sleeping. I think I heard every hour strike from the church tower, as I lay there imagining Amy on her long sad journey westward, pressing on through the darkness with a chill at her heart more cruel than the frosts around her.

What awaited Amy at the end of that dark road?

19. James Comes Home

After my disturbed night I was late in waking. Fortunately, it was Saturday, and my time was my own. I went shakily about the household chores, alert for the telephone bell and a message from Amy.

Outside, a wind had sprung up, rattling the rose against the window and ruffling the feathers of the robin on the bird table. Frost still whitened the grass, but great grey clouds, scudding from the west, promised rain before long with milder, weather on the way.

The hands of the clock crept from nine to ten, from ten to eleven, and still nothing happened. My imagination ran riot. Was James dying? Or dead, perhaps, and Amy too distraught to think of such things as telephone calls? And what about the girl? Was she equally seriously injured? And what result would this accident have upon all three people involved?

I made my mid-morning coffee and drank more than half before realizing that the milk was still waiting in the saucepan. A shopping list progressed by fits and starts, as I made one entry and then gazed unseeingly through the window.

Suddenly, the bell rang, and I was about to lift the receiver when I realized that it was the back door bell. Mrs Pringle stood on the doorstep holding a fine cabbage.

'Thought you could do with it,' she said. 'I was taking the school tea towels over the kitchen so thought I'd kill two birds with one stone.'

I thanked her and asked if she would like some coffee.

'Well, now,' she said graciously, 'I don't mind if I do.'

I very nearly retorted, as an ex-landlady of mine used to do when encountering this phrase: 'And I don't mind if you *don't*!' but I bit it back.

Mrs Pringle seated herself at the kitchen table, loosening her coat and rolling her hand-knitted gloves into a tidy ball. I switched on the stove to heat the milk again. As one might expect, it was at this inconvenient moment that the telephone bell rang.

'Make the coffee when it's hot,' I cried to Mrs Pringle, and rushed into the hall.

It was Amy. She sounded less distraught than the night before, but dog-tired.

'Sorry to be so late in ringing, but I thought I'd wait until the doctor had seen James, so that I had more news to tell you.'

'And what is it?'

'He's round this morning, but still in a good deal of pain. The collar bone is broken and a couple of ribs cracked, and he's complaining of internal pains. Still, he's all right, the doctor says, and can be patched up.'

'What about his head? Did he have concussion?'

I was suddenly conscious of Mrs Pringle's presence and, without doubt, her avid interest in the side of the conversation she could hear. Too pointed to close the kitchen door, I decided, and anyway too late.

'Yes. He was knocked out, and has a splitting head this morning, but, thank God, he'll survive. Now, my dear, would you do something for me?'

'Of course. Say the word.'

'Could you pop over to Bent and take some steak out of the slow oven? Like an ass, I forgot it in the hurry last night. It's been stewing there for about fourteen hours now, so will probably be burnt to a frazzle.'

'What shall I do with it?'

'Let Tibby have it, if it's any use. Otherwise, chuck it out.

And would you sort out the perishables in the fridge? And cancel the milk and bread? I'm sorry to bother you with all this, but I've decided to stay nearby. There's a comfortable hotel and James won't be able to be moved for a bit. Mrs Bennet isn't on the phone, and I don't like to worry her anyway while she's ill.'

I said I would go over immediately, scribbled down her forwarding address, and was about to put down the receiver when, luckily, Amy remembered to tell me where the spare key was.

'I've moved it from under the watering-can,' explained Amy, 'and now you'll find it inside one of those old-fashioned earthenware honey pots, labelled CARPET TACKS, on the top shelf at the left-hand side of the garden shed.'

I sent my love and sympathy to James.

'I'll ring again tomorrow,' promised Amy, and then the line went dead.

Mrs Pringle looked up expectantly as I returned, but I was not to be drawn.

'Have a biscuit, Mrs Pringle,' I said proffering the tin.

She selected a Nice biscuit with care. It was obviously a poor substitute for a morsel of hot news, but it had to do.

Half an hour later, I was on my way to Amy's, and it was only then that I remembered that nothing had been said about James's companion – Jane, wasn't it? What, I wondered, had happened to her?

The wind buffeted the car as I drove southward. The sheep were huddled together against the hedges, finding what shelter they could. Pedestrians were bent double against the onslaught, clutching hats and head-scarves, coat-tails flapping. Cyclists tacked dangerously to and fro across the road, dogs, exhilarated by the wind, bounded from verges, and children, screaming with excitement, tore after them.

The leaves of autumn, torn from the trees, fluttered down like showers of new pennies, sticking to the windscreen, the bonnet, and plastering the road with their copper brightness. Amy's drive was littered with twigs and tiny cones from the fir tree which must have caught the full brunt of some particularly violent gust.

I found the key in the honey pot, and went indoors. A rich aroma of stewed beef greeted me, and my first duty was to rescue the casserole. Amazingly, it still had some liquor in it, and the meat had fallen into deliciously tender chunks. I decided that I should share this largesse with Tibby that evening.

Amy's refrigerator was far better stocked than mine, and much more tidy. There was little to remove – some milk, a portion of apricot pie, four sardines on a saucer, just the usual flotsam and jetsam of daily catering.

There were a few letters which I re-addressed, and then I wrote notes to the baker and milkman, before going round the house to make sure that the windows were shut and that any radiators were left at a low heat.

All seemed to be in order. I checked switches, locked doors, and took a final walk around Amy's garden, before replacing the key. It was while I was on my tour of inspection, that I saw a man battling his way from the gate.

He looked surprised to see me.

'Oh, good morning! My name's John Bennet. My wife works here and asked me to come and see everything's all right.'

I asked after her.

'Getting on, but it's knocked all the stuffing out of her. These children's complaints are no joke when you're getting on.'

'So I believe. Don't worry about the house. Mrs Garfield asked me to look in. She's been called away.'

'Yes, we knew she must have been. That's why I came up. My sister, who lives just down the road from us, saw her setting off last night – very late it was – and looking very worried.

My sister was taking out the dog, and guessed something must be up.'

I had imagined that Mrs Bennet had been concerned for any possible gale damage, but now revised my views.

'Mr Garfield,' I explained, 'has had a car accident, but is getting on quite well, I gather, and should be home before long. Tell Mrs Bennet not to worry. I'll keep an eye on the place while she's laid up, and if she wants to get in touch tell her to phone me.'

We took a final turn round the windy garden together before parting. All seemed well.

I got back into the car and set off for home, marvelling, yet again, at the extraordinary efficiency of bush telegraph in rural areas.

The gales continued for the rest of the week, and the children were as mad as hatters in consequence. Wind is worse than any other element, I find, for causing chaos in a classroom. Snow, of course, is dramatic, and needs to be inspected through the windows at two-minute intervals to see if it is 'laying'. But this is something which occurs relatively seldom in school hours.

Sunshine and rain are accepted equably, but a good blustery wind which bangs doors, rattles windows, blows papers to the floor, and the breath from young bodies, is a fine excuse for boisterous behaviour.

Up here, on the downs, the wind is a force to be reckoned with. Not long ago, an elm tree crashed across the roof of St Patrick's church, and caused so much damage that the village was hard put to it to raise the money for its repair. Friends from near and far rallied to Fairacre's support, and the challenge was met, but we all (and Mr Willet, in particular, who strongly suspects any elm tree of irresponsible falling-about through sheer cussedness) watch our trees with some apprehension when the gales come in force.

The only casualty this time, as far as I knew, was a

venerable damson tree in Ernest's garden. He brought the remaining fruit to school in a paper bag, and the small purple plums were shared out among his school fellows.

I watched this generous act with some trepidation. Damsons, even when plentifully sugared, are as tart a fruit as one could wish to meet. To see the children scrunching them raw made me shudder, but apart from one or two who complained that 'they give them cat-strings' or 'turned their teeth all funny', Ernest's largesse was much enjoyed.

My own share arrived in the form of a little pot of damson cheese, made by Ernest's mother, and for this I was truly thankful.

Apart from fierce cross-draughts, and a continuous whistling one from the skylight above my desk, we were further bedevilled by smoke from the tortoise stove. Even Mrs Pringle, who can control our two monsters at a touch, confessed herself beaten, so that we worked with eyes sore with smoke and much coughing – most of it affected – and plenty of smuts floating in the air.

Amy rang twice during the few days after the accident. The car, she said, on the first occasion, was beyond repair and James had been lucky to escape so lightly.

'And Jane?' I dared to ask.

'Simply treated here for superficial cuts on her face and a sprained wrist. She'd gone home by the time I arrived, fetched by mother. At least she'd had the sense to be wearing her seat belt. It saved her from hitting her head on the windscreen which is what happened to James.'

'And how is he?'

'Still running a temperature, which the doctor thinks is rather peculiar, I gather. He's very restless, and in pain, poor thing. He was terribly worried about Jane, but they've put his mind at rest about that.'

'Any chance of bringing him home?'

'They don't seem in any hurry to get rid of him. He's been

strapped up and the collar bone set, and so on. And I'm afraid his beauty has been spoiled, at least for a time, as a little slice was cut off the end of his nose by the glass of the windscreen.'

'Oh, poor James!'

'He doesn't care about the look of it, but curses most horribly whenever he needs to blow it.'

I sent my sympathy, assured Amy that all was well at Bent, and we rang off.

I had not mentioned it to my old friend, but this was the evening when I had undertaken to give a talk to Fairacre Women's Institute about our holiday in Crete.

Accordingly, soon after her telephone call, I dressed in my best and warmest garments and got ready for my ordeal. The Mawnes had promised to bring a projector and I had looked out my slides into some semblance of order. Amy had offered her own collection, but under the circumstances, I had to make do with my inferior efforts. Luckily, the brilliant Cretan light had guaranteed success with almost all the exposures.

The village hall was gratifyingly full and a beautiful flower arrangement graced the WI tablecloth. Listening to the minutes, from the front row, I studied its form. This was obviously the handiwork of one of 'the floral ladies', expert in arrangement of colour and form with no 'Oasis' visible at all, as is usual with us lesser mortals. The whole thing had been fixed, with artistic cunning, to a mossy piece of wood, and I was so busy trying to work out how it was done, that it came as a severe shock to hear my name called and to be obliged to take the floor.

I began by a brief description of our journey out, and of the attractions of the hotel. The projector, operated by Mr Mawne, worked splendidly for he had brought the correct plug for the village hall socket, a rare occurrence on these occasions, and we were all duly impressed at such efficiency and foresight.

The vivid colours of the Cretan landscape were even more impressive on a grey October evening. The animals evoked cries of admiration, although someone commented that the RSPCA would never have let a poor little donkey *that* small, hump a great load like that! I had to explain that, despite appearances, those four wispy legs beneath the piles of brushwood were really not suffering from hardship and that the load was light in weight.

Knossos, of course, brought forth the most enthusiastic response. The great red pillars and the beautiful flights of stairs made spectacular viewing, and the frescoes of dolphins and bulls were much admired. Even the topless ladies were accepted, except for one gasp of shock from Mrs Pringle in the front row.

I ended in good time, for I had seen Mrs Willet go quietly into the kitchen to attend to the boiling water in the urn, and knew that a coffee break was scheduled.

My final word was of thanks to Mr Mawne, who had so nobly coped with the projector, and to whom I felt I owed an apology as I had been unable to photograph the Cretan hawk for him.

At this, Mr Mawne came forward and began a description of the elusive bird. I must say, his grasp of the subject was profound, and by the time he had described its appearance in detail, its habits, its mode of flight and its diet, a good many ladies were consulting their wrist watches while Mrs Willet hovered by the kitchen door, coffee pot in hand.

Meanwhile, I had sat down in the front row beside Mrs Pringle, the better to enjoy Mr Mawne's impromptu discourse. It is this off-the-cuff situation which gives village meetings their particular flavour. Who wants to stick to such a dreary thing as an agenda? As everyone knows, the *real* business takes place on the way home, or an hour after the meeting finished, in the local pub.

Henry Mawne was just about to begin on the breeding

habits and nesting sites of the hawk, and had broken off to suggest that he would just slip down to his house to fetch a reference book on the subject, if the ladies were agreeable, when Mrs Partridge, as President, bravely rose and checked the flow with her usual charm and aplomb. What was more, she invited her old friend to speak at one of the monthly meetings next year about any of his favourite birds.

'I am sure that they will soon be our favourites as well,' she finished, with a disarming smile, and Henry resumed his seat, flushed with pleasure, while Mrs Willet hastened to bring in the coffee amidst general relief.

I was presented with the magnificent flower arrangement so that, all in all, the evening was a resounding success.

Amy's second call came soon after I returned from school the next day.

'There's a bit of a panic here,' said Amy calmly. 'Don't laugh, but poor James has the *measles*!'

'Oh no! As though he hasn't enough to put up with.'

'Exactly. I suppose he picked it up when he was at home recently. Mrs Bennet was about in the house then. It might have been contact with her. But there, it could have been *anyone*! The point is, the hospital people seem dead anxious to get rid of him before he gives it to the rest of the ward, so they tell me he is fit enough to go home tomorrow.'

'I bet he's pleased.'

'He is. So am I. It's funny they didn't spot this rash earlier, but I think they put it down to a fairly common reaction to antibiotics, and in any case, he hasn't got a great many spots.'

'Can I do anything this end?'

'Yes, please. Could you turn up the heating, and get some milk and bread for us? I'll shop the next day when he's settled in.'

I said I could do whatever was needed.

'He's still at the soup and egg-and-milk stage. A front tooth was knocked out, which gives him a piratical look, and his mouth hurts him quite a bit.'

'He sounds as though he's taken quite a pasting.'

'Well, evidently he was turning right, and a van was coming behind him pretty swiftly, and James caught the full force of the impact. Luckily, nothing too serious seems to have resulted apart from the collarbone and ribs. It's just that he looks rather odd with his sliced nose and gappy smile. And, of course, it is rather ignominious to have the measles in your fifties! In fact, rather a humiliating end altogether to what was going to be a glamorous few days in Devon.'

'Does he feel that?' I asked hesitantly.

'Yes, he certainly does,' said Amy. 'Wasn't it Molière who said: "One may have no objection to being wicked, but one hates to be ridiculous"? Well, that sums up James's feelings at the moment.'

The pips went for the second time, and I felt we should terminate our conversation. 'What time do you expect to be home?'

'During the late afternoon, I imagine. We'll have to see the doctor here, and I shall drive slowly. The poor old thing is pretty battered and bruised. He'll go straight to bed, of course.'

I said that I would put hot bottles in the beds, and we rang off.

An hour or so later, I drove over to Bent to do my little duties.

I took with me a few late roses to cheer the invalid's room, and half a dozen of Mrs Pringle's new-laid eggs. On the way, I left a message at the dairy and collected a brown loaf. The house struck pleasantly warm when I entered, but I duly turned up the heating and set a fire ready in the sitting room for Amy to light on her return.

There was little else to do except to fill the hot-water bottles and to transfer the few letters from the floor to the hall table. I was home again by eight o'clock to join Tibby by my own fire.

Leg upraised, she washed herself industriously, spitting out little balls of goose-grass on to the hearthrug. As cat-slave, I transferred them meekly from the rug to the fire, my thoughts with Amy and James.

They were much in my mind throughout lessons the next day. Soon after five, Amy rang to thank me for my ministrations.

'What sort of journey?'

'Better than I thought. He stood it very well, and feels easier now that he's in his own bed. His temperature is almost back to normal. I shall get our own doctor to call in tomorrow, but I think he'll mend fast now.'

There was relief and happiness in Amy's voice which I had not heard for many months. And I knew, as Amy certainly must know, that, in every sense of the expression, James had come home.

20. The Final Scene

The autumn gales gave way to a spell of quiet grey weather, and we were all mightily relieved. The stoves behaved properly, the children almost as well, and their parents finished tidying their gardens and generally set about preparations for the winter ahead.

Mist veiled the downs from sight. It hung, swirling sluggishly, in the lanes, and everything outdoors was damp to touch. Flagged paths and steps glistened, little droplets hung on the hedges, and nothing stirred.

All sound was muffled. Mr Roberts' sheep, in the field across the playground, sounded as though they bleated from as far away as Beech Green. The dinner van purred to a halt as mellifluously as a Rolls. Even the children's voices, as they played up and down the coke pile, were pleasantly muffled.

The measles epidemic seemed to be on the wane. Children returned, a little peaky perhaps, and certainly with tiresome coughs which persisted long after they were pronounced cured, but seemingly ready for work and secretly glad, I suspected, to have something to occupy them.

James's measles, and his general injuries, kept him resting for some time after his return home. Amy rang me one evening when I was busy with the local paper.

'Getting on quite well,' she replied in answer to my inquiries. 'But I really rang about something quite different. Have you seen the paper today?'

'I'm holding it.'

'Good. Look at page fourteen.'

'Hang on while I turn it over.'

I spread the paper on the hall floor and turned the pages.

'What about it?' I asked.

'Well, look at the photograph!'

Amy sounded impatient. I looked obligingly at some twenty photographs of local houses. At least six pages of the *Caxley Chronicle* are devoted to housing advertisements.

'Which one?'

'What do you mean, which one? There is only one.'

'On page fourteen? It's one of the advertisement pages. There are about two dozen photographs.'

There was an ominous silence. When Amy spoke next it was in the quiet controlled voice of a teacher driven to desperation by some particularly obtuse pupil.

'Which paper are you looking at?'

'The *Caxley Chronicle*. You said "The Paper". On Thursday, naturally, "The Paper" is the local one.'

'I didn't mean that thing!' Amy shouted, with exasperation. 'How parochially minded can you get? Look at the *Daily Telegraph*.'

'I shall have to fetch it,' I said huffily. 'I haven't had time to look at it yet.'

I found page fourteen in the right newspaper, and called excitedly down the telephone.

'Yes! Good heavens! Gerard!'

'As you say, "Good heavens, Gerard!" What do you think of that?'

The photograph showed a pretty woman in a fur coat holding hands with Gerard, who was looking remarkably smug and had a wisp of hair standing up in the wind like a peewit's crest.

Underneath it said: 'Miss Hattie May, the well-known musical comedy actress, after her marriage to Mr Gerard Baker at Caxton Hall.'

'It's staggering, isn't it?' I said. 'And they've even got the names right!'

'It's not the reporters I'm concerned with,' said Amy severely, 'it's poor Vanessa. What will she be feeling?'

'I don't imagine she'll be too upset,' I said. 'I never did think she was in love with him.'

This was plain speaking, but I was still smarting from Amy's high-handedness about parochial minds.

'I don't expect a single woman like you to be particularly sensitive to a young girl's reaction to an attractive and mature man like Gerard,' said Amy, with *hauteur*. She was obviously going to return blow with blow, no doubt to the enjoyment of the telephone operator. I determined not to be drawn. In any case, I had some gingerbread in the oven and it was beginning to smell 'most sentimental', as Kipling said. This was no time for a brawl.

'Look, Amy,' I said swiftly. 'I honestly think Vanessa is completely heart-whole – at least, as far as Gerard is concerned, so don't upset yourself on her behalf.'

Amy accepted the olive branch and spoke graciously. 'I hope you're right. You often are,' she added generously. 'I wondered if I should ring her at the hotel, but perhaps I'll wait.'

'Good idea,' I said, trying to keep the relief from my voice. Amy, in meddlesome mood, is dangerous. 'No doubt, she would prefer to get in touch with you.'

'Yes, yes, that's so!' agreed Amy. She sounded thoughtful.

I rang off before she could start the discussion again, and made swiftly for the oven. The gingerbread could not have stood another two minutes.

I discovered, with some surprise, that half-term occurred the next weekend. So much had happened already this term that I had not really collected my wits sufficiently to look ahead. What with Amy's affairs, the last trivial discomforts of my own injuries, Mrs Pringle's tribulations, the measles and the ordinary run of day-to-day school events, time had whirled by.

Miss Edwards, my infants' teacher, a pleasant girl who had been with me for two years since the departure of Mrs Bonny, brought to my notice the fact that, if we were proposing to have a Christmas concert, as usual, then we should start preparing for it.

She was right, of course, but the thought depressed me.

'What about a carol service with the nine lessons?' I countered weakly. 'We shall have the usual Christmas party in the school.'

She looked disappointed.

'Let me think about it over half-term,' I said, and we shelved the subject.

'And another thing,' she said. 'I'm getting married next Easter, so of course I shall give in my notice, and go at the end of next term. It's early to tell you, but I thought you'd like to know in good time.'

There was nothing to do but to congratulate her, but my heart was leaden. I broke the news to the vicar when I saw him.

His face lit up with joy. 'What good news! She will make an excellent wife and mother.'

'There are too many girls rushing out of teaching to become excellent wives and mothers,' I said sourly. 'Especially infant teachers. Heaven knows when we'll get a replacement. After all, the colleges don't get the girls out until June or July. We shall have a whole term to fill in.'

This is a situation which has faced us often enough, but every time it brings pain and perplexity.

Mr Partridge trotted out his usual optimistic hopes. 'There's dear Miss Clare—' he began.

'Much too old, and not fair to her or the children.'

'Well, Mrs Annett, perhaps?'

'She's two children of her own and a husband, and an old blind aunt coming for the summer.'

'Really? What a kind person she is! Lives for others, and an example to us all.'

I agreed. A heavy silence fell as we wrestled with the problem.

'Now, what about that good friend of yours who is so competent? The lady from Bent? She helped us once or twice, I believe.'

I said that Amy might manage the odd day or two, but was far too busy a person to commit herself to a whole term's teaching.

'Besides,' I said, 'Amy's methods are the same vintage as mine, and I think she'd find our infant room far too chaotic under today's conditions.'

'But I thought that was as it should be these days?' protested Mr Partridge, looking bewildered. 'That last inspector who called – the one with no collar, you remember, and long hair – he said that young children needed to make a noise to develop properly. I recall his words quite clearly: "Meaningful activity creates noise."'

'So do other things,' I remarked tartly. 'The point is that to get a competent teacher for the infant room is going to be a headache.'

'I shall see that the post is advertised in good time,' said the vicar. 'After all, one never knows. Providence has been good to us before, and Fairacre is doubly attractive in the summer. I will have a word with the Office at once.'

'That might help,' I agreed.

'I must go and see Miss Edwards,' he said, 'to congratulate her. Are you sure you can't persuade your friend to come over from Bent for that term? It's not too bad a journey.'

'I will ask her, but I don't think there's much hope there. Her husband is recovering rather slowly from a car accident, complicated by catching measles.'

'Poor fellow,' said Mr Partridge sincerely. 'I heard he had

been injured. He's lucky to have such a good wife to nurse him back to health.'

If he had added: 'And to his responsibilities as a married man,' I should not have been surprised. Clearly, the vicar knew exactly what had been happening at Bent.

One morning, during half-term, I was surprised and pleased to have a visit from Amy.

'Mrs Bennet's back,' she explained. 'Still a trifle wobbly, but it means I can get out now and again. James is in bed most of the day, so he's not in the way of Mrs Bennet's Hoover.'

She presented me with a splendid bunch of late chrysanthemums.

'By the way, you were right about Vanessa. She rang the very same night that we saw the photograph of Gerard and Hattie. I don't know if she was putting on a stout act, or whether she was genuinely pleased, but I must say she sounded so.'

I could afford to be magnanimous in the face of this. 'Well, naturally, as an aunt, you would be more anxious about Vanessa's feelings than I needed to be. But I always thought that Gerard's manner was more *avuncular* than *amatory*.'

'At Gerard's age,' commented Amy, 'it might well be both. He is practically the same age as James.'

We seemed to be treading close to dangerous ground.

'What did Vanessa say?' I asked hastily.

'Well, it seems that Gerard had confided to Vanessa his hopes of wooing Hattie some time ago. You remember she bought that house near the hotel? Evidently he was a constant visitor. Of course, all this is Vanessa's story, you understand. She may well be putting a good front on a somewhat humiliating episode.'

'I don't think so for a minute,' I said stoutly.

'He knew Hattie years ago. In fact, it was his friend who cut him out, so Vanessa says, which is why he's never married. It's rather romantic, isn't it, to think of him being faithful for all those years?'

'Maybe he didn't meet anyone he liked.'

'Trust you to throw cold water on any small fire of passion,' observed Amy, but she was smiling.

'I'm very glad it's ended this way,' I told her. 'Hattie May was always a darling, and the more I see of Gerard the better I like him. I look forward to meeting them both.'

'And so you shall,' declared Amy, 'for I'm inviting them down for a weekend as soon as James has properly recovered.'

She looked at me speculatively, as if weighing up something in her mind. I wondered what was worrying her.

'Have some coffee?' I suggested.

Amy shook her head. 'Not at the moment, thanks. I just wanted to let you know how things have worked out for James and me. You were such a help, when I was in the depths. It's only right that you should know the end of the story.'

'Amy,' I protested, 'there's absolutely no need!'

'Don't get alarmed! I shan't tell you any details that might bring a blush to your maiden cheek, I assure you.'

'Thank God for that! You know I hear far too many confidences for my peace of mind as a spinster.'

Amy looked suddenly contrite. 'I hope I didn't burden you too desperately,' she said, in a low voice. 'Perhaps I imposed on you as thoughtlessly as so many others do. I'm sorry.'

'Your troubles are quite different,' I said. 'And if two old friends like us can't help each other in a fix, it's a pity. You rallied to my support when I needed it. I hope I helped a little when things were tough with you. So, rattle away, and tell me what happened. Of course I want to know. It's just that I don't want you to feel obliged to *Tell All*.'

Amy laughed.

'Well, poor James has had long enough to think about things. I was careful not to press him too much. It was plain that he was desperately unhappy, and one evening after we were back at home he volunteered the information that Jane's affections had been cooling for some time. In fact, it was for this reason that he had insisted on taking her away for the weekend to see if they couldn't make things up. I think he was feeling pretty silly too, as he had asked me for a divorce, and now the girl was about to ditch him.'

'But, surely, it would have been more sensible to have broken with Jane then, rather than pursue her further?'

'Being sensible is not the usual state of mind when a man's in love. Especially a middle-aged man. And you know James! Love him as I do, I face the fact that he is a terrible show-off, and always has been. The handmade shoes, the vastly expensive suits, the fast cars – they're all the dreary old status symbols that James loves to play with. They've never impressed me particularly, as he well knows, and perhaps that's where I have been wrong – in letting him see that I have simply indulged his weakness for his toys instead of letting him think I'm dazzled by them. Well, we live and learn, and we've both learnt the hard way these last few months.'

'It's over now,' I said consolingly.

'Yes, I think it is, as far as our natures will allow it to be. If only we'd had children, I think we should have escaped some of this damage.'

'There would have been other risks. They might have turned out unsatisfactorily in one way or another, and I think that's harder to bear than any result of one's own actions.'

Amy nodded and sighed. 'I suppose the old saying that man is born to trouble as the sparks fly upward, is pretty true. However, our particular trouble had a funny side.'

'Tell me.'

'Well, on the day of the accident, evidently, Jane was being remarkably offhand and James was doing his best to impress her as they drove – much too fast, I gather – down to Devon. According to him, she picked a quarrel about the best route to take, and was actually tugging at his arm when he was turning right, shouting that it was the wrong road.

'I think there may be some truth in this. James isn't a liar about matters of this sort, and it's unlike him to have missed seeing the van coming up behind him. He drives much too fast, I always think, but he prides himself on being a good driver, and really he is.'

'So she may have caused the accident?'

'Who's to say? Anyway, she was furious with him. I heard a bit about her behaviour from the hospital staff. And she wouldn't answer the telephone when James tried to ring her. After some time, he began to accept the position, and it was then that he told me all about it.'

'Was he very miserable?'

'I think he'd begun to get over that. Let's say he was beginning to be more clear-headed, and to face the fact that he'd behaved badly. Also, that he was well out of a situation which would have been distinctly uncomfortable. Jane's mother, I gather, is a holy terror. Anyway, recovery was complete last week when a letter came from Jane. I've brought it for you to read.'

'Oh no!' I demurred. 'I'm sure James would be horrified if he knew you'd shown it to me!'

'Not he! Here, take it.'

She handed over the sheet of bright blue paper. In a large schoolgirl scrawl was Jane's final communication, presumably, to James.

It said:

Dear James,

This is to give in my notice. I don't want to set foot in that office again, or to see you.

My mother says I should sue you for damages, but I've told her I don't want anything more to do with you. I must have been mad to waste my time with someone so old and dotty he can't even drive.

Jane

P.S. Yesterday I got engaged to Teddy Thimblemere in Accounts and we are getting married at Christmas.

'And how did James take that?' I asked, handing it back.

'He lay back on the pillow with his eyes closed, and then he began to shake. I was quite worried, until I realized it was with laughter. He laughed until the tears ran down his cheeks, and of course that set me laughing, too! You should have heard the hullabaloo, and poor James gasping for breath, and saying: "Oh God, my poor ribs hurt so!" And me, wiping my eyes, and saying: "Try *not* to laugh, darling, you'll burst something!" And, after a bit, he would quieten down, and then remember some particular phrase like "so old and dotty he can't even drive", and double up all over again. It did us both a world of good!'

'Not enough laughter about these days,' I agreed.

'It's as good a healer as time,' said Amy, putting the letter into her bag. 'That little bout certainly restored us to happier days.'

'And so, all's well again?'

'As well as one can expect in an imperfect world,' said Amy. 'I daresay James will recover enough to turn to look at a pretty girl again, when he's had his nose patched up and a false tooth put in the gap. And no doubt I shall be as bossy and bitchy as I am at times. But somehow, I feel sure, nothing quite so serious will ever happen again.'

'I'm glad you told me,' I said. 'I like a happy ending.'

'Then let's have that coffee,' said Amy.

A week or so later, I was talking to Mr Willet in the playground after school, when a long low sports car of inordinate length drew up outside the school house. It was a dashing vehicle, bright yellow in colour, with enormous headlamps and one of those back windows on top of the car like a skylight. The bonnet seemed about six feet in length, and the whole thing was dazzlingly polished.

'My word,' said Mr Willet, with awe, 'that must've cost a pretty penny! One of your millionaire friends droppin' in?'

'Strangers to me,' I was saying, when the door by the passenger's seat opened, and Vanessa emerged.

'Hello!' I welcomed her. 'How lovely to see you!'

'We're on our way to see Aunt Amy,' said Vanessa, kissing me, and enveloping me in fair hair and expensive scent. 'And this is Torquil.'

An enormous young man disengaged himself from the interior of the car, and shook my hand so warmly that I wondered if I should ever be able to part my fingers again. He was so good-looking, however, that I readily forgave him, and they came with me into the sitting room.

I thought I had never seen Vanessa quite so lively. It was quite apparent that Gerard's affairs were not worrying her. On the contrary, she spoke of his marriage with the greatest joy.

'Wasn't it fun? That's really why he was off to town last time we called. He really deserves someone as nice as Hattie. He's so *kind*! I can't tell you how good he's been to me. I've *always* asked his advice about *everything*, and he's never failed me. And see what else he did?'

She gazed fondly upon Torquil, who gazed back in an equally besotted fashion.

'He introduced me to Torquil. And here, you see, we are! Just engaged!'

I hastened to congratulate them.

'We're not sure if we're on our heads or our heels,' said the young man. 'We rang Vanessa's father and mother last night, and we're going to stay there over the weekend.'

'And I said,' broke in Vanessa, 'we simply *must* call on you on the way, and Aunt Amy, because we wanted you to know before it was in the paper.'

'Well, I call it uncommonly nice of you,' I said, 'and I very much appreciate it. When will the wedding be?'

'Tomorrow,' said Torquil, 'if I had my way.'

'Dear thing!' said Vanessa indulgently. 'Probably early in the New Year.'

'As long as that?' exclaimed the young man.

I asked them to have a drink in celebration, but they looked at the clock, and each other, and said that they must go.

They fitted themselves skilfully into the gorgeous car. I kissed Vanessa, and kept my hands out of the way as I wished Torquil good-bye.

The car roared away. Mr Willet, who was carrying a bucket

of coke to make up the stoves for the night, set it down, and pushed his cap to the back of his head with a black hand.

'You was cut out, I see,' he observed. 'That young lady saw him first.'

Sadly, I had to agree.

Three days later, Amy rang me.

'Have you seen the paper? And I *don't* mean the *Caxley Chronicle*!'

'Why? Is Vanessa's engagement in it?'

'Yes. Have you read it?'

'I had an accident with the paper today.'

'How do you mean?'

'I muddled it up with yesterday's, and gave it to the children to tear up for papier mâché bowls.'

'Really! The things you do! Sometimes I despair of you!'

'I despair of myself.'

'Well listen! I'll read it to you. "The engagement is announced between Torquil Ian Angus, only son of Wing Commander and Mrs Bruce Cameron of Blairlochinnie Castle, Ayrshire, and Vanessa Clare, only daughter of Mr and Mrs Charles Hunt of Hampstead, London."'

'And will she live at Blair Tiddlywinks Castle?'

'Not for a long time. Torquil's father is in splendid health, I gather, and I don't think the banks and braes are altogether to Torquil's taste just yet. You know what he does?'

'No.'

'He's a band leader. And fairly rolling in money. No, I think London will be the place for those two for the next few years anyway.'

'Have they fixed the wedding date?'

'Yes. It's to be the first week in January. You're going to be invited, so you'd better start looking for that winter coat.'

'I will,' I said meekly.

'We shall be back for the wedding, of course,' said Amy.

'Back?' I echoed.

'From our holiday. James wants to go as soon as he's fit again, and that won't be long now.'

'And where are you going?'

Amy's voice bubbled with laughter. 'Can't you guess? To Crete.'

'*Perfect!*' I cried.

In a flash, I saw again that golden island, and breathed the heady scent of flowers and sun-baked earth. One day, I knew suddenly, I should go there once more.

'Give it all my love,' I said.